Sinful Deceptions

ZOË MILLER

piatkus

PIATKUS

First published in Ireland in 2010 by Hachette Ireland
First published in Great Britain as a paperback original in 2010 by Piatkus

A CIP catalogue record for this book
is available from the British Library.

ISBN 978-0-7499-5330-0

Typeset in Bembo by M Rules
Printed and bound in Great Britain by
Clays Ltd, St Ives plc

Papers used by Piatkus are natural, renewable and
recyclable products sourced from well-managed forests and certified
in accordance with the rules of the Forest Stewardship Council.

Mixed Sources
Product group from well-managed
forests and other controlled sources
www.fsc.org   Cert no. SGS-COC-004081
© 1996 Forest Stewardship Council

FSC

Piatkus
An imprint of
Little, Brown Book Group
100 Victoria Embankment
London EC4Y 0DY

An Hachette UK Company
www.hachette.co.uk

www.piatkus.co.uk

Zoë Miller was born on the south side of Dublin, where she now lives with her husband. She began writing stories at an early age. Her writing career has also included freelance journalism and prize-winning short fiction.

Dedicated with love to my sister, Margaret McEvoy

Acknowledgements

A tremendous thank you to the group of amazing people who have given unstintingly of their energy, enthusiasm and commitment to help bring about the best in this novel: my agent Sheila Crowley, supported by the team at Curtis Brown; my editor Ciara Doorley and the team at Hachette Books Ireland, headed up by Breda Purdue; my new UK editor, Emma Beswetherick, and the Piatkus team; Hazel Orme for excellent copy editing and Kristin Jensen for proof reading. Thank you all so much, your help and support means everything to me.

Special acknowledgement is due to Zoë Clark, make-up artist extraordinaire, who very kindly took time out of her busy schedule to talk me through a day in the life of a make-up artist, and warmly and patiently answered my litany of questions.

Heartfelt gratitude is due to another fantastic band of people who believe in me and look after me so well – my family and friends, especially Derek, Michelle, Declan and Barbara. Thanks a million for all the love, encouragement and understanding.

One of the themes of *Sinful Deceptions* is the wonderful support that sisters can give each other. This book is dedicated to my sister, Margaret McEvoy, who has been there for me in a special way since the passing of our beloved mother and has softened the edges of that empty space with friendship and love.

And thanks to all my lovely readers, and those who have taken the time to contact me on Facebook and at zoemillerauthor@gmail.com. I really appreciate your good wishes and I hope you enjoy *Sinful Deceptions*!

Prologue

Years earlier, in a different life . . .

*I*n this ultra-chic golden-stoned corner of the Cotswolds, the whiff of scandal has never dared raise its sensational head. Until now.

When it explodes across the sunny bank-holiday weekend, it shatters the calm of the quaint, middle-class village, catches everyone unawares, and attracts an invasion of news-hungry media. In the stilled, hushed aftershock, almost everyone closes ranks and holds their silence. But nothing can prevent soft murmurs drifting out on the warm air, gathering substance and crystallising into vivid tabloid headlines:

Tragic Love Triangle Rocks Sleepy Upmarket Village
Student and Teacher Killed in Sex Scandal Tragedy

The accompanying photographs make a mockery of the sunshine spilling across leafy laneways and drenching silent tennis courts; there is the stark image of the crumpled car in the ditch, and the victims, Camille Berkeley, late thirties, beautiful and elegant, her photo reproduced from the university yearbook, and John, the young student, aged just twenty.

Later in the week, the tabloids carry the photo of the student's distraught ex-girlfriend being supported by her friends as she lays flowers in the ditch. There is also the image of the tall, grief-stricken Mr Berkeley arriving at the mortuary. 'The strikingly handsome widower is bearing the scandal with numb dignity,' the caption says.

Other details gradually emerge, courtesy of a local who confirms in hushed tones that Mr Berkeley is Irish and a respected professor of classical history. Camille Berkeley, his deceased wife, was of Canadian origin and had been an equally revered lecturer in the faculty of modern languages. They had moved from Dublin some years ago with their two young daughters who, up to now, have led a quietly sheltered life, to take up posts at a nearby university.

Everyone agrees that it is a step too far when even the girls are caught on an invasive telescopic lens, being comforted by their aunt after the funeral service; the grainy photo shows eleven-year-old Emma, her face dipped and hidden by her long dark hair, and Alix, already tall and leggy for her seven years, showing signs of her mother's classic beauty in spite of her bewildered face.

When the professor whisks his daughters straight back to Dublin, everyone agrees that it is a relief, although it is sad to see the beauti-ful, double-fronted house with the flower-filled gardens lying empty.

Life moves on. The house is sold. The seasons slide past, bring-ing brisk autumn breezes, the drifting snows of winter, a vibrant new spring. Already, a year has flown and it is another summer . . . More years pass, and when the village is developed, the network of roads is upgraded.

For those who still remember, it comes as some respite when the ditch is buried under tons of silencing asphalt so that not a trace remains. But in the hearts and souls of those who care, hazy images and sibilant whispers flutter like a distant pulse and echo faintly through the beat of their lives . . .

Chapter 1

Present Day

*O*n Friday morning it rained in Paris and Alix Berkeley pulled up the collar of her Valentino leather jacket as she sprinted along the narrow cobbled street in the 6th *arrondissement*. So much for her great idea of slipping out to the *pâtisserie* on the corner for fresh, melt-in-the-mouth croissants. She should have resisted the temptation because, whatever the poets said, early springtime in the City of Light could be wet and cold. She tucked her cashmere scarf around her creamy neck, and although her long, jeans-clad legs were snug in knee-high Gucci riding boots, she veered towards the kerb to avoid a puddle, just as a careless driver sent a sheet of rainwater sloshing over the pavement.

Well done, Alix. She laughed to herself.

She was glad to reach her apartment building and, ignoring the rain-bejewelled handrail, took the steps up to the entrance two at a time, fishing in the pocket of her jeans for her security key so that she had it ready as she approached the oak hall door. She took the lift as far as the third floor and marched up the rest of the stairs, feeling virtuous — you couldn't beat stairs for countering the effects of a

3

calorific breakfast. She had just reached the luxurious sanctuary of her sixth-floor apartment in the renovated nineteenth-century building when her mobile rang. 'Hi, Fiona, you're up early,' she said, checking the caller ID. She strode down the hall, inhaling the fragrance of the freesias arranged in the Venetian vase, and dropped the bag of croissants on the glass-topped table in the kitchen.

'*Bonjour*, Alix, so are you. I thought I'd get you before you became caught up in the day. You're back from Milan?'

Alix unwound her scarf with one hand, shrugged out of her jacket, and went to hang them up in the hall cupboard. She ran her fingers through her short, rain-drizzled hair. 'I flew back yesterday evening,' she said as, mobile in hand, she walked into the living room.

'All partied out, I trust?'

'Not exactly,' Alix said. With her free hand she plumped up the silk cushions, picked up a stray magazine and dumped it in the magazine bin. She sank down on the long cream sofa, unzipped her boots and pulled them off. Her legs were warm in stripy woollen socks so she stretched them out across the Spanish rug and wiggled her freed-up toes. 'I went to an after-show event on Wednesday night in some *palazzo* or other and tried not to guzzle too much champagne because it was frantic behind the scenes,' she went on. 'Both days were early starts. Then one of the labels pulled out at the last minute. Naturally, some of the models were very upset, and I had to mop their tears.'

'*C'est la vie.* I can just imagine the bedlam.'

'Bedlam?' Alix said wryly. 'It was carnage. Then we were all struggling for space in front of the mirrors, and for the first time in my career I didn't think I'd have the energy to see it through to the after-show party. I was relieved I was only booked for two days as I'll need all my energy for Paris Fashion Week.'

'Alix! What's this I'm hearing? Where's your va-va-voom?'

'Also,' Alix continued in a self-deprecating tone, 'I don't know if it's just me, but the catwalk models seem to be getting younger and thinner these days.'

'It's not just you, and the same could be said about some of the A-listers sitting outside in the best seats. So, you're resting today?' Fiona said, teasing, fully aware that her friend scarcely ever had a day to herself.

'How did you guess? For about ten minutes. I've a meeting with Henri this morning to discuss the theme for the launch of Alix B and a lingerie shoot at twelve o'clock. The model's a new kid on the block, ravishingly beautiful, but nervous as hell.'

'And Paris's best make-up artist will have her looking exotic and breathtakingly sensual – she'll hardly recognise herself. You're so warm and comfortable that you put them all at ease.'

'It's just part of the job,' Alix demurred.

'Tut-tut. Don't short-change yourself. Not all make-up artists would say the same. I can't wait to try out your new cosmetics range. It's all so exciting.'

'I've already told you that you can have samples any time.'

'No thanks, darling, I'm waiting until the official launch of Alix B. I'll be first in the queue to buy the entire range and I'll make sure the paparazzi get a good shot of me endorsing it. This launch will really boost your career, not that it needs a boost. Have you agreed the date?' Fiona asked.

'Yes, it's all happening at the end of May.'

'Wow. That's just weeks away.'

'Nine, just about. It'll fly in. Everything's on course, thankfully. I don't think I fully appreciated just how much was involved in all of this – the whole production seems to have snowballed beyond my control and some of the planned promotions are a little over the top.'

'This is Paris, my dear. Forget the credit crunch. Ignore *la crise*.

Everything has to be bigger and better, glossier and more extravagant. Your cosmetics brand is going to be huge, mark my words. Alix B at Aurélie will really put your name up in mega-watts!'

At her friend's words, Alix felt an unexpected stab of anxiety in the pit of her stomach. It temporarily silenced her. Did she really want her name up in lights? After all, it hadn't exactly been part of her life plan, had it? How had she allowed this to happen?

'Alix? I hope you're all set for the weekend?' Fiona asked.

'*Oui*, I am indeed all set, but not yet packed,' Alix was glad to change the subject. She made a mental note of what she needed to put into a case for Gstaad: Lainey Keogh knits and leather jeans, her warmest lingerie, and faux-fur-trimmed boots. 'I'm really looking forward to it – it's been a hectic few weeks. Who's going, by the way?'

'The usual gang – you, me, Dave, Sophie, Yvette, perhaps Marc . . .'

'So you want me to act as referee?' It was well known among Alix's Parisian mates that Marc was in love with Sophie but she didn't return his fervour. Sometimes when they all got together, a strategic plan was required to ensure they weren't left alone – Alix often played the role of gooseberry.

'No, I don't,' Fiona said stoutly. 'And to show that I don't expect you to chaperone, I'm reminding you that your invitation also extends to any friend you might like to bring.'

There was a note of curiosity in her friend's voice that Alix swiftly deflected. 'There's safety in numbers, is that it? No, thanks.'

'I've confirmed the flight schedule and we're all meeting in the executive lounge at five o'clock this evening. I'm looking forward to a catch-up,' Fiona said, 'It's a while since we all got together and we'll have some *craic*.'

'Sure thing, can't wait to see you guys as well. Bye for now.'

When she had finished the call, Alix sat silently for a few moments. Then she rose to her feet and looked at her reflection in the Louis XIV gilt mirror over the mantelpiece. *Alix B at Aurélie.* Although a niggle of anxiety persisted, her light green eyes were clear. And that's precisely how it should be, she thought, padding into the kitchen in her stockinged feet.

For someone who had landed in Paris scarcely knowing where she was going, it seemed she was finally about to arrive. And she was beginning to think it was all very scary stuff indeed.

Chapter 2

*A*lix had first met Fiona and Dave thirteen years ago when she moved to Paris to take up a position as a junior make-up assistant in a busy hair and beauty salon. They had been trainee hairstylists serving rigorous apprenticeships, and the three were drawn together by the solidarity of their lowly positions as well as their Irish roots – Alix arriving into Paris from Dublin via London, Dave and Fiona hailing from Cork.

On Alix's first morning, they had shared a coffee break in a tiny cubby-hole, Alix delighted to chat to the bubbly redheaded Fiona and her boyfriend.

'Dave and I are learning the ropes from the ground up as we're going to have our own exclusive business and make a name for ourselves,' Fiona said.

'And where better than Paris?' Dave put in.

'We feel it's the true heartbeat of fashion and style,' Fiona smiled.

'My aim is to help women be who they want to be,' Alix explained, sipping strong coffee, her initial nervousness easing thanks to Fiona's warm manner. 'I suppose you could say it's my passion. I want to help women improve their self-image because it can boost the way they feel about themselves.'

Even though Alix felt herself relaxing in the camaraderie of the tiny canteen, she wasn't entirely honest. It was impossible to explain that it had worked for her: changing the way she looked had helped her to break with the past and the shadow of her mother. She glossed over her background, telling them she'd left Dublin at the age of twenty-two, had trained in London with Estée Lauder, then, at twenty-four, had decided to move to Paris. Neither did she confide that she'd needed to make a fresh start when she began to find London too claustrophobic. 'I suppose for me, given my passion, moving to Paris where there's plenty of work seemed the obvious step,' she explained.

'Here's to our brilliant futures,' Fiona said.

Alix wasn't seeking fame or fortune, but she'd been swept up in the slipstream of Dave and Fiona's enthusiasm. They'd become good friends, supporting each other in their dreams. Now, thirteen years on, without quite knowing how she'd got there or why – never mind acknowledging that the years had simply flown – Alix was thirty-seven and, with hard work, patience and professionalism, plus a talent for creating magic with her fingers and brushes, had made a name for herself. Along the way she'd learned to speak French like a native. Even more importantly, she'd discovered that her craft was less about putting on make-up to enable women to appear completely altered than with bringing out their inner beauty and dramatising their best features to give them an inner confidence. Now she was a freelance make-up artist with a high-profile client list and a fiercely loyal agent, commanding eye-watering fees to transform her models into exotic, radiant creatures. Her work had graced countless catwalks and magazine covers, and one of Paris's top fashion photographers wouldn't shoot without her. When she looked back, she scarcely recognised the vulnerable, insecure twenty-four-year-old she'd been when she arrived in the capital of fashion and beauty.

In the early years of her career, she'd brushed aside remarks that she was working on the wrong side of the camera, with her cropped jet-black hair and high cheekbones, her light green eyes framed with thick dark lashes, and skin as pale as delicate ivory. 'Apart from the looks, you have the height, the exquisite bone structure and the effortless grace. You could be a runway queen yourself,' she'd been told several times, but she'd always laughed it off.

'I couldn't stick that kind of existence,' she'd said to Fiona. 'Your shelf life is depressingly short, unless you're one of the extremely lucky ones. Thin and thinner is mandatory. Could you see me critically examining every mouthful of food before it passed my lips?'

'And that's just for starters,' Fiona had said. 'We won't mention the stressful lifestyle or size-zero debate.'

In any case, Alix had thought, the last thing she wanted was to be on the other side of the camera lens. She'd been there before. She'd smiled and laughed, postured and posed, but those days were long gone and, thankfully, only existed in her memory as a faint film reel.

Dave and Fiona had now realised their dreams and ran their own celebrity hair salon with an ultra-chic address off the Champs-Élysées, where appointments were booked months in advance. Although success hadn't changed them, they enjoyed living life to the full and all the luxuries and fun that came with their affluent lifestyle. Today Fiona had arranged for a private jet to fly a group of friends to Gstaad that evening for a weekend house party in an Alpine chalet to celebrate her and Dave's third wedding anniversary.

'It'll be all very relaxing, log fires, music, a weekend of Michelin-star food, courtesy of our chef,' Fiona had promised when she'd first invited Alix.

'Gallons of chilled Krug?'

'Of course. Shopping too, if you want it. *And* some skiing.'

'If we have any energy left for it,' Alix had laughed.

Now, as Alix took a blue stoneware mug out of the press and prepared some coffee, she was delighted at the prospect of a cosy, relaxing weekend tucked up amid sparkling white snow. She switched on the grill and popped the croissants under the heat, poured the coffee and sat at the table beside the window. She reminded herself that even though she'd be joining her friends as a singleton, she had it all, and more.

Her luxury apartment on the top floor of the nineteenth-century building in the charming and arty 6th *arrondissement* was a far cry from the narrow *atelier* she'd rented when she'd first arrived in Paris. A mixture of classical elegance and homely, Bohemian grace, it was decorated in calm tones of cream and white, with pools of colour supplied by Spanish rugs, ceramic pottery and her growing art collection. She'd come across it by accident and she'd fallen in love with the high ceilings, delightfully exposed beams, terrazzo tiled floors and, most of all, the sunlight that flooded in through the long, elegant windows, which afforded her uplifting and romantic views of the rooftops of St Germain. She had a cleaner who came in twice a week, but unlike her sister Emma's lazy Leticia, Monique was scarily efficient.

As well as assignments in Paris, her career sent her jetting off to other glamorous locations, and whether it was a catwalk event in Milan, a shoot in St Tropez or an exclusive consultation, between preparing clients for fashion shows or weddings, film festivals or cover shoots, she was privy to the secrets of some of the world's most beautiful supermodels and celebrities. After all, you didn't spend time carefully painting a flawless image on someone's face without picking up on their feelings and hearing some of their hopes and dreams.

Alix listened with empathy to the million and one insecurities that were divulged to her, and she had long ago discovered that beneath the luminous skin, whether they were superstars or the latest hot discovery, everyone was the same: they all craved love and affection and a measure of approval. Except her, Alix swiftly reminded herself as she savoured the last flakes of her croissant. This thought cheered her considerably. She didn't need anybody's love or approval. Which was just as well, considering that, deep down, she didn't approve of herself a lot of the time.

She finished her coffee and rinsed the mug. Then she went into the bedroom and tugged the soft white duvet off the bed. There was no evidence of Laurent. No indent on the pillow or resonance of his scent. He'd slipped away before daybreak, as unobtrusively as he had arrived, having sated them both with a night of vigorous sex. There was no question of him joining her and her friends for the weekend. He was like a ghost in her life, there but not there, obscure, distant, slipping in and out on the shadowy periphery of her nights, giving her his full-on, undivided attention when he joined her in bed.

And that was the way she liked it.

Alix smoothed on clean scented linen, plumped up the pillows and scattered them across the huge bed. She filled the laundry basket with the dirty bedclothes and left it ready for Monique, who'd be coming in on Monday. Her Parisian friends had an idea that she had someone in the background of her life, but Fiona and Emma were the only people to whom Alix had confided the nature of her relationship with Laurent. She had anticipated her sister's concern, but was unable to pretend to Emma that she was celibate.

'What about marriage? And children?' Emma had asked, her voice full of misgivings, on one of her visits to Paris. 'Surely you want them.' They were relaxing over a boozy lunch, sitting outside a small brasserie on a quaint side-street where the autumnal trees were turning gold and crimson.

Alix stretched out her long legs, tipped her head back and looked up at the oblong of perfect blue sky above. She felt a refreshing breeze ripple through her hair and slowly let out her breath. 'No, thanks,' she said. 'I'm quite happy like this.'

'I can't help thinking you're leaving yourself wide open to hurt.'

'Relax, hon, I'm able to take care of myself.'

'You might change your mind in a couple of years' time.'

'Not when I love my independence and have a career that keeps me busy.'

'I suppose you're too caught up right now, living the glitzy high life,' Emma said, 'but that mightn't fulfil you for ever.'

'It's not all glamour and glitz. It can be tough, very demanding and back-breakingly tiring. Sometimes you feel as though your arm is about to fall off from constant touching up, and other times you need the patience of a saint. Then there's the occasional four in the morning call time. But I wouldn't swap it for anything.'

Two years later, she felt the same.

She hadn't seen Emma since a brief Christmas visit to Dublin, but once upon a time they been very close, closer than two sisters would normally be on account of their mother's tragic death. Big sister Emma had comforted Alix in the night and wiped away her tears. Together they had stepped around the grey-faced pain of their father and learned to live with their own. Alix caught her breath and, for a long, charged moment, she was back in that frightening place, longing for the scent of her mother and the sound of her laughter, the feel of her arms around her and her warm, cuddly kisses. All gone for ever, the sense of loss made more acute by the pain of betrayal.

Adulthood had sent her and Emma spinning off in different directions. Although Emma had married Oliver ridiculously young at nineteen, she was still married twenty-two years later. Alix was in no doubt that love and family loyalty, steadfast and enduring, were central to Emma and ran like an invisible seam through everything she did, binding it all together.

'You run after your family far too much,' Alix sometimes chided her, whereupon Emma usually laughed.

'It's what you do when you're a mum.'

'Not necessarily,' Alix had once said quietly.

'Don't even go there,' Emma had replied, so firmly that Alix never did again.

Alix went in search of her boots and prepared for her meeting with Henri and the midday shoot, swiftly dismissing another stab of foreboding. She checked the wheelie-case that contained her portable make-up kit. In it, the cosmetics were separated into clear Ziploc bags for speed and convenience, and now, from her store of supplies, she topped up eyeshadows and lip-glosses. Her kit was always kept spotless, likewise her large collection of brushes and sponges, which she scrupulously cleaned after every use.

Alix reminded herself to phone Emma before she left for Gstaad and tell her she'd be away for the weekend. She shoved her Mulberry planner and her mobile into her tote bag, pulled on her jacket and scarf, and drew on the slimmest of soft leather driving gloves. Ten minutes later, she was expertly nosing her red Audi TT onto rain-washed Paris streets.

Chapter 3

If she'd stayed in bed that morning . . .

If she'd cuddled up for a few more minutes, instead of rising from the warmth of the bed to fly down the wide staircase to the marbled hallway where her husband and daughter were leaving for work, bubbles of anticipation almost choking her . . .

Afterwards, when she wanted to turn back time, Emma Colgan closed her eyes and went back to that Friday morning, hoping for more than a snatched kiss from her husband.

'We're off, love,' Oliver said. He flung on his overcoat and tossed a silk scarf around his neck as he walked up the hall. He picked up his black leather briefcase and scooped up the keys of his BMW.

'Yeah, see ya, Mum.' Libby, her blonde and beautiful daughter, followed in his wake, fastening the belt of her Karen Millen coat with the swift, graceful movements that hallmarked her every gesture. She adjusted the collar, carefully shaking out her silky hair, pulled on cream woollen gloves and picked up her Kelly bag.

Emma clutched the mahogany banister as the fizz of anticipation soured. It might have been another ordinary morning. They were so intent on the important business of getting into their Dublin city centre offices before the critical seven-thirty a.m. deadline that they'd forgotten it was a special day for her. 'Wait a minute,' she said, a little breathless.

In perfect unison, father and daughter halted, swivelled around and frowned at this interruption to their strictly timed schedule.

'What's up?' Oliver asked, with barely concealed impatience.

'I know you're in a hurry to catch up with overnight emails from the States . . .' Emma began, paraphrasing Oliver's own words.

'*And* talk to the Far East before they leave for the evening,' he reminded her. He made it sound as though whatever was left of the global investment sector would crunch to a total halt if he wasn't personally directing operations from his enormous walnut desk with the Waterford Crystal paperweights.

'Same here,' Libby said breezily. Fresh from college, and possessing her father's keen analytical brain and trail-blazing ambition, Emma's beautiful daughter was equally passionate about getting to her desk in her prestigious corporate investment office ahead of the rest of her colleagues. Sometimes their combined energy left Emma feeling at a loss. At others, especially lately, she found herself wishing that Oliver would look at her with the same laser-beam attentiveness he bestowed on the *Financial Times*. That was one of the reasons why she wanted this promotion so badly.

'Have you both forgotten?' she asked, wrapping her arms around her slender, négligée-clad body, her voice a little sharper than she'd intended.

Oliver and Libby exchanged a puzzled, conspiratorial glance. It usually heartened Emma that they both looked alike, with intelligent navy blue eyes and resolute mouths. This morning, however, she felt excluded by their shared bafflement.

'Forgotten what?' Oliver's dark brows drew together, deepening his frown. He snatched a glance at his watch and rattled his car keys impatiently.

For a surreal moment Emma thought her husband looked distant and forbidding, already in decisive work mode. She blinked hard and told herself it was just the way he was silhouetted against the leaded glass pane of the hall door. 'The results. They'll be out today,' Emma said, disgusted that her voice felt tight. 'The promotion interview?' she prompted when their faces remained blank.

Oliver looked relieved, as though it wasn't, after all, a matter of national importance that might impact on his inflexible schedule. 'Ah, yes, of course.' He smiled indulgently at his wife. 'Sure you'll get the job, darling. I bet it's only a formality. Let me know, won't you? Send me a text.' He blew her an absentminded kiss and opened the door, causing a draught of cold air to ripple up the hall.

'Yes, Mum, me too – and the best of luck,' Libby called over her shoulder, her blonde hair swirling as she hurriedly followed her father across the threshold.

She couldn't blame them for their haste, Emma told herself, biting back disappointment. She knew their schedule off by heart. They had to be in the car by six forty-five to ensure that they reached Oliver's reserved space in Dublin's financial services centre by seven twenty. This gave them just enough time to grab their second caffeine fix of the day as they headed for the cut and thrust of their adjacent steel-and-glass monoliths. Unlike her. She had ample time to get ready for her day in the far less exciting ambience of Marshalls Marketing.

Despite the chill of the pearly grey morning, Emma lingered in the doorway. Their detached red-brick house on Laburnum Grove in the suburbs of south Dublin was situated at the end of an avenue and surrounded by landscaped gardens. This morning a faint, cobwebby moon drifted benignly in the lightening sky and the first of the tulips were bravely poking their delicate plumes above the soil in the dew-damp flowerbeds. She sniffed the sharp, clear air, listened to the early-morning birdsong, and reminded herself that today was the first day of the rest of her life. Correction: the first day of the new and improved Emma Colgan's life.

Her husband was far too rushed to stop and look at the morning scenery. The engine thrummed in the still morning air as he reversed rather too speedily out of the garage and down the gravel driveway. He skidded out into the avenue, timing his exit through the widening gap in the wooden electronic gates with military precision. He missed the neighbour's pedigree cat by millimetres, causing it to squeal in protest as it scarpered to safety. Oliver beeped the horn just once, and Emma saw the blur of Libby's hand waving regally before the car shot away, whisking the indispensable ones off to their vital roles. She shut the heavy mahogany door and leaned against it for a couple of minutes. The black and white hallway seemed so empty now all the crackling energy had been sucked out.

Chapter 4

*C*harlie was still in bed.

'Hey, Charlie!' Emma went back up the thickly carpeted staircase and knocked on his door. She opened it a fraction, sending a shaft of light into the room. In the semi-darkness, the enormous Metallica poster seemed menacing and surreal. God. She was definitely on edge this morning.

'Thanks, Mum,' Charlie muttered thickly, sounding cross and sleepy. 'I thought I told you not to disturb me.' There was the sound of protesting bed-springs as he turned over.

'What about college?'

'What day is it?' Now Charlie sounded more awake, suspicion and dismay evident in his voice.

'It's Friday.'

'Shite. Thought it was Saturday.'

He scrabbled out of bed and Emma swiftly closed the door. He'd also forgotten that it was the day she was expecting to be offered promotion after serving her time in the background at Marshalls Marketing.

As Charlie crashed around in the bathroom, Emma went down to the kitchen and refilled the cafetière. She opened the door of the cavernous refrigerator that the kids had insisted they needed and poured some juice. Then, even though it was Leticia's morning to come in and clean, she automatically swept up toast crumbs left by Oliver and Libby and tossed their buttery knives, along with their coffee mugs, into the dishwasher. She raised the kitchen blind and glanced out into the landscaped garden, wishing the peace outside would magically wrap itself around her and insulate her from her family's heedlessness.

Charlie loped into the kitchen and rummaged in the fridge. 'Hey, what happened to the blueberry yoghurts?' he grumbled. He pulled out a strawberry mousse and ripped away the lid. 'Are you getting the shopping tonight?' he asked. He licked the foil and dumped it in the bin.

'You've eaten them all and, yes, I'm ordering the groceries.'

'I'm going to a party tonight. I might stay over,' he mumbled.

'Let me know, won't you?' Emma said, but she was talking to his retreating back. She heard him take the stairs two at a time.

She sipped her juice and told herself her family weren't purposely selfish. Right now, Charlie's main concerns were his social life, his part-time job and the trials of his engineering course. And the glorified world of Marshalls's latest teabag campaign didn't even rate on the scale when compared to the ruthless battlefield of gilt-edged mergers, demergers and acquisitions in which Oliver demonstrated considerable talent, or the challenging multimillion-dollar portfolios that Libby fearlessly managed. Although, according to Oliver, Emma wasn't supposed to want a career outside the rarefied atmosphere of Laburnum Grove.

'What are you trying to prove?' he'd asked when she told him she was accepting a job in Marshalls after Charlie had turned fourteen. 'It's not as if we need the money.'

'I'm thirty-five years of age. I'm not just a trophy wife. I want to be able to tell my mouse from my megabyte,' she'd explained, feeling on the defensive. She found it difficult to articulate that, having spent years immersed in domestic trivia, she felt left behind by her successful husband and bright, clever family. Neither did she have the benefit of a university education like them, thanks to the spectacular way she'd dropped out and abandoned her studies. Now she badly felt the need to affirm her own self-worth, something elemental that a kitchen full of stainless steel, sandblasted glass and Neff couldn't provide.

'I suppose . . . so long as it's not too demanding on you,' Oliver had compromised.

'You mean so long as it doesn't interfere with the smooth running of the house.'

'Did I say that?' He'd fixed her with a wounded look.

'Don't worry, I'll be getting someone in to help out a couple of mornings.'

'Good. Look, Emma, it's just that I don't want you running frazzled by the end of the week.'

Now, six years after she'd started at Marshalls, Emma was ready for more satisfaction and more of a challenge. Leticia came in for three hours on Tuesdays and Fridays. At twenty-five, the Filipina was petite and slim, pretty rather than beautiful, and full of a bashful charm. She'd taken over the job from her aunt Marissa four months previously and wasn't the best cleaner in the world by any stretch of the imagination, but she was so pleasant about cleaning Emma's house that Emma found it difficult to fault her.

She went back upstairs to her bathroom, slid out of her négligée and stepped under the power shower. As the refreshing spray and her favourite l'Occitane *crème* flowed down her body, she tried and failed to remember the last time Oliver's hands had massaged her breasts with the same focus they devoted to the keys of his laptop in the evenings. Once upon a time, he couldn't get enough of her. Now their lovemaking was far less frequent and more and more routine. It was natural, though, that the passion of those early years would slowly abate. Or was it?

She switched off the shower, stepped out and wrapped herself in a thick Viennese bath sheet. She reminded herself that, on the outside, she had everything she could wish for. A beautiful home, a great husband – when he wasn't too absorbed in his career – and two fabulous, confident adult children. Yet since she'd passed her milestone fortieth birthday, and as Oliver had become even more distant and driven, there was no denying that she had undergone some quiet metamorphosis. She was becoming increasingly disenchanted with her life. She felt instinctively that there had to be more to Emma Colgan and knew that some of the reasons for her dissatisfaction and need for a fresh challenge lay in the fact that she'd spent her twenties and early thirties ferrying Libby to ballet classes and swimming, Charlie to football, and supporting Oliver in his race to the top. Then she'd accepted a rather mundane job and stayed there, telling herself she was putting career progression on hold until her family were independent.

Surely, now, that time had arrived.

Emma wasn't fooling herself. 'I know I'll never have the distinction of the corner office, company car or expense account like you,' she'd said to Oliver the night before the promotion interview. 'And I'd never relish the perils of wealth management like Libby, God forbid, but promotion in Marshalls would give me a sense of personal achievement.'

'I don't know why you're putting yourself through this,' he'd said, glancing surreptitiously at his iPhone. 'I thought you'd have had enough of Marshalls by now . . .' He must have noticed the way her face dropped for he leaned forward and pecked her cheek. 'Anyhow, darling, the best of luck,' he'd said.

It was the 'darling' that did it: it made her feel as though Oliver was being overly indulgent with his favourite pet instead of supporting his equal. Emma blow-dried her straight, chin-length dark hair and put on her make-up in the way her sister had advised: a light foundation with a dewy finish to lend a glow to her sallow skin, a dash of creamy blush on her high cheekbones, a blend of taupe eyeshadow, smudged for effect to emphasise her almond-shaped soft blue eyes, ceramide mascara and, finally, tinted lip balm in a subtle shimmer.

Once upon a time, Emma had thought that Alix was going to follow in her footsteps and settle down with her childhood sweetheart and fiancé, Tom Cassidy. Then, quite suddenly, he had called off the engagement. After a cry on Emma's shoulder, Alix had picked herself up, left the past behind and never looked back. Now she was free and single and counted celebrity stylists and several supermodels in her circle of friends and acquaintances. She also had a secret lover, of whom Emma outwardly disapproved, yet secretly envied, who delivered clandestine, satisfying and raunchy sex on demand. Alix was always happy and fulfilled, and her life full of glamour and excitement. Sometimes when Emma was ordering groceries online, or she found herself emptying the dishwasher because Leticia had conveniently forgotten, she pictured her sister glugging champagne, jetting off to exclusive appointments and extravagant parties, or whipping around graceful Paris boulevards in her bright red car. On those occasions, a shaft of envy twisted Emma's stomach but she never hinted at it in front of Alix, for it was ingrained in her to keep up a pretence of happy-ever-after with her sister.

Look after Alix for me . . .

Emma heard her mother's voice as though it was yesterday. She felt a momentary dizziness and her cream and gold bedroom with the Limoges lace coverlet and curtains swam out of focus. She took a deep breath. Almost thirty years later, the elusive memory still had the power to transfix her. And that was all it was, she told herself. An ethereal memory, an age-old whisper in her soul that was meaningless, for she had long ago turned her back on her ghosts, along with her mother's betrayal.

Emma stepped back and studied her reflection lifting her chin purposefully. She wanted this promotion because it would give her much-needed validation. And her husband and children would see her in a new light. A more dynamic, sexy, successful light.

Although Oliver *was* proud of her, Emma conceded as she went downstairs. At corporate dinner parties and cocktail soirées, he'd smilingly introduce her as his successful wife, making it sound as though she single-handedly administered the majority of Marshalls's major accounts. She usually smiled bashfully, but in rooms buzzing with affluence and status, she felt like an impostor and never attempted to explain that her authority stopped at the supervision of the accounts team – accounts, as in payroll, debtors and creditors.

But all that would surely change, when the new appointee to the plum job of Marshalls's assistant accounts manager was announced.

Chapter 5

'Do you think Mum will get the promotion?' Libby asked.

They had listened to the seven o'clock news and sport, the weather forecast and traffic report in companionable silence. The morning rush was just starting to build up and the grey sky was brightening, with a glimmer of pale pink sunrise, as her father swung over the canal at Leeson Street, bang on schedule. Libby flipped down the passenger-seat visor and checked her reflection in the lighted mirror. She rummaged in her bag for her lipstick, and while they idled at traffic-lights, she curved the lustrous pink in a glossy bow across her lips. It was brilliant having a Paris-based make-up artist for an aunt – Alix generously showered Libby with an avalanche of freebies and designer goodies, including the Kelly bag, which had been under the tree the previous Christmas.

Her dad waited until the lights changed before he answered. 'I dunno, Libby,' he said, accelerating forward. 'She didn't seem all that pushed about it. I hardly even remember her doing the interview.'

'Dad!'

'Although I sort of recall something . . . one evening recently . . .'

'You *sort* of recall?'

Her father took his eyes off the road long enough to throw her a defensive look. 'Well, you know your mother – she never makes that much of a fuss.'

'You mean you were too busy and she didn't want to bother you.'

Her father sighed. 'You're probably right, Libby, as usual.'

Libby nodded. There were times when her father was far too wrapped up in his own career. 'I *am* right. I hope she's not in for a big disappointment. I'd hate her to feel let down. You know how soft Mum is . . .'

'It would scarcely be the end of the world. We are talking about Marshalls, aren't we?'

Her dad could have been discussing a merger instead of his wife, Libby fleetingly thought. But that was only because he was psyched up for the office. He was immaculately groomed as usual, and she knew from his air of concentration that, beyond being mindful of the traffic, he was mentally gearing up for the challenges of a busy day. Sometimes he had to streamline budgets, introduce cost-cutting measures and even have the balls to fire people – Libby knew she'd hate that. 'I suppose it's not as if there are megabucks involved,' she partly agreed with her father. Then she said, 'You don't really like Mum working, do you?'

'Not particularly. I thought I was sparing her all the extra hassle it brings. I assumed she was happy running our home and being involved with, well, women's stuff . . . lunches and that . . .'

'Dad! That went out with the Ark. You get involved in "women's stuff" when you retire, and you pay someone to clean and housekeep while you're doing more interesting work.'

'Too many good things went out with the Ark, if you ask me. And do you think Marshalls is all that interesting?'

In answer, Libby pulled a face. Immediately she felt a pang of disloyalty towards her mother.

'There's something about Leticia I really don't like,' her father continued, 'apart from the fact that your mother feels the ridiculous compulsion to tidy the house before she arrives.'

'Leticia's okay. At least she keeps her hands off my clothes.'

'See? What kind of a cleaner is she?'

'The best kind. She's friendly and happy and I think she fancies Charlie.'

Her father cut the corner at the top of Harcourt Street rather too sharply. 'How do you know? No, don't bother to answer that or I'll get into a bad humour. Christ. What's the latest on the Hang Seng?'

Libby took out her iPhone and duly reported her findings as her father turned into St Stephen's Green. Twenty minutes later she was saying goodbye to him and marching through the plate-glass entrance of her office foyer, clutching a take-out latte.

She loved coming into work in the mornings with her father: as well as being chauffeured by him in luxurious leather comfort, she enjoyed their special time together at the beginning of the day and the chance to connect with him. Although, on the subject of work, she was with her mum. It was hard to believe that her father – at forty-six, he was younger than most of her mates' dads *and* oozed brains – could be so old-fashioned in his thinking. He was highly principled but, without doubt, he was a hunter-gatherer and an out-and-out alpha male when it came to her mum.

Now Libby felt disloyal towards him so she banished the thought.

She came out of the lift on the fourth floor and walked down the corridor to the wide, open-plan office with the plate-glass windows that looked out onto Dublin's financial hub. All was quiet. Banks of desks and terminals were grouped together in teams extending

27

across the length of the floor and silently waiting for the working contingent to arrive. Soon, they would start to fill, and in thirty minutes' time the office would be a hive of frenzied activity. Another thing Libby liked about coming to work with her father was arriving into the office ahead of everyone else. It made her feel on top of things before the mad scramble of the day got under way.

She'd never admit it to a living soul, but this quiet time in the morning was often the only time she felt on top of things.

She went over to the window and stared out at the expanse of sky where dawn was finally breaking and the colours of the morning – rose, gold and blush pink – were exploding along the underside of soft, billowy clouds and unfurling across swathes of pale blue sky. It was so beautiful that it made her feel like crying. In that moment, she had the inspiring thought that the world was a magnificent place and she would find wings that would somehow lift her up and help her to reach whatever she truly wanted. Her heart jolted and she was filled with a sudden urge to re-create it all on canvas.

Libby let out her breath and called a halt to her fanciful daydreaming. She'd made her choice when she'd applied for a three-year degree course in economics and finance, deeming it far more practical and ambitious than pursuing a favourite hobby – a hobby that had been pushed to one side with the demands of her course, and now her career and busy social life. In a couple of months' time she'd be twenty-two. By the time she was thirty, the economy would have picked up again and she'd be running her own company.

Libby turned from the window and sat down at her desk. For all her airy talk, all her false, cheery confidence in front of her parents, she hated switching on her computer. Sometimes she even felt a wave of nausea as she logged on and opened her accounts for fear of what she might find. A gigantic mistake. Millions wiped off someone's equity. A firm gone bust because Libby Colgan had pressed the wrong button, even though she'd spent ages agonising over the keyboard in a hot sweat before she'd actually depressed the key. Most of the time it was just her imagination going haywire because, naturally enough, she'd been competently trained, there was a limit to her level of authority and there were fail-safe procedures in place to prevent that kind of thing happening.

She'd get used to it, she told herself. She just had to. She owed it to her dad.

'Stealing a march on everyone?' Tanya Wilson said, raising her eyebrows as she strode by Libby's desk.

'Gosh, Tanya, is it that time already?' Libby faked nonchalance.

Tanya's blue eyes gleamed at her through her glasses. 'You don't impress me, Libby, and you've a lot to learn if you think you're impressing the powers-that-be.'

There was no mistaking the malice in her tone, and Libby pulled a face as Tanya stalked across the room to her desk. When she'd started in Boyd Samuel Investments the previous autumn she'd had to contend with a fair amount of envy. Thanks to the downturn in the economy, she'd been the only graduate appointed to the firm that year, and it had been falsely whispered that she'd only been taken on because her father had influence with the CEO. Since then all of her colleagues had thawed, with the exception of Tanya, the bane of her life, and, she suspected, the person who had spread the rumour in the first place. Tanya's sister had graduated at the same time as Libby but she'd had to go to Hong Kong in her search for work.

One thing Libby loved was flaunting her exclusive designer accessories, all courtesy of Alix, in front of Tanya. From make-up to perfume to a chic little purse, she made sure to have it on display whenever she encountered Tanya in the ladies' room. Tanya's reaction was balm to her soul. Best of all, the morning Libby had brought her Kelly bag into work, treating it with a casual disdain, Tanya's eyes had almost popped out of her head and she'd been momentarily speechless. Libby, without shame, had rejoiced in the power surge it gave her.

She finished her latte and dumped the carton in the recycling bin. Then she pulled over her keyboard. Just as well it was Friday. She could legitimately go out on the razz that night, with the excuse that the weekend was here. Later, she'd phone Rob to make arrangements. They might try the new pub in South William Street, relax with a beer or two before going for food. Rob was her boyfriend – she'd met him three years ago on campus in Belfield, the university she'd attended on the south side of Dublin. Like her, he was ambitious and he worked in the IT unit of a rival firm. He was also studying part time for his master's degree, something Libby had put off for the moment – she felt she needed a break from studying.

Even thinking about the night ahead made her wish it was half past five and she had to swallow impatience as well as anxiety as she logged on to her accounts.

Chapter 6

She might have arrived in Paris on instinct, but Alix had grown to love the city and, in particular, the way it seemed to shimmer in the light. City of Light, *la ville lumière* – so-called because it regarded itself as a centre of knowledge and education, but also because it had been the first to adopt street lighting. But Alix had taken that name to her heart because she revelled in the crystalline days when the luminescence fell across the graceful façades of elegant, pale buildings and filtered into the corners of quaint, picturesque couryards, narrow streets and hidden, leafy parks. On sunny mornings the grand boulevards and tiny, intimate squares seemed full of light. It never failed to raise her spirits, and make her feel that life was still there for the taking and held some measure of promise.

This Friday morning, although the early rain had stopped and the sun was breaking through and glinting off the wet pavements, she didn't feel uplifted. Instead, she was gripped with renewed unease as she sat across the table from Henri, the senior marketing manager with Aurélie, in his opulent third-floor office, and discussed the campaign for the launch of Alix B.

Alix B had been conceived almost two years ago when Alix was first approached by a newly formed consortium under the umbrella of Aurélie, one of Paris's most prestigious cosmetics companies.

'*Merci*, Alix, for agreeing to this meeting,' the chief executive had said. 'We appreciate how busy you are and will come straight to the point. We've brought you here today because we'd like to know how you'd feel about helping us to launch a range of eco-friendly, competitively priced cosmetics for today's discerning woman.'

'Wow,' was all she could say. Then again, she had been sitting in the elegant splendour of the Hôtel George V's Le Cinq restaurant, nibbling blue lobster, with Jeanne, the chief executive, Gustav, the financial director, and Henri. She should have suspected something important was afoot.

'We'd love to have you on board – and we'd make it worth your while,' Gustav said.

'In today's crowded market we need something different,' Jeanne went on. 'You, Alix, have found a unique niche. It is well known that the tall Irish girl with the expert fingers is totally sympathetic to the needs of a woman, someone who has no pretensions and is freshly honest in this challenging beauty industry. Who better to front our advertising campaign and endorse our products?'

Although many make-up artists, models and celebrities had diversified into launching their signature brands of perfumes and cosmetics, and many more would have jumped at the opportunity Aurélie were offering, Alix's first instinct was to hesitate. 'It sounds great, but I'm not sure I'd have time for all this,' she said graciously, wondering why her gut was urging caution. 'As you pointed out, I'm an extremely busy person. I don't have a spare moment. Besides, I'm happy with what I'm doing.'

'Which is?'

'Helping women to look and feel better.'

'*Bien*.' Henri beamed delightedly, as though she had given him the five-star answer. 'We all appreciate your mission in life. That is why we are talking to you. We want you to help us to bring the best of today's advances in modern cosmetics within the reach of every woman.'

'Today's advances? You know how I feel about using natural ingredients,' Alix pointed out, trying a different approach.

'That's another reason why we're having this discussion.' Henri looked as though he had done his homework and was prepared to address each of Alix's concerns in turn. 'All our products are being formulated with natural and organic ingredients so that they'll be equally kind to the environment and your skin. You'd have full approval of the ingredients and can be as involved as you want to be in the trials.'

Still Alix hesitated, stalling for time. 'I'm not so sure I want my name to be affiliated with one specialist brand of cosmetics. What I like about my freelance career is that I'm not restricted to certain brands.'

'We're not asking for exclusivity,' Jeanne assured her. 'We understand that in your line of work you have to use a variety of different products. We are looking for your endorsement and your seal of approval to front our advertising campaign. We've already commenced preliminary tests. We're looking at introducing a core line of signature products first – foundations, concealers, eyeshadows, eyeliner, mascaras.'

'Tell me more about the production process,' Alix said, her interest snagged enough for her to ignore her instinctive misgivings. 'You also know how I feel about women being sold a very expensive lie in the name of beauty. I'd like to know just how you're going to put this all together.'

'We'll be competitively priced to suit today's cash-conscious market,' Jeanne said. 'We'll be working with one of Paris's best graphic designers to create a simple yet elegant packaging concept, which won't promise to deliver more than it can. We value the integrity of your name,' she smiled warmly, 'and we can assure you that it won't be discredited. If we could see you in our offices as soon as is convenient for you, we'd like to present to you the detailed vision of our concept. For starters,' Jeanne smiled, 'how does "Alix B at Aurélie" sound to you?'

Alix stared across the elegant dining room to the hotel's bright courtyard outside. She could follow her instinct and walk away from it all, but something about endorsing her signature brand of cosmetics appealed to her. In a moment of vanity she threw caution aside. She raised her hands in surrender and said, her green eyes alight with amusement, 'Jeanne, gentlemen, you are most persuasive. I'll have to talk to Estelle, my agent, and see if she's free to accompany me.'

And so, after more meetings, discussions and reassurances, Alix B at Aurélie was conceived. It had a young, fun, energetic vibe, to ensure mass-market appeal. Supported by a strategic and creative marketing plan, which Henri discussed in detail, Alix B cosmetics were to be launched in Paris at the end of May, then two weeks later in London, and rolled out to key markets in Europe and the US in the autumn. The model who'd be the face of Alix B and who would appear in all the promotional advertising was yet to be revealed to the press. Alix had had input into the selection and even she was impressed with Anika, the twenty-five-year-old stunningly beautiful Dutch model who'd been chosen.

'We've booked the Hôtel Louis XII for the launch event,' Henri explained now. 'The guest list includes Keira Knightley and Stella McCartney, several pop stars and supermodels. The colour theme of the night will reflect our packaging – the palest duck-egg blue, with the brand name Alix B superimposed in gold. Our design team has created a concept for the launch night and we think the visuals are very effective,' he said, passing some sketches across the table. 'It all reflects our wish to strike a balance between market affordability in today's challenging climate while retaining an element of luxury that induces a woman to feel good about using our products.'

'I want women to feel good because the product is doing what it's supposed to do,' Alix said.

'*Naturellement.* We have an excellent product, don't you agree?'

Alix nodded. Henri was right: they had developed a fabulous range of cosmetics using nothing but natural and organically produced ingredients. Eye colours ranged from matte baby pink right through to shimmering cobalt, including citrus orange and sea green, with complementing eyeliners and a range of lip-glosses from nude to deep vermilion.

'As you can see,' Henri went on, 'the name Alix B is strong enough to stand alone, and the product design is very attractive.'

As Henri organised refreshments, coffee for him and a bottle of Evian for Alix, she examined the plan for the launch night, her fingers tracing the outline of her name on one of the sketches. This was going to go global with a big launch in Paris, then London. As Fiona had pointed out, her name would be up there in lights, something she'd never envisaged for herself. She'd come to Paris all those years ago to make a fresh start and had never expected the level of success she'd so far achieved. Neither had she expected Alix B to spiral beyond her control.

The Aurélie consortium thought she had no pretensions: well, she could live with that. But 'freshly honest'? And what about the integrity of her name?

What a laugh.

As Henri handed her a bottle of Evian and a glass, Alix tried to ground her thoughts in reality. It was far too late to call a halt. Why couldn't she look on the bright side instead of allowing imaginary fears to take up her head space?

'Here's to success,' Henri said, waving his mug of coffee. 'I'll have to pretend it's champagne as it's a little early in the day for me. Unless you . . .?'

'Goodness, no, thanks – I'm driving and I have a lingerie shoot later this morning,' Alix said. 'To success.' She told herself there was nothing to be afraid of, raised her glass and put everything else out of her mind.

Chapter 7

*M*arshalls's downtown offices were located in a modern building that Emma knew was supposed to be the height of trendy chic but which she privately considered a little soulless. All morning, in the accounts department, she could feel the tension simmering under the surface. The result of the interviews was being simultaneously emailed to the three candidates just before lunch. Her family might have forgotten it was her big day, but Nikola and Stacy, part of the team she supervised, certainly hadn't. It was a foregone conclusion among her team that Emma would get the promotion.

'You have years of experience and you're by far the most senior,' Nikola reminded her.

Stacy nodded in agreement. 'I'm sure your interview was great,' she said in a magnanimous tone. 'I bet you impressed the board with your conscientious reliability. You're streets ahead of Gillian and Kevin.'

'It won't be long until one o'clock,' Nikola smiled benignly, 'and then you'll be out of your misery.'

Both Nikola and Stacy were in their early twenties and Emma knew, from the mildly sympathetic way in which they regarded her, that they considered her well and truly over the hill. Then again, her life must seem very boring to them, caught up as they were in intoxicating excitements such as hectic speed dating, frantic week-end clubbing and their Herculean attempts to entice Karl, their colleague, into bed.

When Karl and James, the last member of Emma's team, saun-tered past on their return from their coffee break, Emma knew exactly what to expect. Nikola and Stacy perked up immediately. Nikola thrust out her chest so that her boobs jutted saucily through her shirt. 'Hi, Karl,' she simpered.

Stacy widened her eyes. 'Karl, when you get a chance can you email me the February figures?' she said, sounding ultra-throaty and seductive, determined not to be outdone in the face of the com-petition.

Karl slowed and flashed white teeth. Since he had joined Marshalls three months ago, he had caused acute excitement in Nikola and Stacy on a daily basis.

'I just can't stop admiring his brooding Enrique Iglesias face,' Nikola regularly sighed, chin in hands as she stared across the floor to his desk.

'And just listen to his sexy Kerry accent . . .' Stacy as frequently drooled. 'It's one of the reasons I've stayed on in Marshalls.'

'What do you think of our chances, Emma?' Nikola had once asked.

'I don't know,' Emma had replied. 'I'm just glad he sits safely fur-ther down the floor.'

Nikola had smiled tolerantly. 'Oh my God, Emma, don't tell me he does something quivery to *your* pulse beat?'

'Certainly not!' Emma had bristled. 'He's much too young for me. But you pair would never get any work done if he was sitting any closer.' She'd be a little flustered too, Emma had admitted to herself. Karl was gorgeous. He was tall and sexy, brash and breezy, and with a well-toned body, courtesy of the GAA pitch, and messy black hair. He reminded Emma of the daredevil surfboarder in a cologne advertisement. She couldn't help being distracted by his good looks. Occasionally.

She wondered if Oliver took more notice of his female colleagues than he should, colleagues who wore hip-hugging minis and thrust out their breasts at him, who were brighter and more sexily intelligent than his wife, and who could discuss the world's economic problems and the cleverness of his financial deals with far greater knowledge and understanding than she could.

All the more reason to prove herself. She *had* to get this promotion. Emma felt suspended in edgy anticipation as the hands of the clock edged towards the appointed hour.

At five to one, Emma's inbox flashed with new mail.

She froze. The tips of her fingers felt like liquid as they slid across the keys. But as she opened the document, something chilly ran down her spine. It was several breath-holding seconds before she managed to recognise and then absorb the words *unfortunately* and *regrettably*. She looked up and caught Nikola and Stacy watching her, bright-eyed with anticipation. She looked back to her screen. Her heart was pounding painfully, then slip-slid all the way to her toes.

'Emma?' Nikola said. 'How soon are we going to lose our favourite supervisor?'

Too stunned to answer, Emma finally grasped that in Campaign Development, which was further up the office floor as befitted its elevated status, and strategically screened from the lowly accounts section by a row of flourishing potted plants, a different story was unfolding. Gillian, her closest rival for the job, auburn-haired and beautiful, had just leapt to her feet and, despite her skyscraper heels, was doing a little dance in a parody of shocked delight.

A heavy pall fell across the accounts team and settled in Emma's heart.

Libby replied to say she'd talk later when Emma texted her with the bad news, but there was no response from Alix or Oliver. She knew Alix had an appointment, but her husband was obviously far too busy talking to the emerging sub-Sahara or some other sexy territory. That afternoon Emma felt as though she was moving through a fog as work at Marshalls revved back to normal and she answered phones, made calls and tapped revised details into her spreadsheet. Her team was full of uneasy sympathy and solicitous glances. When Gillian invited the whole office out for drinks after work in a voice still squeaky with excited disbelief, Emma took all of two seconds to decide she wasn't going. She'd already endured enough.

She'd stick to her normal Friday night: grocery ordering and delivery, whatever cleaning Leticia hadn't managed to get around to, a takeaway meal from her local restaurant, then two or three glasses of wine in front of the television, bed and routine sex with Oliver. A fairly predictable Friday night.

Sitting at her desk, she was shocked at the way her unhappy thoughts were tumbling. She tried to soothe her bruised ego by counting her blessings. A healthy family who enjoyed a good lifestyle, despite the shaky economy, thanks to Oliver's brains and resourcefulness. His loving support would surely take the sharp edge off her crushing disappointment.

However, when Libby finally phoned in the afternoon, it wasn't to offer the support that Emma needed. 'I won't be home tonight, Mum,' she said. 'I'm meeting Karen and Mandy after work, then going on to Rob's.'

'Which means it'll be tomorrow night before you're home.'

'No, Rob's parents are away for the weekend so I'm staying over until Sunday,' Libby said airily.

In other words, her daughter planned to spend most of the week-end in bed with her boyfriend, enjoying youthful, energetic sex. Emma sighed dispiritedly. 'So neither you nor Charlie will be home tonight. He's off to a party.'

There was the sound of Libby's laughter. 'Is that what he said? I bet it's a private party for himself and his new girl, Melanie. I hope he brings his condoms. Oh, and, Mum, sorry about the promotion.'

'Thanks, darling. Looks like I won't be joining the jet set for now.'

'Well, it's their loss.'

'I'm glad someone thinks that.'

'Don't worry about it. No matter what happens you still have us. We'd never turn you down.' Libby sounded cheery and upbeat.

This was all she needed, Emma flatly decided: the blithe assurance of smug youth that the thrill of their existence was more than enough to compensate for her shattered hopes. Even though Libby was almost twenty-two, there was no sign of her leaving home. She might be managing enormous sums of money on behalf of high-net-worth clients, but somehow her fiscal expertise hadn't yet translated to the accumulation of enough funds for a deposit on a pad of her own. She was only six months into the job, though, Emma conceded, so it was probably early days. And with Rob, her adoring boyfriend, semi-resident most of the time, there wasn't much incentive.

But Libby wasn't finished. 'Mum, would you do me a huge favour?'

'What's that?'

'Could you throw my jeans into the washing machine? I left two pairs in the utility room last night and I forgot all about them. Thanks a mill – you're a star. See ya, Mum, gotta fly.'

Emma gritted her teeth. Libby knew darn well that her mum

would look after the jeans, and – shame on you, Emma – deposit them back in her bedroom, even though Libby and Charlie were supposed to look after their own laundry. Leticia was so terrified even to touch their designer clothes that Emma had gladly taken that job off her list.

Her eyes flicked down the office floor to where Gillian was still holding court with congratulatory colleagues and managers, and she wondered what it felt like to be in her shoes, enjoying the sweet taste of success. The office was buzzing with Gillian's promotion and her plans for the drinks party that evening, including, she almost wept, her traitorous staff. She heard Nikola and Stacy giggling as they made plans to rush out at five o'clock to invest in new and even sexier tops to increase their chances of seducing Karl. So much for their loyalty, Emma fumed, more determined than ever to avoid Gillian's celebration.

'Are you going tonight, Emma?' Karl stopped by her desk and smiled at her in the suggestive way that sent all the young and sometimes not-so-young office staff into a frenzy of eyelash fluttering.

'No, sorry, can't make it.' She tried to paint a nonchalant look on her face. 'I've already made plans.'

'Pity. As far as I'm concerned, the interview board were wearing blinkers.'

'Blinkers?' she snapped. 'It might have been better for me if they'd had on soft-focus lenses.'

'The first rule of competition, Emma, like on the football pitch, is that you must think very positively.' He flashed a grin. 'Next time, talk to me and I'll coach you.'

'There won't be a next time.'

'Of course there will.' Karl marched across to the photocopier, and she watched his progress, her eyes absorbing his wide shoulders, his crisp white shirt, his narrow hips and long legs. She wondered how it felt to be twenty-nine, free, single and super-confident. She'd never felt like that in her entire life.

'I'm only going tonight because of Karl,' Nikola announced.

'Same here,' said Stacy.

'May the best girl win,' Nikola said, eyeing her opponent across the office desk.

'It's every woman for herself,' Stacy solemnly agreed.

'Unless he's hungry enough to want us both. Together, I mean . . .' Nikola joked.

'Yeah, why not? Men like a bit of girl action.' Stacy darted a glance at Emma and muffled her giggles.

'I'd say he's great in bed,' Nikola sighed. 'I go all shivery just looking at him and the way he moves.'

Stacy giggled. 'So do I. Those sexy eyes – he looks as though he's very experienced and knows exactly what to do between the sheets. What do you think, Emma?'

'I don't think I'm qualified to answer that question,' Emma said. Oliver's eyes gave very little away about his sexual prowess. She couldn't admit that she'd only ever been to bed with him.

Then, finally, he phoned.

'It's about time,' she said. She rose to her feet, mobile pressed to her ear, and walked out to the corridor for some privacy.

'About time what? I'm up to my tonsils. I just phoned to let you know that I'll be out tonight—'

'Thanks for the support,' she snapped.

'What?' He sounded puzzled. Then he said, 'Christ. I'm sorry, Emma, I forgot.'

'I thought you were phoning to console me.'

'I'm really sorry if you feel disappointed over the promotion,' he said, 'but I can't help being a little relieved.'

Emma felt stung. 'Relieved? That I was rejected?'

'Don't take me wrong. Surely your life is busy enough as it is.

43

I'm just trying to look on the positive side of this. You'd only have ended up with more responsibility and hassle. Our lives are fine the way they are. Anyway, the last thing I need is a career-driven wife who's burned out on a Friday night.'

'The last thing *you* need? So that's it! We're coming to the real reason why you don't give a damn.' The crushing disappointment of the day rose up and engulfed Emma. 'Are you seriously suggesting I should limit my potential so that I can devote all my energy to running the house and organising the family?'

'I thought you loved the house.' He sounded hurt. 'Leticia takes care of the boring stuff. I work hard enough for the two of us. We always agreed, didn't we, that the family comes first? But now the kids are older, they can organise themselves and you don't need to devote as much energy to them. I'd prefer to see you relaxing more and taking things easy.'

'Taking things easy? So this is it?' she hissed down the phone, conscious of something splintering inside her. 'This is the sum total of my life? I'm not supposed to want any kind of challenge or fulfilment?'

'Calm down, I never said that. I thought you were happy with everything.'

'Maybe I'd like to achieve a little more.' *Maybe I want to feel that I'm important in some way outside the domestic arena. And important to you on a deeper level.*

'I'm sorry if the kids and I don't provide you with an adequate sense of self-fulfilment,' Oliver said. 'And I can't have this conversation now as I'm far too busy. I just phoned to say that I'll be home late because one of the American directors is bringing us out for food and drinks in the Ely.'

'Well for some.'

'Look, Emma, try to cheer up and see the positive side.'

His cavalier attitude stirred her anger. She wondered who would

44

be joining Oliver's group that evening, how many female colleagues would be there – colleagues with inviting cleavages, throaty laughs and clever conversation, whose glances would hold his a little longer than was politely necessary, sending out signals that might cause him to look twice. Oliver was an attractive man and he was bound to have some free and single colleagues, like Stacy and Nikola, who would be keen to get him into bed. In the face of her raw disappointment and rejection, it was too much. 'Get lost,' she fumed, and snapped her mobile shut.

When it rang again ten minutes later, Emma wasn't going to answer it until she spotted that it was Alix.

'Hi, sis,' Alix began. 'I got your text. What on earth were those blockheads thinking of?'

'I can't really talk. I've already been chatting to Libby and Oliver and I've stuff to key in before four o'clock.'

'Sod them. Take as long as you like. How dare they turn you down?'

Her sister was so outraged that Emma almost laughed, but suddenly it turned into a gush of tears. 'It's okay,' she said, swallowing hard and pretending to be detached. 'It's only a stupid job. I don't really care.'

'No matter. How dare they reject my sister?'

'I thought you'd be on your way to Gstaad by now.'

'I will be soon. Fiona has organised a private jet so we'll all go together . . .' Alix chatted on about the highlights of the weekend.

'Very nice,' Emma said, trying to restrain a sliver of envy from colouring her tone.

'Are you sure you're okay?'

'Yes, I'm fine.'

'I have to get going. Just to say I think the interview board were nuts and you should hold your head high and go out and drown your sorrows, not that you should have any sorrows!'

Several minutes later Emma's mobile beeped and she opened a text message from Libby. It wasn't a message to cheer her up or wish her luck, or even a smiley face. It was a reminder to include Libby's special colourist shampoo when she ordered the shopping. Emma felt a blast of fury at her daughter, all set for a sexy weekend while she stapled up her shattered self-image, organised the shopping, separated the laundry for Leticia and obediently sorted her daughter's clothes. Then there was Oliver, all set for flirtatious bonhomie with stimulating colleagues. Even Charlie was out, pursuing the delectable Melanie in a testosterone-fuelled frenzy. And Alix, as usual, was off for a glitzy weekend.

Yet what was stopping her following her sister's example for once? Why couldn't she cut loose and abandon her dutiful Friday night – and where better to hold her head high and show the world she didn't care than at Gillian's party?

Chapter 8

'Harcourt Street, please,' Libby instructed the driver as she slid into the back of a taxi and it pulled away from the financial services centre. She rummaged in her Kelly bag for her mobile and texted Mandy to say she was on the way. Then she sat back as the taxi joined the heavy rush-hour traffic inching across the River Liffey. Despite the lure of the evening ahead, she couldn't help feeling a little annoyed with herself.

It was only when Mum hadn't sounded like her usual, cheerful self on the phone that Libby had belatedly remembered her text about the interview. Trust Libby to ask her to finish off her laundry, then send a crappy, thoughtless text about shampoo, when surely the last thing Mum felt like doing was laundry and grocery ordering?

Libby grimaced.

Then again, she'd been so psyched up at closing off her accounts correctly and sending an important email to Washington that it wasn't surprising everything else had slipped her mind. And her mother never refused Libby. She was far more obliging than most of her friends' mothers. Although that didn't mean Libby had to take advantage of her generous nature, she chided herself. But Mum always said that her family was the best thing in the world, even though, shock horror, she had been only nineteen *and* six months pregnant with her daughter when she'd married Dad. Grandmother Colgan had once frostily hinted to a thirteen-year-old idealistic Libby that her mother had pulled the age-old stunt of trapping him, with his privileged background and glittering future, into a rushed marriage. Libby had been appalled and, in what she liked to think was her private mini-rebellion, had managed to avoid talking to Grandmother Colgan for quite a long time, until she'd had to accompany her father to the old lady's hospital deathbed to say goodbye. But although she might have kissed her and surprised herself by shedding tears at the funeral − because the singing was very emotional, she told herself − her grandmother's comment had run around in her head for a long time afterwards.

Did it mean that her parents wouldn't have married if Libby hadn't been on the way? Was there any truth in what Grandmother Colgan had said about her mum coercing her father into a hurried marriage? Surely not. Had her father felt trapped by her arrival? Libby's entry into the world must have meant the end of his freedom. He'd had to knuckle down and provide a home for his wife and new baby.

Libby thought it was best not to voice these worries to anyone. She sometimes wondered what Granny Camille might have made of her mini-rebellion. She liked to think that Camille Berkeley would have been proud of her granddaughter's feisty stand. However, her maternal grandmother had been killed years ago in a car crash and Libby never spoke to her mum about it because she knew it was a no-go area.

She'd been about seven when her grandfather, Andrew Berkeley, had died and she'd begun to ask questions about the family − like where was her other granny, cos she only had one when most of her schoolfriends had two. Her father had taken her out to the park and sat her on a bench near the ducks, where he'd quietly explained that Granny Camille had died in a tragic accident when Emma was only eleven and it was best not to ask Mum about it as it was all so very painful for her.

Later on, when Libby came across Granny Camille's photograph in old albums, she'd thought at first that she was looking at Aunt Alix. She'd figured out that her aunt would have been only seven when her mother had died, and Libby couldn't imagine how awful it must have been for her mum and Alix, so she was happy to stay away from the subject.

But now it was all ancient history and everything had turned out well in the end. Mum was happy with her family and Alix was a mega-success. Libby was going to Paris with her parents at the end of May for the launch of Alix's new cosmetics range, and she couldn't wait. She'd be meeting all sorts of celebrities and fashionistas, supermodels and stylists, and had to make sure she was as glamorous as possible that night. She still wasn't sure whether to go for a rock-chick look or boho-hip, soft and romantic or timelessly elegant. She'd have to talk to Alix and seek her advice.

Thank God Alix was down to earth. She pictured her aunt's eyes lighting up as they shared a laugh and a joke at some of the more outrageous fashions and hissy behaviour that was bound to liven up the launch night. And afterwards, when she went back to Boyd Samuel, Tanya would get an earful. Better still, she'd put the glitziest photos of the event on her work PC and use them as her screen saver.

Libby brightened up as the taxi neared Harcourt Street and the pubs and nightclubs beckoned. She loved Friday nights and couldn't wait to unwind with a few chilled beers for starters.

When she'd phoned Rob in her lunch hour to suggest going out that evening, she'd been disappointed when he'd refused. 'I can't, Libby. I've a busy night lined up.'

She'd made a face, thankful he couldn't see her expression. 'So? It's Friday. I'm dying to go out and relax with a few drinks. I deserve it after the busy day I've had.'

Rob was silent for a minute, and then he said, 'If you're in need of a drink, you go ahead. I've some studying to do, and if I finish it tonight, it'll leave me free for the rest of the weekend.'

Libby thought rapidly. 'Why don't I come over later, when you're finished? We'll have the rest of the night and all Saturday and Sunday.'

'Okay, so long as it's not too late. Text me when you're on the way.'

Then Libby had phoned Karen and Mandy, her friends from college, and arranged to meet them. She climbed out and paid the driver. It was Rob's tough luck if he preferred an alcohol-free night at home with his books, but she was certainly going to chill out.

And there was no need to worry about Mum, she assured herself as she hitched up her bag on her shoulder. Dad would surely cheer her up. For despite what Grandmother Colgan had insinuated all those years ago, her parents were cool and still together, and she couldn't imagine life in Laburnum Grove being any other way.

Which was great, considering the mess some of her friends' parents had made of their lives.

Chapter 9

'Late again,' Dave joked, pouring Alix a glass of champagne as she walked into the executive lounge wearing a pale grey cashmere overcoat and a soft pink scarf. She was the last to arrive at the airport and her friends were all waiting for her, Fiona and Dave, Yvette, Sophie and Marc.

'Hello, darlings, sorry I'm late but, as you know, I'm the only one who does a decent day's work around here,' Alix riposted, knowing that every single one of them put in long hours at their respective careers – otherwise they wouldn't have been where they were today, successful, recognised and rewarded. Their evening flight left on time, the small jet lifting above the darkening Paris skies and whisking them to the breathtaking beauty and party atmosphere of the snowy slopes. Everyone was in a festive mood, even though it was a rather ordinary weekend at the start of spring. Alix worked out that it was the first time they'd all been together since their New Year's Eve party and everyone seemed keen to relax and enjoy the break.

The chalet was the height of luxury, situated on the slopes out-side Gstaad, a little removed from the hustle and bustle. It boasted underfloor heating as well as an authentic ornate fireplace in the luxurious, open-plan living area. They settled into their en suite rooms and refreshed themselves before coming downstairs for pre-dinner cocktails, where glass walls allowed them to gaze at the moonlit, snowy landscape as they caught up on all the gossip. Then they sat around a big oak table in the dining area where their meal was served by a genial Pierre and his assistant.

Afterwards, the friends relaxed on comfy leather sofas and Marc stoked up the blazing fire. Dave and Fiona opened more champagne and thanked everyone for joining them as they celebrated their third wedding anniversary.

'Cheers! I can't believe it's three years already since we had that wild weekend in Cork,' Alix said, raising her glass. Dave and Fiona had returned to their native Cork to get married and had had a true Irish country wedding, which had involved lots of partying, wild Irish dancing and Guinness by the barrel. The celebrations had lasted the entire weekend.

'Neither can I,' Fiona laughed. 'I don't know where the time has gone. I suppose it's a good sign that it flew by so fast!'

'Congratulations to you both.' Sophie clinked her glass against Fiona's and Dave's.

'Here's to many more years of happiness,' Yvette said.

Sophie and Yvette were Paris-based models. Childhood friends, they hailed from Marseille, and had met Alix when they arrived in Paris hoping to break into the big time. They had asked her to do their make-up for their portfolios and it had been her first private commission. Alix had taken to them immediately and they'd fast become friends. Now, even though they were in their early thirties, they were among the extremely lucky few in their profession who were still able to snare lucrative campaigns. Warmly intelligent, healthy looking as well as beautiful, they had never subscribed to the ridiculous thinner-than-thin industry standard.

Marc was a fashion photographer from Belgium, and had become mates with Dave, Fiona and Alix over the years, running into them on the modelling circuit, where he'd also met and fallen head over heels in love with Sophie. Alix's Parisian social life revolved more around her friends than her career, and they met up for birthday celebrations and Saturday evening meals as well as occasional weekends away.

'Come on, Alix, spill the beans – what really happened in Milan?' Fiona asked when everyone had finished toasting her and Dave.

'Don't ask,' Alix said, tucking her legs up under her on the wide sofa. 'Too many egos clashing. The schedule was rejigged, call times were all over the place, and backstage everyone was falling over themselves. Out on the catwalk it was deemed a sparkling triumph. I wasn't sorry to be coming home early.'

'I'm glad I was too busy to be there,' Yvette said. 'What kind of creations were on offer? Any new trends that we'll be embracing?'

'You'd have missed Valentino, our Maestro, but there's some very exciting talent emerging,' Alix said, and went on to describe some of the key looks and colours for the following autumn.

Sophie sipped her champagne. 'I'm relieved to hear it's business as usual.'

'Yes,' Yvette smiled. 'We all need to hold on to our glamour in these straitened times.'

'So, as usual, no juicy gossip from our Alix?' Fiona said, a mock pout on her lovely face.

'I'm sure there were plenty of cat fights, but you know I avoid the bitchy side of things,' Alix said, then relented. 'Although I might let you in on one or two secrets . . .'

'I should hope so. And how was your week?' Fiona turned to Sophie.

'Okay, if you like wearing a bikini in freezing cold weather!'

Sophie rolled her sapphire blue eyes. She'd recently been snapped up by one of Paris's most glamorous lingerie labels to front their new swimwear and recession-antidote collection.

'How you suffer for your art.' Alix was more aware than most of the demanding and arduous conditions under which the majority of models made a living.

'If I'd been on that shoot, I wouldn't have let you get cold,' Marc said.

'With temperatures of three degrees on the beach in Brittany, even you would have found that very difficult,' Sophie said pertly. 'As if that wasn't bad enough, I also got soaking wet when an icy cold wave almost knocked me over.' She made a face of exaggerated horror.

'*Quelle* disaster!' Marc grinned. 'I could have saved you from *that* calamity.'

'Anyway, Sophie, we're so glad you managed to recover from your near Arctic experience to be here,' Dave laughed. 'And that you, dear Alix, finally managed to make the flight . . . because, besides our wedding anniversary, Fiona and I have something else to celebrate . . .'

Alix sensed what he was about to say before he drew another breath. She knew by the proud contentment on his face and the barely suppressed excitement in Fiona's eyes – and Fiona had barely touched her champagne.

'We're expecting a baby,' Fiona cried.

'We're pregnant,' Dave said simultaneously.

Alix felt jolted into silence. Not only were Fiona and Dave happily married, but now a baby would bring them added joy. She reminded herself that she was quite happy with her life, glad that the next few moments were busy with squeals of delight and hugs as the friends embraced. Sophie and Yvette made up for her silence with their excited questions. She heard Fiona say that she was due

54

in September and would remain at work as long as she could. She heard Dave say that the expectant mother was to learn to put her feet up from time to time, and reduce her working hours as of now, and everybody laughed. After a while, Alix joined the others thronging around Fiona and Dave, gave them both a warm hug, and eventually everybody settled back.

Marc put on some music and Dave topped up everyone's glass, except Fiona's – she had opted for fruit juice. Marc threw more logs on the fire, and the softly lit room filled with the sweet, aromatic scent of woodsmoke. Alix sat in a big armchair, half turned to the window, watching the way the comforting glow of the fire was reflected in the glass walls and seemed to be superimposed on the ghostly night-time drifts of snow outside. 'Alix? You're quiet. You okay?' It was Fiona. She tapped her lightly on the arm and looked at her questioningly.

Alix gave her friend the benefit of her brightest smile. 'Course I am. And your news is fabulous. The best. I'm thrilled for you both. I guess I can't help looking out at the view because it's so beautiful here – you certainly picked the right spot to tell us all.'

'It could be the same for you, you know,' Fiona said gently. 'You could have someone who'd give you a future, someone who'd share your hopes and dreams. I see it when we're out together, the eyes that are drawn to you. You could have any man you want. I know you're happy now, but you could be even happier . . .'

Alix forced a smile. It was convenient that Fiona had assumed she was happy in her singleton state because of Laurent, but it wasn't quite accurate. Not by a murmur did her friend censure Alix's relationship with him. It was something they never talked about, Alix having spelled it out loud and clear when she had first told Fiona that she expected her confidence to be respected.

'I just feel you're missing out on so much,' Fiona went on. 'And I think you'd be a wonderful wife and mother.'

That's where you're so wrong, Alix was tempted to say. I'd be a lousy wife and mother. The very worst in the whole wide world. Instead she lifted her glass of champagne, smiled at Fiona, told her *she*'d be a wonderful mother, and downed the contents in one.

'I hope so. And I'm sorry for lecturing you,' Fiona said. 'I know you're living the life you want. I'm just so bursting with happiness that I want everyone to feel like this. The baby is so important to me and Dave.'

'Of course it is, and I'm so happy for you.'

Afterwards, when she slipped out to the kitchen to get a glass of water, Alix stood for a long time by the window, staring out at the peace and tranquillity of the silent, snowy landscape and the fairy-tale lights of the town twinkling below. She wondered how something so incredibly beautiful could make her feel so incredibly sad.

Chapter 10

*E*mma squeezed up on the jammed banquette to make space for Nikola, and watched a flushed and excited Gillian take orders for yet another round of drinks.

She hadn't known what she'd been missing. All those nights she'd dutifully ordered her shopping online and settled in with a bottle of wine, Dublin's chic youth had been out having fun. Even in these post-Celtic Tiger days, everyone was seriously intent on celebrating the arrival of the weekend with as much alcohol as possible, explosive music, shrieking conversation and, for the females, the least clothing they could get away with. The crowd from Marshalls had taken over the entire back of the pub and were hell bent on celebrating Gillian's success. The atmosphere was loud, frenetic and excited. She wondered if Charlie was out somewhere like this, as a prelude to the party, with the scantily clad Melanie making eyes at him. She wondered if Libby had left her friends and was already in bed with Rob, taking advantage of the empty house to let rip.

As for Oliver, she'd sent him a text to say she was going out after work but he hadn't replied.

'Hey, I'll get these drinks.' Emma stood up and waved her credit card.

'This is my last round,' Gillian shouted back above the roar. She was met with cat-calls and applause. 'After this, it's everyone for themselves.'

Gillian looked great. Emma was furious to realise that it made her feel somewhat diminished. Promotion had given her colleague an instant, shiny confidence, with a glow of self-satisfaction that surrounded her like a halo. Of course, it helped that all the managers and directors had turned up to support her and were even now laughing loudly at her jokes and glancing at her admiringly. Emma stared into her wine and wondered again just where she'd gone wrong.

She was on her third glass of Sauvignon Blanc before she found the courage to move across to where Amanda Jacob, the accounts director and her boss, was seated. After some small talk and hedging around the subject, Emma admitted her disappointment.

'Do you really want to know why you didn't get the job?' Amanda asked.

'Yes, I do,' Emma said, even though she was secretly terrified at what Amanda might reveal.

'You didn't get it because you're just too nice,' Amanda said bluntly.

Something landed with a heavy thud in Emma's heart. 'Too *nice*? What do you mean?'

'You're not ruthless enough. That's why you didn't make the grade. You should have gone into that interview looking as though you were prepared to kick everyone's arse skywards and not as though you'd bend over backwards to help out.'

There was a constriction in Emma's throat. She hated the way her voice sounded thin as she asked, 'Since when did being helpful and friendly debar you from promotion?'

Amanda rolled her eyes. 'You're a great team player, but you just don't have that killer competitive edge to go for the jugular.'

'I didn't think it was required in the job spec.'

'Don't be naive,' Amanda snorted. 'It's a question of walking and talking like a winner, instead of behaving like a people-pleaser. If you really want to get ahead in Marshalls, take some advice from me. Change your whole mindset. The courage and conviction to be a winner has to come from within yourself. Nobody's going to hand it to you on a plate.'

'Thanks for that.' Emma glared at her, then went back to her seat, her head whirling, and the renewed pain of rejection settling again in her heart. She finished her glass of wine and reached for another mini-bottle. Nobody seemed to be asking if anyone actually wanted a drink – rounds were being ordered indiscriminately, the waitress returning to the table regularly with a heavily loaded tray. It was all too easy to sit back and work her way through the mini-bottles lined up in front of her. All too easy to let a soft fuzz descend around her sore heart, insulating her from her family's heedlessness and the painful sight of Gillian chatting brightly to the management contingent as though she already knew them personally. When the CEO himself squeezed through the crowds and gave Gillian a congratulatory hug, Emma excused herself, rose to her feet unsteadily and escaped to the ladies' room.

She frowned at herself in the mirror, at pains to discover just where it showed that she lacked the all-important ruthless streak to make it to the top. Those words of Amanda's had hit a nerve because, whatever about Marshalls, even she knew that she was far too much of a soft touch when it came to her family.

It was nobody's fault but her own if her family didn't understand the full extent of her disappointment. Nobody's fault but her own if she'd taught them to take her for granted and dismiss her feelings so readily. After all, she'd spent most of her married life pleasing others and neglecting her own needs, determinedly playing the part of devoted wife and mother.

It was going to stop right now, Emma decided firmly, raising her chin. She opened her make-up bag and dabbed foundation across her cheeks. Then she applied a fresh coat of mascara and a generous dollop of lip-gloss. In a burst of alcohol-fuelled fervour, she realised that she didn't need promotion to become the new Emma Colgan because the new Emma Colgan was looking at herself in the mirror. She would insist that Libby and Charlie start pulling their weight far more than they did at present.

As for Oliver . . .

This was important. Emma paused and tried to sift through the muddle in her head. She stared at herself in the mirror and tried to connect with herself and her real feelings.

She wanted Oliver . . . Well, deep down, and in her heart of hearts, she wanted him to look at her with the same interested spark that he had when he left for the office each morning. The spark that had somehow become buried under years of domestic stuff, such as moving up the property ladder, the best private school for Libby and Charlie, and the increasingly long hours that he was putting in at the office in the face of economic contraction. The spark that had fizzled out as his all-absorbing career had opened a widening chasm between them.

Last but not least, Emma decided recklessly, the new, improved Emma Colgan was going to sack the lazy Leticia.

Her head felt thick as she worked out how to leave the pub with the minimum fuss and before anyone found out that a few glasses of wine had sent her over the edge. She just had to go back and get her coat, then slip quietly out of the door without saying goodbye to anyone, get into a taxi and, at home, crawl under the duvet.

'Hey, Emma, you okay?'

'Are you feeling all right?'

Nikola and Stacy smiled at her as they marched up to the mirrors and checked their reflections. They looked completely different outside the four walls of the office. Size eight, if they were even that, with tiny cinched waists, sexy, lace-frilled cleavages, make-up still prettily perfect, identical sheets of blonde hair. Early twenties with bright white smiles. No wonder she felt jaded. 'I'm fine,' she said, mustering a smile. 'Great night, isn't it?'

'Yes, but us guys still think it should have been you,' Nikola said stoutly. 'You really deserved the job.'

'Thanks.'

'See you later,' they chorused as she picked up her bag and moved to the door. 'Might see you in the nightclub,' Nikola said. 'That's when the real action will begin.' She gave her an indulgent wink as though to say Emma wouldn't be expected to cope with nightclub mania.

Emma pushed her way through the crowd and felt the sting of self-pitying tears behind her eyes. She knew she'd already had too much to drink, but she went back to the table and, instead of reaching for her coat, sat down and unscrewed the cap of another mini-bottle of wine, pouring most of the contents into her glass. She was easily on her second litre by now, she hazily figured out, and revelled in the warm rush of gratification as a further injection of alcohol kicked in and soothed her ragged nerves. Loud conversation resonated around her and she heard herself speak and saw herself laugh as though she was encased in some kind of bubble.

She heard someone ask the time and was amazed to discover how late it was. She'd been steadily drinking all night. People started to leave, to gather coats, bags, scarves. They were going on to a ritzy nightclub off Grafton Street that she'd never heard of. Stacy and Nikola went to the ladies' room once more, to sex up their faces, she heard them say. She found she was glued to her seat, unable to summon the necessary energy to stand up, walk out of the door and find a taxi to take her home. Worse again was that instead of finding it a matter for concern, she felt nothing, as though she was blanketed in thick fog.

'Emma? You okay?'

Karl's face swam in front of her. He looked anxious.

'I'm fine.' Her voice was high-pitched, slurred, strange.

'You don't seem too good to me.'

She beamed, realising his concern was for her. 'I'm good, really I am. Problem is, I'm too good.' Suddenly her face collapsed and tears sprang to her eyes. Then Karl was beside her, and she was grateful that his body shielded her from the dwindling remains of the office party. 'Just stay here,' she muttered. 'Don't move. Just for a moment, until I pull myself together.'

'I think you need some fresh air.'

'Yes, probably.' She cast about ineffectually for her belongings. Where was her coat? Her bag? God. She couldn't even stand unaided. She was pissed. 'Will you come with me? Just outside for a minute.'

Karl found her coat and helped her into it, located her bag, rescued her gloves from the floor. She knocked against the table as she stood up clumsily, causing the empty wine bottles to rattle. Wild hysteria rose in her throat. Karl took her arm. He was coming to her rescue. He would look after her. He made her feel secure, she thought gratefully. Something like the way Oliver had made her feel all those years ago.

Chapter 11

*O*utside on the narrow pavement the breeze was biting. Emma gulped cool, clear lungfuls of air and tried to steady herself. The traffic snarled and churned by, so close to the pavement that she was almost swept under the wheels of a bus.

'Careful.' Karl gripped her arm, gently propelling her along the street. They came to a junction and waited obediently for the green man, Emma leaning on him when they crossed the road.

The scene instantly changed. Pedestrians surged around, their shapes distorted as they blurred into one another. They spilled out of jam-packed pubs and thronged the pavements. Streetlights were yellow globes suspended in the sky that meshed together in a gaudy necklace. The atmosphere was frantic and full of edgy animation.

Temple Bar.

She spoke through chattering teeth: 'I've always wanted to do Temple Bar on a Friday night.'

'You mean you haven't?'

'No, not like this. My kids have, but not me.' Forbidden excitement burst like a flower inside her, sweetening the sense of loss that had dogged her all day. She hung onto Karl as they negotiated the crowds, skirting the gatherings that spilled out onto pavements, and tasted the energy that reverberated across the thick night air and flickered like a moving tide across the heave of bodies.

'Hey, how about a drink?' she said, conscious that she was suggesting something a little dangerous yet feeling the reckless urge to move beyond the boundaries of dutiful wife and mother.

'I think you've had enough,' Karl said, stalling and looking at her curiously.

The streetlight caught the planes of his face so that he appeared foreign. You could forget Enrique Iglesias — Stacy and Nikola would have cardiac arrests if they could see Karl now. 'I've had enough wine, yes, even I know that,' she giggled, 'but a cool beer would go down very well.'

'If you're sure?'

'Oh, I am . . . and I'm your boss,' she added, with a trace of spunk. 'So you have to follow my orders.'

'Right, boss,' he grinned

Then they were moving into a pub where heat and noise hit their faces, and she followed him, sliding through the space he made between the bodies, feeling as though she had stepped outside herself and into a different and exciting world. It was more relaxed in there, away from Gillian and the office gang, away from her failed attempt at promotion, and she was filled with a peculiar relief. Already the office party seemed distant. It was different, too, to be facing Karl across the small table, watching the way his dark hair waved about his face and his eyes focused on her. The beer was cool and refreshing after the wine and, already tipped over into drunkenness, it was easy to follow one glass with another.

'Emma, I'll have to get you home,' he said.

Despite the fuzz of alcohol, she liked the way he talked to her. Kindly and concerned, as though he had taken her under his wing and was looking out for her. Just the way Oliver had years and years ago.

'Big problem there,' she said, grappling with the words and trying not to sway too much on her stool.

He pushed her glass away from her. 'Come on, I'll get you into a cab.'

'No. I can't.'

'Emma.'

He looked, she thought unhappily, as though he was well practised in assisting helpless females who'd had far too much to drink. And that was precisely what she had descended to. 'I'm afraid I might get sick in the cab.' She forced herself to sit still as the whole pub took flight and swirled around her.

He gave her a long look, then pushed aside his pint, shrugged on his jacket and came around to her side of the table. 'Let's go.'

She was mortified that he had to help her to her feet.

Once again, they were out in the cool, clear night air. Karl guided her up the street very slowly, avoiding the jostling crowds as much as possible. When they had gone a hundred yards or so, he stopped and faced her. They had moved, she sensed, beyond the office dynamic. She was no longer his boss – she could forget about the Emma Colgan who appeared in the office each day in her navy suit and organised the work rota. Right now she was somebody who needed a helping hand, a shoulder to cry on, a listening ear.

'How do you feel now?'

Her teeth were chattering. She couldn't believe how cold she felt. 'I'm okay. I just need to keep walking and get some more fresh air.'

'Would you like to come to my apartment?' he asked. 'It's fifteen, maybe twenty minutes. I can give you some tea and toast, and make sure you feel better before you get a cab.'

She didn't hesitate. She was beyond coherent decision. She heard herself slur, 'I think that's a very good idea.' She saw his teeth flash in a smile, then he held out his arm and she linked it. He guided her away from the crowds and down a cobbled side-street until they came to where the breeze was stronger and saltier and the Liffey was flowing like thick black silk.

They walked in silence for a while, following the course of the river as it surged out to sea and slapped against dark grey walls, orange lights on the opposite bank reflecting on its surface in long wavy columns. Emma was vaguely aware that her nausea was subsiding. She didn't know quite what she was doing beyond that she had embarked on a private adventure.

Karl's apartment was on the fourth floor of a modern block, all clean lines and urban white, floor-to-ceiling glass, recessed lighting, with a huge shag-pile rug and a white corner sofa that ran at angles around two sides of the room, forming a chaise longue at one end.

'Very nice, Karl,' she said, flopping down on the sofa. 'Is this all yours?'

'No, I share with my friend. He's out tonight.'

'It's lovely . . . so spotless.' She couldn't help the surprise in her voice.

'Too spotless for two Kerry men?'

'I didn't mean it like that.'

He roared laughing. 'No worries. We have a lovely Polish girl who comes in every Friday, handy if we're having *friends* in over the weekend.' He gave her a meaningful look, and she wondered had she already fallen into that category. He disappeared into a small galley kitchen and came back a few moments later with two steaming mugs of tea, which he set on a low glass table. 'I'll make some toast,' he suggested.

'No, it's okay. Tea is fine,' she said. 'I don't normally get like this,' she went on, still finding it difficult to form the words because her mouth felt rubbery, yet anxious that Karl should understand.

'Like what?' He gave her a half-smile.

'So pissed.'

'That's because you're upset.'

'Upset?' In spite of her drunkenness, she felt a scalding mortification that he understood.

'Upset over Gillian. It's okay.'

'Do you know what Amanda said to me?'

'Tell me.'

'I'm too nice for my own good. Too *nice*!'

'There's nothing wrong with that.'

'There's everything wrong with it. I let people walk all over me because I'm a people-pleaser.'

'So? We need people like you, people who hold the rest of us together and make this difficult life a little easy.'

'What about *my* life? Maybe I just want to please myself for a while.' Again it seemed vital to shed her skin, to slough off the disappointed and rejected Emma Colgan. She listened to Karl's calming words in his attractive accent.

'There's nothing wrong with pleasing yourself. It's important to be kind to yourself and to treat yourself with affection. Here, drink your tea.' His voice was so kind that it soothed her fraught soul. His eyes, as they looked at her, seemed full of warmth, which her sore heart soaked up. She looked at his hands curled around his mug, the long, lean fingers, then at his jaw, slightly stubbled now so late at night.

'I like being here,' she said, the words rolling out of her mouth with a force of their own. 'I like this, now, us having this talk.' She felt something reckless shear through the baggage of her life, lifting her up, carrying her to a different level and tossing her onto some strange new shore. In that moment she felt a renewed awareness of herself, more vital and alive than she had in years.

'I like it too,' he said. Silence fell. Then, after a while, 'Emma.'

'Yes?'

'Don't feel sad because you weren't hard enough to get the new job. Don't cast aside the way you are or see it as a less . . .' He hesitated. 'I don't know how to say this, but you're just right, perfect, the way you are.'

Something had changed. She sensed it in the way he looked at her. Even through the cloak of alcohol she sensed a difference in the way he was watching her, and she almost jumped when his eyes gave her a top-to-toe sweep. Nikola wanted to sleep with him, she almost said. Stacy thought his eyes were oh so sexy.

'I need the bathroom.' She rose to her feet, appalled that she was still a little wobbly.

Even the bathroom was different. Masculine. Ultra-modern, and full of mirrored glass, with focused lighting and a vast shower cubicle. A pile of black and white towels. She was in a different world, some kind of parallel reality. She had a vision of standing naked under the shower with Karl and her skin flashed with heat. She stared at herself in the mirror and didn't recognise the pale face and expression of elemental desire in her eyes, let alone the excitement that ran like a hot thread through her veins. Emma was conscious of standing on the edge of something. She could leave now before . . . Well, before what exactly? she asked herself. And don't say that the brand new Emma Colgan had already scuttled for shelter. She lifted her chin and rinsed her hands in the deep bowl of the sink, feeling the warmth of the cleansing water as it trickled over her fingers, feeling like a stranger as she left the bathroom and clicked off the light.

Feeling like a stranger when she came back out to the living area, where Karl was still sitting in the same spot on the sofa. This time, she sat next to him.

'You said I was just right the way I am. What do you see when you look at me?' She was pushing away the boundaries now, alcohol lending her false courage as she stepped into new and heady territory, giving her the right to say exactly what she wanted to, with no thought of consequence.

'I see someone with a friendly soul.'

'Friendly?' She pouted like a six-year-old seeking to be indulged.

'Friendly, compassionate, caring.'

'Is that all?' She leaned a little closer, coquettish now, almost flirty. Practising the new Emma Colgan. Trying out her lines.

'No, of course that's not all.'

'Maybe you'd prefer Nikola or Stacy to be sitting here now.'

She felt absurdly pleased when he shook his head and smiled. 'They're too young, too caught up with themselves.'

'They're young and attractive compared to me,' she went on, with a self-deprecating smile, 'I have shadows under my eyes.'

He traced them with his thumb, startling her with a touch that was as soft as a butterfly's. 'Yes, but those shadows under your eyes and your fragile air make you seem soft and gentle,' he said.

'So, Karl, what else do you see?' It had become a game – the game of stepping outside herself. She was carried away with a rashness that caused her to put a finger to his mouth.

Stop. *Now.*

She dismissed, easily, the voice of her conscience. It was coming from too far away. He caught her hand, drew it away from his mouth and held it in his lap. His thumb stroked the soft underside of her palm.

'I see . . .' He thought for several moments, then seemed to come to a decision. 'I see a beautiful woman, of course.'

'How am I beautiful?'

'Everything. The way you talk and move. Your full lips, your curves. It's all beautiful.'

She edged closer, lifted her face, her intention quite clear. A fudgy part of her mind urged caution, whispered danger. She would stop, she told herself as she closed her eyes, but not just yet.

A kiss, a caress, a hug, something to comfort her, something from this sexy young man to validate the beautiful woman she was, something to give her back her sense of self. Then she would leave, go outside into the night and call a cab, return to being a dutiful wife and mother. These few minutes were time for her to be good to herself and to look after her own needs for once.

When his mouth swooped down on hers, hot, seeking, lusty, she knew she had misjudged everything. All thoughts of warm solace dissolved. For this was pure, unmitigated lust. She leaned into him, tasted the warmth of his lips and tongue, and opened her mouth. All that mattered was the physical, and the sensation of his lips on hers. The depth of his long, hard kiss reached into her and ignited a forgotten spark.

'Emma.' It was a sigh against her ear, a question, an endearment.

'Ah, Karl . . .' It was permission.

His fingers found the buttons on her shirt, peeled it back off her shoulders, revealed her lacy bra. His eyes locked on hers as his fingers slid down her bra strap, his intentions quite clear, but she didn't make a move to stop him. Then he eased down the satiny cups, exposed the creamy skin, the nipples ripening in the charge of the moment. Something caught in her throat.

Just this, and then she would call a halt.

'This?'

She felt the shock of his hands on her breasts. 'Yes.' He bent his head, and as his lips locked onto her aching nipples a responsive need echoed deep inside her. After that, she was lost.

She allowed Karl to remove her skirt and slide off her silk underwear. She watched his face through half-closed eyes and saw his eyes glaze as she lay back for him, finally naked, and languidly stretched out across the chaise longue.

After that everything was a blur. His hands were all over her body, his fingers, then lips, touching intimately, seeking and finding a response in the very essence of her. Her chest fluttered as she heard herself moan. Then the hot, swelling rush gathered inside her, before it finally, mercifully, rose to a long, quivering peak.

Just this, nothing more. Her thoughts drifted, like tattered silk on the breeze.

'Emma . . .'

She heard him from far away. She was swept up on some distant shore where every cell in her body vibrated. But there was more. He touched her again. She flopped obediently onto her tummy. She saw her hands splayed out in front of her like starfish, her nails pink and oval against the white of the sofa as she lay there and heard him unzipping his trousers. It wasn't really happening. It wasn't really her. It was as though she was dreaming. She felt hands underneath her hips, lifting her, heard his rasping breath, and knew by his strangled groan what was about to happen.

Oh, Oliver . . .

Far away in the distance an ice-cold instant of clarity told her that it was too late, much too late, to call a halt, and everything would be altered from now on.

Chapter 12

*A*lix lay wide awake in solitary splendour, enfolded in the downy comfort of the enormous sleigh bed. Saturday morning, and all was quiet in the luxury chalet in Gstaad. She lay very still as she slowly connected with the day, and watched the bright light pressing through a chink in the window drapes, sending a ray across the room. She knew that if she pulled back the curtains, she would be treated to the most magnificent vista of the Alps and the bright glare of the sun, dazzling on acres of pure white snow. After a while she heard doors opening and closing quietly, muted voices, the far-off clink of pots in the kitchen. Breakfast would soon be served for those who were keen to go out onto the slopes. Last night, before bed, Marc and Dave had said they'd be setting out early for a couple of hours on the piste and all were welcome to join them. She should get up and jump into the high-pressure shower. Instead she lay on, enfolded in the warmth, and stared up at the pine ceiling, as Fiona's news settled into her head.

She could hardly be envious, could she? Marriage, and all it entailed, was firmly off her agenda. She was just a little out of sorts, she told herself, flinging back the covers and putting her bare feet to the floor. Fiona was her friend. She owed it to her to be as fully supportive as she could be, and as she stood under the refreshing spray she vowed to laugh and smile in all the right places.

'The snow is perfect, so I want to see as many of you as possible out enjoying the fresh air,' she heard Dave announce as she arrived in the kitchen for breakfast, dressed in a thick purple jumper and black jeans. Dave and Marc had already been out for a scout around, going as far as the village for a selection of magazines for Fiona.

'Fiona won't be joining us, unfortunately,' he grinned. 'She's still in bed, sipping tea and nibbling toast.'

'Actually, I'm up,' Fiona announced, appearing at the doorway, her face pale and washed out. 'There's no such thing as morning sickness,' she said wryly. 'It can keep you awake half the night as well.'

She had a soft, serene glow about her, and Alix wondered why she hadn't spotted it until now. 'I'll stay here with you,' she said immediately. She'd been awake half the night, too, and couldn't summon the energy for even the nursery slopes this morning.

'I don't want to spoil your weekend, Alix. You go out and enjoy yourself.'

'I'm fine staying here, honestly.'

They waved goodbye to the rest of the house party and relaxed in the armchairs, which were drawn up to the glass walls and the magnificent sweeping view that stretched beyond. Alix fetched extra cushions for Fiona.

'I'm not an invalid,' Fiona smiled. 'I'm just having a baby. If I feel a little pukey, it's perfectly normal.'

'It's a good excuse to spoil yourself a little.'

The chef brought out coffee and croissants for Alix and more tea for Fiona, which she sipped very slowly. Then Alix went over to the coffee table to fetch the magazines that Dave and Marc had bought. She flicked through the bundle.

She was transfixed by the front-page photograph of a six-year-old child standing in the demolition dust of her war-torn Middle Eastern village. The image captured innocence amid the ugliness and she knew instinctively, without checking the copyright line, that it had been taken by Tom Cassidy, once upon a time her boyfriend – correction, her ex-fiancé – and now a respected, world-renowned photojournalist. Every so often, she chanced upon his insightful pictures in the media and, without fail, they caught her off guard. Her hand shook as she stuck the magazine back.

'Here you go,' she said to Fiona, carrying the bundle of glossies to her. 'You've a choice . . . Let me see . . .'

'Oh, something light, please. Something I don't have to devote too much energy to.' Fiona selected a magazine with a photo of Brad, Angelina and their family on the cover, and lay back in her armchair to read.

Alix automatically turned the pages of another magazine. Ten minutes later, Fiona's slithered to the pine floor and Alix saw that her friend had fallen into a light doze. She got up and riffled through the pile again until she found what she was looking for. She sat back into the squashy sofa cushions, tucking her long legs beneath her, and stared at Tom Cassidy's photograph.

He must have been lying flat on the ground to capture the angle, the child's proud, dignified stance so at odds with the bewilderment in her eyes. He'd probably waited quite a while to freeze-frame that fleeting expression. She knew how long he'd wait. Knew only too well the kind of stoic patience Tom was capable of displaying when it came to getting the perfect picture.

Her friends would be surprised to know that once upon a time she had spent hours in front of the camera, posing unselfconsciously as Tom Cassidy practised his photographic skills on her, painstakingly saving every penny from his part-time job to buy a succession of cameras, each one a step up from the one before until he had finally managed to secure a third-hand Hasselblad.

Then again, there were lots of things about Alix that would surprise her friends, she mused. Surprise? More likely shock. She closed down that dangerous train of thought and flicked through the magazine. Inside, there was a four-page spread about Tom, including a selection of his photographs, some of which she'd already seen in other publications. Her heart jumped. The article was publicising his forthcoming exhibition – in Paris.

She closed her eyes.

Tom. In Paris.

Their paths had crossed occasionally since she'd left him behind in Dublin. She'd bumped into him the first year she'd gone to assist at London Fashion Week – when she'd taken a quick break from the organised chaos of backstage, she'd been turned to stone when she'd seen him in discussion with other photographers just a few feet away. She hadn't realised that he'd made the break from Dublin too, and when he'd looked round, he'd stared at her as though she was a stranger for several long seconds before turning his back and striding away.

Alix had been so distracted that she'd mixed up her brief for the make-up and incurred the wrath of the high-profile stylist. 'You silly girl,' she'd pounced. 'Karina was supposed to be sultry and sexy, not soft and natural!'

After that experience, she'd made sure to find out the names of the photographers who'd be on the same job as her so that she could avoid Tom as much as possible and, in the main, she had managed to keep her distance. Then, four years after they'd split up, and when Alix had been in Paris for two, she'd heard on the grapevine that Tom had left fashion photography for the dangerous fields of war and battle. As time went on he developed a reputation for his raw and honest portrayal of humanity amid the wreckage of war. Alix became used to recognising his work. She no longer had to worry about bumping into him unexpectedly on the modelling circuit, but a corner of her mind fretted about the often dangerous situations he appeared to relish.

'Hey. Did I fall asleep?' Fiona's voice was husky and she rubbed her eyes, struggling into wakefulness.

Alix shoved the magazine behind the sofa cushions. 'You were snoring your brains out,' she joked.

'I wasn't,' Fiona protested.

Alix smiled at her. 'Would you like some coffee now?'

Fiona sat up straight and pushed her hair out of her face. 'Actually, I'm ravenous. Coffee, gateau, whatever.'

'Pierre is out. Stay there and I'll get you something. Although maybe not gateau. How about a plain pastry?'

'Lovely, thanks.'

Alix was glad to escape to the gleaming kitchen and busy herself preparing coffee and a pastry for Fiona. She had another bad moment later on, after the skiing party had returned, healthy and glowing. Everyone went upstairs to shower and change and Marc, who was first to come back down, wanted the magazine. 'It must be here somewhere,' she heard him saying as he poked around the room. 'It had an article about Tom Cassidy – that's why I bought it.'

The sound of her ex-fiancé's name on someone else's lips crashed like a wave inside her. 'Is this what you're looking for?' Her face felt hot as she plucked it from behind the cushion, but Marc didn't notice her discomfiture.

'Hey, Alix, would you like to give me some support in my heroic quest for Sophie?' he asked.

'I've already told you, there's nothing I can do. Anyway, Sophie's my friend.'

'That's why it's better I go with you. It just might make her think a little more about me and see me as someone who's worthy of a date.'

'What are you talking about?'

'I have tickets for a photographic exhibition next Wednesday week, a fellow countryman of yours, Tom Cassidy? You've seen this?' He waved the magazine at her.

'Yes, I know about it.' Her voice was clipped.

'Then you'll come?' Marc sounded enthusiastic. 'It might make Sophie—'

'I don't think it'll make Sophie anything. And I'm not really interested.'

'Aw, Alix. C'mon, be a sport . . .'

'Yes, go on, Alix, you'd enjoy it,' Fiona said.

'Look, Marc, why don't you just ask Sophie directly?'

'I've already asked her. She laughed. Right in my face. *Merde!* The pain!'

'In that case, I don't see how I can help.'

'Okay, forget about Sophie.' Marc sounded a little defeated. 'Why don't you just come with me anyway? No strings. This guy's supposed to be good. I've met him before and I know you'd like him . . .'

Marc chatted on about Tom's career, oblivious to Alix's silence. She felt torn in two, one half of her secretly dying to see Tom again, to find out if he'd changed, if he was happy and fulfilled now that he'd followed his dreams so successfully . . . if there were any gaps in his life. But the other half of her, the inner, pragmatic voice that had once – no, *twice* – salvaged the mashed-up pieces of her life, was warning her to stay very far away.

'Look, isn't this a wonderful piece of art?' Marc thrust the magazine in front of her.

She glanced at the photograph, at the child's posture, and

something about her resonated deeply within Alix. It was as though Tom, through his camera lens, had reached out and held a mirror up to her shadow self. Sensing she was taking a tentative step into a dangerous abyss, she heard herself telling Marc that, yes, she'd go.

What had she done? Alix asked herself giddily. Why had she agreed to be within a certain radius of Tom again? Her friends were laughing and ribbing each other about their skiing. Then again, maybe it wasn't so crazy. After all, Alix reminded herself as she stomped into the kitchen, Tom Cassidy meant nothing to her.

Absolutely nothing.

Chapter 13

$\mathcal{E}$ mma opened her eyes. She was drifting in a warm cocoon and something was muffling her face. She heard the sound of running water as though from far away. Gradually she realised she was snuggled under the creamy, lace-edged duvet in her queen-sized bed. Oliver was in the shower. She lay there, drowsy, half in and half out of consciousness, suspended between the dark velvety womb of sleep and the beckoning day ahead.

She was wearing her shirt. She'd fallen asleep in her *shirt?* Silly her. Moving her hands down her body, she realised her bra was missing and that she was naked from the waist.

Shards of memory coalesced into a long, silent scream. Pain exploded in her head and surged into her chest. It locked her breath and reached out a strong hand to squeeze her heart. Her mind was spinning so fast that it made her dizzy. Slow down. Take deep breaths. *Breathe.* She felt the air coming in through her mouth in short gasps. Then paralysis crept through her limbs, some kind of suffocating mixture of dread, guilt and sorrow that overwhelmed her, locking her in its vice-like grip. In spite of the duvet, she was freezing cold.

'Emma? Are you finally awake?'

Oliver loomed over her, one white towel slung low around his hips, another in his hands as he roughly dried his hair. Oliver. Her husband. Her beloved.

Emma turned into the pillow. She heard her voice croak, 'No.'

'Are you okay? You have me worried. It's after midday. I'm already back from the gym.'

'What?'

'Jeez, you seem to have had a right blast. Was the office party that good?'

'No.' The muffled word was all she could manage through the nausea.

'It must have been a helluva bash.' She heard Oliver opening drawers. 'I was home around one o'clock, and you were much later than me.'

'Was I?'

'Don't you remember? Although you probably don't.' He chuckled. 'I think it was around four in the morning when I heard you come in. What happened? Did you all decide to take the party to the nearest nightclub?'

She heard Oliver stepping into his jeans, pulling up the zip, fastening the buckle on his belt. The sound made her feel even more nauseous. 'Yes, something like that.' The words hurt her throat.

He came to her side of the bed. She caught his clean, lemony scent. 'I was glad when you texted me to say you were going out with the office gang and that you weren't just home alone licking your wounds.' She felt the weight of the mattress subside under him as he sat down, reached out a hand and brushed back her hair. Sometimes at weekends Oliver disappeared into the office for a few hours but otherwise the Saturday Oliver was different, relaxed and human in his casual clothes compared to the suited, brisk and resolute Oliver who marched out of the house at six forty-five every weekday morning. 'I'm sorry about yesterday, love. I couldn't talk to you because the head honcho from New York paid a surprise visit and we had an emergency meeting. Then after he'd scooped out our entrails, he insisted on bringing us all out for food and drinks. Me and the kids think you're great. If those arseholes in Marshalls can't see your potential, then it's their loss. Do you want to stay on in bed?'

She kept her eyes squeezed shut. 'Yes, I feel terrible.'

'You're not used to going on a bender, you silly thing. Can I bring you up anything? Water, Solpadeine?'

'Just water, thanks.'

She heard him leave the room. Several moments later he returned with a glass of water, which he placed on the bedside locker. 'Would you like some soup for lunch?' he asked.

'No, I—' She forced her eyes open. Another rush of nausea – this time at the sight of her husband gazing at her with concern. Okay, he was often work-obsessed, but he was always, without exception, solid and dependable. He threw her a look of alarm as she hauled herself out of bed and headed to the bathroom. When she came back he had opened the curtains and was standing by the window, gazing out at the bright Saturday afternoon. She crawled into bed and flopped down.

'Were you so upset about the promotion that you had to go and get pissed?'

The promotion. *The promotion.* Hysterical laughter trembled inside her.

He came back to the bed. 'I'd hate to think that my wife was so upset over a silly job that she got herself into a dreadful state about it. How much did you have to drink?'

'Too much,' she said.

'What made you go off the deep end? Did the new job really mean that much to you?'

On a level far removed from the sickening guilt that consumed her, she managed to say, 'Not that much, no. The drinks were just flying and I lost count. Don't ask me how it happened . . .'

Don't ask me how or why it happened. It just did.

'Emma, a job is just a job. At the end of the day you're only a few digits on a personnel file. I've been there myself, and I know how horrible rejection is. When you get over the initial disappointment, you'll realise what's the most important—'

'When were you turned down?' she asked, casting her mind back, trying to recall his disappointment, but unable to pinpoint any time in the past few months that her husband had been anything other than his career-dedicated self.

'It doesn't matter now,' he said, bending to drop a kiss on her forehead. As he tucked the duvet around her neck, Emma caught the glint of his wedding ring. 'You might as well take the chance to have a rest,' he said. 'You do far too much running around. You should give yourself a break every now and again, even if it is a self-induced, self-inflicted standstill. I'm off to hit a few balls at the driving range, then calling into the garage to get the car valeted. So there's no rush, you can take your time getting up. And Charlie's home. He came in last night around the same time as I did. We'll be watching the match this afternoon, so just shout if you need anything.' He left the room, closing the door quietly behind him.

Emma lay still as a roaring tide surged around her head. The packed pub, Gillian holding court, the mind-numbing effects of the alcohol. She didn't know how many of those small yet lethal bottles she'd consumed. The taste was still in her mouth. She'd never be able to drink Sauvignon Blanc again. And then, terrified to go there in her mind, chaotic, noisy Temple Bar with Karl, and afterwards his urban white apartment.

Karl.

She saw herself spread across his chaise longue, naked and

unashamed, heard her giggles as she went into the shower and felt the water hitting her body, then Karl stepping in beside her.

Jesus. God Almighty.

She couldn't remember getting dressed, going down to the street, hailing a cab or arriving home. Nausea hit the back of her throat, watering her mouth and causing her face to perspire. She struggled out of bed and barely made it to the bathroom in time. Afterwards she leaned her head against the cool white tiles, trying to rid herself of the memory of other tiles under her feet, cool and slippery under her hand, hard against her shoulder blades as Karl balanced her against the wall of the shower. *Oh, God.*

She was surprised to see that her own bathroom looked just the same, loo rolls piled higgledy-piggledy in the basket, toothbrushes in the holder, the tube of toothpaste uncapped, fingerprints on the mirrored cabinet – her own, or perhaps Oliver's, from the day before when everything had been innocent, familiar and perfect.

She stared at her reflection in the mirror, her pallor, and in her eyes a hard and painful knowledge that hadn't been there before. She sluiced her face, rinsed her hands, plucked a yellow towel from the rail and dried herself, catching the familiar scent of her favourite conditioner. She tore off her shirt, dumped it in the bin and wrapped a bathrobe around herself, trying to hug the fabric of yesterday's life around her, comforting, warm, familiar, perfect. Then she leaned over the bath, put in the plug and turned on the taps.

'Mum?'

She opened the door a little. It was Charlie, her lean six-foot son, an amalgam of herself and Oliver, with Oliver's height and navy blue eyes and her oval face, dark hair and fine bone structure. She struggled to find words. 'I'm fine, Charlie. I'll be out in a minute.'

'Dad said to keep an eye on you, that you're a little under the weather . . . Jeez, Ma, you look in tatters. What's up?'

Her son seemed so wholesome and honest that she couldn't think what to say. Already she was conscious of an invisible barrier between them, shifting the energy and altering her usual response.

'Hey, you were out on the town, right? Dad didn't tell me you had a hangover. Must have been some night for you to get wasted!'

Wasted. If only. She clutched the bathrobe to her chest. 'Charlie, don't think—'

'Huh! Ma, I'm not going to think any less of you for going on a bender,' he grinned. 'I'll still respect you, okay? Just means that the next time I have a blast you spare me the lecture. Anyway, I can't afford to drink too much,' he added, moving away from the door. 'My part-time job doesn't pay me enough.'

Emma locked the door and immersed herself very slowly in the warm water. She sat in the bath, watching a column of white sunlight dance through the frosted window pane and bounce glittering rays off the taps in the washbasin. It was so bright and cheerful that it seemed alien.

What's up, Ma?

Everything.

She looked down at her body, saw the water swishing against her limbs, between her legs, foaming against her breasts, leaving patterns in the swelling creaminess; breasts that Karl had kissed and sucked only a few short hours ago, deceitful legs that had shamelessly opened against Karl's taut hips, inviting him in.

How had she been so careless with everything so dear and familiar? How had she screwed up so badly? The bathroom spun around her. Waves of panic rose and fell, crashing into her tummy and shooting into her head. She just wanted to crawl into a hole of nothingness and die. But there was no such blessed relief. The minutes ticked by and the prism of sunlight shifted a little and she was still sitting in the bath, only now the water was cooling.

'Mum?'

It was Charlie again, outside the bathroom door.

'Yes, Charlie?' Her voice was strained, high-pitched. Even uttering his name was different from how she'd been able to utter it yesterday. Yesterday she'd been his loving mum, entitled to a modicum of respect. Today any claims she had on him in that regard were counterfeit.

'I've left a banana on your bedside locker.'

'A *banana*?'

'Yeah, the potassium's good for a hangover.'

She wished, more than anything in the world, that all she was suffering from was a massive hangover. 'Ta, Charlie.'

'I'm putting on the kettle if you'd like tea or coffee.'

'No, it's okay. I'm going back to bed for a while.'

The bathroom spun again as she levered herself out of the bath, teeth chattering, body shaking, and she swaddled herself in a jasmine-scented bath sheet. She felt a moment of sharp clarity in the midst of her distress.

Oliver must never know.

She dried herself and cleaned her teeth. In the sanctuary of her bedroom she pulled on a clean nightie, and her heart stopped when she saw the banana Charlie had left for her. She stared at the walls of her bedroom, the security she'd taken for granted. She'd not only betrayed her husband, Emma agonised, she'd also betrayed her children.

For a long, aching moment, she wondered if this was how her mother had felt. She groaned and crawled beneath the duvet. Exhaustion overcame her and she drifted into an uneasy sleep.

Chapter 14

*E*mma's dream of her mother is always the same.

Camille Berkeley is standing in the open doorway, her face soft and luminous, her body edged in fizzy sunlight, as though someone has drawn around her contours with a golden pen. She looks beautiful, vibrant, happy. She smiles at Emma. 'I have to go out, darling. Helga will keep an eye on you. Look after Alix for me, won't you?'

'Yes, Mum.' Then her mother steps through the door and closes it behind her, shutting off the light from the hall, and it is the last time Emma sees her.

Look after Alix . . .

Until then, life had been perfect. Emma had heard many times how her parents had bumped into each other in the quadrangle of Trinity College, Dublin. Camille was from Canada and, an only child, all alone in the world. Andrew Berkeley had swept her off her feet and in less than a year they were married. Two years later Emma was born, followed, four years on, by Alexandra, and her parents were thrilled with their perfect little girls. Emma couldn't quite get her tongue around her baby sister's name, so friends and family adopted the pet name she'd given her, and Alexandra became Alix. Then, when Emma was six, the family moved from Dublin when her parents accepted jobs in an English university.

The elegant house in a leafy cul-de-sac of an upmarket Cotswolds village rang with laughter and happiness. Emma was proud of her tall, good-looking father. Even prouder of her mother, who was beautiful as well as clever. Mrs Green, the daily, ran the house with a thorough efficiency and Helga, the au pair, looked after Emma and Alix and brought them to horse-riding, ballet and tennis lessons. Her parents held dinner parties with like-minded academics, and the dining room rang with sparkling conversation and lively debate as well as her mother's silvery laugh. Sometimes students dropped in to talk to her parents or look for further tutorial advice.

Then one fateful weekend, when Emma was eleven and Alix was sick in bed, everything changed.

Now, in her sleep, fragmented dreams revolve around the same disturbing memories – the angry words between her parents one Friday evening and her beloved father storming out of the house, her mother's tear-stained face as she tries to pretend all is well, the young man calling to see her on Sunday evening, and the whispered words between them that see her mother leaving the house to follow him out to his car in the sunny evening. Later that night, the horror of her father arriving home with his sister Hannah, a nurse in a London hospital. She hears her father's sobs, and sees Aunt Hannah standing in front of her with such sadness on her face that Emma's heart drops.

She is confined to the playroom under Helga's care for the next few days, hearing the ringing of the doorbell, the slow tread of footsteps and the hushed, respectful voices. And when Emma goes down to the kitchen while Helga is busy with Alix, she sees newspapers sticking out of the bin. Curiosity draws her forward to lift them out and, for a frozen moment, she stares at the terrible headlines and the photos underneath. Then she shoves them back, runs into the playroom and curls into a ball in front of the television.

Aunt Hannah brings her and Alix to the funeral service, and from murmured conversations, Emma gathers that John, the student, had been a pupil of her mother's, and very gifted. Clara, his ex-girlfriend, also a student of her mother's, is inconsolable. She turns up at the church and launches herself at Emma's father, crying loudly on his shoulder until she is led away by concerned relatives. In her dreams, Emma still sees the paleness of Clara's long hair against her father's dark suit and his remote face.

The family move back to Dublin and Aunt Hannah comes with them, giving up her nursing job and postponing her plans to emigrate to Australia. Her father finds work in a publishing firm and his considerable talents are ploughed into editing college textbooks. The edge of his deep sorrow is clouded with the help of a whiskey bottle. Emma, with Alix in her wake, learns to brave the Dublin schoolyard where they sound different from everyone else and where they elicit shock and pity when their classmates find out that their mother is dead.

Very occasionally, when the whiskey gives him false courage, their father talks about their mother. 'It was all my fault, you know. I'm responsible for what happened . . .' He looks so upset that Emma doesn't want to talk about it, especially when Alix quietens and starts to bite her nails, her huge green eyes troubled. Occasionally she overhears Aunt Hannah telling him rather sternly that there is no point in looking backwards and dragging up old wounds, that he has a duty to his daughters to look to the future, to their future, whatever about his own.

Then, when she is seventeen, Emma meets Oliver at a friend's party and everything changes again.

Chapter 15

*L*ibby negotiated her way through the shopping-centre doors and out into the raw, breezy day. Her arms were laden with a huge bouquet of flowers, a bottle of wine and a box of chocolates. Waiting outside in the car, Rob opened the passenger door. Libby settled herself, carefully placing the flowers in the space by her feet so as not to crush the blooms, and balancing the chocolates and wine on her lap. After she had put on her seatbelt, Rob reversed out of the parking space.

'Are you feeling guilty about something?' he asked.

Libby made a face as they drove out of the car park. 'What have I got to feel guilty about?' she countered, unwilling to admit that he'd hit a raw nerve.

'We're taking it for granted that we can turn up at your place for lunch having spent the weekend enjoying ourselves.'

'So? Isn't that what the weekend is all about? We're young and carefree. We work hard all week. We're *supposed* to be enjoying our-selves,' she said coolly, thinking that, lately, his version of enjoyment seemed to differ vastly from hers.

Rob was her first serious boyfriend and Libby liked to think he was also her soulmate. He was clever. They shared the same sense of humour, even followed the same soccer team, and they had a fantabulous sex life. Well, she thought it was fantabulous, although she'd no experience apart from Rob. He was a good listener and she could tell him everything. Almost everything, she qualified. She'd never confided in him about her fanciful day-dreaming or her dissatisfaction with her job. Sometimes she thought it was hilarious that she couldn't admit her innermost feelings to her soulmate. Rob knew she'd loved art in school, but there was no room for castles in the air in the face of his sensible ambitions, ambitions she'd told him she shared.

Now her problem with her work seemed to be messing up her relationship with him. Recently there had been moments when she'd found him extremely head-wrecking, to say the least. Like when he insisted on putting his studies before everything else, reminding her that not so long ago she'd been quite happy to study alongside him when exam time was looming. And he'd begun to pass comments on her drinking habit. Drinking habit? Like, since when did she *have* a drinking habit? And there were moments like this, when he knew her so well that it was almost as if a boring big brother was keeping an eye on her.

The weekend they'd just shared had left her feeling a bit flat. It hadn't helped that by the time she'd got a taxi to Rob's parents' house on Friday night she was flying, after a few shots and beers with Karen and Mandy. Her friends had gone on to a nightclub and she'd been almost sorry she hadn't gone with them to let her hair down, for Rob had been stone-cold sober and unhappy with the way his studies had gone – or not gone, as he had irritably pointed out.

On Saturday afternoon, when she'd hoped they'd go shopping together or even for a romantic stroll in the park, he'd spent a long time on the Internet doing research for his college assignment. He had to do it this weekend, he explained, as he was further behind than he'd realised, and he had a strict timetable to keep to. Libby had put on the sports shoes she kept in Rob's wardrobe with a couple of changes of clothes, and stomped out of the house to go for a walk by herself. Later they'd ordered in pizza and sat in front of a DVD to eat it. Not the exciting weekend she'd envisaged, so she would hardly have rated it a success. She also had the sinking feeling that the rest of Sunday would fly and all too soon it'd be Monday morning and the start of another demanding week. Now they were heading home to Laburnum Grove for lunch.

'We're not arriving out of the blue,' Libby said, a bit chastened. 'I texted Mum, so she's expecting us. She loves having us for Sunday lunch and seeing the family all together.'

Another problem was that, as Rob had guessed, her guilty qualms where her mother was concerned had persisted over the weekend. Now, as Rob had so kindly pointed out, they had invited themselves for lunch. But Emma loved having them, so, Libby brightened up, she was almost doing her mum a favour.

Rob indicated left and drove up the avenue. 'I'm not family and I don't like taking for granted that I can turn up for lunch,' he said.

'You know you're always more than welcome. Look, Rob . . .' Libby's voice softened. She reminded herself that it was precisely because Rob was so thoughtful and considerate that she was still with him. *And* he was brainy. Much like her dad, she supposed. 'Mum wasn't in the best of humour on Friday, on account of some stupid job she didn't get, so I'm just trying to cheer her up. But don't let on you know about it. Okay?'

When they arrived at Laburnum Grove, Libby went down to the kitchen where Emma was peeling vegetables. 'Hi, Mum. I know these flowers won't make up for not getting that job,' she said breezily, lowering her bouquet into the Belfast sink, then placing the wine and chocolates on the granite worktop, 'but I hope they'll help to cheer you up a little,' she went on, inwardly cringing. Why should a few supermarket flowers make up for not getting the job she'd wanted so much? Then she turned and saw her mother's face. 'Jeez, Mum, what happened to you?'

'Your mother was out partying with the office gang on Friday night.' Her father chuckled as he came into the kitchen. 'She enjoyed herself rather too much. Isn't that right, Emma? And now, unfortunately, she's paying the price.'

Libby felt as though she was off an invisible hook. 'Hey, cool, Mum, good for you! Glad you were out having a blast and not sunk in gloom over that silly job. You should go out more often – then it wouldn't be such a shock to the system. It's about time you lived it up a little. You should be taking it easy today, though.' Her mother looked as though she hadn't slept for a week. Her eyes were red-rimmed and her face was pale and tight.

'Charlie and I offered to make lunch,' her father said, 'but your mum insisted on doing it herself.'

'Is there anything I can do?' Libby asked, feeling apprehensive as she threw her eyes in the direction of the shiny cooker with the intimidating bank of switches. Mum was an expert on Sunday lunch, timing everything to perfection and producing marvellous food with tempting sauces. Libby was hopeless at that sort of thing and she hated the mess she made when she tried, very occasionally, to cook for Rob.

'No, I'm fine,' Emma said, to Libby's immense relief. 'And thanks for the flowers. They're absolutely beautiful.'

'It's okay if Rob stays?'

'Of course. You don't have to ask.'

'I'll set the table,' Libby offered, sliding off her jacket. 'And I'll put the wine in the fridge – although,' she hazarded a joke, 'you probably won't feel like any. There's nothing worse than a rotten hangover.'

Sunday lunch was served on the polished mahogany dining table that overlooked the landscaped garden through big picture windows. Libby had set the table with crystal wine glasses, gleaming cutlery and folded napkins, a water jug and a vase of flowers, and they sat down to roast lamb, mint sauce, a selection of vegetables and roast potatoes. While her father was discussing Saturday's match with Charlie and Rob, Libby turned to her mother. 'Where did you go on Friday night?' she asked.

'Go?' Her mother looked at her uncomprehendingly. God, she really was in bits, Libby thought. She must have suffered a hell of a hangover, perhaps even some form of alcohol poisoning if those pained eyes were anything to go by. Mum wasn't used to going on a bender. On the rare occasion she went for a drink with Libby, after a shopping spree or a chick flick, she stuck to two glasses of wine.

'Yeah, what nightclub? You did go to a nightclub, didn't you?'

'I – em – yes, we did, but let me see, now, what was it called?' Emma's voice sounded funny, kind of shrill, and she looked totally frazzled. There was a sudden silence as Oliver broke off his football conversation and frowned. Even Charlie threw his mother a puzzled look.

'You mean you can't remember,' Libby said, trying to lighten the mood. 'Oh, Mum, you probably can't remember anything if you were that sozzled.'

It was the wrong thing to say. Her mother fixed her with a wounded stare, then dropped her eyes to her plate and picked at her food. Libby met her father's eyes and he shook his head. 'Hey, Charlie,' Libby turned to her brother, 'how did your party go?'

'What party?'

'Your private party with Melanie?'

93

'I wasn't at a private party with Melanie,' he said gruffly, looking daggers at her.

Another wrong thing. Libby groaned inwardly. So much for the relaxed family Sunday lunch.

'Did you see the *Business Post*, Libby?' Her father came to the rescue. 'There's a good article in it on the latest divestitures and acquisitions in the US. There have been several billion worth of transactions alone in the last quarter.'

'Sounds promising. I must have a read,' Libby said. 'Do you think the supply of private equity will ever match the pre-downturn days?'

'It's hard to tell,' Oliver said as he poured more wine. 'Certainly not in the short term.'

Her mother was sticking to water, Libby noticed, and she was clearly a million miles away. 'Hey, Mum?' She gave her a big, bright smile.

'Yes, Libby?'

'How about going shopping soon? We'll get some glam for Paris and Alix's make-up launch. Maybe next Saturday? I've no plans yet and Rob will be in college.'

'That's fine,' Emma said, and Libby congratulated herself on finally bringing a half-smile to her mother's lips.

'We have to push the boat out and do her proud. I'm not turning up in anything other than pure, elegant designer sophistication.'

Charlie laughed. 'You'd better get a face transplant so.'

Libby cast him a supercilious glance. 'Alix will be looking after my face, thank you very much. She's already told me my bone structure is perfect for a feminine, ethereal look.'

Charlie guffawed even louder.

'And the house will be free when Mum, Dad and I go to Paris, but don't get any big ideas,' Libby went on.

'Who says I need a free house?' Charlie seemed upbeat now.

Libby threw him a mocking glance. 'Yeah, as if.'

Her father obviously decided it was time to change the subject. 'Who's for coffee?' he asked as he rose to his feet.

'What happened to dessert?' Charlie said, so indignantly that everyone around the table laughed.

Emma made herself join in the laughter. She had gone through the motions and got as far as Sunday lunch without buckling completely under the strain of her deception. Everything about her life seemed strange, as though she was walking in a dream or viewing it in black and white. It was a rather ordinary Sunday afternoon with her family. Yet now she knew that its very ordinariness made it special, beyond price. On Friday she had fully belonged here, in this house, to this man, was the mother of her children. Now she felt as though she was separated from the reality of it by a sheet of darkened glass.

When everyone laughed at Charlie's indignation, she would have given anything to hold that moment, to freeze-frame it so they could stay in that golden capsule of time where everything was all at once brilliant and normal. But even as the thought formed, time marched on. It was already the next moment, and the moment after, and they moved out into the kitchen. Oliver filled the cafetière, Charlie poked his hand into the depths of the freezer and triumphantly withdrew the frozen tiramisu, and Libby, with the undeniable air of a martyr, carefully stacked plates in the dishwasher.

They said confession was good for the soul, Emma agonised, but her confession would just bring all their lives tumbling down around them. And for what? It would never make her feel better or, more importantly, change what had happened.

Yet how could she live such a lie and blatantly deceive her husband?

Chapter 16

*A*lix slid off the body of her lover, lay panting for several moments, then turned towards him, raised herself on an elbow and tucked the duvet around her tummy.

Laurent reached out and wound tendrils of her dark hair around his finger. 'You're wild tonight, *chérie*, and you don't usually see me on Sunday nights. What's the matter?' He released her hair and brushed the palm of his hand across her swollen nipples, giving her the equivalent of a mild electrical jolt.

'Why should anything be the matter?' she asked flippantly, in perfect French.

'Alix,' he said, caressing the side of her face, 'you're insatiable, you're demanding, but you're not really with me tonight. I know by now when something is troubling your pretty head.'

Alix lay back against the lace-edged pillows and gazed at the ceiling as she spoke to him. 'I'm fine. Really, Laurent. I just needed this, needed you. Badly.' She'd called him on impulse, needing him to distract her from the thoughts swirling in her head, but she couldn't tell him so.

'Just this? The sex? Or do you sometimes think you want more, the marriage and the togetherness? You know I can never give you those things. We agreed, didn't we?'

'I know. It's fine.' She turned towards him and put her arm around him, snuggling into his chest. 'I like us just the way we are, no more, no less. I don't want marriage. I've never wanted it. We're perfect, you and I.' She angled her long leg, winding it around so that it was tucked between his thighs. She pressed the length of her body against him. In a few minutes, Laurent was aroused again, and this time he pinned her beneath him, and she lay with her back pressed to the sheets, her hips flexing to meet his beautifully slow thrusts. But even though her body was once more flooded with the sharp, sweet throb, Alix found it totally meaningless.

'That was good, yes?' he asked, lifting her hand and kissing the palm.

'Lovely.' She forced a smile.

'Thank you for calling me. I enjoyed it.'

'So did I,' she said automatically. It hadn't been a question of enjoyment. She'd needed the distraction, the physical release, greedy for the few heady moments of bliss that brought oblivion to her restless mind. After a while Laurent reached for her again and Alix closed her eyes to focus on the sensation of skin against skin, the heat and hardness of his body, trying to ignore the fact that it was so mechanical and devoid of emotion.

Later she lay quietly in bed holding back tears as Laurent went into the shower. He came back into the room, rubbing his hair vigorously, then swiping the towel across his toned torso and down his limbs. He was ridding himself of her scent and any remaining traces of their lovemaking before going home to his wife. It made her feel sad, as though she was no longer of any use to him. She wondered what it would be like if he were to spend the night in her bed, if they were to cuddle together after making love, in a messy yet comfortable tangle, a squeezy and relaxed embrace. But that would never happen. For Alix was Laurent's mistress, and had been for the last two years.

At forty, Laurent was a rising star on the French business scene, with an interest in several European companies. His wife and two young sons meant everything to him. But not so much that he couldn't help being bewitched by Alix Berkeley.

They'd met at a French society wedding in a Fontainebleau hotel where Alix had been booked to look after the make-up for the bride and bridesmaids. She'd bumped into Laurent when she was taking a short break in the rose garden. She'd been sitting on a centuries-old stone wall, tilting her face to the sun and a bottle of Evian into her mouth, when he'd appeared in her line of vision, as if he was attempting to escape from the tedious speeches and endless wedding protocol.

He'd phoned her several times, finding out all about her and telling her about himself, including that he was married, before she agreed to talk to him in the privacy of her apartment.

'I'm filled with longing for you, Alix,' he said. 'You're beautiful, graceful, desirable. I can promise you fantastic sex on a fairly regular basis, if you're interested.' He'd laid his cards on the table that very first evening. 'But absolutely nothing beyond that, you must understand.'

'Just sex suits me perfectly,' Alix had told him, happy with the prospect of regular, enjoyable sex with no strings. 'But first let's see how fantastic you really are,' she said, leading him into her bedroom.

Afterwards she sighed with satisfaction and happily agreed with his self-assessment. He explained that after the birth of their second son his wife had lost interest in the physical side of their marriage and didn't really care if he had a mistress, as long as he was discreet. She maintained her position as his wife and was spared any details.

His wife's family had thrown the full weight of their honourable and influential name, as well as their powerful position, behind him in his quest for power, and he didn't want to rock the boat. Neither did he want to cause her or their children any distress. Alix and Laurent met up three or four times a month, often in Alix's apartment and sometimes in a discreet hotel. He brought flowers and champagne, chocolates and treats, and gave her expensive jewellery on her birthday and at Christmas. In between times, they maintained completely separate existences, Alix busy with her career and Parisian social life, and Laurent maintaining a façade of integrity as well as making a name for himself in business circles.

Naturally enough, and much as Alix had expected, Emma flatly disapproved of their relationship. 'Has this anything to do with our mother?' That she'd brought up the forbidden subject showed Alix how upset she was.

'Why would it have anything to do with her?' Alix was shocked.

'Well, you're sort of getting your own back in a roundabout way.'

'Getting my own back? Sorry, you've lost me,' Alix said.

'I'm confused myself,' Emma admitted. 'I guess I feel you're pressing a self-destruct button, something like the way she did. But you're getting your own back on her memory by steering clear of marriage.'

Alix strove to stay calm and unemotional in the face of her sister's suggestions. 'You're being too analytical,' she said firmly. 'As far as I'm concerned, I'm entering into an agreement with Laurent that suits us both.'

'I can't help feeling you're being used.'

'We're using each other,' Alix said. 'We're sex buddies. We're not hurting anybody else. It's enjoyable and fun. He's very sexy and brilliant in bed. Mostly he calls me, but sometimes I call him.'

'I can't say I approve, but if you ever want to talk about it, I'm here.'

By now Emma was used to the status quo and the subject of Laurent was rarely raised between the sisters. Alix and Laurent knew each other as friends as well as sex buddies. Fully dressed and ready to go home to his wife, he sat down at the edge of the bed and stroked her hair. 'You are happy with this, with us?' he asked.

'Yes, thank you for coming. I hope Simone—'

He put his finger to her mouth at the mention of his wife. 'She's out. At the opera. Thank you for this evening. I hope you have a good day tomorrow.'

'I'll be busy,' she said. 'The glitzy tournament of Paris Fashion Week begins.' In the middle of it all, she also had a date with Marc, Alix silently reminded herself. As if she needed reminding. It was one of the reasons she'd needed the distraction of Laurent tonight. The prospect of coming face to face with Tom again was more alarming by the day. Now she wondered if she had the guts to see it through.

'Enjoy the excitement,' Laurent said.

For a wild moment she thought he could read her mind, but he was, of course, talking about Fashion Week. Then he was gone, and even though he left her with a pair of diamond earrings straight from Van Cleef, along with the drift of his aftershave, Alix's apartment echoed with a chilly emptiness, much like the beckoning night.

Impatient with herself, she got out of bed and straightened the duvet, plumping up her pillows and telling herself that *of course* she had the guts to come face to face with Tom. They were both so much older and wiser that it would surely be a doddle.

Chapter 17

$\mathcal{I}$n the flurry of the Monday-morning rush, Emma was filled
with a death-like calm. From a distance she observed Oliver
hunting for his car keys, Charlie looking for his mobile and Libby
fretfully rummaging through the pile of ironing for a freshly washed
shirt. Libby was crabby and unusually disorganised and Oliver
vented his impatience by slamming the hall door behind them.
There was no trace of the happy, relaxed Oliver who had sat by her
bedside on Saturday and stroked her forehead.

It had been very tempting to go sick but Emma had bleakly reasoned that she couldn't guess what Karl might hint to Nikola or
Stacy in her absence. It had been tempting to forget about going to
work in Marshalls ever again, but a sudden departure would cause
huge controversy in the office and draw attention to her, which was
the very thing she wanted to avoid. Better to confront Karl, however difficult it would be, and warn him off – or, worst-case
scenario, get some idea of the kind of gossip that was being aired.
If necessary, she'd be on hand to deny everything.

She was first to arrive in the office, her heart pounding like a trip hammer and her scalp prickling as she walked down the floor. Everything was exactly the same as it had been on Friday, yet now workstations, computers and filing cabinets seemed filled with some terrible threat that made her feel sick. Even her desk, as she sat down, seemed alien and menacing.

Nikola arrived next and plonked down her bag with a glossy magazine. She shook out her long blonde hair, reminding Emma of Libby, then caught it back in a scrunchie. 'Good weekend? It always runs in too quickly, doesn't it?' She passed her normal Monday-morning comment and smiled her normal smile as though nothing was amiss.

Emma exhaled. 'Yes, it does,' she said.

Nikola shrugged out of her jacket and hung it up. 'Friday night was great, wasn't it? Gillian certainly pulled the crowd. I think everyone turned up.'

'Yes, they did.' Emma tried to sound casual, bracing herself for what Nikola might say next, ready with a whole pile of excuses and false explanations.

'I don't remember seeing you leave. Were you among the first to go?'

'Probably.' Emma felt weak, but aware that her anxiety had less-ened just a little. She hadn't caused a noticeable scene. More importantly, she hadn't been spotted heading off with Karl. If she had, the grapevine would have let Nikola know by now.

She sensed Karl's arrival in the office before she saw him. It was in the charge of tension that leaped across the floor, the prickle at the back of her head, and the slow, painful thud of her heart. She forced herself to turn very slowly and watch as he took his mobile out of his pocket, pulled off his jacket, slung it on the nearby coat-stand and sat in his chair, fitting his long legs under the desk. He switched on his computer and pulled his keyboard towards him. She wasn't sure if her legs would carry her, but after a short while, and before the office filled up, she forced her trembling fingers to pick up a file and slowly walked over to him.

'Karl – I . . .' She could go no further. Her carefully rehearsed speech dried in her constricted throat.

He smiled up at her with the blue eyes that had flashed with passion on Friday night and roved over every inch of her naked body. She thought she was going to faint. She gripped the edge of the desk for support as the file shook alarmingly in her other hand. Then she realised the eyes were friendly, cheerful, relaxed. 'Hi, good morning, Emma,' he said.

He was used to this, she thought. Used to one-night stands and careless weekend sex. Used to facing female colleagues on Monday mornings after spending a night in bed with them. There was no trace of embarrassment or any degree of shame on his upturned face. A rush of self-preservation formed a hard resolve inside her.

'Can we have a chat, please?' she said, keeping her voice even. 'In the meeting room? Now?'

'Sure thing.' He rose to his feet.

'Nikola, I'm just having a quick meeting with Karl,' Emma told her, waving the file. She walked down the floor, conscious of Karl behind her. She closed the door of the meeting room and sat down opposite him.

'Friday night, Karl . . .' she began.

'You got home all right?' A knowing smile.

'Yes, but it shouldn't – we didn't . . .' She was unable to continue.

'Sure. We didn't.'

She knew by the casual grin on his face that the episode had meant nothing to him. 'You don't understand, Karl. Friday night didn't happen. OK? If one word gets out . . .' She swallowed her rising hysteria and gave him a steady, determined look, anxious to impress on him the gravity of what she was saying.

'Don't worry, I know it was just one of those nights when you go a little crazy, do stuff you wouldn't normally do . . .'

'I'd had too much to drink, unfortunately,' Emma said. 'I didn't really know what I was doing.'

He smiled at her. 'Didn't you? I'd had more than a few drinks as well. But from what I remember—'

'You don't remember anything, right?' she snapped. 'If I hear that one word, one *whisper* has leaked out, I can spread my own rumours. And I think my word would be a lot more credible than yours.'

'I told you not to worry. You can't even see the whip marks. I have them well hidden.'

'The *what*?'

He leaned back lazily in his chair. 'Sorry, that was a joke. We didn't get as far as bondage. Not quite. But you were good, Emma, really great,' he said before she had a chance to silence him. 'Thanks for a brilliant night. I'd no idea of the passion you hide behind your calm front. Your husband is a very lucky man.'

She closed her mind to the image of Karl lifting her up in the shower. Bile rose in her throat. 'Keep my husband out of this,' she said, squaring her shoulders and swiftly deciding there was no point in trying to appeal to his better nature. His off-hand manner told her that his moral compass was different to hers. 'And God forbid that I hear the slightest whisper. I hope for both our sakes that there'll be no need to have this conversation again.' There was little more she could do or say, Emma realised. If she attempted to threaten or intimidate Karl into silence she'd make the situation far worse.

And if word leaked out she'd hurt her family immeasurably – blow their comfortable, secure world into smithereens. Oliver, Libby and Charlie didn't deserve that. Okay, they drove her mad at times and took her for granted, but that was nothing compared to the gravity of her sin.

'Chill, Emma – I've forgotten about it already,' Karl said. He appeared to sense her anxiety because he went on, 'It's okay, relax. When I say I've forgotten, that's just for everybody else. Because I haven't. You were brilliant, Emma. But,' he smiled ruefully, 'as you wish, it didn't happen. And you're the boss, after all.'

'Just remember that,' she snapped, her voice trembling a little. She picked up her file, walked out of the room and returned to her desk, feeling as though her legs were going to give way.

She thought the morning would never end, astonished by the way normal office life went on around her. The phones shrilled louder than ever, the photocopier went on the blink and the post was late. She was painfully aware of Karl in a way she'd never been before. Her composure was jolted each time he passed her desk – so much so that she decided in a moment of hysteria that her only option was to resign and get as far away from Karl and Marshalls as she could.

As soon as she felt composed enough to talk to Amanda without bursting into tears, she would hand in her notice.

Somehow, miraculously, Monday came to an end. Tuesday arrived and, once more, the minutes and the hours began to slide past. Then it was Wednesday, and all the time, life in Laburnum Grove and work in Marshalls unrolled much as usual – but Emma felt as though she was living on a knife edge.

She was also physically exhausted, because the luxury of eight hours' untroubled sleep seemed an elusive fantasy. In Marshalls, she couldn't bear to look at Karl, yet perversely she found herself carefully monitoring his every movement. She couldn't live with this constant reminder of her infidelity, yet she was still nervous of breaking down in front of Amanda if the latter questioned her decision to leave.

'He's really gorgeous, isn't he?' breathed Nikola when she

noticed Emma's eyes automatically follow Karl out of the canteen at lunchtime on Wednesday. She cupped her chin in her hands and went on wistfully, 'We're still trying to figure out where he disappeared to last Friday night.'

Emma had been watching the way Karl moved his hips, and was suddenly appalled by the realisation that he knew full well she was watching him and was deliberately swaggering a little more than usual.

'So, what do you think, Emma? You're the expert, after all.'

Emma choked on her coffee. 'What?' She'd missed what Nikola had said.

Nikola went on, 'You're the one who's married and living with a bloke, so you're the expert on sex. Stacy and I don't have it on tap like you,' she laughed. 'Can you tell by a bloke's hips just how good he is in bed? Do swively hips translate to sexy moves in bed?'

'Sorry, girls, I wouldn't know,' Emma said, her heart rate subsiding.

'Or else you're not telling,' Stacy said. 'You must know by Oliver's hips if he's up for it.'

'Yeah, I bet he has that certain swagger when he's in the mood,' Nikola said.

'Hey, I wasn't talking about his *swagger*,' Stacy giggled.

Emma rose to her feet and picked up her coffee cup.

'Hey, we're only joking.' Stacy flapped a hand. 'Didn't mean any harm.'

'No worries.' She smiled lightly as she wove her way through the canteen.

Oliver. She pictured her unsuspecting husband directing operations from behind his walnut desk, talking to global clients and going about his efficient day blissfully unaware of what had transpired between his wife and Karl. Feeling secure and in control of his life, he was oblivious to the fact that the worst had already happened. It was terrifying to know that it would take only a few words to change everything, to destroy his peace of mind, wipe out his trust, demolish the contentment that underpinned his home life and his relationship with Libby and Charlie.

In a moment of firm resolve, she emailed Amanda as soon as she got back to her desk and asked for a meeting with her. Amanda emailed back: she'd see her at three o'clock.

'You're resigning?' Amanda frowned.

'Yes, that's right,' Emma said, holding her trembling hands firmly in her lap. 'I want to leave as soon as I can.'

'This is a surprise. Has it anything to do with the promotion?'

The promotion. She felt a wave of gratitude. The whole of Marshalls, even her family, would assume she was resigning on account of her failure to be promoted. 'I think I've gone as far as I can in Marshalls,' she said, wondering where the words were coming from.

'Hmm. Where are you moving to? You do have alternative employment lined up?'

'No, not yet. I need time to think about where I go from here,' Emma said.

Amanda pursed her lips. 'You realise you'll have to serve two weeks' notice?'

'Two weeks?' Emma tried to hide her dismay.

'Yes, according to the terms of your contract. Look, Emma, I must admit you've taken me by surprise,' Amanda said, her tone softer. 'You're a real team player and I hate to lose you. Is anything else bothering you that's contributed to your decision?'

Emma felt Amanda's eyes search her face. She shook her head. 'Nothing. I really feel the need of a change of scene. As soon as possible.'

'You're owed some annual leave,' Amanda said. 'If you're that anxious to get going it could be factored in. I'll check that out right now.' She drew up a spreadsheet on her computer and, after a short while, said, 'You could resign with effect from next Thursday. Does that suit?'

'Yes, thank you.' She'd survive a week, just about. If it became too stressful, now that she'd faced Karl and made her feelings clear, she'd go sick. 'I'd really appreciate it if word of my resignation was kept quiet for now.' It was bound to cause a fuss and focus the spotlight on her. Neither would she tell her family yet. She'd wait till she could mention Marshalls casually.

'I can't promise you that,' Amanda said. 'Once the paperwork goes through, staff are bound to talk. I can hold it back for a couple of days – that would give you a bit of time to reconsider, too.'

'I won't reconsider,' Emma said.

Maybe Karl would talk after she left, Emma fretted. Maybe with her off the scene he'd boast about what had happened after Gillian's booze-up, but it was entirely possible that no one would believe him. After all, it was incredible to think that happily married, prim and proper Emma would allow herself to be seduced by the randy Karl. Likewise, it was difficult to believe that Karl would allow his raffish, sexy image to be coloured by admitting he'd bedded Mrs Colgan.

Or maybe he'd see it as a plus. For, according to Karl, her full lips, her curves and the way she talked and moved were beautiful. He'd found her passionate behind her calm exterior. Watching him sit across the room, or stroll to the water cooler, or laugh at something Nikola said, hazy memories of the response he'd evoked in her rose in her mind. At odd moments, when she saw him sitting back in his chair, the phone to his ear, her heart squeezed with the memory that she'd behaved in a totally wanton way with him, flaunting and revelling in her sexuality in a way she hadn't done for years.

If she wanted to make it up to Oliver, and be the best wife she could be, what better way to redeem herself than by showing him she loved him more than anything? She would forget about enhancing her true potential and embracing new challenges. All she wanted was to be happily married to Oliver and the best mother she could be to Libby and Charlie.

And now that she knew the kind of passion she was still capable of, why not work on that to lift her marriage out of the rut it was presently mired in? It would be one way, surely, of making it up to Oliver . . . wouldn't it?

Chapter 18

Alix swore as her mascara caked into splodgy lumps on her long, feathery eyelashes. Bloody hell. She, the supposed expert in the field, was making a complete mess of her own make-up. She looked down at her hands and saw her pink manicured fingertips trembling ever so slightly. If she was like this now, what would she be like in an hour's time when she came face to face with Tom again?

From what she had gathered, the Tom Cassidy retrospective was the hottest ticket in Paris. The exhibition was bound to be crawling with celebrities and hangers-on of all descriptions. So in all probability, Alix considered, she might not even come within air-kissing distance of Tom. The studio was bound to be heaving with beautiful people, filled with their own importance, who had never heard of Tom before now. It would no doubt be noisy, with jazzy music pumping, and of course there would be the ubiquitous canapés and a river of wine and champagne served by scantily clad hostesses. She took a bracing gulp of her vodka and cranberry before carefully cleaning the messy mascara. She counted to ten as she lined up her makeup brushes before starting again.

When she was happy with her face, she pulled her leather trousers up around her slender hips and slid her arms into a cream lace top. Even selecting what to wear had reduced her to an insecure teenager, but the leather trousers had hit the right spot – somewhere between classic elegance and sexy siren. After all, God knew how many bimbos Tom would have hanging on his arm and she needed all the ammunition she could get her hands on to shore herself up against the vulnerability that was making her stomach contract.

Earlier that evening she'd popped into Dave's and had her short hair blow-dried in an uncompromising funky upswept style. 'Heading out on the town with Marc?' he'd laughed. 'What on earth will Sophie have to say?'

'So far she doesn't seem to care,' Alix said. 'However, if we're snapped by the paparazzi and end up in some glossy mag together, as a couple, it might be a different story.'

'Maybe it could be you and Marc?'

'No way, sorry to disappoint you.'

'On the outside you might be the glittering Alix Berkeley, with Paris at your feet, but I see another side to you, a side that would be brilliant with commitment and babies. Hmm?' He paused, angling the dryer away from her. When she didn't reply he went on, 'Fiona and I are the happiest we've ever been.' He switched off the dryer and raked styling gel through her jet-black hair, checking her reflection in the mirror. Alix just wanted him to be finished so that she could make a swift exit. 'I can't explain how awesome it is to be expecting a child of your own with the person you love most in the world. I'd love to see you with that kind of amazing happiness.'

'Thing is, Dave, I'm amazingly happy as I am,' she'd quipped.

She *was* amazingly happy just as she was, Alix instructed her sexy image in the bedroom mirror, and that was what she needed to project when she saw Tom again. She pouted her cerise lips one last time before she turned away. Then she sat down on the bed and zipped up her five-inch stiletto boots, slipped on a cream cashmere jacket and threw her mobile into her Chloé bag.

Anxiety mushroomed into full-blown panic when Alix stepped out of the taxi with Marc to find no huddle of paparazzi, let alone the snap of a single flashbulb. 'Are you sure this is the right address?' she asked him. The drive through the busy evening streets had been all too swift, giving her scant time to breathe deeply and calm her fluttering pulse.

'Yes, this is it,' Marc said, ushering her into the modest foyer and showing his invitation to the concierge.

'But I thought—'

'You were expecting something more glamorous?'

Alix shrugged, trying to adjust her thoughts and anticipate what lay ahead. 'I thought we might have had a photo opportunity. Something you could show Sophie? Isn't that what you wanted?'

Marc shook his head. 'I wanted to come regardless, but Tom Cassidy doesn't operate like that. These tickets were like gold dust because so few were issued – mostly to colleagues and a few friends. And Tom issued strict instructions that his paparazzi mates were to honour his wish that, on account of the sensitive subject matter, the exhibition be held in a respectful manner and not turned into a media scrum. I hope you're not disappointed?'

'No, this is fine,' Alix said shakily.

As the lift doors hissed open on the top floor, she was almost blinded by fear and anxiety. Marc once more produced his invitation for inspection, the door to the exhibition room was opened and they stepped through.

Alix's eyes flashed around the huge loft area, taking in the discreet lighting angled on the various stands where the photographs were mounted, the table in the corner laid out with refreshments, and hearing the low buzz of conversation. There was no tinny jazz, and scantily clad hostesses would have been sacrilege in the room's sober ambience. Instead, piano music drifted quietly in the background, rippling notes that made her think of the swell of the sea on a calm evening or a light breeze ruffling the leaves of Paris's plane trees.

There was no sign of Tom.

Marc joined some of his colleagues and introduced Alix, and they began to circulate, studying the photographs, all showing the human face of war.

She should have known. Alix bit her lip. Tom Cassidy's work was not celebrity fodder. Instead, his insightful images portrayed some of the most heartbreaking scenes imaginable. Alix felt her heart melt. Yet through it all there was a message of hope: the pictures revealed the indomitable face of humanity in spite of the many ills visited upon it, a triumph of the spirit over the horrors and ravages of war.

She and Marc moved slowly from stand to stand, absorbing the graphic, mostly black and white prints. They were halfway around when she sensed Tom behind her and knew he had spotted her.

'Hey, Tom,' Marc called as they moved to the next stand. '*Bonsoir* and welcome to Paris. This is bloody incredible stuff – well done.'

'Marc? Marc de Burgh? It's a long time since our paths crossed.'

'It sure is.'

She had no option but to turn and face him, mentally preparing herself, but nothing could have readied her for the sheer force of his presence.

Her heart squeezed.

In his youth, Tom had looked every inch the rock star, with his rakish, dark blond hair and air of edgy preoccupation. His nose had been slightly crooked since a hurling injury, and he retained his slim, lean build, with the intangible aura of mercurial energy that had attracted her to him in the beginning. In some respects he hadn't changed, but she intuitively realised, from his lived-in face and watchfulness, that he was more reflective and self-disciplined than the impetuous young man who'd captured her image from all angles.

Marc was talking from somewhere far away. 'Tom, may I introduce Alix? Alix Berkeley . . . Tom Cassidy . . .'

He was wearing a sharp charcoal-grey suit. Ice blue eyes skimmed across her face like quicksilver. 'Hello, Alix.' His voice was smooth.

'Hi, Tom,' she said.

They didn't shake hands.

'I'd like to introduce Melissa,' Tom said, indicating a diminutive, beautiful blonde by his side, who made Alix feel like a clumsy giant and who didn't, she immediately saw, rely on any cosmetic procedures to enhance her smooth, flawless skin or bright, sparkling eyes.

'Hi, Melissa,' Marc said, leaning forward to kiss the blonde bundle of perfection on both cheeks. Melissa was wearing a classic white Chanel dress, cinched in at an impossibly small waist and emphasising the soft curves of her breasts and hips. She wasn't clinging to Tom or simpering at his elbow but it was obvious from the way they stood together that there was a connection between them. Tom went on to explain that Melissa was an award-winning foreign correspondent who was just back from Chad. While Marc chatted to Melissa, Alix braced herself to steal a glance at Tom. She caught him staring coldly at her, but as soon as her eyes collided with his, he looked away.

'Can I get you a drink?' Tom asked. Now he was smiling pleasantly at Marc and gesturing towards the table in the corner. All trace of the antagonistic stare had vanished.

'Thanks, Tom, but this is your night. Alix and I will look after ourselves,' Marc said. 'We'll let you circulate and catch up with your friends and colleagues.'

Tom inclined his head and Melissa gave them a brilliant smile as he drew her away to chat to some new arrivals.

Alix felt as though she'd been punched in the solar plexus as she followed Marc over to the table. He handed her a glass of chilled white wine. 'You look as though you could use this,' he said.

Alix's teeth were chattering and clinked against the glass as she held it to her lips. 'Yes, the subject matter is a little unsettling.'

Marc shook his head. 'Man, it's sensational. You can't look at any of those images and not be moved. And Tom is so modest about it all. He doesn't seem to care about the danger he puts himself in. He must have nerves of steel as well as a huge heart.'

'A huge heart?' Alix asked, gripping the stem of her glass. 'What makes you say that?'

'Sure he must have a huge empathy with humanity in all its aspects, good and bad, or he'd never be able to portray it as movingly as he does.'

Marc was right, of course, she thought, feeling a little faint. It was obvious from the photography that behind the smooth, self-controlled veneer he presented tonight, Tom Cassidy was all heart and soul; maturity and his hair-raising experiences had enhanced rather than eclipsed these qualities. In that respect – Alix gulped her wine – he was on the other side of the spectrum from Alix, whose soul had long ago been consigned to the deep, dark abyss.

Marc said he was keen to chat to some of his photographer mates and there were also some prints he wanted to examine in closer detail. Alix encouraged him to go ahead and do his own thing. He had to be conscious at some level of her tension and withdrawal and she was better off on her own as she drifted around the exhibition.

She heard a melodious ripple of laughter, then Tom's answering chuckle, and turned in time to see Tom curl his arm around Melissa's shoulder as they chatted to some friends. She looked so petite and blonde and snug in his arms that Alix ached inside. Tom laughed again, a carefree, infectious laugh that Alix remembered of old, and she pulled herself up sharply.

Why was she doing this to herself? Raking up hurtful images of the past and letting Tom affect her in this way? Anything there had ever been between them was finished – over and out, done and dusted.

Not quite, a little voice mocked, the voice she usually managed to ignore in the busy glitz and glamour of her life. Now, as she kept a covert eye on Tom and watched him circulate with the beautiful Melissa, the little voice was loud and clear in her ear: it reminded her that it was imperative for her sanity to keep the biggest distance possible between the two of them.

After a while Marc reappeared. 'Melissa's just told me they've reserved a couple of tables at Les Deux Magots for some food,' he told her. 'Are you interested in coming along?'

Alix shook her head. She needed to cry her heart out, like a six-year-old child. 'You go, Marc. I'm sure you'll have lots to discuss with your colleagues. I'll find my own way home.'

'Are you sure? I don't want to abandon you.'

'Not at all, I insist you go. I'll be fine. Thanks for the invite,' she added as an afterthought, summoning some conviction to her tone.

'You're the one who did me the favour.' He smiled, kissing her cheek. 'I hope you got something out of it.'

Out of the corner of her eye, Alix caught Tom looking at them before he turned his back to her. She felt there was something coldly deliberate in the way he ensured she was out of his line of vision and shivered. 'Oh, I did,' she insisted. But not exactly what you'd think. On the one hand it might have been a mistake to come here tonight, but it had been a temporary lapse, a timely lesson and an urgent reminder to her to stay very far away from Tom while he was in Paris.

There was no respite when she reached the sanctuary of her apartment. The spacious rooms rang with a strange kind of emptiness. She pictured Tom and Melissa, flushed with the success of the exhibition, heading to the restaurant with their friends for a relaxing meal where wine and chat would flow late into the night, and felt a surge of irrational loneliness. Irrational because she hadn't been part of Tom's life for so long. She stared at herself in the gilt mirror and wondered what Tom had thought of her – her clothes, her sexy image – but when she looked at her perfectly made-up face, it was as though she was gazing at a mask.

Chapter 19

The world of beauty and cosmetics has been Alix's fantasy escape since she was twelve.

She begins experimenting, saving her pocket money for tubes of cheap foundation, mascaras that promise to transform your eyes, palettes of glittering eyeshadows, pencils and lip-gloss. And she finds she is able to make a whole new face for herself when she looks at her reflection. A face that bears no resemblance whatsoever to the seven-year-old face in the mirror whose owner wondered why her safe, comfortable world had suddenly exploded.

More importantly, a face that bears the least resemblance to her mother's.

She spends hours examining herself from all angles, noting the way the extra-length mascara and blend of purple eyeshadows with the dramatic sweep of black liner make a mystery of her light green eyes. She paints her lips traffic-light red, adding a beauty spot to the side of her nose for good measure. Then she wipes off every scrap and begins again, this time using a paler foundation, white high-lighting cream on her brow bone, and a dark, almost russet lip-gloss.

When she looks in the mirror again, she tells herself she need never be afraid when her father or Aunt Hannah says she is the image of her mother.

They think she doesn't know. They don't realise that, even at seven, she could pick out the words in a newspaper headline – words she'd spotted as well as the photographs that told a story of their own when she'd slipped out of bed and tiptoed down to the kitchen for a glass of milk. At first she wasn't quite sure what 'love triangle' meant, but it didn't take her long to figure it out, between Emma's closed-up face, what people were not saying and the hastily averted yet curious eyes at the funeral gathering. And it didn't take her long to realise that it was something that must never, ever be spoken about.

Back in Dublin, her father and Aunt Hannah talked about Mum as though there was nothing untoward about her death, apart from it having been a tragic accident. Her framed photograph took pride of place on the mantelpiece. And when Alix had nightmares in the night, Emma comforted her as well as her father. He told her she should always remember her mother and how much she'd loved her and Emma. That now she was in Heaven, which was a very special place, like a beautiful garden, and Alix and Emma were still her little girls and she still loved them and was taking care of them in an even better way.

Alix didn't want her mother in the beautiful garden. She wanted her here, now – in the mornings checking her school bag and in the evenings checking her homework and telling her she was wonderful. Aunt Hannah was good and kind but she wasn't her mother, her dinners didn't taste the same and her hugs were different.

When Alix is thirteen, she eventually speaks of her fears to Emma. 'Do you ever think about Mum? And what really happened?' she says, her heart hammering.

'What do you mean, "what really happened"?' Emma rounds on her almost angrily. 'She died in a car crash. It was a terrible accident.'

'Yes, but . . .' Alix's voice drops to a whisper. 'What was she doing in the car with somebody else? She wasn't with Dad.' There. She has voiced the worst of her fears. She waits in trembling horror to hear what her sister will say.

'No, but she was on her way to get Dad,' Emma says, as though nothing whatsoever is wrong. 'So Aunt Hannah told me.'

Then when she is fifteen, and before Emma gets married, Alix brings up the subject again. This time Emma breaks down and cries. 'You're not supposed to know,' she says. 'I tried to keep it from you.'

Emma finally admits that she suspects their mother had had an affair. There had been a big row between her parents that weekend, when Alix was sick in bed. Emma has done her best to hide her suspicions from her because the last thing Mum told her on her way out of the door was to look after Alix.

'Look after me?' Alix questions.

'That's right. I know Helga was around as well but that was the last time Mum spoke to me, just as she went out the door.' Emma's eyes fill with fresh tears.

'And you've been keeping an eye on me all this time. You mad thing.' Alix hugs her tightly.

'I just wanted you to remember good things about her. It was bad enough that she was gone, never mind the dreadful way it happened. Dad never talks about it.' Emma gulps. 'And I've never talked to him or Aunt Hannah about the details. But listen, Alix, don't ever let on you know, and don't dare say anything to him, because it would break his heart all over again. Promise me you'll stay quiet?'

'Okay, don't worry. I'm not going to breathe a word. Promise. Do you think . . .'

'What?'

'Well, do you think I'm like her?' Again, she waits, fearful, to hear what her sister will say.

'Yes, I guess you are. And not only in looks. You have the same mannerisms. Sometimes the way you laugh and walk . . . and you're neat and tidy like Mum was, not like muddly me, and very clever as well, so, yes, I suppose you are like her in lots of ways.'

After that, Alix experiments more and more with her makeup brushes and palettes of colour and deliberately leaves her bedroom in a chaotic mess. When she is sixteen, she becomes very popular with her schoolmates. The quiet, private girl who usually hangs back because she feels less than cool is suddenly everyone's best friend. It begins quite by chance when she bumps into Jackie one Saturday morning in town. Jackie is the most popular girl in the class and the self-proclaimed leader of the bright, confident in crowd who incite envy with the way they are first to have everything and who hang around together to the exclusion of everyone else.

'Hey, Alix, I hardly knew you! Where did you get your make-up done?'

'I did it myself,' Alix says, floundering and embarrassed that she's been caught out wearing her sexy and seductive look. Make-up is forbidden in the classroom so she's not too surprised that Jackie almost fails to recognise her.

'Cool. Any chance you could do my face like yours?' Jackie asks. 'I'm going to the disco tonight and I want to look special. There's this guy I fancy . . .'

'Sure. I can make you look any way you want,' Alix shrugs.

'Brill. Could you call around to my house before the disco and we'll go together?'

Jackie's new look is an instant success and Jackie's friends beg Alix to work her magic on them. It becomes a regular event, the select gang of mates descending on Jackie's house where Alix sets to work with her brushes and colours, mascaras and pencils, and they all head off together to the disco. Alix revels in the feeling of belonging.

And that is where Alix meets Tom.

One night she's out on the floor, dancing with her mates to the sound of Madonna, when she spots a lanky, jeans-clad guy with dark blond hair and an air of restless energy darting glances in her direction. She automatically turns to check behind her to see who might be the subject of his scrutiny, but the floor is clear. Something hot washes over her when she realises that his glances are all for her. After a while he disappears. The following week she dresses extra carefully, her heart lifting when she sees him there again and feels his eyes on her. She is full of a heady expectation. She is just growing out of her gawkiness into her tall slenderness, and the way he looks at her makes her feel excited and ultra-special, as if she is the only girl at the disco. The third week her heart drops when she sees him chatting to one of Jackie's friends. But her envy lasts all of ten seconds because Jackie's friend nods and points in Alix's direction. Then he comes over and starts to chat.

'Hi. I've heard about you. My sister's a friend of Jackie's, and –' he pulls a self-deprecating face '– that's a pretty crap chat-up line.'

In spite of her racing heartbeat, she can't help a soft laugh. She is hopeless at flirting, not having had much practice, and it's refreshing that he doesn't pretend.

'I'm not too good at this kind of stuff,' he says.

'Neither am I, but I think you're doing okay.'

'Good. I've been trying to screw up the courage to say hi . . .'

'Really?' She warms to his honesty, finding it endearing.

'Yep.' He gives her a lopsided grin. 'I'm Tom.'

'Hi, I'm Alix, with an *i* instead of an *e*.'

'How did that come about?'

'A family pet name.' She laughs. 'I was christened Alexandra.'

'Alexandra,' he echoes. His blue eyes scan her face and he speaks her name as though it is a blessing.

Chapter 20

'Your last day, Emma. How do you feel?' Nikola asked.

'I don't know,' Emma admitted as she slid off her coat and sat down at her desk. 'A bit weird, to be honest.'

'You certainly took us all by surprise,' Stacy said, putting down her lip-gloss and raising her eyes from her compact mirror. 'How long had you been planning it?'

'Not too long,' Emma hedged.

Word of her resignation had flown around Marshalls on Monday afternoon. For once she'd shocked Nikola and Stacy out of their indulgent tolerance. And even though it had taken every ounce of her resolve, Emma had gone over to Karl's desk to have a few words with him.

'I heard you're leaving,' he said, rather cheekily.

'That's right. I want to spend more time with my family,' she said, speaking very softly so she wasn't overheard. 'I don't want to know about Marshalls any more, or hear anything I might not like to hear,' she went on, quietly and deliberately. 'If I do happen to hear something I don't like, well, I might be tempted to say a few things you wouldn't like.' Her threats were empty and futile, but she forced herself to meet his eyes and fix him with a meaningful stare so that he got the message. He merely grinned at her impudently and shrugged.

Now she looked around the office floor, immensely relieved that by the time she walked out that evening, her awful, gut-wrenching days in Marshalls would be over. Better still, Karl hadn't been on hand for most of the week to set her nerves jangling as he'd been on a training course – Emma hadn't needed to resort to sick leave.

'And you definitely can't come out after work for a booze-up? Even a mini booze-up?' Stacy asked hopefully.

'No, I'm going to some office thing with Oliver,' she lied.

'Now that you're free of here, think of all the time and energy you'll have to devote to him.' Nikola raised knowing eyebrows.

Emma turned on her computer. For all her libidinous plans to make it up to Oliver, it hadn't been so easy to initiate the great marriage revival and encourage impromptu sex. So far, her attempts at redemption hadn't gone anywhere near as successfully as she'd hoped.

She'd planned a seductive, romantic meal for Monday night, but when he'd arrived home from the office, Oliver had been totally taken aback. 'What's this in aid of?' he'd asked.

Candles flickered, reflecting on the polished mahogany surface of the table and the crystal glassware. A vase of yellow roses and baby's breath thrust out vibrant plumes of colour beside a carafe of cherry red Chianti. The succulent aroma of roast beef filtered in from the adjacent kitchen. Emma was dressed in a soft chiffon blouse and a mid-length wrap skirt, and her pulse spots were scented with her favourite Vera Wang perfume.

A love song was playing softly in the background.

'What have I forgotten?' Oliver looked worried.

'Nothing.' She painted a smile on her face, touched his arm in a familiar gesture. 'I thought it would be nice for us to have a romantic meal in our own home. Just the two of us together. For once in our lives.'

Oliver looked unhappy now. 'You should have warned me.'

Emma's heart plummeted and fear ignited her anxiety. '*Warned* you? Since when should I have to warn you? I thought it would be a nice surprise.'

'It is. It's just . . . well, look, I wasn't expecting all this on a Monday night.' He nodded at the table half-heartedly.

No, Emma thought. Her husband had expected to bury his head in the laptop for a while and then grab something to eat while he watched Sky Sports. 'That's the whole point,' she said. 'We've fallen into a rut and we should shake ourselves up a little. Try and be a bit more adventurous. The kids are out tonight so I thought we'd take advantage of it and have some romantic time together. Look, Oliver,' she caught her breath, 'I feel we've lost sight of each other, lost sight of the excitement we used to have in our relationship.' She voiced all the things she'd told herself in the dark of night in a pathetic attempt to validate her behaviour. Now, listening to the words falling from her lips, she knew they fell very short of expiating a sin such as hers. The music changed to Seal's 'Kiss from a Rose', reminding her of an earlier summer, years ago, when Charlie was about five and she was beginning to feel free of the restrictive days of babyhood. She was caught in the grip of painful nostalgia.

Then Oliver left the room and she heard him go upstairs. A few minutes later he reappeared. He'd entered into the spirit of things by having a shower and changing into his black shirt and jeans. 'This is all very nice,' he said, smiling at her across the table. 'And you're right, we're both too caught up in stuff and the weeks just seem to fly by. Then you're running the house, and taking care of us all.' He lifted his glass in a silent toast. 'I don't know where we'd be without you. I'd never find my car keys, or where Leticia hides my socks. Charlie's football kit would never be ready on time and even Libby . . .' His voice softened. 'I know you spoil her a little, we both do, but she'll be gone from the house soon enough, and she mightn't show it, but she looks up to you big time.'

Emma's food lodged in her throat. He was trying to make her feel good and she didn't deserve it. Neither did she deserve Libby looking up to her. And this wasn't going to work. It was crazy – absurd, even – to think she could obliterate the events of a fateful Friday night and set their marriage back on course with soft music, candlelight and a pseudo-romantic meal. Oliver looked so solid and trustworthy – and so sexy – that Emma felt doubly ashamed of herself and her subterfuge.

'By the way,' she began, knowing it was now or never, and hoping she could talk about it without her voice quivering, 'I'm quitting Marshalls. I'm finishing up on Thursday.'

He looked startled. 'You're what?' He was giving her the full benefit of his laser-beam attention, and not because of a possible promotion but because she was resigning from her job.

'You were right,' she said. 'I don't really enjoy the hassle of Marshalls.'

'I'm delighted for you. You'll have more time to yourself,' he said.

'I'm going back to Pilates and joining a book club,' Emma told him. Although surely she'd be more sexy and adventurous to Oliver if she learned to pole dance or ice skate?

'Great. Annabelle might need you on one of her worthy causes,' he said, referring to the wife of one of his colleagues. With Oliver's backing, she had tried to enlist Emma's help in one of her many charitable projects before Emma went to work in Marshalls.

'I won't be giving Annabelle or her friends a call just yet,' Emma said, reluctant to explain how inferior the domineering woman and her cronies had made her feel, and how terrified she'd been in their company lest she committed a social faux pas.

'Whatever makes you happy, darling,' he said, smiling as he shared the last of the wine between their glasses.

When he smiled at her like that her insides turned to mush. 'What kind of dessert would you like?' she asked, emboldened, infusing her voice with a trace of huskiness and determined to see the romantic evening through to its natural conclusion. So far, since Karl, she hadn't made love to Oliver. Now it was more important than ever to re-establish intimacy with him in order to block out that other forbidden intimacy. And she wanted her husband to thrill and excite her. She wanted to feel the spark of desire that Karl had rekindled, only this time with Oliver.

'What kind . . .?' He looked wary now of this new, coquettish wife.

She opened a button on her silk blouse, revealing a generous eyeful of cleavage.

Oliver's brows shot up.

A door banged, a bag thumped onto the hall floor and footsteps approached. Charlie burst into the room, his figure silhouetted in the doorway against the bright kitchen light. 'Hey, what's going on?' His single glance took in everything – the slight charge in the atmosphere and the undone button on Emma's blouse. His face was a mixture of disbelief and embarrassment.

'I thought you had football practice,' Emma said, quite unnecessarily, when it was obvious to Charlie that his parents had thought the coast was clear.

'Football?' He was still staring at them. 'It was called off. The pitch was waterlogged. So what are you two up to?'

Emma exchanged glances with Oliver. For a moment she thought he seemed slightly relieved. He said, 'We were just having a pleasant meal together.'

'Yeah, right.' Charlie backed into the kitchen. 'Sorry I interrupted you.'

'It's okay, Charlie, you're not interrupting anything. We're just finished. And your mother is celebrating – she's finally leaving her job so she made a special meal for us both.' He winked at Emma.

Father and son retreated into the kitchen, discussing match fixtures and training times. So much for impromptu sex. Emma leaned forward and blew out the candles. A single puff, and the flames were extinguished, all sparkle gone in an instant.

She wished it was as easy to erase her sins.

Although her first attempt to revive spontaneous passion in her marriage had been doomed, Emma tried again. On Wednesday evening she filled the bath, swirling the warm water around, blending the fragrances of bergamot and lavender. She sprinkled on a handful of petals and watched them float on the surface. She lit two dozen tea-lights and arranged them on the windowsill and along the side of the bath. Mindful of notifying him in advance, she'd told Oliver she had another romantic treat in store for him, and it involved the bathroom.

When the bath was ready and the room filled with a sensual aroma, she went out onto the landing and called down to her husband. 'You can come up now,' she said, suddenly dry-mouthed. She slipped back into the bathroom, out of her robe and, feeling decadent and lascivious, slid into the warm, scented water.

'What's this?' he said, standing in the semi-darkness.

'It's our own very private spa but we don't make enough use of it. The kids are gone to a gig,' she said, swallowing her nerves and trying to sound playful. 'If you'd like to join me, we'll have some champagne.'

'Champagne?' His eyes flew to the bottle jammed into a cooler beside the bath. She tried to ignore the fact that his first comment had referred to the champagne and not to joining his naked wife.

'It's about time we started enjoying ourselves more. Come on in . . .' She managed to inject a sultry, seductive note into her voice, amazed at how she pulled it off.

'Hey, Emma,' he grinned, 'I can't remember the last time we shared a bath . . .'

Gripped by hot shame, she watched Oliver shrug out of his clothes. She looked at his familiar body, admiring the broad sweep of his shoulders and the way his powerful frame tapered to his narrow hips. What the hell had she seen in Karl? She must have been out of her mind. In a sense she had been, thanks to a glut of alcohol.

Oliver climbed in at the other end of the bath, dislodging petals and displacing the water so vigorously that some of it sloshed over the side and extinguished half of the tea-lights. 'Oops,' he laughed. 'Never mind, maybe it's better that not too much light is cast on my toned-up six-pack.'

There wasn't enough room for both of them to sit comfortably. In Emma's romantic visions, she hadn't realised that Oliver's knees would protrude above the scented water or that the taps would dig so uncomfortably into her back.

All of a sudden she felt incredibly nervous at the thought of Oliver's hands on her treacherous body. 'Champagne coming up,' she said hastily, reaching for the glasses and the bottle. But the bottle, stuck fast in the cooler, refused to budge.

Oliver came to the rescue. 'Here. Let me.' He reached out and put the glasses on the tiled floor and lifted out the champagne. He poured it and handed Emma hers. They clinked. 'Here's to our private spa.'

Emma took a long sip and spluttered, almost choking on the bubbles.

'Are you okay?' Oliver asked. He knelt up in the bath, petals stuck to his hips, and reached behind her to tap her on the back.

'I'm fine,' she managed, feeling hysterical with a mixture of longing and heartache at the sight of her husband. She, too, knelt up in the bath, the better to lean against him. Somehow, though, in the movement of her legs she dislodged the plug and the water began to drain away.

Oliver got out and reached for a bath sheet, brushing the petals off himself. 'We've been kicked out,' he said. 'We're not wanted here. Let's move somewhere we're a bit more comfortable.' He wrapped the towel around his waist, pulled Emma out of the bath and swaddled her in another towel, hugging her close so that her face slotted into the hollow of damp skin at his neck. He pushed her gently into the bedroom, then went back to the bathroom.

So much for the great bathroom seduction, Emma fretted as she sat on the side of the bed and watched him bring through the glasses and champagne. He still had the towel around his waist, she noticed. He hadn't got dressed. Yet.

'Are you sure we won't be disturbed?' he asked. She thought he seemed a little uneasy, but maybe her anxiety was colouring everything.

'Positive,' she told him. 'Libby, Rob and Charlie are all gone to a gig in the O2.'

With calm deliberation, he locked the door. 'Just in case.' Then he refilled their glasses and sat down beside her. She felt an instant of pure terror as he peeled away the edge of her towel to reveal her damp breasts and bent his head to them.

Afterwards she lay awake into the small hours of the night and muffled her tears. Oliver had made love to her with his usual tenderness, and it had all been much as normal, yet frighteningly easy to fall into the familiar rhythm, and to move her limbs in the right places. But her responses had been wooden, her face hot with shame, and deep inside she'd felt full of self-loathing.

Now, the following morning, as the hours blessedly ticked away on her last day in Marshalls, Emma was exhausted. Moreover, it was painfully obvious to her that she could never redeem herself fully. She would have to live with her self-disgust, her shame, and hide it from Oliver as best she could. She loved her husband with every cell in her body. Nothing must be allowed to come between them. And, she vowed, she would never take him for granted again.

She owed him far too much . . .

Chapter 21

*H*e is the tall, rangy, quiet guy, standing in the kitchen at her friend's birthday party. His dark hair is tousled, as though it needs a trim, and his navy blue eyes are calmly alert. Emma can't help giving him furtive glances, noticing the way he leans against the worktop with a bottle of beer in his hand, laughing and chatting with his friends, looking as though he is quietly in charge of the world and totally in tune with himself, which is something she badly wants for herself.

He catches her staring at him and she blushes furiously and looks away. But, time and time again, she finds herself drawn to his face and his air of relaxed self-possession. After a while he puts down the beer and, to her amazement, introduces himself and leads her into the shadowy sitting room where the lights are dimmed and the music is playing. They press together in the dim light while 'Careless Whisper' wafts across the room and she feels as though she's wrapped in a magic spell. Afterwards she calls it their song. He tells her that he was immediately attracted to her – something in the way her soft blue eyes look at him make him feel ten feet tall.

Emma can't believe that the talented Oliver Colgan, with the quiet, modest manner and calm smile, feels like that about her, or that he is happy to bring her out for meals, to the movies and for walks by the sea. When he teases her, makes her laugh and kisses her hungrily, it's exciting, terrifying and thrilling. But there's something about him, too, that makes her feel safe and protected. She can't believe it when he tells her he loves her. Oliver has already sailed through college and is now working in the banking sector. Emma is in her final year in school, the long months of exam cramming fizzing at the edges with the sparkling knowledge that Oliver is there for her. Getting to know all about him is a heady new adventure. His circle of friends becomes hers. She learns to enjoy the same music as him, the same television programmes, much the same books.

Even more exciting is the long, hot summer following her final school exams when she and Oliver start to sleep together, Emma shy at first, and Oliver eager enough to sweep both of them along in his raw, lusty passion. Life takes on a whole new dimension, lifting her up and excising the past with all its sadness. Oliver's lovemaking silences the unhappy murmurings in her soul and for the first time in years she feels joy in her life. But although on the one hand she feels truly cherished and desired, on the other she is terrified lest it is all snatched away from her.

She has barely settled into an arts degree course when she discovers she is pregnant. 'We'll get married,' Oliver says as soon as she breaks the news.

She feels terrified and pleased in equal measures. 'Oh, Oliver, are you sure? I don't know what my father will say – and what about your parents?'

'You're not to worry your little head about my parents. I'll talk to them. I'm sure they'll understand. I love you, Emma, and it'll all work out fine, I promise.'

Emma's father is philosophical about it, but Oliver's parents are quietly furious. She marries him on a cold, bright February day, and Libby arrives three months later, Charlie less than two years after that. And he is just a few months old when Aunt Hannah decides to follow her dream and emigrate to Australia. 'I'll be fifty next year,' she says to Emma. 'Alix and you have turned into lovely young women so you scarcely need me any more, and if I don't go now, I never will.'

Emma hugs the aunt who'd unselfishly stepped in to fill some of the space left by her mother. When her father dies five years later of liver cancer, Emma tells herself that the past and all its sad history is buried with him. By now, Alix is making a new life for herself, the children are out of that busy baby stage, and she and Oliver are blissfully happy with their young family and each other. Emma is learning to shop in the right shops, and Oliver is climbing the ladder in the bank, wearing more expensive suits and shorter, neater hair.

Thanks to Oliver, life is full of promise and far, far better than she'd ever expected.

Chapter 22

*L*ibby glided out of the fitting room and struck a pose. 'Ta-da! What do you think?'

She waited, full of exuberance, as her mother put her head to one side and admired her in the Miu Miu cotton shift with the bubble skirt. Libby loved what she saw in the mirror – the dress was funky and its rosy blush hue brought out her delicate skin tone.

'You look gorgeous, Libby, and that dress is a maybe,' her mother said. 'It's glam but it's fun and youthful.'

Libby adjusted the sash and did a twirl. 'Yay! That's what I thought too. The most important piece of advice that Alix gave me was not to go too formal or attempt to dress older than my years.'

'When were you talking to her?'

'I emailed her during the week for advice before we went shopping for the launch. Little did I know what you had up your sleeve, Mum!' Libby gurgled.

Her mum smiled warmly. 'I know that Alix's launch will be one of the most glitzy nights in your life so far. I want it to be perfect for you, and I want you to feel that you're looking sensational. Not that you need designer glam for that. You're already very beautiful, Libby. Quite perfect, in fact. Even your hair.' She reached out and flicked the ends.

'Mum! Are you sure you're feeling all right?'

'Course I am.'

'But all this!' Libby swept her hand over the swathe of dresses waiting for her approval, from silky purple to pale blue georgette, from body-skimming crêpe to floaty chiffon.

'Take your time, there's no rush,' Emma said. 'Decide which you like best and we'll have them put aside. Then we can go to lunch while you think about it and make your final decisions. You'll need two or three outfits, and matching shoes and bags.'

Libby shook her head. 'But all this, Mum. I didn't know we were going on a serious shopping blitz! You'd swear we were auditioning for leading roles in *Sex and the City*. Hey, we'll blow them out of the water.'

'Good. You deserve a treat.'

'A *treat*? Some treat this is!'

Her mum was certainly going over the top, like someone hell bent on a mission – the mission in this case being a revamp of Libby's glad rags. They'd planned to hit the shops early and her mum was organising her tote bag and slipping on her camel-coloured wool jacket when Libby had come downstairs just before nine o'clock that morning. But instead of getting into Emma's Golf and heading to Dundrum town centre as she'd expected, her mother had arranged for a cab to whisk them into the city.

'We'll hit the Grafton Street area first, then we can head out to Harvey Nicks and the House of Fraser in Dundrum,' she'd said. 'I've decided we're not just going shopping for a dress for the launch. We're going to treat ourselves big time.'

'No way, Mum!'

'And you're not to worry about money, Libby. Today is on me.'

First port of call had been an exclusive hairdressing and beauty salon tucked into a laneway off Grafton Street that was normally too expensive for Libby. Emma had booked them both an appointment. 'If we're going shopping for serious glam, we have to look the part,' her mother said, smiling at Libby's pleasure as they were escorted across to the basins and swathed in thick towels. Two scalp massages, hair-conditioning treatments and glamorous makeup later, they hit the streets.

Now it was almost lunchtime and Libby was having the time of her life. She went back into the dressing room, took off the Miu Miu and hung it up on the padded hanger. Next was a black velvet Dolce & Gabbana. It looked promising too, with a sweetheart neckline, spaghetti straps and a mesh frill peeping out under the mini skirt. She slipped it over her head, smoothed it down over her curves and knew straight away that there was no need to go looking any further, no need to try on anything else. This was *it*. The mini dress fit her like a glove and Libby didn't have to look at her reflection to know it was perfect on her.

When she came out of the changing room, her mum's face flashed with emotion. 'That's the one, that's it – it's beautiful, Libby,' she said, her eyes suspiciously bright.

'Mum, you're not going to cry, are you?' Libby's attention was torn between the dress and the look on her mum's face.

'It's so perfect that I can't help feeling a little mushy. It's chic but fun, and I'm buying it right now – there's no need to even think about it. It'll look great with the spiky heels I spotted outside and the matching clutch that I'm also going to buy you. Then we'll shop for underwear and perfume.'

'Mum, no way,' Libby objected.

Emma waved away her protests. 'Just enjoy it, Libby, let me spoil you. Please.'

'I will on one condition,' Libby smiled.

'What's that?'

'Lunch is on me, and then I want to buy *you* something special to wear.'

Emma smiled. 'Lunch is already booked in the Town Bar and Grill, so it's my treat.'

As the day went on, Libby was overcome by her mother's extravagance. Emma had already bought her some designer jeans and shirts, but she took the wind out of Libby's sails by buying her the blush cotton shift as well as the black velvet dress, a beautiful Grecian-style midi, a pair of the thinnest, spikiest heels that Libby had ever seen as well as the clutch bag. She followed that with three sets of the sheerest, softest bras and knickers.

'There's no better way to feel like a glam goddess than to have fabulous lingerie next to your skin,' Emma pointed out. 'And you need something special for under those dresses.'

'It's all so lovely that I don't want to cover it up,' Libby sighed as she watched the assistant carefully swathe the whispery silk in soft pink tissue. 'Paris isn't going to know what's hit it.'

She was relieved when Emma picked out two gowns for herself, a Vivienne Westwood draped dress in shimmering turquoise and a Helen McAlinden lilac cocktail number in silk and chiffon.

'I'm not sure what colour Alix is wearing,' Emma had said as she dithered over the two gowns. 'I want to complement her outfit, not clash with it.'

'We're taking both,' Libby told the assistant firmly. Turning to her mum, she smiled impishly. 'Let me pay for one of these. I'm treating you this time.'

'No, Libby, that's far too much,' Emma shook her head.

'I insist,' Libby said, waving her credit card. 'And I want no arguments.'

*

By the time they finished up in Dundrum town centre that evening, they were laden with a raft of lavish carrier bags and the last stop of the day was the bar in Harvey Nicks.

Libby ordered a Cosmopolitan, but Emma said she was happy to stick to still water with ice and lemon.

'You're not still getting over that Friday night?' Libby asked. 'I thought you'd have recovered by now.'

Although her mother's dark hair was sleekly glossy after the hairdresser's that morning, and her face was expertly made up, Libby thought she looked strained. Emma shook her head and her blue eyes were full of irony as she said, 'Sometimes, Libby, I feel as though I'll never recover.'

She reached over and squeezed her mother's hand. 'I hope you're not embarrassed at getting hammered. It was only one night and we all fall off the rails from time to time.' Then something else occurred to her. 'You didn't – Mum, you didn't leave Marshalls on account of that, did you?'

Her mother sipped her water, the expression in her eyes neutral. 'Goodness, no, Libby. I wanted to leave anyway.'

'Dad's pleased at any rate.'

Emma still seemed a little downbeat so Libby went on, 'Look, Mum, it's just that he wants you to have a hassle-free lifestyle.' She smiled encouragingly, wondering where the bright, bubbly atmosphere of the day had suddenly gone.

Emma smiled back. 'Yes, you're right.'

'Think of it, you'll have a whole new life away from Marshalls, as well as more time for shopping and beauty treatments. Why shouldn't you enjoy the nice things in life for a while? You've certainly worked hard enough.'

Her mum was silent for a moment, and when she spoke, Libby had the strangest feeling she was trying to get a hidden message across to her. 'Whatever about my life, all I ever want is for you, Charlie and your dad to be happy. I love you all so much, Libby.'

'I know that, Mum. We all do.'

'I think you're all brilliant,' Emma went on. 'No matter what happens, remember that. And I'm not being mushy. Sometimes these things don't get said enough in the busyness of life.'

'It's fine, Mum. We think you're brilliant too.' Libby sipped her cocktail and felt a stirring of unease. Her mother didn't normally bare her soul. Maybe her night on the tiles had triggered some kind of mid-life crisis. Then again, it could be the other way around, Libby considered. She'd allowed herself to get pissed because she'd reached a crunch point in her life. And if her mother went on like this, Libby was afraid she, too, might let her guard down and reveal the catastrophic news that she was unhappy in her stellar career. Sometimes she felt her restlessness was so close to the surface that it would burst out in a huge torrent of words as though it had a life of its own. Problem was, whatever about her mother leaving Marshalls, Libby chucking in her brilliant career on what was surely a whim would be something else entirely. Her parents would be devastated.

'Anyway, darling, I treated you today because I want you to realise how special you are to me and how very proud I am of you.'

That did it. She certainly couldn't unburden herself now, Libby decided. Not only had her mother blown a hole in her credit card for Libby, but she'd done so because she was so very proud of her clever daughter. No way could she throw that back in her face.

She picked up one of her swish carrier bags and peeped inside at her black velvet dress, reminding herself of how sparkly it had made her feel, and allowed the excitement to wash over her again. Then she beamed at her mum. 'You're special too and, thanks to you, we're both going to take Paris by storm. Hey, bring it on!'

Chapter 23

On Sunday morning Alix was just out of bed and standing at the kitchen worktop in her bright red slippers and favourite comfy PJs when Emma phoned. 'Hi, Alix, how's things?' her sister said. 'Can you talk or did I disturb you?'

'Disturb me at what?' Alix joked. 'I'm not in bed having torrid sex, if that's what you're afraid of.'

There was a brief silence at the other end of the phone. Then Emma said, 'Let me guess, you've already sent him home?'

'No, he wasn't here last night.' Alix filled the kettle with her free hand and plugged it in. 'How are things *chez* the Colgans?'

'Fine,' Emma said. 'Sorry for phoning you so early but I'm catching you now while the coast is clear.'

'No prob. I'm just up. So tell me why you need the coast to be clear? I'm intrigued.'

'I'm phoning while Oliver's out on the golf course, Libby's still in bed and Charlie's in the den glued to his computer.'

'What's up that you don't want your gang to hear?'

'I know we'll be over in a few weeks' time for the launch, but

I'm planning on bringing Oliver to Paris soon for a surprise visit. However, much as I love you, darling sister, I'm booking us into a posh hotel – I'm hoping we could meet for lunch, maybe, on one of the days?' Emma spoke very quickly and Alix knew her sister was anticipating her response and anxious to explain where she was coming from.

'So you'd rather not stay with me?' she said, feeling a tiny stab of rejection. 'You know I've oodles of room and would love to have you.'

'Yes, I know you would, but this is an unexpected treat for Oliver, a kind of second honeymoon of sorts . . .'

Emma sounded apologetic and Alix was tempted to give her a shake. Her sister had surely nothing to apologise for – but that was Emma all over, anxious to please. 'Are you celebrating anything special? Birthday, anniversary?' Alix cast around lest she'd forgotten a milestone, but nothing came to mind.

'No, I just want to treat him. It'll be a surprise – that's why I'm phoning you now. I know he loves Paris, and it's very romantic, so I want to do the real hearts-and-roses stuff, but it would be nice to have a chance to catch up with you also . . .'

'How soon were you planning on coming? It's a little cold over here at the moment. Not that that will bother you, I suppose. Second honeymoon and all that . . .'

'I'm hoping to book flights for around the end of April, depending on when you're free.'

'Let me check . . .' Alix went into her bedroom and rummaged in her holdall until she put her hands on the thick Mulberry Filofax that went everywhere with her. She should really surrender to modern technology, she supposed, and use mobile computing to store her notes and engagements, but her Filofax was akin to a bible, filled with an accumulation of precious jottings and details that would be difficult to refile. She knew exactly where to put her finger on whatever she needed and she had her see-at-a-glance cal-endar opened in a jiffy.

'Yes, that's fine with me. I'm busy Fridays, and a couple of Saturdays, but so far free on Sundays. If you and Oliver can tear yourselves away from your love nest, how about meeting for Sunday lunch?'

'Perfect. I'll organise flights, and if you want to book somewhere special, it'll be my treat – and Alix, I'm really looking forward—'

'To seeing me or your love-in with Oliver?' Alix couldn't help teasing. 'I suppose it must be hard getting private time together, with your two adult kids still at home. Not to mention the boyfriend.'

'We don't mind having Rob,' Emma said. 'It's Libby's home, too, and it won't be for ever. And, yes, it is hard to get time alone – but I'm dying to have a chat and get up to date on the launch of Alix B. Thanks for understanding why we won't be staying with you.'

'Give over, it's fine,' Alix said warmly. 'You don't have to explain. At least we'll get to have lunch in spite of your seduction plans. I suppose you could have brought Oliver to Rome or Vienna . . .'

'There's something magical about Paris and it'll be good to catch up with you as well.'

'How do you feel now you've left Marshalls? Any plans for your new life?'

'Right now I just want to take time out, enjoy being at home and do a few different things with Oliver.'

There was a definite catch in her sister's voice. 'Are you okay?' she asked. 'You sound a little tired. You're probably doing too much, as usual. How's Leticia? Has she pulled up her socks yet or are you still bailing her out?'

'I've had a talk with her and gone over her duties again. I was almost going to give her the sack,' Emma said, taking Alix by sur-prise.

'You were?'

'But I just couldn't bring myself to do it.'

Quelle surprise. 'Don't let her away with stuff. And do a few things for yourself. Go shopping and update your wardrobe. Revamp your make-up, the tried and tested therapy.'

'I'm waiting until Alix B is launched to update my make-up, but I've already been shopping. I went out with Libby yesterday and we bought up the town. We'll do our best not to upstage you on the night of the launch, but you might as well know that, according to Libby, *Sex and the City* won't hold a candle to us,' Emma said, sounding a little more cheerful.

'Good,' Alix said. 'That's the way to go. I had an email from Hannah – she's coming to Europe for a holiday and will definitely be in Paris for the end of May.'

'Hannah's coming? That's brilliant. We haven't seen her in years. And I haven't talked to her since Christmas so I must give her a call.'

Afterwards Alix wondered why she'd brought up the subject. Some perverse need to say his name and test Emma's reaction, she supposed. 'Tom Cassidy's in Paris, for an exhibition of his work.'

'Tom?' Emma sounded puzzled. Then, she went on, a worried note in her voice, 'You're hardly going to see him, are you?'

'I already have,' Alix said airily, digging her short, even nails into her palm. 'Marc had an invitation to the exhibition and invited me to go with him.'

'Oh, Alix, after everything that happened he doesn't deserve the time of day from you.'

'That was years ago,' Alix said lightly. 'I've moved on since then.'

'If you just went to show off how well you've succeeded, that's okay, I suppose.'

'I scarcely got to talk to him, and I went with Marc to make Sophie jealous.'

'I was half afraid you were foolish enough to imagine that you and Tom could pick up where you left off . . .'

'Rest assured, that will never happen.' Alix was able to say this with utter conviction.

When she finished chatting to her sister, Alix made some herbal tea and, still in her PJs and slippers, sat at the window and gazed out over the rooftops bathed in sunshine. This morning the view failed to uplift her. She felt rattled, dissatisfied, almost. The day yawned emptily ahead, with just a walk in the calm oasis of the terraces and avenues of the Jardin du Luxembourg to look forward to. After that, she could pick up some organic fruit and cheese at the nearby open-air market, and if any of her friends were free, she could meet up with them for a couple of hours that evening. But she would still be returning to an empty apartment.

She tried to ignore the curl of envy she felt at the thought of Emma bringing Oliver to Paris for a love-in – or a sexathon, more like. It was the least Emma deserved. Her sister's life was busy, with her ambitious husband and adult stay-at-home kids. Up to now she hadn't had a minute to herself, between her job in Marshalls, running her home in leafy Dublin suburbia and putting up with Leticia's shortcomings.

Yet sometimes in the dark hours that sprang out of nowhere, and when Alix was being achingly honest with herself, she admitted that Emma had everything that was important and valuable in life. A dependable, steadfast guy, a fabulous son and a beautiful daughter. She wondered what it was like to make love to the same person over and over again, time after time, so that you would know them so well, be almost part of them, attuned to every inch of their body and nuance of their soul. Sometimes in those dark hours she faced the painful fact that she'd had the opportunity to have all that, but she'd turned her back on it many years ago.

Now an unexpected wave of regret took Alix's breath away and brought a hollow pain to her stomach. She asked herself why on earth she was feeling like this on such a beautiful Sunday morning, and decided a bad fairy was up to mischief. A bad fairy who was slowly but meticulously putting her life, past and present, under a microscope and turning it inside out. She refused to allow it to upset her. Right now she would have a long, luxurious soak in the bath with her favourite patchouli-scented bath oil before she went for her walk.

As for the bad fairy? Well, it could do whatever the hell it liked.

Chapter 24

*E*mma sat at the kitchen table and watched Libby putting on her Zara jacket and lifting her blonde hair over her shoulders.

'Where did you say you were meeting up, Mum?' Libby asked.

'Some new restaurant in Dawson Street, La Venetia, I think,' Emma said. 'We can have a meal there and a few drinks.'

'Drinks? I might pop in for one or two, just to say hello. From what I remember, Nikola and Stacy are a bit of fun.'

Emma's mind raced. 'When did you meet them?'

'Last Christmas. Don't tell me you've forgotten.' Libby paused as she reached into the fridge for a can of Red Bull. 'We were shopping in town, remember? We popped into Samsara for a drink to rest our legs and soak up the atmosphere and they'd had the same idea. We ended up staying far longer than we meant to and having far too many Cosmos,' Libby laughed, 'even for me.'

Emma caught her breath. The memory almost choked her; Libby's carefree face against a backdrop of sparkly street lighting, shops windows blazing warmth and inviting them in, the relaxed ambience of the festively decorated pub.

Libby was still talking as she pulled on her gloves. '. . . and I'm at a loose end tonight as Rob's in college. Again. You can send me a text and let me know where you are.'

'There's no real need,' Emma told her. 'I expect it'll be an early enough night.'

'What? No nightclub?' Libby teased. 'In that case I'll have to join you to make something of the evening. *And* I'll be there to keep an eye on you. What do you think, Dad?'

Emma felt Oliver's arm going around her in a quick hug. She caught his lemony scent as he bent his head and briefly nuzzled her neck. 'I couldn't agree more, but don't enjoy yourself too much without me,' he said.

Libby rolled her eyes and marched out into the hall. 'Dad, we'll be late. You'll have plenty of time for smooching Mum later.'

'Coming, Libby, right now.' Oliver grabbed his briefcase and blew Emma a kiss as he backed out of the kitchen door.

Emma tightened the sash of her silk dressing gown and sipped her orange juice.

'Mum, did you see my mobile anywhere?' Charlie loped into the kitchen.

'No, Charlie, I didn't.'

He picked up the cordless house phone and punched in his mobile number, then bounded out of the kitchen and back up the stairs, pursuing the sound of his *Rocky* ring tone.

Another Thursday morning in the Colgan household and what a difference a couple of weeks made. She should have been a little more at ease now that the nightmare of Marshalls and Karl was behind her, but Emma found she was still getting up at the same time each morning, the swirl of her guilty thoughts urging her on. Once out of bed, however, it was difficult to motivate herself to do anything.

Leticia had been alarmed to find her employer at home when

she'd arrived the previous Friday for her usual three-hour stint. Emma found it stressful to have her cleaner brandishing cloths and mops with exaggerated enthusiasm, as though she was doing her utmost to impress with her strenuous efforts in bathroom and kitchen.

As for Oliver . . . He still left for the office as though he was heading into Nirvana, but now he was a little more considerate, a little more loving and attentive. On the surface everything seemed fine, but she still felt as though an axe was about to fall. Her episode with Karl would never be over, she thought as she stood up and pushed her chair back. For the rest of her life, she would carry that awful knowledge in her heart and keep it a secret from Oliver.

She was seeing Stacy and Nikola that evening. They had phoned and insisted that they wanted to bring their favourite supervisor out for a meal and a few drinks to celebrate her release from the regime. It went against all her instincts to go, but they had wheedled and cajoled until she finally agreed.

After that, Marshalls would be history.

Nikola sloshed more wine into her glass. 'Drink up, although you don't deserve this, not after what you've done.'

Emma flinched, a slice of bruschetta halfway to her mouth. 'What have I done?'

Nikola sipped some wine. 'You've gone and left us to the mercy of that cow Amanda Jacob.'

'Amanda's not all that bad, is she?' Emma watched them exchange glances.

'You don't want to know,' Stacy eventually said, attacking her tagliatelle.

'At least you're out of it now.' Nikola's eyes were envious.

'What do I not want to know?'

'Amanda hasn't replaced you yet because she wants to streamline the unit,' Stacy said, putting down her fork. 'She thinks we should be operating far more efficiently, that we were allowed to get away with murder. So we're all in uproar at the moment.'

'If this is about me, I don't want to know.' Emma gulped her wine, sorry now that she was raking over the remnants of her dismal career.

'She hasn't actually come right out and blamed you,' Nikola said. 'It's just the way she's swarming all over us and analysing every detail of our processes, as well as picking holes in our targets. Even Karl's getting fed up, and you know how easy-going he usually is. I thought he was going to lose his cool the other day when she demanded an in-depth explanation for his February figures.'

'Karl.' Emma felt faint. This get-together had been rather a bad idea.

'Yes, he was going ballistic because she threatened him with his P45 and he's hoping to apply for a mortgage and buy a place of his own instead of renting.'

Stacy added with relish, 'So he feels he has an axe to grind with you as well.'

Emma waited until a wave of dizziness passed, then said, 'I'm half sorry I agreed to this meal. Is there any good news at all?'

'Well, we were exaggerating a little about Karl,' Stacy said, her eyes suddenly gleaming. 'He said he had a few tricks up his sleeve. And the really brill news is – wait for it . . .'

Emma felt prickles of alarm as she realised what Stacy was about to announce, for there was only one thing that made her eyes light up in that particular fashion – or, rather, one person.

'He's going to join us later in the pub,' Nikola said, fluttering her elongated eyelashes. 'When he heard we were meeting, he insisted on coming along to say a proper goodbye to you.'

'After all our attempts to get him to ourselves, we have you to thank, Emma,' Stacy squealed. 'So, no hard feelings about dumping bitchy Amanda on us. Not tonight at any rate.'

Libby stared at the figures flashing on the screen in front of her and her heart thudded. Some kind of white noise was taking up all of her head space. Then she tore her eyes away and stared down the floor. Most of the desks were empty with the terminal screens shut down for the night. It was almost eight o'clock and a lot of the staff had gone home for the evening. She'd been at her desk since seven thirty that morning, trying to fix a mistake she'd overlooked the previous day. It hadn't worked. And now she was about to make the biggest fuck-up of her entire career as well as screwing up one of her major clients' accounts.

'Still here, Libby?' Tanya Wilson breezed by her desk, infusing the stale air with a waft of expensive perfume. She was freshly made up and wearing a short mini displaying enviable long legs. Tanya. The expert on everything, with a glittering career and an equally glittering social life. Right now, she totally freaked Libby out.

She swallowed hard. 'Won't be far behind you,' she called carelessly.

'Good. Otherwise I'd be watching my back,' Tanya laughed. 'Can't have whizz-kid Libby giving me a run for my money.'

There was no fear of that happening, Libby thought grimly. She, Libby Colgan, was just about to be found out for the fraud she was: that she hated the type of work she did, and dreaded each day in the office with fresh anxiety. She felt like putting her head down on her desk and having a good bawl. No one knew. No one had a clue. Not Rob, not her mother – and certainly not her father. At the thought of his face, Libby tried to pull herself together. He was her role model, her inspiration, her trail blazer. She'd deliberately followed in his footsteps and chosen a career in finance, hoping to make him proud of her, hoping to live up to his name and reputation. She couldn't let him down. She sat up straighter as her eyes darted back and forth across the screens and her fingers sped furiously across the keyboard. Then the synapses in her brain spun – she had seen a way out of her mess. It might be slightly unethical, but what the hell? She needed this sorted. Libby pressed a few more keys and eventually stood up, aware that her shirt was sticking to her and that her legs were wobbly.

Out in the ladies she freshened up. She badly needed a drink. She picked up her mobile and speed-dialled her mother.

Emma answered her mobile automatically and swore under her breath when she heard Libby's bright voice.

'Are you still in La Venetia? I can jump into a taxi and be there in five minutes.'

'There's no need, Libby. We have the table until nine so we'll be leaving shortly.'

'Course there is. I have to make sure you go out with a bang. And I'm just finished in the office and looking forward to a drink or two. So don't head anywhere until I get there.'

She should have left before now, Emma realised. She should have pretended she felt sick and left after the main course, because this was turning out to be the worst night of her life – correction, the second worst. The worst had already happened and that was precisely why she found herself in this position. Neither did she need to pretend sickness – her stomach was doing somersaults because Karl had arrived, full of apologies for disturbing their meal, but Emma knew immediately he had come early on purpose in case she had heard he was joining them and decided to forgo the pub.

'Karl, hi!' Stacy purred, giving him a blinding smile. 'No prob if you're early. We've just ordered dessert. I'm sure you can have some, if you like? The chocolate chip ice cream looks positively decadent.' Her eyebrows rose suggestively.

'And let's get another bottle of wine,' Nikola put in. The waiter hovered, prepared to set another place and bring a chair, but Karl had already jumped into the booth beside Emma, and right now his thigh was jammed hard against hers.

'We were just filling Emma in on Amanda's carry-on,' Nikola said. 'She's been a perfect bitch, especially to you.'

'Do you think she's picking on me?' Karl asked, flashing Emma a grin. Her stomach lurched.

'Kind of.' Nikola thrust out her boobs. 'Maybe she secretly fancies you and wants to get you into her office. Alone . . .'

'Nikola! Don't be giving him ideas,' Stacy gurgled.

'He'd hardly find Amanda sexy – or do you like your women like her, Karl?' Nikola asked in silky tones. 'Kind of hard-edged and bossy, the dominatrix type?'

'Me? I prefer my women soft, of course.'

'That rules you out then, Nik,' Stacy said, quick as a flash. 'You're as hard as nails.'

'Sometimes I like the older woman,' he said, deliberately baiting them and laughing when they responded with shrieks of mock horror. 'Although if Amanda had me alone in her office I'd call it discrimination. What's the other one? Sexual harassment? Maybe I could make enough money for my deposit after all.'

'Oh, Karl,' Stacy giggled and ran a hand through her hair, 'you're a scream. The big problem with our office is that there's nowhere near enough sexual harassment.'

'No matter how hard we try . . .' Nikola pouted.

'Emma doesn't think I'm funny, do you, Emma?' Karl said.

Everyone's eyes swivelled to her. She'd been frantically calculating whether or not she could make it out of the restaurant in time to intercept Libby and prevent her from coming face to face with Karl. But Karl's last remark had frozen her to the spot. Any ideas she had for escape shrivelled.

'So, Emma?' he asked.

'Stacy's correct. You're absolutely hilarious,' she said, eyeballing him furiously.

'And you don't think it's a good idea to tell Amanda I feel harassed?'

She saw the glint in his eyes and knew the implication. A pain in her heart rendered her incapable of speech, let alone articulate conversation. Was this the axe that had been waiting to fall? She hadn't been imagining it. She strove to face him down. 'I think that would be a very bad idea,' she said softly.

'Do you?'

'Yes, Karl.'

Sexual harassment. How dare he? Okay, so she'd been his boss at the time and it had been highly unethical but, if anything, he was harassing *her*. He was being outrageous. Then he gave her a private smile and she realised he was playing with her, goading her, like a cat teasing a mouse.

'Hey, let's forget about snotty Amanda for tonight,' Nikola said. 'Quit talking about work. We're out to enjoy ourselves.' She picked up the wine bottle and topped up their glasses. 'Emma, you've hardly touched yours. Knock that back and we'll hit the pub.'

'I'm going home. I'll let you three carry on without me,' Emma said, anxious to get as far away as she could from Karl.

'Hi, Mum.' It was Libby, her tumble of long blonde hair sleek and shiny, her make-up perfect and her smile so transparent, trusting and innocent that Emma was shaken.

'Ah, Libby.' She made herself smile. 'Good timing. I was just leaving, so we can get a cab home together.'

'Home? No way,' Libby laughed. 'It's Thursday night, more or

155

less the start of the weekend. Hey, I haven't met you yet, have I?' She turned to Karl, her eyes appraising him swiftly.

'No, you haven't. And you are . . .?'

'Libby, Emma's daughter.'

Karl turned to Emma and smiled a devilish smile. 'I didn't know your daughter was so beautiful, Emma.'

'Who's for drinks?' Libby asked, reaching into her bag for her purse. 'Or will we wait till we get to the pub?'

The rest of the evening was a disaster. The five of them went to a pub in South Anne Street, where there was standing room only and they had to shout to be heard. Emma was swept along, feeling totally out of her depth, yet knowing full well that she daren't go home and leave Libby in Karl's clutches. Nikola and Stacy were flashing mutinous looks in Libby's direction. They thought they were up against major competition now in capturing Karl's attention. Emma felt like telling them they were wasting their time: their biggest challenge was not Libby but her mother.

She was stuck trying to make small talk to the now deflated Stacy and Nikola, as alarmed as they were that Karl was paying quite a lot of attention to Libby, trying and failing to catch the threads of their conversation in the general chatter going on around her. Thank God her daughter was in a relationship with Rob, she thought as she watched her trying to chat to Karl, impeded by the noise levels. Not that being in a relationship meant anything any more, was her next, rather dismaying, thought. And Libby was drinking a lot. She was ready for her second, and then her third vodka and white lemonade before anyone else. The sooner she got her home, the better.

She finally snagged her daughter's attention. 'Libby, come on, it's time to go home.'

'We're heading as well,' Nikola said, looking downcast as all her flirtatious plans lay in ruins, thanks to Libby's luminous presence.

'What? No nightclub?' Libby asked.

'Not tonight.' Stacy's eyes said there was no point in extending the agony.

'We have work tomorrow, and with Amanda on our backs we don't want to be too hung-over.' Nikola looked meaningfully at Karl.

'And you have work tomorrow as well, Libby,' Emma reminded her daughter.

Libby's face clouded a little. 'Yeah . . . Let's have one more drink and then we'll call it quits.'

One more drink. She could just about cope, Emma decided, watching her daughter signal to the barman. Then she would make sure she never laid eyes on Karl ever again. When Libby slipped out to the ladies' room, Emma grabbed her chance to give him a pep talk. 'We're going as soon as Libby comes back,' she told him 'I don't want to see you again, and God forbid I hear that you've been making any more of your veiled threats.'

'Threats?' He gave a short laugh. 'I'm not threatening you. You're far too nice. I've already told you I think you're very special. I'm more interested in getting a place of my own. But I need to come up with a deposit.'

She felt weak. 'Deposit?'

He leaned in close to her. The scent of his aftershave made her feel sick. 'Problem is, I'm short five thousand euro.' He smiled.

The axe fell cleanly, shearing the past and all its golden promise away from the blunt and brutal present, cleaving a great divide in Emma's consciousness. Bile rose in her mouth and she stepped back, as if he had attacked her physically. 'You're out of your mind. Is this how you get your kicks?'

'All I said was that I'm finding it difficult to put my deposit together. Whereas you, Emma, have money to spare. That is the big difference between us. Your daughter says you didn't even need your job in Marshalls because her father earns more than enough. She said you have a beautiful home and are looking forward to spending more time in it. How lucky you are.'

'I don't have that kind of money.'

'Did I ask you for it?' Their eyes locked. His were dark and intense as they held hers. 'I just said you were very lucky.' He smiled wolfishly. 'A lovely home and a husband with a big banking job in the financial services centre. What more could you ask for?'

Then he left her, shaken to the core.

Chapter 25

Sofia was amazing: seventeen years of age, six foot one, acres of sleek dark hair and velvety legs that went on for ever. It was her first big event, she'd nervously confided in Alix.

'You'll be fine.' Alix smiled reassuringly as she dipped a brush into matte translucent powder and swirled it around the contours of the girl's face. 'I'll have you looking like an Egyptian princess in no time. You just have to sit there quietly and we'll do all the work. Then you can go out there and blow them away.' She picked up her wand of ultra-lustre mascara and leaned in a little closer. 'Now, Sofia, I want you to look straight at me.'

Alix had been flown to Rome that morning to do the make-up for the exclusive unveiling of Florence-born Bianca Bruno's autumn/winter collection. Word filtering back from exclusive previews had hinted that her designs were sensational and would take the fashion world by storm.

Out front, everything glittered. A gaggle of press and hawk-eyed buyers rubbed shoulders with Rome's fashion élite, sipped champagne, nibbled canapés and waited with zealous anticipation to see what trends would emerge on the super deluxe, beautifully styled catwalk – and if Bianca would live up to the rumours.

Behind the scenes, the atmosphere was no less charged. The key look Alix was creating for the show reflected the colours in the couture collection, which called for dewy complexions, red lips and Cleopatra eyes. She felt a slight pang as the girls she transformed seemed younger and more innocent than ever: the smoky seductive eyes and bright pouting lips she gave them turned them into fully fledged vamps.

In her usual work attire of comfortable jeans, ballet flats and a light jersey top, Alix worked swiftly, using her fingers, brushes and sponges, highlighting and illuminating, blending eyeshadow and lashings of kohl, while the hair team worked on Sofia's dark hair. Just as Alix stroked on the final coat of lip-gloss, the girl began to sway.

She'd seen it before. The nerves and excitement, plus the fact that she probably hadn't eaten a decent meal in days, had caught up with her at the crucial moment. Luigi, one of the stylists, threw up his hands in horror and stalked off.

'Wait – just give me five minutes!' Alix begged.

'We don't have five minutes. Our running order will be ruined,' Luigi snapped.

'Two, then,' she pleaded. 'It'll be quicker than prepping anyone else.' She turned to Sofia. 'Don't you dare faint. When was the last time you ate?'

'Yesterday,' Sofia whispered, spots of perspiration now showing on her forehead.

Alix bent down, rummaged in her case and handed her a carton of banana and mango smoothie. 'Here, get this into you. All of it.'

'Won't I wreck my face?' Sofia sounded like a child.

'I'll have you touched up in no time,' Alix said, reaching for the rice paper. 'It's either that or you forget about your golden opportunity. Drink that, take a few deep breaths, and don't dare skip breakfast again. Promise? And I mean a decent breakfast, not just a lettuce leaf and a double espresso. Otherwise you'll never last the pace.'

A couple of minutes later Sofia had recovered enough to go and strut her stuff. Alix stretched to her full height, flexed her arms and legs and rubbed the small of her back.

'Well done,' Thérèse, the style director, said, coming across from the clothes rails. 'You saved her arse. Luigi would've stomped all over her inert body.'

Alix had worked with Thérèse before and respected the other woman's thorough professionalism and creative vision. It was a sobering reality, she thought, that quite often people at the top of their profession were far more approachable and pleasant to deal with than those clawing and fighting their way up the ladder. 'No prob,' she shrugged, 'although if I had my way, three meals a day would be compulsory.'

'Sofia doesn't know how lucky she is that you were looking after her,' Thérèse went on. 'You're a natural mother hen, Alix. I've seen the way you look out for those girls and you seem to know instinctively how to relate to them. You tune into them unconsciously.'

'I think you're talking about my sister, she's the mother hen in the family. I haven't a maternal bone in my body.'

Thérèse raised her eyebrows.

'I just can't help feeling a little sympathetic,' Alix went on, 'especially when you know how young they are, how lonely it can be travelling around from job to job, wondering if you'll have work next week or the week after. *And* paying a huge chunk to your booking agent. Sofia looks stunning and she'll pull off Bianca's collection like no one else. I had to have her out front. But I think I'm getting jaded with runway fashion,' she said, surprising herself with her admission. 'Right now the backs of my knees are giving way. Anyway, enough about me. Who's next for the sultry-siren look?'

The after-show party was held in a five-star hotel adjacent to the via Veneto and Alix had arranged to touch base there with Estelle, her agent, who had also flown across for the show. Estelle Picard was slim, petite and sexy in the way only a Frenchwoman could be. Despite her diminutive stature, she could strike a mixture of awe and terror into the hearts of the fashion world with her indefinable air of success and business acumen. Nothing escaped her dark, intelligent eyes, and she was fiercely loyal and supportive to the clients whose careers she had elected to manage.

Alix had swapped her comfy workwear for a Diane von Furstenberg classic red dress and spiky Ferragamo heels. She'd put on her silver jewellery and sprayed her favourite scent. Her hair was loosely sculpted around her head. Now, champagne in hand, she threaded her way through the mob of glitterati, PR and press to where Estelle was chatting to a friend. When she spotted Alix, she excused herself. 'Alix!' She kissed her warmly. 'Congratulations on a wonderful show. You were amazing, and you created magic with all the models, especially Sofia. She's the one to watch.'

Alix looked across the room to where Sofia was surrounded by a throng of well-wishers. 'I wouldn't be surprised if she's already been snapped up.'

'Good. So, how are you?'

'Fine.' Alix smiled.

Estelle studied her face. 'You look a little tired, *ma petite*.'

Alix tried not to grin. Estelle had a habit of addressing her as *ma petite*, even though Alix was by far the taller of them. 'It's been non-stop since the start of the year,' she said. She plonked her empty glass on the tray of a circulating waiter, helped herself to two more and passed one to Estelle.

'No wonder we had to arrange to meet up in Rome.' Estelle tipped her glass to Alix's. 'And your life is going to get busier,' she continued. 'I've been talking to Henri about the launch of Alix B and he has updated me on everything. I was sorry I missed your meeting with him, but I was in New York.'

'I guess someone has to buy up Fifth Avenue.'

'*Mais non*, it was strictly business,' Estelle told her. 'Anyway, busy and all as you are, I've had a request you might like to consider, although I admit as personal consultations go, it's slightly off your usual line of work.'

'Fire away,' Alix encouraged, knowing that Estelle would never steer her in the wrong direction.

Estelle put a hand on her arm and guided her away from the press of people. 'I've been approached by a Mr James Cooper, from Essex in England, who says he is willing to pay over the odds to reward you for doing the make-up for his daughter on the occasion of her eighteenth birthday.'

Alix took a swift gulp of her Dom Pérignon. 'Go on, tell me more.'

'He's some kind of mobile-phone tycoon, *nouveau riche*, so money is no object and she's his only daughter, Jemima. She knows you've looked after her idol Lily Allen so, according to her father, it would make her the happiest girl in the world. The party is being held in the newly renovated Savoy Hotel in London the week after next. Yes, I agree, the short notice is absurd,' she said, in response to Alix's look, 'but he has been most eloquently persuasive in putting his case to me.'

'Send me through the details and I'll have a think,' Alix told her.

'You won't have much time for that,' Estelle said. 'Men like James Cooper don't seem to realise that you're usually booked up months in advance.'

'Right. I'll let you know ASAP. All of a sudden I need food.'

Alix cast her eyes around the busy function room. 'Any sign of something decent to eat? Preferably laden with calories.'

Alix flew back to Paris the following morning, her mind occupied with Estelle's latest request.

London.

Having left the city all those years ago, she preferred to avoid it but, given her profession, she had to be there from time to time. And whenever she was, and found herself filling in the couple of hours between make-ups and after-show parties, she couldn't ignore the reminders of the twenty-two-year-old girl who'd fled there after the break-up of her engagement to Tom.

Oxford Street, where she'd stood in the milling crowd feeling alien and alone; Paddington, where she'd stayed for a week in a budget hotel until she'd found a tiny bedsit of her own; the lake in St James's Park where she'd sat, painfully missing Tom and recoiling from the shock at the way her life had turned on its head. It was more than fifteen years ago, Alix mused as the plane droned on to Paris and she stared out of the cabin porthole at puffy white clouds. It was a lifetime ago, another era. Yet the memory was so sharp that in some ways it seemed like yesterday when she'd told Emma she was heading off.

Emma and Oliver's first home is a pleasant three-bedroom house within commuting distance of Dublin.

'Alix!' Emma says, opening the door one Saturday afternoon in early February. 'I wasn't expecting you.'

That much is obvious. Emma looks exhausted. She is wearing a navy tracksuit that has seen better days, with what looks like sticky puke on the shoulder. Her dark hair is scraped back from her unmade-up face and she has grey shadows under her eyes. She is just twenty-six yet, for the first time, Alix sees lines of tension in her forehead. Seven-year-old Libby flies up the hallway and, screaming with delight, wraps herself like a limpet around her aunt.

'Get back, darling,' Emma says patiently, trying in vain to prise off her daughter.

'She's okay.' Alix reaches down and scoops her niece into her arms, whereupon Libby immediately scrambles down and races into the kitchen.

'She's not okay,' Emma says. 'She has some kind of tummy bug and so has Charlie. I'm supposed to be keeping them quiet, but it's impossible.'

Emma's kitchen is a mess. Libby's toys are scattered across the floor and Alix has to step gingerly as she makes her way to the table. Five-year-old Charlie is throwing a tantrum as well as his toy cars, and when he sees Alix he bawls even louder and flings them with renewed vigour. Damp laundry is hanging from a wooden clothes horse and is also slung over the back of two chairs.

'Don't mind things,' Emma babbles. 'We're all upside down as I was awake half the night changing sheets, pillowcases and pyjamas.'

'How on earth do you cope?' The words come out involuntarily and Alix feels like kicking herself.

'It's not as bad as it looks.' Emma is defensive. She rubs at a patch of dried-in cereal on the table. 'The tumble-dryer packed up – it couldn't have picked a better time.'

'Where's Oliver?'

'He's in college.'

'For the day?'

Emma nods. 'Yes, and most of tomorrow as well.'

'So you'll get no real break this weekend.'

'It's just hectic at the moment, with Libby and Charlie being sick. Oliver's up to his tonsils in the office and has lectures most weekends. But it'll be worth it in the end. Next year, thankfully, will be his last for studying and he's already been promised a good promotion. So I just have to put up with it for now.'

'You should have phoned me. I'd have come over to help you out.'

'Not at all. You should be enjoying yourself and making the most of your carefree single years. They don't last for ever.'

'Anyway, I have some news.' Alix is unsure where to begin.

'Oh?'

'I called in to tell you I'm off to London.'

'London? When? Is Tom going with you? I wouldn't mind a holiday myself.'

Emma is busy making tea, so Alix is grateful that she doesn't have to look at her face as she takes a deep breath and says, 'It's not a holiday. I'm going for good – and, no, Tom isn't coming with me. The engagement is off. We've split up.'

'You've *what*?' Emma whirls around and drops the tea caddy on the tiled floor, where it smashes. Libby bursts into tears and Charlie runs across to stare at the mess in fascinated horror. Emma screams at him to stay away from the broken pottery and he promptly opens his mouth to release a thick stream of yellowy puke. Libby cries even harder. By the time the pandemonium is brought under control and the sisters have time to talk, Alix realises that Emma has wrongly assumed Tom originated the split and that she is going to London to heal her broken heart.

Chapter 26

Oliver gave the cab driver Alix's address.

'*Mais non.*' Emma gave the address of the hotel.

'What's going on?' Oliver asked as the driver sped away from Charles de Gaulle airport and joined the stream of traffic sweeping around the night-time streets.

'Another surprise.' Emma forced a smile. She was finding it increasingly difficult to put up a front and a weekend in Paris, alone with Oliver, was the last thing she needed, but she couldn't have cancelled without arousing his suspicions. It was just over a week since the Thursday night she'd seen Karl and at first she'd been so shocked by what he had implied that she'd been incapable of normal communication. Back in Laburnum Grove, she'd managed to camouflage her stricken silence with domestic trivia, burying herself in a full wardrobe declutter, then a kitchen spring clean, with Leticia's over-enthusiastic help, and preparations for their Paris weekend. But all the while myriad anxieties bubbled just beneath the surface.

What was Karl up to? What could he do? There was no way he

could take things further. Or was there? Just what exactly was he capable of? She'd even switched off her mobile for a few days and stuck it in the back of a bedroom drawer, telling her family it was temporarily mislaid. Silly, she knew, for Karl could easily find a way to contact her if he wanted to – both Nikola and Stacy had her landline number and house address. Now it was Friday evening, the romantic weekend in Paris beckoned, and she felt incredibly edgy, her nerves stretched to breaking point. To make matters even more difficult, she'd brought Oliver here under the guise of visiting Alix, all the time planning an alternative weekend.

'We're not actually staying with Alix,' she said now.

He looked at her questioningly.

'I wanted to treat us to a special weekend,' she said, trying to sound upbeat. 'We're meeting Alix for Sunday lunch, after we've had some time together.'

'I see. At least I hope I do.' Oliver stared at her for a long moment, and then he turned to look out of the window.

Emma bit her lip. She'd rehearsed her words with a casual, non-chalant air. *We're not staying with Alix after all. I thought it would be nice for us to have some time alone in the city of lovers.* But she'd shied away from mentioning lovers. *Lovers!* Surely Oliver would be madly suspicious? With the candlelit meal she'd foisted upon him, an attempted bathroom seduction and now a surprise weekend in a five-star hotel, it screamed that she was trying very hard to compensate for something.

She felt helpless as the cab swept along the gracefully proportioned Paris boulevards, with glittering streetlights and elegant buildings. When they eventually drew up outside their hotel in the chic 1st *arrondissement*, a uniformed concierge sprang to open the cab door. Oliver paid the driver, stepped out and gazed up at the imposing edifice.

He *had* to know that something was wrong. And she was a total fraud, portraying herself as a dutiful, loving wife when she was anything but. But now she had gone over the top in her attempts at deception. The splendid hotel lobby drew them in, and wrapped them in layers of luxury. Her hand was shaking as she signed the form at Reception and she dropped her handbag. It flew open and the contents skittered across the marble surface, her lipstick ending at the feet of a stern bell-boy. Her legs were trembling as she and Oliver stepped out of the lift onto a deeply carpeted foyer, strung with crystal chandeliers and decorated with a succession of enormous mirrors that reflected her crimson face as they walked to their suite.

When the bell-boy had gone Oliver observed the thick velvet curtains, the acre-width bed and silken coverlet, the mountains of pillows and cushions. A veritable love nest. Emma's heart quailed.

'Well. This is some surprise,' he said eventually.

'I thought we deserved a little pampering,' Emma told him. She had to pull herself together, forget about Karl. She was in Paris with Oliver, trying to repair the gigantic hole she'd put in their marriage. She owed it to him to make the best of the weekend – and on their return to Dublin she'd find some way of dealing with Karl and getting shut of him, even paying him off, if it came to that.

Oliver wrapped his arms around her, pulling her tightly to his chest. He dropped a kiss on the top of her head. Emma closed her eyes. 'You're perfectly right,' he said softly. 'This is a fantastic idea. I'm just sorry I didn't think of it to celebrate your new freedom.'

Emma smiled up at him. 'Let's go out on the town. Hey, we're in Paris. Just you and me, all by ourselves.'

Paris was full of different sounds, a medley of exotic scents, busy restaurants, honking traffic, scurrying pedestrians, strolling tourists, windows glowing with tempting pastries, pavement cafés heaving with life. A cool breeze came off the Seine. It was a busy, exciting

Friday night. So very different from that other Friday night when she'd staggered through Dublin against a milling crowd. She pushed the memories away and hung onto Oliver as they crossed the road in the shadow of the glittering Eiffel Tower, and walked towards the restaurant that Alix had recommended. It was quiet and intimate, a place for couples or lovers.

Emma was making small talk about Libby and Charlie in the interval between their main course and dessert when Oliver asked her what was wrong. 'I'm not stupid, Emma,' he said, his relaxed demeanour vanished. 'There must be something up. All this . . . the weekend . . . other stuff . . .' A muscle clenched in his jaw.

Emma was unable to form a word, let alone a sentence. She sat, dry-mouthed, as Oliver rested his elbows on the table, laced his fingers and leaned forward attentively, the expression in his navy eyes keen and perceptive. 'Is there any particular reason for all of this? I'm concerned as to what exactly is going on.'

Emma gripped her trembling hands. 'There's nothing going on. I just thought it would be a good idea for us to get away.'

'Really?' He gave her a shrewd glance. 'I think there's more to it than that. I know this might sound off the wall but, God forbid, did you by any chance . . . well, darling, did you think I was having an affair?'

Oh, Oliver. She couldn't talk. She felt dizzy. She saw the creamy curve of her naked arm, her hand stretched out in front of her, pink nails against a white backdrop.

'On second thoughts, scrap that.' Her husband sat back and laughed. 'I don't know how I could be so thick. If you thought I'd played away, you'd be after me with the sharp end of a knife. You'd scarcely be planning second-honeymoon stuff.'

She managed to make her lips move into the semblance of a smile, grateful that Oliver seemed oblivious to her deep anxiety. 'No, probably not.'

He quirked an eyebrow. 'So, um, is this just all for you and me?'
She nodded.

'Is anything else bothering you? I know that lately I've been a bit distant and preoccupied . . .' He gave her a lopsided grin, which made him look suddenly young and carefree, the kind of grin she didn't deserve and that snagged at her heart. 'I know I've been going through the motions, only half there some of the time, but there was a good reason for it.'

Eventually, through the mist of her nervousness, Emma realised he was trying to tell her something about himself. 'What is it? What are you trying to say?'

Oliver looked at her, a rueful expression in his navy eyes. She watched his long, lean fingers as he picked up the wine bottle and drained what was left into their glasses before he continued. 'Thing is, darling, I'm sorry I wasn't supportive enough or there for you in a more meaningful way when you were turned down for promotion. But problems in the office that particular week took up too much of my time and energy. Although that's no excuse.' He shrugged. Then he looked at her steadily and his voice was quiet as he said, 'You see, I know exactly how you felt, because I've gone through something similar recently. But I was too embarrassed and humiliated to tell you. Too gutted, really. So now you know.'

She stared at him, her heart thudding. 'I don't believe this. Why on earth didn't you tell me?'

Oliver gave her a half-smile and his eyes glinted. 'My pride was hurt. I felt enough of a failure as it was. Talking about it would have reinforced that. I preferred to move on, put it behind me, and try to forget about it.'

'And when did all this happen?'

Oliver scanned the restaurant. He threw down his napkin. 'Let's go for a drink somewhere quieter – if there is such a place on a Friday night in Paris. Maybe we should head back to our lovely hotel suite. I don't want to spoil your romantic illusions but you'll find out that your husband isn't such a hot-shot after all.'

'Don't be ridiculous. I want to hear everything. *Everything.* Okay?'

They passed on dessert, left the restaurant and hailed a cab back to their hotel. The sitting room in their suite had soft lighting and plenty of big, cushiony sofas that were perfect for intimate conversations. Oliver opened the mini-bar and poured two cognacs, passing one to Emma. He pulled off his tie and undid the collar of his cream cotton shirt. Then he sat down beside her and told her about the departmental head vacancy that had been up for grabs and how he'd thought he was the man for the job.

'The last couple of years have been extremely difficult, Emma. Every area's been squeezed and I worked bloody hard and assumed I'd earned more than enough Brownie points to deserve a step up the ladder.'

'I thought the bank was doing okay?'

'I've had some huge challenges. I didn't like to bother you because,' his voice softened, 'you had more than enough crap all those years ago to last a lifetime.'

She was touched. 'Oliver! I'm not a fragile flower, you know.'

His mouth turned up at the corners. He reached out a hand and brushed back her hair. 'Aren't you? I always saw you as my soft but big-hearted wife in need of tender, loving care. Call me old-fashioned, but I used to fancy you looked up to me as your knight in shining armour.'

Oh, I did, I did! You've no idea how much! 'I still wish you'd shared this with me,' Emma said.

'Believe me, I did enough worrying for the two of us. I've also been putting in longer and longer hours to maintain the same targets. I was next in line for promotion before the market went

172

belly-up and promotions are few and far between these days. So when the vacancy was announced I was sure I'd be rewarded for all those nights I stayed late and all those difficult rationalisation programmes I helped to implement.' He paused.

'And?' Emma asked, already knowing in her troubled heart what he was about to say.

'I was passed over in favour of a younger blow-in,' he said. He knocked back the last of his cognac. 'A whizz-kid, they're calling her. Six years younger than me with twice the energy. Buzzing with new ideas for cost-cutting and further rationalisation. Brimming with the latest managerial strategies that are sharper than her stilettos. *And* she's the youngest departmental head we've ever had.'

Oliver. Passed over. In favour of a woman six years his junior. What a blow to her alpha-male husband.

'It was a bitter pill after all the years I've given the company and all the recent ball-breaking initiatives I've implemented.'

Emma said, her voice faint, 'When did this happen?'

'Three to four months ago.'

'You should have told me at the time.'

'I didn't want to think about it. Bloody hell, I was told I didn't have the creative vision or imagination to lead the department to the next challenging level. I never heard such rubbish.' He shook his head. 'The bottom line is the size of the profit at the end of the balance sheet. Fact is, I've been sidelined at a crucial time in my career.'

'Oliver, your time will come again. You'll have more opportunities.'

'Will I? I'm not so sure. Globally, things have got far more cut-throat in the banking sector. And a lot of the new blood coming up through the ranks have the latest buzzy qualifications and are far greedier for success. What's even more galling,' he laughed, 'is that despite my disappointment I'm working harder than ever. Sometimes I wonder what the hell I'm trying to prove. I know I don't have enough time for you, Libby and Charlie, but right now, I can't see the pace letting up.'

'I can imagine how disappointed you were,' Emma said, her throat tight. 'But you're far too hard on yourself and I'm really sorry you didn't tell me at the time.'

Oliver put his arm around her. 'Do you know what I've realised, though?'

'What's that?' She felt his fingers on the nape of her neck, teasing the ends of her hair.

His voice was low and calm as he went on, 'That it doesn't matter. Not deep down. The most important thing in my life is us and the kids. So, I'm sorry if I was a bit off or distant these last few months. It was just my deflated ego. You, Libby and Charlie are far more important than anything else. And I do love you, Emma, even if I don't show it enough.' His right hand cupped her chin while the other skimmed the contours of her body, and his navy eyes were mesmerising as he said, 'Most importantly, I still fancy you like mad.'

There was a moment of charged stillness between them. Oliver's dark-lashed eyes were heavy-lidded and full of desire. His finger traced the outline of her mouth. Emma's heart pounded. She had no option but to meet his gaze and prayed he wouldn't see traces of guilt in her eyes. She closed her mind to Karl. He didn't exist, not in this reality, the reality of Oliver looking at her like this while his hands sent shivers of pleasure through her.

He pulled her to her feet. She felt his lips on her forehead and her eyelids.

'Do you know what I was afraid of, Emma?'

'No?'

Another kiss, this time on the side of her neck.

'You thought we were stuck in a rut, but, hell – all the time I was afraid I'd lost it . . .' He folded her tightly into him.

'Lost what, Oliver?'

'This.' He held her even tighter, welding their hips together, and a flame of excitement ran through Emma at the unmistakable feel of his arousal. She heard the steady thump of his heart.

He gave a low chuckle as he slid down the zip of her dress. 'I was afraid it had done a bunk. But thanks to your recent attempts at seduction, and now this . . .' He stood back and her dress fell to the floor. His eyes flickered over the curves of her breasts and hips, thinly veiled in silk underwear. 'I'm glad I was wrong.' Her body was suffused with longing for him as he pulled her close again, threaded his fingers in her hair and ran his tongue lightly around her lips before he kissed her, a long, deep kiss that went from tantalising to seductive to demanding. Then he reached down and slipped his hand underneath her silk French knickers.

She leaned into him as his fingers teased, dipping into her moistness, making her throb with need. 'Darling Emma, I'm going to show you just how much you mean to me,' he breathed, 'even if it takes all night . . . Thanks to you, we're away from everyone and can make up for lost time with as much noise as we like . . .'

Emma's body melted with desire. This was Oliver as she had known him years ago, but now a stronger recognition of his dear familiarity and a powerful awareness of his male physicality thrummed through her. She pulled at his shirt, but her trembling fingers were too slow for him – Oliver tore off his clothes and plucked off her underwear. He propelled her across to the bed, sending the pile of pretty cushions flying with a sweep of his arm. She fell onto it and Oliver gave her a smile of mixed triumph and desire. He lifted her to him and turned her body to fiery liquid as he swiftly sank into her.

Afterwards, they lay entwined. Then he scooped her to him and rolled over so that she was sitting astride him. He reached up to kiss her breasts, rolling his tongue around her nipples, gently tugging at them. 'Sorry if that was a bit hasty,' he said, a glint in his eyes. 'No, I'm not sorry. I needed you badly. So I guess we'll have to start all over again . . .'

She sighed with pleasure.

They eventually slept, spooned together in the vast, luxurious bed.

Chapter 27

'What's up with you, Libby?' Rob asked, as though he was barely containing his impatience.

'Nothing. Why?' Libby asked belligerently. She stabbed a piece of red pepper with her fork, scraping her plate, the jarring noise giving her a certain grim satisfaction.

'Nothing? Please don't insult me. You've scarcely looked at me all lunch hour. You don't seem to be with me at all. I raced out of the lecture hall so that we could meet up. I've to get back to college for two and I've to study tonight, so the least you could do . . .'

Libby tuned out again. She was finding it harder and harder to stay alert and interested. It was Saturday afternoon, and even though she'd been out with her mates on Thursday and Friday night, burning the candle at both ends, normally a couple of Red Bulls did the trick. Today she'd arranged to meet Rob for lunch to break up the day for him, and everything was getting on top of her.

She was still shaken by the narrow escape she'd had the week before in Boyd Samuel, on account of the strictly unorthodox strategy she'd tried that Thursday evening. It had worked out all right –

this time. God forbid it happened again, with a larger, more complicated account. Then she really would be in deep shit.

And for someone who'd been about to go off to Paris for the weekend, her mother had been in very peculiar humour all week. There had been something weird about her, something that Libby could only describe as thinly veiled desperation. Maybe Mum was feeling anxious at joining the massed ranks of the unemployed. Libby sincerely hoped that didn't mean her easy-going mother would become depressed in the weeks ahead.

'I might as well leave now,' Rob said, his face thunderous.

'Sorry, Rob.' Hurriedly, she pulled her thoughts together and put a hand on his arm. 'I've had a few problems in the office and I can't help thinking about them. You know how it is . . .'

'No, I don't. When we're out for lunch I think I deserve at least some of your attention. This has been a complete waste of time.'

She felt like telling him to go to hell. But a row with Rob was more than she could take right now. She hadn't the energy for confrontation. Her head ached and she wondered if she could take some more Paracetamol. And tomorrow was Sunday and then it would be Monday again, and she'd be lucky to get out of the office before seven thirty in the evening. She was almost seven months into her job now and she kept hoping it might get easier. But if anything it was growing harder. She'd spent three years studying economics and now there was no ignoring the fact that she detested the world of finance and figures.

How was that for a major waste of time?

And why couldn't she tell Rob how she felt? She'd been with him since college and she was beginning to wonder if that had been a waste of time too. She'd never experienced those free and easy student days when you hung around in a group and had a few different boyfriends. She'd never been swept off her feet. Like her college course and her career, Rob was the boyfriend who ticked all the right boxes. She tried to dismiss the thought that they weren't really her boxes.

That still didn't explain why she felt so edgy and irritable. Unless . . . and Libby found it difficult to follow this train of thought but she made herself go with it, even though her face felt a bit hot and her heartbeat accelerated. Unless her general edginess had something to do with Karl.

She'd found him very attractive and very beddable. She could see why Stacy and Nikola lusted after him. Not that she fancied him. Nikola and Stacy could probably handle him but he was too smoulderingly sexy for her. Libby wouldn't have a clue what naughtiness he might expect in bed. Surely more than she'd be prepared to deliver. And at almost thirty, he was a little too old for her.

But she'd discovered to her surprise that she'd liked being chatted up by another man. Karl had flirted outrageously with her, and even though it had been a little unsettling, she'd found it amusing without wanting to take it further. It had made her wonder how much she'd enjoy it with a man she fancied. A man she lusted for enough to want to throw caution to the winds.

All of a sudden, throwing caution to the winds seemed like a most exciting prospect.

Chapter 28

The restaurant was busy with couples and family groups. It
had an excellent Sunday lunch menu, extensive wine list and
superb view of the Seine. Sitting beside Oliver in the coveted
window seat that Alix had reserved, Emma watched her sister's
arrival.

She was a vision in understated elegance, outclassing many of the
chic Parisian women in the restaurant. She slithered out of a fabulous amethyst brocade jacket and handed it to the staff at the door.
Then her tall, svelte figure, immaculately dressed in a beautiful gold
top and black crêpe trousers, threaded through the tables. Alix
kissed Oliver and hugged Emma before sliding onto the leather
chair opposite them. 'And what exactly have you been up to?' she
asked.

'What do you mean?' Emma replied, startled. She'd never kept
secrets from her sister, but surely her betrayal wasn't *that* obvious.

'Have you been on the F-plan diet or something?'

'Why?'

Alix frowned, put her head to one side and silently studied her.

Emma laughed to ward off twinges of anxiety. 'Well, you look stunning,' she said. 'I love your amazing top.'

Alix smiled and stroked the sleeve. 'It's rather fun, isn't it? This is a Bianca Bruno, the new kid on the block in Rome, and I think she's going to give D&G a run for their money. But look at you, darling, you've lost weight. Definitely. You're trimmer. Oliver,' she fastened her laughing eyes on his face, 'what have you been doing to my sister?'

Oliver's eyes flickered over Emma. 'I'll let my wife tell you for herself.'

'The new diet is all about green tea.' Emma tried to recall something she'd recently read on the health pages of a glossy magazine. She'd known already that her zips were sliding up with a little less pressure, which was no surprise considering she'd lost her appetite. 'Five cups a day improves your metabolism so you can lose ten pounds in six weeks.' She paused. 'Or maybe it's six pounds in ten weeks.'

'Really? I don't think that's quite what Oliver meant,' Alix joked, 'but I must pass that gem on to some of my girls. They think the espresso and nicotine diet is the only way to go. Anyway, down to the real business of the day. Cocktails, everyone?'

'I'll get these,' Oliver insisted.

'You guys are looking great.' Alix looked from Emma to Oliver. 'Did you enjoy your love-in? Or should I say your sexathon? I hope your bedroom was suitably decadent with pillows and nice things. And I hope you've left some life in the bed-springs.'

'Alix!'

'Never mind.' Alix was unabashed. 'I can see that all's well in the Colgan marriage. What did you do with yourselves yesterday, or am I not allowed to ask that question?'

'Well, no, you're not – it's private and confidential.' Oliver chuckled, winking at Emma.

'We did stuff that was off the usual tourist trail,' Emma supplied, anxious to change the subject. 'We found quaint little churches and tucked-away parks and squares. Then we succumbed to the lure of the Seine and took a private *bateau mouche*. It was bliss.'

'And your meal last night was okay?' Alix asked.

The previous evening they had dined in a Montmartre restaurant with music and dancing. Emma had worn a midnight blue cocktail dress that skimmed her knees and Oliver looked sexy in a white shirt and dark trousers. Then afterwards, back in their hotel suite, he'd slowly undressed her, as though he had all the time in the world to devote to just that, his renewed passion filling Emma to the brim with delight.

'Yes, we'd a lovely evening,' Emma said primly, exchanging a glance with Oliver that Alix pounced on.

'You guys look like the cat that licked the cream. You won't want to stay with me ever again when you come to Paris. It'll be five-star hotels with enormous bouncy beds from now on . . .'

'Who said we needed a bed?' Oliver cut in, and Emma's heart gave a little flip. He slung his arm along the back of her chair. He was attractive in a pale grey shirt and Emma felt a sudden urge to lean back into him, feel his arms around her and his steady heart-beat against her cheek.

Their cocktails arrived and Alix tipped her Mojito against Emma's and Oliver's. 'I knew it! Two sex maniacs you are – you should be ashamed of yourselves!'

Oliver laughed. 'Alix, for once I couldn't agree more!'

'I think we've had enough on that subject,' Emma said, deciding it was best to steer the conversation in another direction entirely. 'How about you, Alix? Have you seen Tom since the exhibition?'

Alix shook her head.

'I still find it hard to believe that you risked bumping into the guy who broke your heart into smithereens just to make

Sophie jealous,' Emma went on. 'Come on, what was it really all about?'

'Okay.' Alix raised her hands in surrender and waggled her fingers. 'I was curious. That's all. I haven't seen Tom in years. There's no crime in that, is there?'

'Oliver, try and talk some sense into your sister-in-law. How could she be curious to see the guy who broke off their engagement out of the blue?' The guy who had put such despair on her lovely sister's face that Emma had had to be restrained from seeking him out and exacting a very cruel revenge. Even now, years later, she couldn't forget the haunting heartache that had been etched across Alix's face and her tears when she'd sat in the kitchen that Saturday afternoon and told her it was all over with Tom.

'I'd better stay out of this,' Oliver said. 'I'll get busy checking out the wine list.'

'Look, Emma, that was all ancient stuff.' Alix flapped her menu. 'We just said hello and that was that. It was all very civilised. I probably won't bump into him again for another ten years or so. Anyway, I was with Marc.' She shrugged.

'I just hope he didn't stir up any bad memories for you,' Emma said. 'You know I don't want you getting hurt.'

Alix shook her head. 'You can't fix everything, you know. Or always make it right. I'm thirty-seven, and I was cured of Tom Cassidy a long time ago.'

Time certainly heals, Emma thought, looking at the nonchalant expression on her sister's lovely face.

'Anyway, changing the subject, I've been talking to Hannah about her trip to Paris,' Alix went on. 'She's really looking forward to seeing us again. The more I think of it, the more I realise how great she was to put her life on hold for us. God forbid, Emma – if anything happened to you, I couldn't see myself jacking in my job to keep an eye on Libby and Charlie.'

'Libby and Charlie are much older than we were then,' Emma said.

'And it's not as if you'll have any bust-ups.' Alix grinned.

'I should hope not.' Oliver's arm went around Emma's shoulders and he gave her a quick squeeze.

The recollection of her infidelity surged through Emma. She felt full of self-disgust. The possibility of Oliver discovering her adultery hung over her head like a decapitating sword. She had a vision of Libby's hurt face, of Charlie's shock, and her love for her children gripped her heart. Her hand shook as she raised her glass of water: a wave of loss combined with exhaustion swept over her.

She felt vulnerable and exposed in front of her sister and husband, terrified that her anxieties were transparent, and asked herself if it was possible to maintain the paper-thin façade that had somehow brought her through the last four weeks. Had she really survived four weeks? Sometimes it seemed like a lifetime. She buried her face in her menu and wished that the waiter would bring the wine.

'Hey, Emma, are you okay?' Alix refilled her sister's water glass. 'Here, take a sip. You looked as though you were going to faint.'

'Emma?' Oliver's face was concerned.

'I'm fine.' She forced a smile.

'I'd say it's just as well you two love-birds are heading back to Dublin,' Alix joked. 'I think my sister needs a good night's sleep.'

Emma couldn't remember the last time she'd had a good night's sleep. Was this how married people got away with infidelity? By simply behaving as though it wasn't happening?

Well, so be it, and tough shit if she found it unbearable. She pulled herself together, stuck on her brightest smile and turned to Alix. 'Tell me about Hannah. And I want to hear all the gossip on

Alix B and the launch. You should see the dress Libby picked out. It's just adorable. She's so looking forward to it . . .'

On Sunday evening, just as her parents were arriving home from Paris, Libby looked around the jammed disco bar and decided that a mini-break from Rob was what she needed. After she'd met him for lunch on Saturday, the rest of her weekend had been boring. She'd called around to him on Saturday night, ready to go out in a Stella McCartney dress Alix had given her, but Rob had insisted on staying in and watching a movie on the television.

'I'm tired, Libby,' he'd said to her disappointed face. 'I'd far rather sit in with you and relax than battle through a crowded bar in town.'

'Then why didn't you come around to my house?' She felt as petulant as she sounded, for with Rob's parents in the living room they wouldn't have much privacy. 'It's free – Mum and Dad are in Paris, and Charlie will be doing his own thing.'

'Sorry, I didn't realise.'

'Oh, forget it,' she said, flouncing into the television room.

Rob put on the television and took some bottles of beer out of the fridge, then reminded Libby that he had college again in the morning and his whole future was at stake. As if he hadn't enough qualifications already, Libby huffed. She was fed up with him spending most weekends glued to his books as he studied for his Master's. It was about time he packed in the books and had some fun while he was young. He could always go back to his studies later on. After all, her father had gone back to college and studied when she and Charlie were young. Only, of course, she crossly reminded herself, that was because he was so young getting married and starting a family. Partly thanks to her.

She'd spent Sunday at home and now she was glad to be out with Karen and Mandy in the energetic music of the disco bar. It was obvious that Sunday was just another party night to judge by the crowds knocking back shots and cocktails as if they were going out of fashion. She flagged a waiter and ordered another round of Cosmopolitans, laughing when Karen and Mandy exchanged a look of exaggerated surprise.

'Relax, girls, chill a little.'

'I'm just thinking of tomorrow morning,' Mandy said.

'Me too,' Karen agreed. 'Mondays are bad enough without having a massive hangover.'

Maybe it was time to move on from her college mates, Libby thought. After all, Karen and Mandy weren't the most exciting party animals. She hadn't noticed it so much in college, but now that they were out in the real world, set free from the constraints of projects, assessments and exams, Libby wanted to taste edgy, glitzy life. She caught a sexy-looking guy giving her the once-over, and sat up a little straighter.

Maybe, too, it was time to move on from Rob.

'Whatever you do, make the most of your youth,' her mother had encouraged her, several times, when Libby was nearing the end of her college years. 'That interval between college and settling down is precious. Those years should be the most fun-filled time of your life.'

'You missed out on all that,' Libby had said once. 'The college experience and the fun years afterwards. Did you ever regret that?'

Without hesitation, her mum had smiled and given her a hug. 'How could I when I had you? You, my dear, were far more precious than any of that – you still are. But I'd like you to have it all, the fun and adventure, and then the beautiful babies in due course. The world is your oyster, Libby, never forget that.'

Right now she wanted some fun, Libby decided. And adventure. Hey, she was almost twenty-two and the world was at her feet: what could be more exciting than that?

She knew what could be more exciting when she saw him press through the crowds on his way to the bar. She knew in the instant that passed between him placing his order with the barman and turning to survey the crowd. It was the reason she'd persuaded Mandy and Karen into the disco bar in the first place – they had never frequented it before and almost turned up their aristocratic noses at it. It was the venue, he'd told her, ever so casually, that he often dropped into on a Sunday night.

For she'd changed her mind about him. About him not being for her. Over the weekend, Libby had found she couldn't help thinking of Karl. She kept seeing his eyes as they had smiled lazily into hers, kept seeing his gesticulating hands, kept hearing the intoxicating Kerry cadences in his voice. He was sexy and alluring, and she sensed something dangerous about him, which made him all the more exciting. And she found herself wondering what kind of naughty adventures he'd expect to get up to in bed.

He wasn't too old either. What had made her think that? Maybe because she'd been comparing him with Rob. But there was no comparison between Rob's gentle passion and the smouldering desire she sensed in Karl. And then, just as she had known he would, and much as she had intended, he spotted her in the crowd.

Chapter 29

She should have ordered a cab, Alix chided herself. She should have known that the car park adjacent to the popular Paris studio would be full. Now she had to double back and swing around the block and find a space in the next car park. *And* lug her kit that bit further. She indicated her intention to pull into the right-hand lane at the last minute, and from behind her, an angry driver shot past and almost sliced off her wing mirror. Someone else leaned on the horn.

Dammit.

Of course, none of this would have happened had she managed to wake up on time. Or if she'd had a decent night's sleep. Or if she hadn't been awake at four in the morning with the usual dark thoughts crowding in. She spun the wheel, took the corner too sharply, and accelerated down the road.

Alix was suitably stressed out by the time she slewed to a halt in the car park, thankful to find a vacant space. She lifted her kit out of the boot and, mobile in one hand, dragging her case with the other, she hurried out onto the street and cut a haphazard path through the pedestrians. Her phone rang, and she breathlessly informed Minette, the stylist, that she was on the way.

Turning up thirty minutes late for a magazine shoot was an unforgivable offence. Studio time was booked; the photographer and assistants, the hair people and the stylist were waiting. As was the model, Claudine, who had flown up from Nice that morning.

'Apologies.' Alix flung off her jacket and opened her case.

The photographer and his assistants were busy checking the lighting and reflectors, and the stylist had already started on Claudine's hair. Alix opened her brush roll and laid out her Ziploc bags, containing foundations, eyeshadows, eyeliners, lip-glosses . . .

She was short of make-up. She scrabbled through the bags, unable to believe the evidence of her eyes. Somehow or other she had managed to leave the lip-liners at home or at the last shoot. She felt a trickle of perspiration run down her back. She could improvise. She'd have to. Most of the look was concentrating on Claudine's stunning cheekbones and huge dark eyes. But what a silly mistake to make.

'Everything all right?' Minette asked, noticing Alix's silence.

Alix beamed. 'Yes, fine, just embarrassed at being late.'

'So was the photographer,' Minette told her quietly. 'And I think he's having a problem with his camera battery.'

By the time everyone was ready and the faulty battery had been replaced, they were an hour behind schedule. Claudine was brilliant, a total professional, unfazed by the commands that the photographer was throwing at her, or that the wind machine was freezing cold, and that some of the glamorous eveningwear she was showing off was held together with pins.

Alix sipped two cups of plastic-tasting coffee, stretched her wrist and knee joints and waited to move forward with a touch-up. She took a quick break to run to the ladies' room, skipping down the stairs to the next floor. On her way back, she was hurrying up the stairs two at a time when she almost collided with someone.

'*Excusez-moi!*'

'Alix?'

'*Tom?*' She shot him a look of alarm.

Tom Cassidy. All six feet of him, sexy and gorgeous in a white T-shirt and stone-washed blue jeans that were snug on his hips. Right beside her, barely two feet away on the narrow stairs. So close that she caught the clean scent of him, saw the fine lines fanning out from his quicksilver eyes – saw those blue eyes momentarily startled. All her senses went into meltdown.

'What the hell are you doing here?' she said, incapable of controlling her apprehension. She folded her arms across her body, holding herself tightly as if that would somehow stop her churning insides falling out.

He stared at her for what seemed eternity, his face now expressionless. 'I'm here because I'm using the darkroom equipment today. Is that a crime?'

'The *darkroom*? I thought that went out with the dinosaurs.' She forced a careless laugh to cover her shock but knew by the way his eyes were suddenly hostile that she'd hit a nerve. She was talking nonsense. She knew full well from articles she'd read that Tom sometimes worked with darkroom equipment, turning out fabulous sepia-toned prints.

'Or are you one of those dinosaur species?' she asked, her anxiety making her heedless.

'That's a cheap shot and it doesn't suit you,' he said. In the glare of daylight, his hair was shorter, neater than he used to wear it, and up close she could see glints of silver at the temples. Something quickened inside her, the knowledge that the twenty-two-year-old youth she'd said goodbye to was long gone and that he, too, was at the same stage in the voyage of life as she was.

How had he fared? she wondered. Had he achieved all he wanted to? Fulfilled his dreams? She realised, with a pang, that she'd love to sit down and compare notes with him, ask him how he was really doing, but that that was impossible.

'Sorry, no doubt you like to be true to your art,' she went on, with an edge of sarcasm. It was the only way she could protect herself against the hammering of her heart. Putting up defensive barriers would keep him far away from her, both physically and emotionally.

He looked puzzled. 'I don't get this. We're grown adults. Where did your cynical agenda come from? Why can't you at least be civil to me?'

She shrugged. 'Sorry. There's nothing to be ashamed of if you strive to be true to your profession. I admire your integrity.'

He stretched out a hand to the wall, preventing her progress up the staircase. 'Do you know what I'd really like?'

She could see he was angry from the set of his jaw and the flash in his blue eyes that flicked over her like a whiplash. 'What, Tom?' she managed – just about – to sound flippant.

'I would like,' he went on, his voice measured and coldly deliberate, 'if you and I could sit down some time and you could kindly explain why you're still so hostile towards me. I never really understood why you threw back my ring and screwed it all up for us. I'd kinda like to know what I did to deserve the treatment I received at your hands. And from your attitude now, which I find quite appalling by the way, it's something that's still obviously festering away inside you. What could I have done to cause you to treat me in this manner? What did I say? Or not say? I can't help feeling curious, that's all, so some sort of explanation would be rather useful for me.'

'I wouldn't lose any sleep if I were you. It's scarcely a national issue, is it?' she quipped. 'I would have thought that nowadays you'd have far more important concerns on your mind than an ancient romance. I'm sure you've had plenty of relationships since.'

'I've had my share,' he said, stonewalling her with his gaze. 'But at least when they came to an end there was mutual understanding and, in some cases, antagonism as to why they failed. In your case . . .' He paused.

'I was the one who got away, is that it? Or is it that I was the one who called it quits and you just didn't like being on the receiving end?' She was being totally off the wall, Alix knew, because her guilty conscience was eating her. Her instincts came together in a frenzy of anxiety that urged her to push him away and close this down. She prayed he'd never discover that she'd allowed Emma to believe he'd broken up with her instead of it being the other way around. But that was only a mini-deception compared to her greater, far more grievous sin of breaking up with Tom in the ruthless manner she had. It was something she'd never forgiven herself for and it was far too late to put it right.

He shook his head. 'This is a load of crapology. I just don't get you. You're not the Alix Berkeley I knew once upon a time.'

'You're perfectly right. I'm not. Now may I be allowed to pass?'

'You may.' He dropped his arm and she went to step around him, steeling herself to walk tall and proud. She heard his next words as she drew level with him, and wheeled back to catch him regarding her with a supercilious curl of his lips.

'Would you care to repeat that?' she demanded.

'You heard. But just to reinforce it, I said that the girl I knew would never have compromised her ideals by lowering herself to play the role of mistress.'

'How dare you?' She had to restrain herself from slapping his face.

'You needn't worry, Alix, it's a well-kept secret.' He gave her a look of derision before he turned on his heel and marched down the stairs.

Compromised her ideals? Alix was shaking when she returned to the studio. But she had to drag her composure together as the stylist was looking for her to touch up Claudine's foundation. 'Where were you, Alix? We need you *maintenant!*'

She was edgy as she hung around for the rest of the shoot, wondering how long Tom intended to be in the building, cursing her bad luck at running into him. However, there was no sign of him for the rest of the day and she reached home without any further skirmishes. She opened her make-up kit on the kitchen table, took out her brushes and set to cleaning everything, the repetitive actions keeping her fingers occupied – but her mind was buzzing, flickering off in a million different directions, thinking about Tom and wondering anxiously how long he intended to remain in Paris. The city surely wasn't big enough to keep the two of them apart.

Chapter 30

The night he introduces himself to Alix at the disco, Tom Cassidy is sixteen, just like her, and still at school. She finds it easy to chat to him and, with his endearing honesty, almost forgets he is the awesome male of the species as she relaxes and laughs at his jokes. She feels even better when he coaxes her out onto the floor and puts his arms around her. When he takes her home at the end of the night she feels she is walking on air.

She hesitates at the gate. As she looks at him under the street light he is suddenly alien and very masculine.

'We had some fun tonight, didn't we?' he says.

'Yeah,' She makes herself sound careless. She steels herself to hear that he won't want to see her again. She sees him looking at her mouth and her throat dries. Then he leans over and kisses her so softly and tenderly that, for the first time, she feels a flood of excitement lift her heart.

'Will you be at the disco next week?' he asks.

Next week. Her heart sings. So it wasn't just tonight. 'I might be,' she says.

'I'll see you then,' he says, finally releasing her and opening the gate.

Next week he is waiting for her when she arrives, sick with nerves, along with Jackie and the gang. He wastes no time but comes straight over to her and kisses her cheek. Alix feels as though she is wrapped in a hot, exciting whirl of joy.

It is the start of their romance and they become good friends as well as lovers. She finds him easy to talk to and she tells him about her mother while he holds her close and wipes away her tears. They talk about their dreams and hopes for the future. Tom is going to be a photographer. He's already building up a portfolio and he's going to travel the globe and take amazing pictures. Alix tells him she's going to work in the world of beauty and image, portable skills that will take her anywhere she wants to go.

'My sister tells me you're very clever,' he says. 'Don't you want to do something more academic?'

'No way, definitely not,' she says, without elaborating.

He takes her hand in his and squeezes it tightly. 'Well, then, together, me and you, we'll be a team and we'll take on the world.'

She finds him kind and humorous, and he bristles with a restless energy that makes him fun to be with, but when he's focused on taking the perfect picture, he's patient and very much the perfectionist.

She poses for him: they trek the Dublin Mountains and she stands by the ridge of the valleys, on top of outcrops, by rushing streams, her face whipped by the cool air, her hair flying in the wind; they spend long hours in the shimmering haze of the seashore and the endless sky, all the time in search of the perfect shot, the perfect backdrop. He brings her out into autumnal woods and cold, crisp snow, where fields are hushed with a blanket of white as he experiments with light and shade, colour and contrast.

When he says he loves her, her heart bubbles over with joy.

After a few months, it is the most natural thing in the world for them to become lovers. For Alix, sex isn't the drama that some of her schoolmates seem to think. It's all about her and Tom feeling closer still, skin to skin, trusting each other, and showing each other the depth of their love in the best way possible. When she feels his lean, hard body claiming hers, it's like nothing else on earth and every vein in her body turns to fire.

When Alix leaves school, she enrols for a course in a beauty college. Tom goes on to study media skills, specialising in photography. On her twenty-first birthday he surprises her with an engagement ring, which he has saved up for with his wages from his part-time bar job.

'We can't get married for a couple of years,' he says, trailing his fingers through her hair. 'I'll be finished college soon but I'll be earning peanuts for a while.'

Alix leans into him and admires the tiny but perfect solitaire diamond. It sparkles on her finger. She feels a lump in her throat. *I'm engaged. Engaged to be married. I'll be Tom's wife. Tom's loving, devoted wife. And in time the mother of his children.* 'There's no rush,' she reassures him. She reminds him that she is still on trainee wages in the beauty salon, with a long way to go before she is established.

He holds her tight and kisses her. 'I can't wait to explore the world with you. As soon as I have a couple of years' basic experience under my belt, built up my portfolio and my bank balance, we'll get married and head off.'

Then, just a year later, Alix ends it.

'I'm going to work in London,' she tells Tom. She hasn't seen or spoken to him for two weeks, deliberately avoiding him and not answering his calls. Now, on a February afternoon, she sits across the table from him in the sterile and anonymous first-floor café in St Stephen's Green Centre, and tells him she hadn't seen him because she's been busy making plans. Plans to start work in London the week after next. She rushes her words, almost breathless in her urgency to get them out. 'Dublin's too small – there aren't enough openings. I need plenty of experience at the cutting edge, proper on-the-ground training, and London's where it's at right now.'

'Hey, Alix, you're scaring the shit out of me. What about us?' She looks at him wordlessly.

He runs a hand through his hair and stares at her, agitated. 'You know I can't wait to get out into the world, and travel the length and breadth of it, but we'd planned to do it together. After our wedding. When we have enough dosh. Which I don't at the moment. Neither do I have enough experience or contacts to launch myself out there just yet. What's the big rush? Surely you could wait. Here, look.' He pulls a few pages from the inside pocket of his jacket and pushes them across the table to her. 'I've been checking out InterRail for starters. And a few hostels. We could get around Europe quite cheaply, but I'd need at least another year . . .'

Alix stares down at the information unseeingly. She eventually raises her eyes to his and her voice, when she speaks, is very soft. 'Tom, you know I want to freelance, but I need loads of suitable experience and that means getting to where the real action is, the fashion shoots, the catwalk shows, movie premières. I can't do all that in Dublin . . . not at the same high-profile level. I've a chance of starting with Estée Lauder in London – it's a fantastic opportunity for me and I can't say no to that.'

'An opportunity for you? Are you cutting loose? Breaking us up?' He sounds incredulous.

She shrugs.

'Because that's exactly what you're doing – you're breaking us up. What about our engagement?' Tom is clearly bewildered.

Alix forces the words out through her constricted throat. 'I guess it means we won't be engaged any more.'

Now he looks stunned. He casts his eyes around the busy café. '*What?* You can't mean that. No way. And here of all places. Goddammit, Alix, you can't mean it. Don't you love me?'

Alix stays silent. She begins to slide the tiny diamond off her finger. It comes off far more easily than she had expected it to.

Tom shakes his head as though he can't take it in. 'I don't believe this. Not here. You really picked your moment to kick me in the teeth.'

'Sorry. It wasn't . . . I just wasn't thinking.' It's a lie, of course. She has thought it out carefully and it seems easier to tell him in a public place where there is less chance he'll let fly.

'What the fuck did I do?' he hisses across the table. 'And I don't apologise for the French. Where did I go wrong? *Did* I go wrong somewhere?'

'No, you didn't,' she says desperately.

'I don't believe you. There has to be more to this—'

'I thought you'd understand that this is my big chance, a huge opportunity,' she says, drawing a deep breath. 'I can't turn it down.'

'Don't give me that bullshit. You know there'll be plenty of other opportunities for your talent.'

'Not this particular one.'

'Chrissake, is this your sadistic way of dumping me?'

Sadistic? How awful it sounds. Yet Tom is right. But there is no easy way to tell him that, much as she loves him, she is terrified of marriage and of following in her mother's treacherous footsteps. With her mother's blood running through her veins, how could she be capable of becoming a loyal, steadfast wife, never mind a loving mum? No matter how many different faces she might make, or how much she alters her appearance, at some intrinsic level she has no trust in herself as a wife or mother and it's far better to end it now before life gets too complicated.

But she tells Tom none of this. The words stick in her throat: although he loves her, he wouldn't understand the depth of her anxiety. He would try to paper over the cracks, but in time they'd surely fracture. So the angry words fly back and forth across the space between them until Tom flips his spoon across the table in a futile gesture of anger. 'If you walk out on me now, it's goodbye,' he says, injured male pride coming to the fore.

Alix makes herself face him down. 'Then that's what it is.'

She tells herself it's better this way as she closes a door in her heart, puts her beautiful ring on the plastic table top, rises to her feet and leaves. When she reaches home, she finds she is clutching a crumpled InterRail timetable between her white-knuckled fingers.

After she tells Emma she's off to London, she breaks the news to Andrew Berkeley.

'I suppose I saw this coming,' he says.

'Sorry, Dad, to be leaving you on your own . . .'

'Don't be silly, love, you have to live your life. I'll have plenty of work as well as my books to keep me going.'

'Dad, did you ever . . .?' She's about to ask him if he ever considered having a friend, a woman friend, but she stops herself just in time, for it would raise the ghost of her treacherous mother, the ghost Alix is trying to keep at bay, who mocks her at every turn.

'I'm glad you're making a new life for yourself,' he says. 'I'm sorry Tom won't be with you – he's a nice young chap. But I just want you to be happy. I know life hasn't been easy for you, or indeed for Emma, and for that I take full blame.'

'It's all in the past now,' Alix says, wondering what part he had played in her mother's infidelity. 'I'm just looking forward to the future.'

She's relieved that Tom doesn't attempt to contact her before she leaves, as she has no idea how she would respond to him or if she'd be able to maintain a careless façade in front of him. As it is, the great day dawns and she feels torn between regret, sadness and the need to get away.

She isn't sure what the future will hold when she arrives in London. She's just grimly determined that it will be entirely different from the past.

Chapter 31

Something somewhere chimed distant unease as Emma watched Libby step carefully down the thickly carpeted stairs, mindful of her vertiginous stilettos.

'Out again?' Emma tried to sound light and disinterested.

'Yeah – so?' Libby paused.

'But not with Rob?' Emma prompted.

'How did you guess?'

'Weren't you out with him last night? And the night before? It's not like Rob to be gallivanting three nights in a row in the middle of his thesis and in the middle of the week.'

'Yeah, well, I saw Rob on Monday night – but what made you think I was out with him last night?' Libby asked.

Emma bit her tongue. She had almost said it was the way she had been dressed: her daughter had hardly put on that slashed-to-the-navel chiffon top and a pair of tight leather jeans for the benefit of her girlfriends. Now, this evening, as Libby came down into the hall, Emma saw that she was wearing a different yet equally revealing bustier that left little to the imagination – it barely covered her nipples. Her make-up was exotic: eyes smoky, lips red and pouty.

Libby was dressed for sex.

If it wasn't Rob, who the hell could it be? Safe, dependable Rob, who was almost like a son to her and Oliver. She hated to think that her daughter felt the need to cavort like this to attract some strange guy. Whoever he was, she disliked him already for inciting Libby to dress in such an overtly seductive manner. Luckily for Libby, Oliver had flown to London that morning for a conference and wouldn't be back until the following evening. So it was up to Emma to deal with this.

But Libby wasn't a teenager she could order back to her room. And the last thing Emma felt like was confrontation. Since her return from Paris she hadn't heard a word from Karl and she was frazzled enough to say the wrong thing altogether. She'd had a huge row with Leticia yesterday morning when she'd caught her snooping in Charlie's bedroom, which, with Libby's, was supposed to be off limits. Then Emma had totally forgotten about a wedding that she and Oliver were due to attend the following Saturday until he'd reminded her about it last night. The daughter of one his clients was getting married and he had accepted the invitation weeks ago. A few of the senior management in his office would be there. Even though it was supposed to be the A-list wedding of the year, it was the last thing Emma wanted to attend right now. It also meant they would stay overnight on the Saturday so she wouldn't be around to keep tabs on the new, vampish Libby.

Now she was floundering in front of her daughter, who was already at the hall door. 'I guess I just assumed you were out with Rob.' Emma shrugged.

'Didn't I tell you? Rob and I are taking some time out,' Libby announced. 'That's why I saw him on Monday night. To agree to a trial separation. Effective immediately.'

'Off with Rob?' she said. 'Whose idea was that?'

'Mum! If you must know, it was mine. But it shouldn't make any difference to you.'

Emma couldn't ignore that. 'Hang on a minute, it's the difference between my daughter going out gallivanting to get over a broken heart, in which case I'd tell her to be careful she doesn't drown her sorrows too well, or my daughter going out to enjoy herself with someone new, in which case I'd advise her to take it easy.'

'You mean not jump into bed on the first date?' Libby jutted out her bottom lip, like a stubborn child. Only now her lips were glossed and painted with a crimson stain. 'Don't worry, I didn't. Jump into bed on the first date.'

'So it's someone new. Are you going to tell me who he is?' Emma asked.

Libby gave her an impish grin that unnerved her. 'No, not yet. I want to keep him to myself for a little while. So you needn't worry about seeing him on the landing in the morning. Anyway,' her careless laugh grated on Emma, 'he has his own place, but even if he didn't, I don't think he's the type who'd want to sleep under Mummy and Daddy's roof.' Her eyes sparkled.

What type was he? Emma wanted to ask. A work colleague? A friend of a friend? How well did she know him? And, worse, why was she dressed up like a sex siren for him? But Libby forestalled any questions by saying that her cab was waiting outside. Then she left, negotiating the gravel driveway as best she could in her dangerous skyscraper heels, looking somehow, to Emma, very young and far too vulnerable for the sharks that were out there.

When Libby had spotted Karl the previous Sunday night, he'd given her a huge smile. He'd come straight over to the table she was sharing with Mandy and Karen, and insisted on buying drinks. Mandy and Karen had refused as they were about to leave, and pulled on their jackets, sending meaningful glances in Libby's direction. She'd been amused at their astonishment when she'd said she wasn't going home and that she'd be delighted to have a drink with Karl. He was a former colleague of her mother's, after all.

Karl was in the same kind of flirty mood he'd been in the first time they'd met, making Libby feel free and light-hearted, far away from Rob's tiresome exams and the dismal prospect of the office the following morning. She'd laughed encouragingly at his jokes and felt a thrill course through her when his eyes met hers and scanned her body.

This was it. This was the excitement she craved and, judging by the look in his eyes, he was hers for the taking. They'd had a couple of drinks together and afterwards he'd walked her to the taxi rank. She was a bit surprised at his chaste goodnight kiss, expecting more in the way of passion from him. He was obviously holding back, she reasoned.

'Tomorrow night?' he'd asked.

She'd hesitated. She was supposed to be seeing Rob and, in fairness, she wasn't about to two-time him. Libby Colgan did have some standards.

'Tuesday night?' he'd suggested hopefully, and she'd agreed. It would give her time to talk to Rob, and clear things with him.

Rob had been very silent when she'd mentioned the temporary split. They were supposed to be meeting in town, but instead she arranged to call over to his house. She had known by his face when he answered the door that he'd guessed something was amiss.

'It's just a temporary break, to see how it goes,' she'd repeated, staring at a spot on the wall.

He'd given her a long, thoughtful look. 'If that's how you feel, the last thing I'm going to do is try to persuade you otherwise. You can have your break. For as long as you want.'

She'd felt kind of bereft and at a loss when she'd got home but equally annoyed that Rob had let her go so easily. She'd cheered herself up thinking of her date with Karl the following night and the prospect of taking a huge step into the unknown.

On their first proper date, Karl brought her to the movies and for drinks afterwards. He chatted about his home in Kerry, his life in Dublin and the job in Marshalls now that her mother had left. He spent a lot of time boasting about his apartment. It didn't take her long to sense that he was self-obsessed as well as self-confident, and she found that her normal effervescence dried up a little in the face of the glances she intercepted from him when he thought she wasn't looking. Calculating, speculative glances, as though he was sizing her up. And not, she thought with disappointment, for bed. Even his goodnight kiss was friendly rather than passionate.

In the taxi going home on Tuesday night, she wondered if he thought she was too young, too inexperienced, despite the see-through top and the sexy make-up tricks Alix had shown her. Maybe she was giving off the wrong vibes. Maybe she just wasn't sexy enough for him.

Now, tonight, she was wearing a daring bustier and he was already waiting for her in the restaurant. Even though it was their second date, when Libby walked across to where he was seated a shiver ran down her spine as though she was entering some strange and unfamiliar landscape.

He stood up and kissed her. 'Hello, again.'

'Hi, Karl.' She felt the whisper of his lips on her cheek, caught the drift of his aftershave. Exotic and musky, it quivered on her senses.

He touched her hand, squeezed it briefly and invited her to sit down. 'I hope this is okay?'

Libby looked around the Temple Bar restaurant. The tables were rather too close so there was barely enough room for her to pull out her chair, and with an uproarious hen party nearby, and rock music thumping from speakers in the ceiling, it was much noisier than she would have liked. 'Yes, it's fine.'

'Temple Bar is great, isn't it? I like it here.'

She smiled in agreement, privately thinking that there were far nicer and far more sophisticated venues in Dublin city centre where you could bring someone for a getting-to-know-you meal besides the busy restaurants in the maze of side-streets off the Liffey – they were usually jammed with tourists and boisterous party groups.

'You look good tonight, Libby. You're very attractive,' he said, deliberately allowing her to see his eyes lingering on the soft swell of her breasts.

'Thank you,' she said, waiting to feel ripples of excitement at the direction of his glance, but instead she became uncomfortably aware of just how low her top was cut. All of a sudden she was glad to be in such a lively restaurant. It was better to have some noise and distraction because she didn't know quite what to make of Karl.

As the night went on, Karl was chatty and attentive but she sensed that he wasn't quite with her. Not in the way she would have expected. He'd said she was attractive and he'd allowed his eyes to linger on her cleavage, but it had seemed an automatic response. There was no genuinely shared laughter, let alone the intimate exchanges that might have acted as a forerunner to sex. You knew when a man was really interested in you, and when he wanted to sweep you off to bed. And Libby didn't sense that about Karl. Yet.

Then again she might have it all wrong, Libby thought as she sipped her wine and chatted about her favourite movies. Maybe she was just too young and naïve to pick up on his cues. She'd little or no experience of worldly-wise men like Karl, men who'd been around the block a little. Maybe he was afraid to rush her, and felt she needed time and space to get to know him. Before they took things any further.

Chapter 32

The black limousine slowed to a crawl as it negotiated the teeming, neon-flashing West End streets. It swung onto the Strand and glided to a halt in front of the opulent edifice of the Savoy. Alix swung her feet out onto the pavement and wondered if she needed her head examined. The driver fetched her wheelie-case from the boot and passed it to an attendant.

She'd flown from Paris in James Cooper's private jet, sharing the champagne-fuelled journey with some well-heeled party guests who couldn't be expected to avail themselves of a scheduled flight. In a couple of hours' time, she'd been informed, three hundred guests would be descending on the newly renovated Savoy where the pink-and-white-themed party of the year was being held in the ballroom.

Alix had initially decided to refuse the booking until she'd read the email that James Cooper had sent to her through Estelle. 'It would mean the world to Jemima,' he'd written. 'You've no idea how chuffed she'd be to have you do her make-up for the most special, most fairytale night of her life so far . . . Alix Berkeley, make-up artist to the stars, hot from Paris . . .'

Yes, Mr Cooper, Alix thought, her mouth curving in a smile, flattery will get you everywhere.

'My daughter is beautiful, but I'd like to engage your services to ensure she goes off to her special night looking as divine as possible . . . and as happy as I can make her.' He went on to tell her a little bit about Jemima, filling in the background.

Alix felt like saying that you couldn't *make* anyone happy – they had to decide that for themselves – but his heart seemed to be in the right place. She wondered how it would feel to have her make-up artistry mean the world to an eighteen-year-old girl. To bring about such a difference to her fairytale night. Emma had enjoyed that privilege with Libby down through the years, Alix experiencing it only at a far-removed second hand. Curiosity had urged her to accept.

Upstairs, in Jemima's suite, she refused tea or coffee and asked instead for a glass of spring water. Then she was ushered into Jemima's lavish bedroom, with a view of the Thames, and her adjacent, equally lavish dressing room, where a mid-length pink tulle dress took centre stage, wrapped in protective gauze. Jemima greeted her as ecstatically as she could, given that she was swathed in towels while a jeans-clad male stylist worked on her long blonde hair, adding glossily curled extensions that snaked down as far as her waist.

'Alix! Thank you so much for coming. It's brilliant to see you!' She made it sound as though Alix was a long-lost friend who'd just arrived from Western Australia. 'When I heard you'd done Lily Allen's make-up for her cover shoot I told Daddy I *had* to have you. And this is Robin from John Frieda. Only the best will do for Jemima Cooper – isn't that right, girls?'

Her two friends giggled. The hairstylist gave Alix a grin that said, 'Hey, man, let's just indulge them and go with the flow.'

'And Daddy always does what I tell him. You can start with Jane and Lorna,' Jemima said regally. 'They're my two VBFs, and see?!' She poked her dainty wrist out from the folds of towels and displayed a diamond-encrusted watch. 'They bought me a Tiffany watch for my birthday.'

'Very nice,' Alix said.

'So I'm allowing them to have their make-up done by you. On one condition.'

'Which is?' Alix asked, checking the lighting before she set up.

'They can't look as good as me.' Jemima giggled, reaching out again, this time for her champagne glass. 'I'm the birthday girl so I deserve to be spoiled. Oops!' Some of her drink slopped over the edge of the glass. 'Never mind,' she said, her manicured fingers mopping up a stray bead of liquid and popping it into her mouth. 'There's plenty more where that came from.'

Alix arranged a small table and chair to take the best advantage of the light in the room. Then she opened her case and invited Jane to sit down. 'Well, Jane, what would you like? Any particular look?'

'Something sexy,' Jane said hopefully.

'Not too sexy, though,' Jemima interjected.

Alix got to work, smoothing Jane's blemish-free skin with a light primer, then applying foundation, using a brush for ease of application and blending with her fingers. She contoured the girl's face, giving the illusion of strong bone structure. And all the time she worked, she listened to the chatter going back and forth between the friends. About the hip-hop group that Jemima had *insisted* on having and for whom Daddy had pulled out all the stops . . . the two dozen bare-chested waiters who would be wearing white trousers with *I Love Jemima* printed in Day-glo pink across the buttocks . . . the pink Cadillac that had brought her to the hotel and would deliver her safely home tomorrow . . . Yes, there was going to be a chocolate fountain, she'd had to fight with Daddy over that, but not an ice sculpture, as they were so passé.

Maybe Jemima was trying to make it into *Hello!*, but Alix had expected something different from an eighteen-year-old who had just spent a year on a Swiss baccalaureate and whose father's business seemed to be recession-proof. Jemima was now busy reciting a long list of birthday presents she'd already received, including, naturally, a car from Daddy. She would have to learn how to drive it next, she giggled. *And* he was treating her and her two very best friends to a fortnight in the Seychelles.

'You must be having the birthday of the decade,' Alix said when the hairstylist had left and she was assessing Jemima's sun-damaged skin.

Jemima pouted. 'All my friends are. Lorna was eighteen last month and she arrived by hot air balloon at a silver and white marquee in the back garden of her parents' family home. And Jane ferried us all by helicopter to an Oscars-themed weekend in the Isle of Wight. Don't worry, when the birthdays are over we'll all go back to our recessionista status,' Jemima laughed.

'I see,' Alix said, feeling totally out of touch. 'Is that what it means to be eighteen nowadays?'

'It depends on how much money your father managed to safeguard before the credit crunch and how far you can twist him around your little finger.'

As though on cue, James Cooper bounded into the room. Tall and well built, he looked as though he was used to getting his own way. 'Hey, poppet, your mum's phoned to say the room's looking really sensational and the five-tiered cake . . .'

'Daddy,' Jemima squealed and jerked around, 'you're supposed to knock!'

James looked slightly taken aback. He swiftly recovered. 'I knew you were getting beautified, not that you need it – and hello, you must be Alix. How's it going?'

'Fine, Mr Cooper,' Alix said. She felt like telling him to encourage Jemima to wear adequate sun protection the next time he treated her to a holiday, but she didn't think it would go down too well.

'Good. Hope everyone's looking after you okay.' He waved a hand expansively. 'You're welcome to join the party, you know, plenty of room for more, have some drinks . . .'

'Thanks, but I've already booked a return flight,' Alix said. It would be a regular scheduled flight this time. The use of the private jet had ensured her safe arrival in plenty of time, but it didn't stretch to the return journey.

'Whatever makes you happy – once Jemima's happy, of course!'

'I *am* happy, Daddy. Alix is going to transform me into a princess. Aren't you, Alix?'

It sounded like a plea from the heart and Jemima's eyes sought Alix's in the mirror. No matter how much money Daddy had, or how privileged her upbringing, his daughter still carried the same insecurities as women the world over. Suddenly Alix felt like putting her arms around her, and telling her that the most genuinely beautiful women she'd ever worked with were those who made the best of their features but were ultimately comfortable in their own bodies and confident with their inner selves.

The moment passed. Jemima tilted her face trustingly towards Alix and closed her eyes, making herself seem even more vulnerable. Alix felt a sudden frisson along her spine and told herself to concentrate on the job. Jemima had regular features and the typical English-rose complexion, but with the state of her skin, she had her work cut out. She swept on a primer and applied a medium foundation. Then she camouflaged spots and blemishes with a light reflecting cream. She concentrated on Jemima's deep blue eyes, giving her a dramatic smoky look, and balanced it by keeping her lips natural, with a light pink gloss.

She found herself chatting to Jemima as she worked, instilling in her the importance of using a high-factor base all year around, and recommending some products to her. 'And plenty of still water,' she said. 'Especially between alcoholic drinks if you're out at night. It'll pay dividends in the long run. It's up to you to look after your skin and that means starting now, before you're twenty, not waiting until the first wrinkle appears. And cleanse every night, even if you only use baby lotion. It's so important.'

When she had finished, she encouraged Jemima to look at herself in the mirror. Alix had delicately emphasised her cheekbones and made the most of her blue eyes.

'Oh, wow, that's fantastic, Alix – thank you so much!' Her enthusiasm was engaging and Alix couldn't help feeling gratified. 'I'd kiss you only I'd smear this lovely job.' Jemima twirled happily around. In spite of her spoiled precociousness, she exuded a young, eager innocence. Once again Alix's heart was snagged – she felt a surge of protectiveness towards the younger girl. Her life had been handed to her on a plate, no doubt about that. Her only experiences so far were happy and positive and her trusting heart was still very much intact. Alix had been four years older than Jemima when she'd first come to London but now, looking back, she seemed to have been world weary compared to Jemima's fresh vitality. Nature versus nurture, Alix sighed, and the hand of Fate played a gigantic part as well. She tidied her make-up, replacing tubes and pencils in the appropriate Ziploc bags before packing them away in her wheelie-case as, with squeals of delight, Jemima turned her attention to her frothy party dress.

'All done?' James Cooper was waiting in the sitting room when Alix came through from the dressing room.

'Yes, I've finished and Jemima is happy.'

'Good, good. Are you sure you won't stay for the party? It seems a lot of travelling in one day.'

'No prob. It's all part of my job,' she told him. 'I can easily get a cab out front and I'll be home in no time.'

'I'll have someone take your case down for you,' he said, moving across to the phone.

Alix forestalled him. 'It's no problem, Mr Cooper, I can manage.'

'I'm sorry I can't offer my driver but he's needed for—'

'Of course,' Alix said smoothly, heading towards the door.

'You must think Carol and I have Jemima spoiled rotten,' he said.

Alix smiled. 'I think she's a very lucky girl – it's obvious she means the world to you.'

'That she does. I'd do anything to make her happy. Because from the time they're a tiny mite, all *your* future happiness and peace of mind is tied up in them. Terrifying, really. Serious stuff.'

Serious stuff indeed, Alix reflected as the cab trundled through busy Friday-evening London suburbs en route to the airport. Not all parents felt like James. Or loved their children with quite the same unselfish passion. Her mother, for example.

Once again she was treading the usual well-worn path when it came to judging Camille Berkeley. Camille hadn't considered her children when she'd embarked on her affair. She hadn't even thought about the repercussions on Emma and Alix – the distress, the fear, the feelings of abandonment. Naturally, she hadn't expected to be found out in such a tragic and very public way. But she had been selfish – she hadn't sacrificed her lust to ensure her children's security.

Alix sighed and reminded herself that she'd let it all go when she'd started a new life. By the time she'd reached Paris she'd sundered her ties with the past and the legacy of her mother. She might be a carbon copy of her, with her looks and temperament, but she'd made damned sure not to be in a position where she could hurt a husband or children of her own.

But what about other children? For example, Laurent's?

Her flight was delayed by thirty minutes and she was annoyed that she had to hang around in the soulless environment of the airport, where the coffee was watery and tepid. She abandoned it in favour of a glass of wine. She also found she had too much time to reflect on Tom Cassidy's parting shot earlier that week. She'd been completely shaken after the encounter with him, but the next couple of days had been filled with ten-hour sessions and back-to-back photo shoots for magazine spreads. It had been later in the week that her fog of anxiety had cleared a little and the full meaning of his words had sunk in. Now the scene replayed itself in her mind.

A well-kept secret.

They'd been so careful, she and Laurent, so meticulous with their arrangements, rarely venturing beyond Alix's apartment to ensure their affair never became public knowledge. God knew how Tom had discovered it. And if he knew, then other, less honourable photographers surely did. She didn't care that Tom had found out or that he had slated her lack of integrity. It was the least she deserved.

But God forbid Laurent's innocent children ever got to hear of it. Why hadn't she seen it before? How come she'd been so thoughtless? Whatever about his wife, who turned a blind eye, Laurent's young children would suffer if the affair became public knowledge. Up to now, Alix had been so wrapped up in herself and her own needs that she'd failed utterly to give them due consideration.

Something else that bugged her was Jemima's nude face and her almost childlike faith in Alix's ability to transform it. Alix dealt with models and celebrities of Jemima's age all the time, but the cosy dynamics of a family environment were a million miles removed from the hectic, businesslike modelling circuit and it had all been very personal.

It was obvious that Jemima's trust had never been shattered by an unfaithful parent. There had been something vulnerable about her face, tilted towards Alix, something defenceless that had mocked her. She could hardly bear to acknowledge the surprising wave of maternal protectiveness she'd felt towards Jemima – it had pulled the rug from under her.

I haven't a maternal bone in my body. Her recent words resonated.

She was relieved when her flight was finally called. She rose to her feet, grateful for the distraction of the shuffling queue and the rummage for her passport, opening it at the appropriate page and staring at her unsmiling image.

Alexandra Berkeley.

Sudden tears pricked her eyes as she stepped through into the aircraft to be met by the flight attendant's cheery smile and she blinked them away furiously. Alexandra Berkeley had put all her feelings away when she'd left Dublin, enclosing her heart in a protective bubble, which had safely insulated her from connecting with anyone on a meaningful level. But now it was in danger of bursting.

Chapter 33

'What's wrong, *chérie*?' Laurent asked. He stroked her cheek as they sat at the table by the window where, outside, pinpricks of light studded the velvety Paris night.

Alix had texted asking to see him as soon as her Friday-evening flight from London touched down in Paris. He had arrived an hour after she reached home with a small gift-wrapped package.

It had all been so convenient, Alix sighed to herself, sex without strings, no commitment and a skilful lover who came and went and made no emotional demands. Convenient but selfish, and now everything had altered.

'We have to talk, Laurent,' she said, pushing her glass aside.

He looked at her speculatively. 'You are bothered about something, *oui*?'

'I am. I'm afraid . . .' Her voice faded. She began again, 'We have to stop seeing each other, you and I.'

Laurent was immediately on guard. 'Stop this? Us? You are unhappy with me?'

She leaned her elbows on the table and cupped her chin in her hands, her heart sinking as she realised that this was going to be a lot more difficult than she'd anticipated. 'No, but I don't think we can continue our – our relationship. You see, I bumped into . . .' something caught in her chest, but she made herself continue, 'an old friend during the week and he knows about us. I suspect others may too.'

Laurent's face darkened. '*Merde!* What old friend?'

It was still painful to say his name. It stuck in her throat. 'Never mind, just someone I knew years ago in Dublin. He's a photographer.'

'A photographer?' Laurent looked startled. 'And he knows about us? You are sure of this?'

'Yes, he said – he said— Well actually, there's no point in pretending. He said it was a well-kept secret.'

'*Mon Dieu!* Why didn't you tell me immediately? How many people know?'

'I don't know,' Alix said, picking up her glass and twisting the stem in her hands.

'You must have some idea!'

'I don't.' She shook her head.

'How did your friend find out?'

There was a hard edge to his voice and she didn't like the way he had emphasised the words *your friend*, as though Tom was more than a friend and, by implication, perhaps Alix had confided in him.

'He's not my friend, not any longer. I bumped into him in a photographic studio last week . . .' She trailed off.

'You know what this means.' Laurent's face was set. 'I can't afford to take any chances.'

'I agree. I don't want to be responsible for causing any hurt to your children.'

'They are too young,' Laurent snapped. 'They would not understand.'

217

Alix gave a bitter smile. 'You're never too young to have your trust destroyed.'

He rose to his feet as though he hadn't heard her last words. 'But if it became public my wife would never forgive me. And as for my father-in-law . . . What can we do? This is a disaster!'

Alix remained silent.

As she'd waited for Laurent that evening, one part of her mind had imagined that he might take her into her arms and tell her how much he loved her. He would tell her that he wouldn't – couldn't – give her up, no matter what. Then he would take her to bed and show her how much she meant to him. And hold her all night long.

Get real Alix, she'd told herself. That was only a ridiculous fairytale. The other, more rational, part of her expected that they might make the most of their last night together, enjoying each other's bodies one final time, with Laurent thanking her for all the pleasure she'd given him and expressing huge regret that it had to end.

But that wasn't happening either. And in a funny – no, shocking – way, she was relieved.

Laurent stared out of the window for long moments, then wheeled around. 'Do you think your friend will talk?'

His voice was icy and Alix's anger sparked. She stood up, the better to face him. 'How do I know? I certainly didn't tell him. I haven't seen him in years and I've no idea how he found out.'

'Perhaps, Alix,' he raised a cynical eyebrow, 'you were a bit careless.'

'I was never careless, dammit. I knew there was too much at stake,' Alix fumed. She'd been so scrupulously careful that she'd never left any evidence of Laurent for Monique to come across. 'Maybe *you* were. Maybe you were boasting to your friends about having the perfect set-up – your wife and family in addition to sex on tap.'

'Don't be ridiculous. I've too much to lose.'

Yes, your father-in-law's support. Laurent might be great in bed but his first thought had been for his reputation and not his innocent children. Why, oh why, hadn't she seen this before? She was equally bad, so obtuse and wrapped up in her own frame of reference that she had failed to see anyone else's. She said, giving him a steady determined look, 'I think it's best if you leave.'

'I am leaving. This could ruin me. I wasn't here – I've never been here, understand?'

Alix gripped the back of the chair and watched silently, feeling sick, as he picked up his jacket and walked towards the door. He had the decency to turn around and give her a look of regret before he shrugged and marched out into the hallway. She heard the outer door slam behind him and, with that expressive gesture, the last two years dissolved into the ether.

Bastard!

She picked up his gift-wrapped package and flung it at the wall. Although she couldn't really blame him. Laurent had set out his terms quite clearly at the beginning and now that they had been breached he was acting accordingly. She was furious with herself for being so blinkered, and angry with the cold, clinical way that two years of careful assignations and satiating sex had ended. And she was enraged with Laurent for implying that she had told Tom.

Far too wound up to cry, she tipped the last of the Sancerre into her glass. She had a mental picture of Tom on the stairwell of the studio and his troubling words came back to her again

A well-kept secret. Who else knew? Had Fiona talked? Was there any danger that their relationship would become public knowledge, even though it was now over? Both Laurent and Alix had high enough profiles for their affair to become tacky fodder for the gossip media. And if any enterprising photographer had managed to take snaps of Laurent entering or leaving her apartment building . . . God forbid.

There was only one way to find out who else might have known of her involvement with Laurent. She could try to see Tom and ask him outright, but she hated the idea. Even though she'd imagined herself and Laurent having great sex one last time, she was relieved that he'd simply left. For sitting across the table from him, watching him as he chatted, it had been suddenly impossible to visualise going to bed with him. And the reason for that was because – much to Alix's consternation – pictures of Tom, and the indescribable way it had been between them, kept getting in the way.

The room swayed. How could she see him, let alone try to talk to him, when even the thought of him sent her into dangerous meltdown?

Chapter 34

'Emma! You were supposed to be here an hour ago,' Helen, the receptionist, exclaimed as Emma walked through the door of her local hair and beauty parlour.

Emma felt cold. 'Was I?'

'Yes, we had you scheduled in for nine thirty. Wash and blow dry, wasn't it? I rang your mobile when you didn't appear but got no answer.'

That wasn't too surprising, considering her mobile was once more switched off and secreted in the depths of her bag.

'Is there any chance you could do me a huge favour and fit me in?' Emma asked desperately. 'Oliver and I are off to a wedding today and I can't go with my hair looking like this. The bed-head effect is scarcely appropriate.'

'We're quite full but I'll see if I can squeeze you in,' Helen said. She scrolled a long fingernail down the appointment book and cast an eye around the busy salon. 'If you can hang on for twenty minutes or so, I'll see if Joan can look after you.'

In the end Emma waited half an hour before she was enfolded

in towels and a voluminous black gown and led to the basins. A long thirty minutes during which she had to fish her mobile out of her bag, power it up and reluctantly phone Oliver to tell him of her mix-up. Then she was subject to the blast of canned music and the buzz of half a dozen hairdryers, which exacerbated her rising anxiety.

Her confusion meant they were delayed leaving Dublin. Oliver was tense and silent as they hurtled down the motorway, his foot heavy on the accelerator of his powerful black car. Emma sat equally tense in the passenger seat, her hair sleekly styled and her hands tightly clasped in the lap of her knee-length tulip Dior dress as she watched the Irish countryside sweep by the window.

The ceremony was taking place in a church with a view of the breathtaking grandeur of the Mayo countryside. They were just about to shoot past the side-road leading to the church when, at the last minute, Oliver spotted the line of gleaming cars that flanked the kerb and glinted in the pale sunshine. There was a squeal of brakes as he took the turn with inches to spare and screeched to a halt.

At the entrance to the churchyard, they were met by a cordon of security men and a posse of reporters and photographers. 'I don't know what all the fuss is about,' Oliver said, annoyed, as he withdrew their invitation from the inside pocket of his Armani gunmetal grey suit and flashed it.

'It's not every day that this church sees the only daughter of a stud farmer getting wed,' the security man laughed, waving them through.

'A wedding is just a wedding,' Oliver replied testily as he ushered Emma up the path and into the charming, flower-decked church where Ireland's most fêted soprano was already in full flow.

Oliver's irritation was all her fault, Emma told herself as she sat stony-faced in the pew and tried not to cry at the tear-jerking singing. She had caused their delay that morning, but the warmth and emotional closeness that had sprung up between them in Paris had been slowly dissolving anyway. It was now just over two weeks since she'd faced up to Karl in the South Anne Street pub and still there had been no word from him. Instead of feeling relieved, Emma was becoming increasingly edgy and she knew Oliver had picked up her vibes.

She couldn't help it. One minute she told herself that all was well, that Karl had been merely playing with her. It wasn't as if he'd actually threatened her with anything, just passed a few remarks designed to rattle her, and she'd overreacted. But other times she sensed that disaster was waiting. She was becoming more obsessed with Karl and his thinly veiled intimidation than the fact that she'd cheated on Oliver. And today, the last thing she felt like was attending this gilt-edged event.

Libby had been extremely envious of her parents heading off to the society wedding in the heart of Mayo, where the exclusive, five-star Duncan Castle had been booked out for the weekend to host the fabulous reception and accommodate all the guests, and where the hottest Irish rock band were rumoured to be taking to the stage later in the evening.

'Hey, Dad, can you smuggle me through in the boot of your car?' she'd asked Oliver.

'You wouldn't enjoy it, Libby,' he'd said. 'It's just a networking opportunity for me.' Oliver and several of his senior colleagues had been invited in the interest of maintaining beneficial business links. Emma felt like telling Libby she'd swap places with her. Apart from the fact that she still wasn't sure what Libby was up to, with Rob off the scene, she didn't want to attend a sentimental wedding ceremony, full of white lace and promises and happy-ever-afters, when her own marriage was in danger of falling apart. Who would?

Now she found it impossible to keep her emotion in check as

she listened to the happy couple promise to love and honour each other and watched their triumphant march down the aisle, the bride in a mist of happiness and Vera Wang. Once upon a time, she'd glided down the aisle with a proud young Oliver by her side, feeling they could conquer the world, never dreaming that those vows would be tainted by her reckless behaviour. Once upon a time, she'd been the smiling bride, radiant with happiness, and nostalgic memories of that long-ago innocent and optimistic day were churning now in her head.

The reception in the resplendent luxury of Duncan Castle was sumptuous in every respect, chilled champagne flowing, cocktails flying, the bride's face lit with joy. Everything about it twisted the knife in Emma's heart.

'Emma! Oliver! I was hoping you'd be here. How adorable to see you!'

'Hi, Annabelle.' Emma braced herself as she greeted the wife of one of Oliver's colleagues, who pounced enthusiastically on them, wrapped in layers of fuchsia silk.

'Isn't this a wonderful celebration?' Annabelle gushed, her plump, ring-encrusted fingers waving her glass to encompass the beautifully decorated ballroom, which was themed in silver and white. 'Where would we be without marriage? In these days it's great to see young couples taking the plunge. So few marriages last, wouldn't you agree?'

'Not necessarily,' Oliver said, curving his arm around Emma, obviously in an attempt to show a united front.

She felt ice cold.

'How sweet you are! They say plenty of sex and money is the glue that keeps most marriages together. What do you think, Oliver?' She flirted coyly with him.

'Sex and money? I can't answer that, Annabell,' Oliver laughed.

'You haven't denied it, so that's a positive in my book.' She turned to Emma, her cool gaze flicking over her from top to toe. 'You lucky thing, to have the winning combination. Hang onto that man of yours, or there'll be a queue forming! By the way, I heard on the grapevine that you're a lady of leisure these days. How interesting!'

Emma knew immediately where this was heading. Annabelle prided herself on her charitable commitments and if she sensed you had any spare time on your hands she regarded it as her mission to relieve you of same and hijack you onto some board or other. 'It's not all leisure.' Emma summoned single-minded resolve. She was determined not to get involved with the likes of Annabelle, her socialite cronies and their schemes, and suddenly she hadn't the patience even to pretend interest.

Annabelle pursed her lips. 'Really? I'm setting up a committee to examine the possibility of raising funds for a knitting circle for Africa. I was hoping you'd get involved. A little effort on our part would make such a difference to the lives of the poor. You might find it a relaxing change from the cut and thrust of the corporate . . .' She raised an eyebrow. 'Or was it marketing you were dabbling in? Not quite as demanding, anyway, and possibly more your milieu?'

'I'm just taking a temporary break from the boardroom scene,' Emma said firmly. 'I'm considering my future career options very carefully and I'd rather not get involved in a project that I might not be able to follow through.'

Annabelle tossed her champagne-free hand dismissively. 'Suit yourself. I suppose your career must come first.'

Emma was relieved that the gong sounded then for dinner, and further talk with Annabelle could be avoided. Better again was that the seating at the round tables was arranged so as to mix the guests and encourage them to mingle: she found herself sitting beside an uncle of the bride. During the six-course meal she was grateful that he kept the conversation flowing by regaling her with colourful accounts of his travels. When the meal and speeches were over, there was a lull while the tables were cleared and rearranged and guests moved out around the foyer and bar.

'It mightn't have been any harm to get involved with Annabelle's project,' Oliver said as they came out of the ballroom. 'It would be good for your profile.'

'What profile exactly?' Emma turned on him. 'The profile of Oliver's wife, you mean, the kind of wife you'd like to have in the background, playing with charity events, dallying with long liquid lunches that end up costing far more than any funds that would be raised for the poor unfortunates. Do you know it's frowned upon to wear the same designer outfit twice to some of these so-called benevolent dos? How's that for charity?'

'Not so loud,' he hissed, gripping her elbow and directing her through a gap in the crowd towards a quiet corner of the foyer.

'Emma,' he put his hands on her shoulders and turned her around to face him, 'when are you going to tell me what's wrong?'

'There's nothing wrong,' she said, dredging up a smile.

'Really?' His navy eyes searched her face. 'I thought we could talk. I thought we had a fantastic weekend in Paris, but this week I've a feeling that you're blocking me out of something. And something's upsetting you. Take yesterday, for example . . .'

'I was just a bit forgetful.'

'So leaving your credit card behind on the boutique counter and walking away is forgetful?' he said. 'Excuse me, Emma, supposing I left my credit card on the petrol station forecourt because I was a bit *forgetful*? Then this morning you mixed up the times of your hair appointment. And that's a first. Look, honey,' Oliver went on warmly, 'I just wish you'd tell me what's up. I thought you'd have a whole new lease of life when you left Marshalls, no worries or pressures, time to do what you wanted, and last weekend in Paris was very special, but you're going around this week like a lost soul.'

'I suppose I've kind of lost my bearings,' she eventually said, striving for some element of the truth in an attempt to appease him. 'I've lost the focus to my days and it's a bit strange.'

He was looking at her as though he didn't believe a word. 'I'd have thought that packing in your job would help you to relax more, give you freedom and more time to do what you really want to do.'

'Or more time to rub shoulders at frivolous lunches with your colleagues' wives?' she asked.

He frowned, as though he was at a loss to understand. 'Is that such a problem?'

She'd been there before, during the free time she'd had when Charlie and Libby had started school and before she'd started working in Marshalls. She'd been sucked into attending lunches and charity bashes with Annabelle and others. Oliver had encouraged her, but the events had filled her with unease because she'd felt inferior to the women she met. She'd never revealed this to Oliver. It was one of the reasons she'd started working in Marshalls: her job gave her a cast iron excuse to avoid them and it meant she was free of Annabelle's long reach.

She said, 'I don't want to get involved with Annabelle's gang – no, thanks, Oliver. They make me feel . . .' She hesitated.

'How?' He was looking at her intently, as though it really mattered. 'Speak to me, Emma, tell me what's bothering you.'

Emma looked about the crowded foyer, at the wedding guests swarming around, the bride in her lovely dress, laughing with her friends, her new husband handing her a glass of bubbly and kissing the tip of her nose.

Oliver had kissed her like that on their wedding day.

Something collapsed inside her. 'Sometimes – oh, Oliver,' she was appalled to hear herself blurt, 'sometimes I feel I'm walking a tightrope.'

Oliver's dark brows drew together as he scrutinised her for a long moment. Then he cast a swift glance around the gathering. 'Let's go outside. We'll grab a glass of whatever's going around on that tray and split.'

Chapter 35

*O*utside, the western sky was streaked with the gold and crimson of a spectacular sunset. The gardens were dotted with couples strolling in the evening air and the sounds of laughter and conversation drifted on the scented breeze. Emma clutched her flute of champagne and strove to put Karl aside so that she could concentrate on Oliver and explain away her outburst.

He led her across the castle courtyard to where a path cut through the colourful gardens to the lake.

'So, Emma,' Oliver began, 'you're not happy.'

'You should be inside, networking with your colleagues,' she said, wary now of what she might say. He might have glossed over her bolshiness and pretended all was well with the Colgans, but he had taken time out to stop and listen to his recalcitrant – correction, deceitful – wife who had all but thrown a tantrum in the gilded foyer of Duncan Castle.

'I'd rather find out what's bothering you. What do you mean by "tightrope"?'

Emma pulled her thoughts together. The mellow evening was

still and calm and, with the light fading from the sky, it seemed to invite confidences. But not too many.

'Why don't you start by telling me how Annabelle and her friends make you feel?' he asked. 'What's going on there?'

'To be honest, they've always made me feel as though I'm some kind of blow-in, and not quite at their level . . .' It was easy to talk about this, to share feelings she'd never before admitted to him.

'Are you serious?' Oliver flashed her a look of surprise as they strolled down the path, which was bordered with flowerbeds. 'Why on earth should you think that?'

'For starters, I've not been to private school or college, unlike most of them.'

'Good grief, that's hardly the be-all and end-all . . .'

She sipped some champagne. 'I sensed they never understood what you saw in me, or how the rather ordinary Emma Berkeley managed to snag the brilliant Oliver Colgan.'

'I hope you told them I married you for your lovely curvy body.' He chuckled softly and tightened his grip.

'You did in a way, didn't you? I was pregnant, after all,' she said quietly, turning to face him.

There was a long silence.

She was conscious that a barrier had come down – a barrier she'd long ago erected in her mind: topics she'd been afraid to bring out into the open were suddenly easy to discuss now that she had her back to the wall and nothing left to lose. She'd already been unfaithful to Oliver, and now that the worst had happened she felt a certain liberation to air subjects she'd usually avoid. The whys and wherefores didn't really matter any more – a lot of stuff didn't really matter any more. The realisation was bittersweet.

'Yes, you were,' Oliver eventually agreed. 'But, Emma, I loved you, we loved each other. The fact that Libby was on the way, okay, it made things a bit rushed . . .'

'Would you have married me anyway?' Emma pressed.

'I could ask you the same question – would you have married me? Who knows what we might have done the following year, or the year after?' He grinned and stroked her cheek. 'What does it matter now? People get married for all sorts of different reasons and none is more legitimate than another. In our case, we loved each other, and the important thing is we made a go of it. We're together, we have our family, the kids love you,' he continued softly, 'and I love you more than ever. Don't spoil all of that with over-analysing things that happened years ago or inventing baggage for yourself – silly baggage I can't believe you were carrying around.'

They had reached the lakeshore. The evening was drawing in and the slight breeze whipped up the silky surface of the water, ruffling the reflection of the golden sun that streamed across it in a fiery, molten column of light. The panoramic backdrop of dark purply mountains, clothed here and there in swathes of dense pine forests, was silent and brooding in the fading light. Back in Castle Duncan the wedding celebrations were moving up to the next level: there would be dancing and singing, the hot-shot rock group and, afterwards, on the second floor, their luxury room with a canopied bed awaited them. There, no doubt, Oliver expected to take her in his arms and make love to her like he had in Paris the previous week, urgently and hungrily.

'What did you mean by "tightrope"?' he asked again. He drained his champagne and looked at her closely.

Emma shivered. Oliver slid off his suit jacket and threw it over her shoulders. She was grateful for the warmth against her skin. 'Sometimes I feel it's all a balancing act,' she said, picking her words carefully. 'That the children don't really appreciate me because I've always tried to keep everyone happy and everything on an even keel, even if it meant putting myself last.' She felt conscience-stricken as she spoke, aware that she was talking about the earlier Emma, who had been dissatisfied before everything had changed.

'Neither am I appreciated by the kids,' he joked. 'Although you've been there for them far more than I have. I guess you've spent too much time running after them.' He wrapped his arm tightly around her. 'Why do you feel you have to smooth the path of their lives so much? You should let them look out for themselves a bit more. Make them take responsibility for themselves.' He fell silent. Then he said, 'Emma, do you think it has anything to do with the way your own mother . . .?'

She didn't deserve it, but she allowed herself to feel the warmth of his embrace. 'I want Libby and Charlie to feel perfectly happy and secure in knowing how much we love them.' That, at least, was the fundamental truth, even if it didn't directly answer his question.

He dropped a kiss on her forehead. 'Look, darling, that's something else that's far behind you. You shouldn't let something that happened almost thirty years ago have any bearing on the present. The kids won't break if you put yourself first more often,' he continued. 'On the contrary, it would help them to develop a healthy respect for you. And you can't make them happy, no matter what you do. Their happiness is up to them, not you, okay?'

'There's more to it than that,' she said. 'I look at you and Libby and think of the great success you've made of your careers. Charlie will do so too, in time. I look at Alix, fulfilling her dreams. You must all feel happy that you're living full lives, using the best of your talents, and going after what you really want. Me? Sometimes I feel left behind by my clever family.' She was conscious that she was still talking about the earlier Emma, and that she should have had this conversation with Oliver weeks – no, months – ago, when it had been important to her.

'Left behind?' he said. 'Christ, Emma, I can't believe you were so unhappy. How come I didn't know? What kind of an insensitive brute have I been? I'm really sorry if I was too caught up in my own career to notice that something was troubling you. But I don't understand where all this is coming from,' he continued. 'You've been wonderfully clever in making such a great success of raising Libby and Charlie. They're a credit to you, so don't dare put yourself down or feel left behind. You're still young. There's a whole new future out there for you. Maybe you feel a little at a loose end right now, but this time and space is giving you a chance to see what you'd really like to do with the rest of your life. And whatever you choose, you know I'll be behind you all the way. Know, too, that the kids and I love you.'

Oliver lifted her chin and kissed her. She kissed him back, savouring the moment of closeness.

'We're just in time for the sunset,' he said, 'and I want you to promise me something. See that sun slipping below the horizon? I want you to pack up your tightrope, your doubts and your worries. I want you to promise me that when the last of the sun disappears from view, it will take all your baggage with it. Every last scrap.'

By now the sun was a perfect red ball poised just above the orange-streaked horizon. It started to glide down, staining the sky and the lake water with yet more colour. They waited on the foreshore until the brilliant disc was but a tiny crescent. One minute it was still there, clinging like a gleaming jewel to the edge of the evening sky, then it was gone.

Oliver smiled and led Emma back up the path. She looked back, just once, but already the sky was darkening to purple. It was funny, she thought sadly, the way she could view her whole life with perfect clarity and see what was important and what was just window-dressing now that she had almost thrown it all away.

But only almost, she reminded herself. Surely if Karl had intended to do any mischief, he would have come after her by now. Surely the worst was over.

Chapter 36

*T*uesday night was cool in Paris, with a fine misty rain. Alix's heart was thumping as her long legs swung elegantly out of the taxi. She stepped onto the pavement and drew herself up to her full height. She paused for a few moments and took slow breaths of the damp air. She was wearing her red Versace velvet jacket over slim-fitting jeans and Louboutin heels, quite oblivious to the fact that she was standing in the path of pedestrians who had to skirt around her. She had never felt so nervous in her whole life.

Well, she had, of course, and not once but twice. The first time was when she knew that her father was telling her something utterly terrible about her mother going to live in Heaven instead of coming home; and the second . . . Alix straightened her shoulders and reminded herself that she had no one but herself to blame for that.

She'd got through those times and she'd get through this now, she decided as she lifted her chin and stepped into the foyer of the hotel where Tom was waiting. She was doing the right thing, even if it caused her endless anxiety – she couldn't leave the discovery of her relationship with Laurent to chance. She'd already more than enough on her conscience.

She went through to the bar and when she saw him seated at the counter, looking moody in a biker jacket with a glass of beer in front of him, Alix felt a moment of sheer gratitude that he had bothered to reply to the email she'd sent to his website address. He sensed her approach and turned, the spark in his eye swiftly replaced with caution as she drew near.

'Alix.' His greeting was coldly formal. No polite air-kisses. Not even a handshake.

'Tom. Thanks for coming.'

'Can I get you a drink?'

Alix rummaged in her bag, her fingers chasing a suddenly elusive purse. 'No. I'll get this, thanks,' she said, conscious that nerves made her voice sounded stilted.

'Don't be so snooty.' He was brusque. 'Just tell me what you're having.' He ordered a martini for her and was silent until the barman placed her drink on the counter. Then he picked up her glass with his own. 'Let's sit somewhere more comfortable,' he said, and went over to a table for two.

'So, Alix, to what do I owe the honour?' he asked. He was older, any boyishness gone for ever.

'A drink for old times' sake?' she hazarded. She took a sip to ease her constricted throat. Dammit, he was still as sexy as hell with his blue eyes and tight haircut. But, then, she'd never thought otherwise.

'Old times' sake? Yeah, right.' His eyes were unforgiving as they examined her face. Her stomach contracted. 'In that case we should be drinking vinegar,' he remarked laconically.

'I wasn't sure if you'd be still in Paris,' Alix said, twisting the strap of her Chloé bag where it rested on her lap.

'I'll be here for another six weeks or so,' he told her. 'I have a couple of projects on.'

'And after that?'

'Who knows?'

'Tom, isn't what you do a bit, well, dangerous?' Her question was involuntary. She could have bitten her tongue.

He shrugged, his quicksilver eyes laughing as they met hers. 'Of course. That's part of the charm.'

'Don't you worry about your safety?'

'Why should I? There's no point in worrying. It's a waste of energy. Besides, I don't have anybody waiting for me at home.'

'What about . . .' She paused.

He held her eyes.

She looked away. 'Don't you have a partner, girlfriend, whatever?'

He sank almost half of his beer before answering. 'Are you referring to Melissa? She's a good friend. But no, Alix, I don't have any permanent ties. I'm free to do just as I like, when I like. And I know you didn't ask me to meet you to lecture me on the finer points of keeping my precious hide safe from a stray bullet or two. Never mind the machetes.' She knew he had registered the shock in her eyes. 'So, curiosity's killing me. Why did you email me?' The look he gave her was anything but friendly. Once again she was reminded that she was dealing with a fearless, uncompromising man, not the hurt twenty-two-year-old she'd left sitting in a café in St Stephen's Green. She recalled the ruthless way she'd left his beautiful ring on the plastic table and shivered.

He tilted his head. 'Unless, dare I say, you've finally decided to enlighten me as to why you thought it best to drop me without a proper explanation and really fuck me up in the process?'

She shook her head, felt tears snag at the back of her eyes and a wave of regret rise in her chest. 'Tom. Please. It was years ago and

I didn't mean it to happen the way it did. I don't think I really knew what I was doing. I was young and foolish and impetuous. And selfish. I wasn't thinking of you, just of myself.'

He looked at her shrewdly. 'In a way you did me a favour, because it toughened me up big time. But you still haven't explained why you threw back my ring and left me high and dry.'

'I felt – I felt smothered,' she said. It wasn't even half the truth and she tried to look convincing. 'I wanted to spread my wings.' She was grasping at words and warming to her theme. 'I needed to feel free and unfettered. And when I had the chance to go to London, I jumped at it.'

'I was stupid enough to think we were going to feel free together. Free as birds as we travelled the world. I burned all my photos of you, you know. Had great fun making a bonfire one night.' He stared into space for a long moment, then seemed to pull himself together as though he regretted the confidence. 'But, hey, it was cathartic and I've moved on since then. I got me a helluva life. You didn't get very far, though, did you?' He gave her an ironic glance. 'London and Paris. Just a hop and a skip away.'

She shrugged. 'Yeah, well, it's my line of work.'

'Thought you might have broken out and ventured as far as Tokyo, New York or LA.'

'I do travel now and again, mainly to London, Milan and Rome, but I love living in Paris.'

He had declared a temporary truce and was willing to talk without any further recriminations. For that she was grateful. It was stressful enough to be sitting beside him without trying to direct the conversation to the topic she had to discuss. And that was without acknowledging the familiar chords he was striking in her heart, or giving space to the memories that threatened to overwhelm her.

Tom ordered another beer and a martini for Alix, which she insisted on paying for.

'So, you love living in Paris,' he said when the fresh drinks arrived.

'I do. It suits me here,' she told him, deciding not to reveal that it had a cast a spell around her, much as he had long ago.

'Yes, it appears to meet all your needs,' he said meaningfully, giving her the opening she was looking for.

'Look, there's something I have to know . . .'

'So now we're getting to it. The reason you wanted to see me.'

'Yes, and I really appreciate that you took the time out . . .'

He gave her a steely look. 'I must be the greatest sucker going, huh? You weren't interested in seeing me or talking to me at all, were you?'

She was silent in the face of his anger.

'You're wondering how much do I know about your . . . ah . . . private life. Isn't that it? Jeez, I should have guessed you didn't want to see me to express concern for my welfare. Or even to have a drink for old times' sake. But, then, I've always been brainless and stupid where you're concerned. I even went down the route of fashion photography in case it managed to bring me into some kind of contact with you.'

'Tom!' He hadn't lost any of his disarming honesty, she noted.

'Only the first time I ran into you I was so angry I had to walk away. After that, it didn't take me long to figure out you were avoiding me.' He gave a short laugh. 'Anyway, as I said, you did me a big favour. And now,' he threw her a lopsided grin, 'you want me to do you a favour . . .'

'Look, I thought I was being careful – obviously I slipped up somewhere. I'm concerned about what you know – and who else might be privy . . .?'

'But not the least bit concerned about what I might think?'

Alix spread her hands in surrender. 'That, too, in a way.'

'Huh! Why?'

'Look, it doesn't matter.' She closed her eyes briefly, then opened them again to give him an imploring glance. 'I've tried to keep my – my private life strictly that. I can't afford any word to leak out.'

'Why not?'

'I'm not able to explain.'

'That doesn't give me much reason to reveal my sources.'

'Tom. It's complicated.'

'Then give me one reason,' he snapped, 'one good reason, why I should grant your wish?'

She took a deep breath, cast around for words, and then said, 'There are innocent children involved. I don't want them to get hurt.'

'Christ! I don't believe you. You've been having an affair with a married man and now you're using kids to twist my arm. Give me a break.'

'It's the truth. That's why I'm concerned about being exposed.'

'I can't believe you've suddenly developed a conscience.'

'I know what it's like to be betrayed by a parent. I don't want to be responsible for inflicting that harm on someone else.'

'Ah, you know how to manipulate, bringing that into the equation. I wondered how long it would take you to fall back on your old childhood nemesis. Something else that should have been water under the bridge a long time ago.'

Alix was helpless. How could it be water under the bridge when her own dark conscience was living with a constant reminder?

'Tell me this,' he said, and once more she was treated to his implacable stare. 'Why didn't you think about these innocent children before now? Surely it's a bit late in the day to be having a crisis of morality.'

'I know.' She was subdued. 'I was too wrapped up in myself and what I was getting out of it.'

'Which was?' He arched an eyebrow.

'What you normally get out of an affair,' she said, with a catch in her voice. 'I don't have to spell it out, surely. Or are you looking for an intimate confession?' Even though her heart was thumping she forced her eyes to meet his and he was the first to look away. 'So are you going to tell me?' she asked.

He grinned. 'I'd love to keep you guessing, get some of my own back on you.'

'Tom!'

'Relax. I don't know anything much beyond the fact you've been seeing a married man for the past couple of years. I don't know who he is, where he lives, how often you meet up . . .'

She was slightly relieved. 'How did you find out? I need to make sure it's not going to become common knowledge and nobody goes digging to dish out the dirt.'

'They won't find out from me. I couldn't care less what you get up to in your leisure time. Or who you screw. I've forgotten already. As for who told me, it was Marc.'

'Marc?'

'Yeah. He phoned me the day after the exhibition to say how much he'd enjoyed it. I asked him if you two were an item.'

'Why?'

'I was going to warn him off, why else?'

She shook her head.

'See, Alix, I was curious to know if my ex-fiancée was still going around collecting engagement rings and breaking hearts. But he told me he was in love with someone called Sophie, and when I pressed him about you, he gave me a heads-up and said it was a well-kept secret among your friends that you had a part-time lover somewhere in the background and he trusted me to keep that information to myself.'

'And that's all.'

'Yes, that's it. I guessed the married bit. It was worth it to see the look on your face.'

'You bastard.'

He grinned. 'I still can't understand why you settled for something like that. I never would have thought you'd accept second best.'

That's because I don't deserve anything more, Alix thought.

'I'm not going to lose any sleep over it,' Tom went on. 'And your innocent children are safe. For now at any rate. So, I guess you've got what you came for. And I won't be divulging any of our secrets. You can toddle on home and relax. Okay?'

Relax? She could hardly stand up, her legs were so shaky. Her fingers were trembling as they reached ineffectually for her bag. In the end Tom came to her rescue by lifting it up and handing it to her. 'Are you all right? Can I see you into a taxi?' he asked.

'No, I'm fine,' she lied. 'I'm going to the ladies' room first anyhow.'

'Right so, I'll see you around some time,' he said breezily, uncoiling his long, lean body and rising to his feet.

'See you, Tom, and thanks.' She hurried away, concentrating on putting one foot in front of the other and making her escape before he could see the sheen in her eyes.

Once she reached the cubicle and shut the door behind her, she stuffed a ball of tissue against her mouth and let the tears flow. Tears for herself and for Tom; for the young man whose heart she'd broken and for herself – she had done what she'd thought was for the best, but that decision was now causing her huge waves of regret and remorse. After a while she stopped crying, blew her nose, cleaned her face and repaired as much of her make-up as she could. When she had fixed the worst of the damage she went outside to the mirror and finished the job, glossing her lips and running her fingers through her hair, spraying her favourite Dior scent.

Then she threw back her shoulders, lifted her head high and marched though the hotel foyer to the pavement outside.

And Tom detached himself from the granite pillar flanking the hotel entrance where he'd been waiting.

Waiting for her.

Chapter 37

'Tom? What's this?' Alix halted.

Hands in his pockets, he gave her a slightly bashful grin. 'I just wanted to make sure you were okay. Old habits, I suppose. I'd a feeling you were a bit fragile.'

'Fragile? Me? Never!' Alix swept away into the throng of pedestrians, horrified that her eyes were once more filling. She kept up a steady pace, her long legs sidestepping pedestrians on the busy boulevard, all the time trying to remain ahead of Tom. He caught up with her at the junction, standing beside her shoulder to shoulder, throwing her amused glances as the traffic roared past and they waited for the lights to turn green.

'So you don't want to talk to me now that you've got your wish?'

She glared at him through the tears. 'You were the one who told me to toddle on home.'

'Alix! You're upset.'

The lights blinked green, the pedestrians surged forward and Alix grimly looked straight ahead as she crossed the road, trying to contain the tears that threatened to pour down her cheeks. At the other side of the intersection, Tom gently took her arm and turned her to face him, heedless of the crowds swirling round them. 'Hey, what's up?' With infinite care, he reached out a finger and touched the crystalline tear that had run down her face and was now trembling at the corner of her mouth.

Alix froze.

Something flashed across Tom's face, lighting up his eyes. Then, as if recalling where he was and who he was with, he stepped back and threw out his arms in capitulation. 'Sorry, I didn't mean to invade your space.'

Alix shook her head and the moment passed. 'It's okay. And I'm fine, really.'

Traffic surged around the corner, car horns honked, motorbikes roared. Alix started to move away.

'Are you rushing anywhere?' he asked.

She looked at him, a tiny bubble of excitement caught in her throat, but her head reminded her that, for the sake of her guilty conscience, she was better off getting as far away from Tom as was humanly possible. But looking at him now, his quirky smile, she was already lost, all resolution dissolved.

'Why?' she asked, thinking how inane the word was, considering the wealth of possible answers.

'Are you hungry?'

'So-so.'

'I just thought you might like a bite to eat – strictly for old times' sake. And this wasn't planned, Alix, so I don't know where we'd even get a table for two in Paris at this hour, but I . . . Hell!' He grinned mischievously and her heart did a double flip. 'I thought it was worth a try. I just fancy taking you somewhere for a meal. Off the record, so to speak.'

'I dunno.' She was playing for time, feeling mesmerised as well as suffused with bittersweet memories.

'Come on, let's just surrender to the moment and go eat. Let's park all our collective baggage for now and call a temporary truce. There'll be no talk of recriminations or regrets from me, not tonight, and you have my solemn promise on that.'

This was all wrong. She'd asked Tom to meet her that evening for the sole purpose of finding out exactly how much he or anybody else might know about her private life. The anonymity of a hotel bar had been ideal. She hadn't expected to prolong the evening by joining him for a meal, much less be sitting here now across the table from him in the intimate surroundings of a small exclusive Montparnasse restaurant. The intimate surroundings in which his proximity was dissolving her defences. In which heat shimmied up and down her skin every time his eyes came to rest on hers. In which she felt tongue-tied and vulnerable when he laughed and displayed tender tiny lines at the sides of his eyes. She felt like reaching out and touching them with the tips of her fingers.

He'd removed his leather jacket and was wearing a soft Calvin Klein shirt. He discussed the menu and the wine list with her, seemingly unperturbed that she was quiet and subdued as her eyes took in the hard strength of his tanned forearms, the neat dusting of dark blond hair.

'So tell me,' he said when their orders had been taken, 'you've been living here quite a while. What do you love about Paris?'

She steeled herself to give him a friendly, superficial smile. It was on the tip of her tongue to prattle on about shopping and haute couture, the glitz and glamour of her job. But something in the way his eyes held hers and searched for an honest response caused her to reach deep inside herself for a more considered answer.

'I think the city is beautiful,' she began haltingly, trying to make him understand how she felt. 'I love the way the light shines across the elegance of the buildings, the roofs of St Germain from my apartment window, and the sight of Paris from the top of the Eiffel Tower. I love Saturday evenings in the Louvre after most of the tourists have gone, Sunday mornings in the Jardin du Luxembourg, winter or summer. It's all so peaceful and calm. Even Place de la Concorde is full of a magical kind of peace despite its history . . . and it makes me feel as though I'm part of that serenity.' She stopped, slightly shocked at her revelation but unable to continue breathing because Tom was looking at her in much the same way that he'd looked at her when they were sixteen. He stared at her for a long moment before dropping his eyes and fidgeting with his cutlery. She was grateful for the interruption when their wine arrived and their starters were served.

'You surprise me,' he said after the waiter had left them in peace.

'Do I? Why?' She concentrated on stirring her pea soup.

'I thought you'd be telling me about the razzle-dazzle night life and the alluring fashion shows and, of course, your glamorous job.'

'My job's not all that glamorous.' She was relieved to move on, to chatter about other things besides her feelings,

'It has to be,' Tom said, picking up his fork and attacking his tiger prawns. 'Bringing out the inner goddess in everyone? It has to hold an element of fascination.'

'It's also long hours on your feet, waiting to apply the right brushstroke at the crucial moment, if you're on a shoot. Or spending all day tripping over everyone and vying for space behind the frenzied scenes at a fashion show.'

'Hmm. I suppose that's why you need a measure of peace and calm.'

She watched the way his fingers broke some crusty bread and felt far from calm. 'And I don't have such a scintillating night life.'

'Really?'

Once again, she wanted him to understand – she couldn't fathom why. 'I meet up with some friends and other ex-pats and

246

we go for meals. That's how I'm friendly with Marc, and Sophie's a friend too. There are always invites to parties and promos, and I attend them occasionally, but I'm not usually out painting the town red. What about you, Tom? What attracts you to the dangers of your job? Some kind of death wish?'

'On the contrary,' he said. He seemed to be putting his thoughts in order as though he, too, was looking for a real answer and not a textbook explanation to fob her off. Then he asked, 'Have you ever, in your life, been in any kind of mortal danger?'

Alix shook her head. Danger, yes, she acknowledged, but not of a mortal nature, although it had seemed at times that her heart would break and she'd never survive it.

'You see, I have been. But because of that, my job makes me feel very much alive. You've no idea how extraordinary it is to see people like you and me living on the very cusp of life and death, how humbling to witness displays of basic dignity and daily bravery. There's an awesome beauty to be found in the middle of conflict, in the courage and heroism of ordinary people, and it's important to search for it, seek it out and show it to the world. And it's compelling to find yourself part of history in the making.'

'Yes, I can accept that and your exhibition blew me away. I found it very moving and profound.'

'Really?' He looked pleased.

'Yeah.' She mentioned her favourite pictures, the ones she had found most powerful, and Tom elaborated on a few, putting names to faces, bringing his subjects alive for her. Their plates were cleared away and the main course arrived, duck confit for Tom, red mullet and sea bass in saffron cream for Alix. She felt a little nugget of pleasure when he ordered another bottle of wine.

'How about the situations you find yourself in?' Alix pressed. 'Aren't you frightened some of the time?'

'I'm not reckless, if that's what you mean,' Tom said. 'I cleared out of Iraq before it got too dangerous. Apart from the safety aspect, you have to develop a certain amount of mental resilience – spending any length of time in a conflict situation where innocent adults and children are killed or maimed by cluster bombs and bullets can take a huge emotional toll.'

This time Alix was silent because the images he was conveying were simply too difficult for her to formulate a response.

'Here,' he filled her glass, 'drink that up and eat your fish. I didn't bring you out to frighten you or put you off your food. The only person you're depriving is yourself if you waste that excellent meal. Anyway, I'm taking a break from conflict photojournalism for the moment. I feel a bit burned out, a little fatigued, so I'm recharging the batteries.'

'Do you think you'll ever give it up and settle for something less dangerous?'

'I don't know,' he replied honestly. 'I can't answer that question right now. Maybe if I had family, dependants . . . who knows? But that's enough about me. Tell me how come you managed to rise to the top in such a cut-throat profession? I always knew you had a rather grim determination and that nothing would stand in your way – and I'd never question your talent – but how did you break and conquer Paris?'

'I'm sure you'll find the details of my job extremely superficial compared to yours,' she said.

'Not so. The more I move around, the more I see there's room for everybody in this world. Where would we be without the wheels of commerce? The dream of beauty?'

She relaxed a little and told him about her progression from those first days when she worked in a busy salon and lived in the cramped *atelier*. Before she knew it, they had drained the second bottle of wine and the night was drawing to a close.

'Well, thank you,' Tom said after he had settled the bill and they had gathered their jackets. 'It was nice to be able to put the past to one side and have a proper conversation.'

'Yes, it was.'

Outside the night air was chilly. They strolled to the intersection, where it was easier to hail a cab. 'Mind you,' Tom laughed, 'there's still a part of me that hasn't forgiven you.'

Alix paused. 'I guess I deserve that.'

'It would take a while to repair all the damage,' he said lightly. His eyes searched her face and she felt suddenly shy. 'Do you know what might help?'

'What?'

'This.'

Before she realised what he was up to, Tom had enveloped her in a hug. He held her close for several moments, and she absorbed the sound of his breathing and the hardness of his arms around her. Then, on the Paris street, he laced his fingers in her hair and kissed her. At first Alix resisted, but as his mouth moved slowly against hers, tracing the outline of her lips, dropping little kisses at the corners, she ignored the alarm bells shrieking in her head and gave herself up to the magic, to the taste of him, and the hunger of his mouth as he deepened the kiss until he was crushing his lips to hers.

'Wow,' he said, after they came up for air. 'You're still one hell of a kisser.'

Alix's head was swimming and her mouth on fire. Mostly she was furious with herself for allowing Tom to kiss her. Correction, she silently chided. Furious with herself for her reaction. It was impossible to talk. She stepped away from him, almost tripping over herself in the process. Her eyes darted across the surging traffic, searching for a cab, intent on getting away. She raised her hand and one slewed to a halt in front of her.

Tom escorted her across the pavement and gallantly opened the passenger door. 'In you get, and thanks for a lovely evening,' he said.

Alix clambered in on shaky legs.

'He's a lucky man, whoever he is,' Tom said.

'He's not so lucky any more,' Alix snapped as he went to close the door.

'Sorry?'

She stared at him for a moment and shut the door. Then, suddenly reckless, she zapped down the window. 'Yeah, didn't I say? We've split.' And she had the immense satisfaction of seeing surprise flash across Tom's face as the cab pulled away from the kerb.

It was a satisfaction that lasted until she reached her apartment and wondered what exactly she'd done.

Chapter 38

*K*arl ordered wine and a bottle of still water. 'So, how's your mum?' he asked.

'She's fine,' Libby said, trying to decide between lasagne and a carbonara dish, wondering which would be the easiest to eat while she chatted to Karl. 'She's seems to be enjoying life so far.' She studied her menu again, wondering if stringy cheese made less of a mess than the pasta – she didn't wanting to get traces of food on her chin in front of him..

'Really? That's good. You must tell her I was asking for her,' he said.

She looked up and caught him smiling. For a sour, funny moment it seemed to Libby a lecherous smile. But that must be her, and the fact that she was most definitely out of her depth with him. 'Yeah, sure, and I'll tell her that Marshalls seems to be doing quite well without her,' Libby tossed in. 'Though on second thoughts, maybe not. That might make it sound as though she was dispensable.'

'Your mother was anything but dispensable.' Karl smiled – again it seemed a peculiar smile. 'We were all very sorry when she left so unexpectedly.'

It was a week since she'd seen him. He'd explained that he was going home to Kerry for a long weekend when he'd kissed her goodbye outside the noisy Temple Bar restaurant. Another chaste kiss that had left her feeling vaguely uneasy as well as wondering where she had fallen short. She'd gone out with Karen and Mandy over the weekend, and had read at least three glossy magazines, scouring them for sex tips and articles on how to seduce your man. Then earlier today he'd texted her and arranged to meet.

The waiter appeared with the bottle of red wine and a litre of water and filled their glasses. It was another cheap and cheerful city-centre restaurant, though not as noisy as last week's had been. Tonight, despite the advice Libby had gleaned from her magazines, she felt uncomfortable when Karl's eyes zoomed in on her cleavage of Wonderbra-supported breasts. She had a funny feeling he was doing it out of habit and not because he was interested in her.

It was her. It had to be her. She was too inexperienced to relate to him properly on a sexual level. She might be almost twenty-two, but convent school, then three years of college and the relative shelter of her involvement with Rob hadn't exactly prepared her to play the sexy-temptress game that Karl surely expected.

'Did your mum ever tell you why she left?' Karl asked. 'We were all taken by surprise.'

Libby shrugged. 'I think she'd just had enough. She's enjoying being a lady of leisure right now. She had a great weekend in Mayo at a glam wedding with my father.'

'Very nice. I'm glad for her. Does she know that you and I . . .?' Karl asked, lifting his glass and touching it to Libby's.

Libby shook her head. 'Not yet. I want to keep you to myself for a while.'

He laughed. 'Keep me to yourself? Now that sounds interesting.'

Her face pinked. Maybe he had picked up a different meaning from the one she'd intended. 'I don't tell her everything that's going on in my life.'

'Or do you think she might not be too happy that you and I are—'

'Are what?' she asked, seizing on the opening and trying to give him a sultry look.

'Friends?' he suggested, quirking an eyebrow.

She felt a moment's disappointment and tried to hide this by sipping her water. 'It's actually none of her business,' she said loftily.

He laughed. 'I forgot. You're an adult. Of course it's none of her business.'

He'd forgotten she was an adult? What the hell did that mean?

Holding her eyes, Karl reached across the table, lifted her hand and slowly raised it to his lips. Then he put it down, picked up the menu and signalled to the waiter once more. 'You ready to order?'

At the last minute Libby opted for a pizza, and as the night went on, she decided that she had made a dreadful mistake in assuming that Karl was the excitement she'd craved to fill a gap in her life. Her evening with him was full of underlying tension and she was unable to relax. She'd thought he was sexy, but it was all on the surface. And she realised that sexiness had more to do with how you related to someone, how they communicated with you and made you feel inside, not staring at your cleavage or throwing you pseudo-meaningful glances. She'd nothing in common with him, no talking points, didn't connect with him on any level whatsoever and it was difficult to keep up a conversation. By the time she was halfway through her pizza she'd exhausted everything there was to talk about – her job, her family, the holidays she'd enjoyed, music she listened to. And it wasn't even an age thing. It was just that Karl wasn't really listening to her. Oh, he smiled and laughed and asked her questions, but all the time his mind was elsewhere. It was impossible to draw him out. It was almost as though he was being deliberately secretive.

'How long did you say you've worked in Marshalls?' she asked, conscious that she'd asked him on the first night they'd chatted. What had happened to the light-hearted, flirty chat? Where was the buzz she'd felt as his eyes had met hers? Was it her fault that it had fizzled away?

'I suppose about four months now.'

'Do you think you'll stay on there?'

'I'll have to, if I want to be approved for a mortgage. It's not too bad, I suppose. Although I miss your mum – she was great to work for.'

'I'm sure she was. It's good that you're buying your own place,' Libby went on, changing the subject. She didn't like the way he kept bringing her mother into the conversation. It was almost like being on a date with her in tow. And she sensed intuitively that Emma wouldn't approve of Karl. Neither would she approve of Libby's seductress ideas. Her dad, she knew, would thoroughly dislike him on sight.

'I hope it'll work out. I need lots of money.'

She found she wasn't happy with the way he was looking at her, as though she was going to provide him with it. Surely not. Libby pulled herself together and told herself that her imagination was running riot. Just as she had given up on having any decent conversation, Karl opened up a little.

'I was supposed to be buying an apartment with my girlfriend,' he went on, much to her surprise. 'We both came to Dublin to work and save money. She had a very good job. But those plans have been scuppered.'

'Oh. How come?'

He shrugged. 'She lost her job and she's no longer my girlfriend.'

'I see.'

'How could you? I bet you've never cheated on a boyfriend, the way she cheated on me. She slept with the boss. That's how she lost her job. Have you ever cheated?'

All of a sudden she didn't like the way the conversation was going. 'No, Karl,' she said airily. 'Never.'

'And how about your parents? Have they cheated on each other?'

'My *parents*? Of course not.' Libby couldn't wipe the shock off her face.

'So your father has never cheated on your mother? Nor she on him? They must be quite perfect.'

Libby was dumbfounded. This was crazy. How dare he? *She* was crazy to be sitting here, putting up with this crap talk. She also felt hugely uncomfortable when she thought of her eye-popping cleavage and had an urge to cover herself up. 'I think you're being far too personal,' she said huffily, and realised how ridiculous that was when she'd secretly been considering going to bed with Karl. How personal was that?

'Sorry, Libby, have I upset you?'

Yes, you wanker, she almost said. She tried to stay calm. 'I'm sorry if your girlfriend has hurt you, but I don't think my parents' relationship is any of your business,' she said witheringly. 'And thanks for everything, but you and I are going no further and it's best if I leave. Immediately,' she continued, even though they were only halfway through their meal.

'Ah, Libby, stay and have your dinner. Please. I'm sorry for saying the wrong thing.'

'So am I,' she sniffed indignantly. 'But I'd prefer to leave now. There's no point in wasting your time or mine.'

He regarded her silently as she rose to her feet, picked up her bag and shrugged into her jacket. She had the feeling that he was looking at her as a cat might a cornered mouse. And she still felt his eyes on her as she stuck her chin into the air and wove her way through the tables to the door.

It had been a dreadful, humiliating mistake, Libby told herself as she reached the pavement. She breathed in lungfuls of fresh air and congratulated herself on her timely escape.

'Libby! Is anything the matter?'

Emma's heart squeezed as her daughter marched through the hall door on impossibly high heels, her face like thunder and her fingers clutching her jacket tightly over her semi-naked bosom. Once again she'd felt apprehensive as she'd watched a provocatively dressed Libby leave the house earlier that evening. Once again Oliver was away, this time in Galway, and not due back until Friday. As soon as she heard Libby's key scrape in the lock, far earlier than she'd expected, Emma came out into the hall but nothing had prepared her for the sight of a clearly outraged Libby stalking through the door.

'It's okay, Mum, don't fuss. I'm perfectly fine.' Libby pulled off her heels and made to dash up the stairs.

Emma stalled her, putting her hand on her arm. 'It's not fine and you're far from okay. What happened?'

Libby gave her a rueful smile. 'Oh, Mum, I suppose you could say I bit off more than I could chew. But I've learned my lesson.'

'Are you hurt?'

'Nah, I'm okay. Let's just say I made a mistake and I had a disaster of a night. Well,' she qualified, 'it didn't turn out the way I expected.'

'So long as you're not hurt.'

'Only a bruised ego. And before you ask, absolutely nothing happened. Not even a goodnight kiss. I wouldn't have wanted to kiss him goodnight anyway. Not after what he said, the creepy bastard!'

'Libby!'

'Well, he was! I suppose you might as well know . . .' Libby's voice trailed away.

'Know what?'

'You might get to hear of it through Stacy and Nikola.'

The fearful apprehension that had followed Emma around for weeks solidified as she felt a tightness in her scalp and heard a roaring in her ears.

'I was out with that guy Karl,' Libby was saying.

The words pounded and receded in Emma's head. 'Did you say Karl?' she said faintly.

'Yeah. Never again. You really escaped him when you left Marshalls. If you ask me he should be going around with a health warning across his chest. He might be terribly sexy and have something significant dangling between his thighs, but there's absolutely nothing between his ears. I left him sitting there halfway through my pizza because I couldn't bear to listen to any more of his silly rubbish.'

'What was he saying?'

'I'm too angry to talk about it.'

'Tell me, Libby.'

Libby sighed in exasperation. 'His girlfriend cheated on him. So he said. He told me they were supposed to be saving up for an apartment together, but they've split. Then he started asking me questions about you and Dad – had Dad ever cheated on you. The nerve of him, talking about my parents like that . . .' Libby stomped up the stairs in her bare feet. 'How dare he? As if Dad – never mind you . . .'

Emma clutched the banister for support, but nothing could prevent her from falling into the pitch-black abyss.

Chapter 39

She could keep pretending it had never happened. She could blink, once, twice, and try to make it go away – much like her father used to suggest long ago when she was afraid of things that went bump in the night. She could act as if this was a normal Friday evening, when Oliver has just returned from Galway, and because the evening is unexpectedly warm they have decided to sit in the back garden. Now she has just come into the kitchen to fetch a bottle of their favourite Chianti.

She could keep pretending it had never happened but she is only fooling herself with her terrible deception, quite apart from Oliver, Libby and Charlie.

On the outside everything seems fine. Her face looks much the same, the shadows under her soft blue eyes as carefully concealed as the dangerous knowledge spinning in her head. Her sleek dark hair is caught back in a silver clip and she is wearing her favourite DKNY jeans with a crisp white shirt. Thanks to the blazing row she had with Leticia that morning, every surface in her stylish kitchen is gleaming, from the acres of granite worktop to the raft of high-end appliances to the limestone floor. Evening sunlight slants through the French windows, sending glittering prisms dancing through the crystal sun-catcher. They sparkle like colourful spangles.

'It'll bring you good luck,' the shopkeeper had said as she pressed the tissue-wrapped crystal into her hand on that sun-kissed holiday in Sicily when all was perfect. Only she hadn't quite grasped at the time how utterly perfect it was.

Or just how ridiculously easily it could all go so horribly wrong.

She feels her breath rising in her body and lodging in her constricted throat. Somewhere deep inside her, the throb of sheer undiluted panic pulses in time to her fluttering heartbeat. As she looks around the kitchen, memories crowd and she tries to capture them in her soul, but they flit like ephemeral ghosts – memories of all the precious times, the good times, Christmas and birthday mornings, the time Libby tore into the room brandishing the flimsy scrap of paper with her brilliant results, Charlie's set face as he ate his breakfast the morning of his first big exam and, most cherished of all, the ordinary times . . . Libby's furrowed brow as she irons her shirt for work, Oliver hunting for his car keys with the toast between his even white teeth, Charlie trailing football-pitch mud across the floor . . .

Enough.

Upstairs and out of sight in the spare bedroom, her case is packed, ready for a swift departure. Her flight details – single ticket, one way – are folded into her passport, which is safely in her bag. Outside, in the garden drenched with mellow evening light and resonating with birdsong, Oliver is waiting. No doubt he is wondering what has happened to the wine Emma has offered to fetch. Yet she lingers in the quiet of the kitchen, holding tightly to one last moment of his blissful ignorance before she speaks the unutterable, remembering life as it had been, just one more moment, then another, unwilling to go back out into the calm evening and voice the words that will shatter his heart and bring everything crashing down about them.

More than anything in the world, and like a tide of humanity before her in other times and places, she wishes she could put the clock back, spare the pain. But it is already far too late. And impossible for her to pretend any longer.

As Emma steps through the door, the crystal sun-catcher tinkling cheerfully against the glass and shooting dizzying shards of light across the polished floor, Oliver slowly looks up and she watches him become terribly still as he sees her deception written all over her face.

Afterwards Emma couldn't bear to remember the precise moment when she called Oliver into the kitchen and shattered his life. Or the look in his eyes as she stumbled over her halting explanations and flimsy excuses. Shock, incredulity, helpless distress formed a mask on his features and he cut her short. He strode out of the kitchen and into the study, slamming the door in her face and turning the key in the lock.

She tried to talk through the wood, her breath heaving painfully as she attempted to articulate how sorry she was, how stupid she'd been. She stopped short at telling Oliver how much she loved him, knowing it would sound trite and meaningless in almost the same breath as her confession.

'I'm going to Paris in the morning,' she called through the door, wrapping her arms around her trembling body as she stood there. 'I'll get out of your way for a few days. I'll tell the kids I'm going to Alix for a short while until we know . . . Oliver – God – I'm really sorry . . . I can't believe how silly I was . . . the ridiculous mistake I made . . . It was so incredibly stupid . . .' Her voice, high-pitched with emotion, echoed thinly in the marble hall.

From the other side of the door there was silence. Nothing but a heavy, impenetrable silence.

She drifted around the house for the rest of the evening, glad that Libby and Charlie were both out. Later, she lay down on the spare bed, unable to sleep, hearing them returning home in the small hours and going straight to their rooms, unaware that their mother was in the spare bedroom and their father still locked in his study. As soon as she touched down in Paris she'd text them to let them know where she was, making it seem as though nothing unusual had happened beyond her last-minute decision to grab a cheap flight to visit Alix.

In time they were bound to discover that their mother had betrayed them, but that was for another day . . .

Chapter 40

'So, are we officially over, then? We're not just pretending it's a temporary split?' Libby grabbed her courage in both hands and came right out with it instead of pussyfooting around. 'I know you're very busy with college and work, so with me off your agenda you'll have a clearer mind. I won't be annoying you to come out and party.'

'You never annoyed me,' he said, 'but I wasn't sure where we were headed either.'

It was Saturday evening and Libby was sitting curled up on the armchair in Rob's bedroom, having called around to return some of his books and CDs and collect the last of her clothes. She found that it was good to have a decent talk with him, to put a proper closure on things, unlike the shabby and dismissive way she'd initially broken up with him, which had left a very sour taste in her mouth. Thankfully, she'd got the whole embarrassing episode with Karl out of her system too. She was so glad that they had never gone beyond a few kisses, and already she felt she'd picked herself up and moved on. With Karl off the radar, it had felt cleansing to chat honestly to

Rob about her feelings and admit that she thought she was too young to be tied down to her first ever relationship.

'I think it's better to have a clean break,' Rob agreed. 'That way you won't be looking over your shoulder if you want to date somebody else. And at least we both know exactly where we stand. I'll be going to Germany shortly on a study trip and it'll leave me free to do whatever I want as well as concentrate properly on my thesis.'

Looking at his sensitive face, Libby felt a little sad. He'd been her first real boyfriend, her first lover, but she'd outgrown him during the past few months. And she hadn't really loved him, not in the true, passionate sense of the word. In a way she'd fallen in love with the idea of Rob because he'd ticked all the right boxes.

'Germany is a good opportunity,' he went on. 'It's a chance to see a bit of life and have a change of scene. When I thought about what you'd said I saw you were right, Libby. We were tying each other down. I'm still very fond of you, and that will never change, but I'm looking forward to seeing something of the world, and being free and easy for a while.'

'Go for it, Rob,' she replied. 'It sounds exciting and it'll be a whole world removed from Dublin. Keep in touch and I might catch you for a drink before you go, to give you a decent send-off and to wish you the best of luck.'

She felt a little sad that they'd reached the end of the line. Rob was clever and talented, he'd go far in his career, and with a caring nature, he wouldn't be short of girlfriends. But he wasn't for her, Libby reflected, surprised to find herself feeling at a loss. On the one hand, while she'd enjoyed making love to him, and found him good fun and a great mate, she'd taken him a little for granted and secretly yearned for more excitement. Chances were she'd never find someone quite as genuine and caring as he was. They'd shared those unique college years and he'd always been there for her during stressful exam times and student fun. She felt a few tears sliding down her cheek and dashed them away with the back of her hand. Rob, too, seemed a little sad.

'Oh, Rob, what are we like?' She grinned. 'One day when you're a famous web designer you'll look back and laugh at all this.'

'And when you've turned over your first million, I hope you'll have fond memories of your old boyfriend.'

'I don't know when that's likely to happen.'

'Why the uncertainty? You'll go far, Libby, I know you will.'

It had been liberating to speak honestly to Rob about her feelings. So she was just taking that a little further when she said, 'I'm not so sure it's what I really want to do with the rest of my life. The kind of work I'm doing at the moment, I mean. I'm finding it a bit boring and suffocating.' She'd never spoken to him of it before, any more than she'd admitted to her dad that her life was in the wrong groove. Whatever about her father, surely it was something so fundamental that she should have been able to talk it through with Rob. It had been easier to pretend to share the same ambitions as him, and remain in a certain comfort zone, rather than have the guts to admit that her dreams were so different to his. Further proof, if any were needed, that he wasn't the right man for her. Now she had voiced her worst fears and the sky hadn't fallen in. Rob didn't look shocked or appalled. Instead he merely shrugged.

'Whatever you choose to do, I'm sure you'll be a hundred and ten per cent successful.'

'Really?' she asked, seeking reassurance.

'I've no doubt about it. You have a can-do attitude, a quick, determined mind and a kind of inner motivation. That's more important than anything else.'

They chatted for a while, both unwilling to say the final goodbye. In the end she gathered up her stuff, and Rob kissed her at the hall door, wishing her the best of luck and saying he'd keep in touch.

She walked home from Rob's house, feeling a sense of freedom. He'd offered her a lift but she'd refused, preferring to stretch her legs and enjoy the fresh air and bright, lengthening evening. It was calm and sunny, and it reflected how she felt inside: calm, now that she'd had a heart-to-heart with Rob and sorted things out between them so that they had parted as friends, and sunny, a new optimism that the rest of her life was starting now. For once, she wasn't tearing into town on a Saturday night. She was in such an upbeat, positive frame of mind that she was tempted to have a word with her father, maybe tell him straight that she wasn't entirely happy with her job and see where it led. Her honesty with Rob had shown her it was the best way to go.

But when she arrived home something shrouded Libby's positive frame of mind and quelled her newfound resolve to talk to her father: something was wrong at home – or, more precisely, something was wrong between her parents.

She'd never known Mum to go tearing off at such short notice before. Trips to Alix, away from the bosom of her husband and children, were usually premeditated and meticulously planned weeks in advance. They involved trolley loads of shopping deliveries, a freezer jammed with meals and a long list of instructions. Libby hadn't thought too much about it until she arrived home and read another bland text from her mum, then saw her dad's face as he emerged from his study. Her heart skipped a beat and she knew that anything she wanted to say to him would have to be put aside for now.

Her dad needed a shave and his eyes were red-rimmed as though he had been crying. She'd never seen him look so devastated except when his parents had died. He made some coffee and slunk back into his study, like a wounded bear seeking refuge in his cave. And Charlie was no help.

'What's going on?' she asked him later that evening.

'What do you mean?'

'Hello! Mum's gone to Paris in a hurry and Dad's in bits and hiding out in his study.'

'Is he?'

'God, you're useless. Or else you're just too wrapped up in your sex life to see what's going on under your nose,' Libby fumed.

'What sex life?' Charlie practically snarled.

'So it's all off with Melanie?'

'It was never on with Melanie. She's gross – get it?' He stormed out of the kitchen, leaving Libby staring at the space where he'd been standing.

Libby went up to her room and began to tidy her clothes, her mind churning. On impulse she lifted her black velvet Dolce & Gabbana dress out of the wardrobe where it was carefully stowed and tried it on again. She stared at her reflection. The dress made her feel really special: it promised parties and fun times, yet it was cute and classy. She couldn't wait for the night of the glitzy launch. Her mother had planned to go over a couple of days in advance to meet up with Aunt Hannah, while she and Dad were flying out early on the morning of the launch. Then they were all staying overnight in the Henri XII hotel off the Champs-Élysées.

Which made it all the more unusual for Mum to make a quick visit now, Libby thought. She looked at her anxious face in the mirror and told herself to calm down.

Sunday was as bad, with her father staring at her as if she had two heads when she asked him about dinner, nabbing him as he came into the kitchen to make fresh coffee.

'Isn't there anything in the freezer?' he'd said abstractedly.

'Not much, just some pizzas.'

'Fine. I'm not hungry so you and Charlie can have them. I'll grab something later on.'

Whatever had happened – Libby's thoughts whirled – her

mother was trying to play it down by sending silly texts from Paris. And she'd never known Dad to spend most of the weekend immured in his study. On the few times he came out, he looked as though the roof had fallen in. All the way into work on Monday morning, he didn't utter a syllable, not even enquiring about the stock market latest. Libby eventually gave up trying to make conversation, and she knew from his face not to ask what was going on.

By Monday evening there was still no word from Mum as to when she might come home. Another bad omen. Whenever she'd visited Alix before, she had always, but always, made a big deal of ensuring that everyone knew her return flight details, usually going so far as to clip them with a magnet to the front of the fridge. The best place to put them, she'd joked, for it was the one place where everyone was sure to see them. Libby was tempted to pick up the phone and ring Alix – maybe she knew what was going on – but her courage failed her. It was all making her feel incredibly nervous. More nervous, even, than when she sat in front of her computer in the mornings, half afraid to switch it on.

Chapter 41

*A*lix put down her lip brush, stood back and examined Anika's face from every angle.

The Dutch model had sat patiently throughout the trial run while she had worked with her brushes and sponges, creating an image that would do justice to the glittering launch of Alix B. Now she appraised the dewy translucent glow of Anika's skin, where she'd brought out a subtle natural blush, the wash of soft peachy glow and frosty shimmer on her eyelids and the dramatic way that she'd swept out the shading to meet the exaggerated wing at the socket lines.

Alix had already created a look for the advertising and promotional material that would be released prior to the launch, but the effect she was creating for the launch night was slightly different from that required for the glare of bright studio lights and the wide-angle camera lens.

'That's quite perfect,' Henri said. 'Very striking, yet not over the top. We want a look that every woman can identify with and feel is within her grasp.'

'Have you settled on the gown?' Alix asked as she began to pack away her brushes.

'We've narrowed it down to the white Chanel column or the ivory crêpe.'

'The ivory crêpe would be a softer foil for Anika's skin tone.'

'We've just over two weeks to go. It's all very exciting. Have you chosen what you will wear?'

'I've something in mind,' Alix said, knowing she sounded a bit flat. Part of her wanted to pull the plug on the whole project, to forget about Alix B and the launch night.

She was glad when the session was over, relieved to be out in the fresh air of a sunny midday Tuesday in Paris. Instead of hailing a cab to bring her straight back to the apartment and Emma, she began to walk, turning down by the Seine and following the curve of the river back up towards Île de la Cité. Normally she enjoyed a browse among the riverbank stalls, but today its chic Bohemian feel passed over her head. She crossed over the Pont Michel and headed towards Notre Dame.

She sat on a bench in the small peaceful square behind the great medieval cathedral: its silhouette dominated the skyline, impenetrable, secure, unmoving; idly, she watched the tourists swarm around the building, cameras at the ready, and heard streams of conversations in foreign languages. She sat for a while, feeling the warmth on her face, relieved to have some time on her own, some time to get her head around all that had happened in the last few days.

Meeting Tom had been the height of stupidity. And her last throwaway remark – what had possessed her? As if the bad fairy hadn't done enough damage to her life.

Tom had phoned her on Saturday and she'd almost jumped out of her skin. She'd forgotten she'd given him her mobile number when she'd asked to meet him – she'd fully expected he wouldn't want anything further to do with her.

'I enjoyed talking to you,' he'd said, surprising her with his warm tone and making her feel gratified in spite of everything. 'It was good to suspend hostilities long enough to have a catch-up and a laugh. Hey, Alix, who would have thought it? I was just phoning in case there was any chance we might meet up again, just casual, for a meal and a chat, while I'm in Paris.'

She'd closed her eyes when she heard his familiar voice. Her heart had lurched at his suggestion. 'I don't think that's a good idea,' she'd told him, her fingers clenched around her mobile.

'That's a pity.' He'd sounded disappointed, and she'd almost relented. There was a silence between them.

In a rush to fill the vacuum, she'd said, 'In any case, I have Emma visiting me this weekend. She's arriving later today and I'm not sure how long she's staying.'

'So why don't we all go out for a meal together? It would be nice to say hello to Emma.'

'No, Tom, I'd rather not,' she'd said sharply. Tom and Emma together was something to be avoided at all costs. Emma was bound to be hostile towards him – she held him responsible for their break-up. God knew what she might say.

'Okay, so.' He'd sounded dissatisfied. 'Guess I might see you around some time.'

'Yep, sure.'

She should never have seen Tom last week, Alix fretted. Being with him again had resurrected memories that were best forgotten. Then, in the middle of all this, Emma had arrived in Paris.

Alix had thought that her sister was merely indulging in a last-minute break until she'd opened the door to her early on Saturday afternoon and seen her white, haunted face. Alix had been genuinely shocked to hear her shattering news. One part of her felt extremely sorry for her sister – you couldn't look at Emma's face without your heart going out to her. And the awful thing about it was that it wasn't only Emma who was hurting but Oliver as well – and as soon as they found out the truth, if they found out, Libby and Charlie would be too. Another part of her felt angry with her sister for throwing it all away so carelessly. But she couldn't talk, Alix grimly reminded herself, rising to her feet and sending some pigeons wheeling into the air.

When she got back to her apartment, Emma was holding a magazine in front of her but Alix knew full well that her sister wasn't attempting to read it. She still looked ghastly. She'd admitted to Alix that so far she'd been unable to cry. Alix hadn't revealed that she knew exactly how that felt.

'Still feel like going out tonight?' she asked Emma, summoning a bright voice. Fiona had invited them for dinner as soon as she'd heard Emma was over and Alix had jumped at the chance of distraction.

Emma put down her magazine. 'Yes, it'll be nice to see Dave and Fiona again. But I packed in such a hurry that I'm not sure if I brought enough glam clothes. Do they know about me?'

'Not much. I told Fiona you'd had a bit of a row with Oliver and you're staying with me for a few days, just so they won't be asking you about him. And I'll find you something glam to wear.'

'Thanks, Alix, you're too good to me. When is Fiona's baby due?'

'The middle of September.' Alix went into the kitchen to put on the kettle. Fiona's pregnancy, on top of her secure and happy marriage, was something else she had to face. If she was to be any kind of support to her friend over the coming months she had to square up to it and make her peace. And then look happy when the baby arrived. She dropped sachets of white tea into two mugs and poured in boiling water. After a minute she scooped out the sachets and brought the mugs to the low table in front of Emma.

'Sip this, it'll do you good. Then tonight put on the glitz and I'll do your make-up,' Alix offered. 'You must have been going through torture these last few weeks. It'll be no harm to have a different focus for a few hours.'

'You're right.' Emma smiled wanly. 'And thanks for having me over like this.'

'Don't be ridiculous.' Alix touched her arm comfortingly. 'Have you heard from anyone yet?'

'I had texts from Libby and Charlie. They think I'm just over here on a spur-of-the-moment visit. I'm not expecting to hear from Oliver.'

'So you don't think he'll tell them what's happened?'

'Not for the moment. He's still in shock. And the last thing he'd do is upset the kids. It's mad.' Emma laughed mirthlessly. 'I feel as though I'm discussing a torrid soap opera instead of my marriage.'

'And, dare I ask, what about Karl?'

'What about him?'

'Do you think he'll pursue Libby any further? Does Oliver know he was seeing her?'

'Good grief, no. I couldn't bring myself to tell him and I didn't want to drag Libby into it. Besides, I didn't get as far as naming Karl to Oliver. He thinks I confessed because I was feeling guilty. Libby told me she wants nothing more to do with Karl and you know Libby – once she makes up her mind about something, that's it. Just as well, otherwise I would've had to tell her what happened. He was only using her to get to me, and he can't very well spill the beans to her because then he'd have nothing to threaten me with. Maybe I should have paid him off in the first place.'

'No way, Emma. You'd never have known when he'd come looking for more. I'm glad you felt you could turn to me. You need to give yourself and Oliver some space. And I agree with you – he'll scarcely tell Libby and Charlie just yet. Karl sounds like a nasty piece of work. If you don't mind me saying, you must have been really pissed to go to bed with him.'

'I was.' Emma winced and drew a ragged breath. 'Although he's not bad or evil. He's quite confident and very sure of himself and I think he just found himself in a certain situation that started as a prank and somehow got out of hand. Unfortunately when he did hook up with Libby, I couldn't live with it any more and the threat was always there that he might just . . .' Her voice faltered.

Alix sighed. 'Do you think you might have stayed quiet about it otherwise?'

'That was the idea. I was hoping to live with it and put all my energy into our marriage. I know I sound like perfidy incarnate but I was desperate. I didn't see the point in tearing our lives apart on account of a once-off reckless mistake. And I owe Oliver so much.' Her voice choked.

'Oliver owes you just as much. Don't lose sight of the fact that you're the one who's held your family together and supported him all these years. He must have been neglecting you at some level. Otherwise you would never have been unfaithful.' Alix fell silent. Then she said, staring into her mug, 'And I suppose we're all entitled to a crazy, reckless mistake. You don't have the monopoly on that.'

'You mean you and Laurent?'

'Of course.'

'Are you sad that you've broken up?'

'Not really. I called a halt because there was a chance we were going to be found out,' Alix said. 'And Laurent ran as fast as he could. But you don't want to hear all this now. I'm not letting myself dump on you.'

'I want to hear it. Don't worry about dumping on me – that's what I'm here for. Are you missing Laurent?'

'No, we were never emotionally involved. I had a wake-up call when I thought about his kids, who might be hurt.'

'But surely you knew that when you took him on?'

'Not really. At the time I was just thinking in terms of my own needs and wants. I was more concerned with the fact that I didn't want emotional ties, and that I'd no kids of my own to hurt . . . you know . . .'

'Like Mum?' Emma prompted. 'Is that what you're getting at?'

'Yes. You see,' Alix gulped, 'I've always been conscious that I'm so like her it's not funny. Look, forget what I said. Anyway, this is a mad conversation to be having.'

'Hang on, darling – you've hardly let that define your life? A resemblance to our mother?'

'How would you feel if you'd grown up being constantly compared to her,' Alix said defensively, feeling a chasm opening between them, 'and found to be almost identical in looks and temperament? Wouldn't that leave its mark?'

'Hey – God, you shouldn't feel like that. If anything I'm the one who's fallen off the rails and followed in her footsteps.'

'Look, sis, you can't let this break the two of you up for good,' Alix said, relieved to focus on Emma. 'Right now Oliver needs time to lick his wounds, but eventually you pair will have to sit down and talk it through. I presume you still love Oliver?'

Emma's blue eyes were pained. 'I do. More than I ever realised. After I was . . . unfaithful, I saw my whole life with him in a completely different light – the small things, the silly incidentals, all the stuff I'd taken for granted. Only problem was, I was appreciating all those precious things a little too late.'

'Those times are still precious. All those silly yet important things haven't gone away. Don't let a moment of madness wreck the rest of your life,' Alix urged.

She'd had her moment of madness, she reflected. She knew how it tasted years later when the guilt and remorse continued to eat away at her. How, though, could she impress on Emma the importance of doing her utmost to sort out her marital problems before the bitterness set in? There was one way. She could tell her sister the truth about her break-up with Tom. She could tell her how hopeless she'd felt, about the stupid, reckless thing she'd done when she'd felt vulnerable and low, and how it haunted her in the small hours, and even more so on bright sunshiny days. She didn't want Emma to embark on that kind of stark, lonely road without trying everything in her power to heal herself and Oliver and make some kind of peace with what had happened. Alix felt a dizziness in her head and a numbness in her face, and although her mind was swirling, her mouth felt frozen, and she sat quietly for a few moments until the sensations passed.

Later she worked her magic on Emma's peaky features, making her pallid skin look soft and warm, drawing out the colour in her eyes with a smoky wash and outlining her lips in a natural pink. She was glad to sense her sister relaxing a little in front of the mirror.

'Mmm, your fingers are very soft and soothing,' Emma said. 'I could sit here all evening. I should get my make-up done more often. How exactly did you get rid of those circles under my eyes?'

'Trade secret,' Alix joked. 'Let's find you something sexy to wear now.' She gave her sister a loan of her slinky DKNY top, and a generous splash of Dior's J'adore and together they got a cab to Fiona and Dave's. 'They moved last year,' she told Emma as they sped across the city. 'Their new apartment is something else – the last word in luxury. You'll enjoy having a poke around.'

But the last thing Alix expected as Fiona ushered them along the hall to the large, welcoming kitchen with the beautiful solid oak table was to see Tom rising to his feet.

Chapter 42

𝓕iona, in a softly draped pale green kaftan that complemented her red hair, was talking brightly. 'Even though it's Tuesday night and some of us have work tomorrow, we thought we'd get the gang together . . .'

Somehow, above the noisy hammering of her heart, Alix caught the gist of her words as Dave took her jacket. Out of the corner of her eye, she could see Marc sitting in conversation with Sophie. Yvette was there also, setting the table with glasses and cutlery.

'Sophie and Yvette are just back from Rome, and Marc asked if it was okay for Tom to join us, so I said the more the merrier . . .' Fiona chatted on, completely oblivious to the fact that Alix was feeling sick. 'Hi, Emma, good to see you, you're very welcome. Do you know Tom? He started out in fashion photography but then he abandoned the world of high glamour. Now he's rather gainfully employed elsewhere . . .' Fiona pulled out chairs, waved her hand encouragingly, 'Sit down, everyone, and remember, I'm still feeling a little fragile so it's all very casual . . .'

Alix was sorely tempted to grab the jacket that Dave was bearing off to the cloakroom and get the hell out of there. She was vaguely aware of Emma's shock, but her sister masked it as Tom shook hands with them as though he was meeting them for the first time.

At all costs, Alix calculated frantically, she must keep Tom and Emma apart. Hopefully neither would make any reference to their shared past while they were in company. Emma was far too gracious to voice any animosity while they were guests in someone else's home. It would be up to Alix, though, to deflect the conversation away from anything remotely sensitive.

Dave poured wine and Yvette helped Fiona serve plates of *boeuf bourguignon* and salad. There were assorted breads and jugs of olive oil, bowls of plump vine tomatoes, cheese platters, rice and pasta.

'Come on, everyone, don't be shy – help yourselves,' Fiona urged.

Alix made sure she was sitting at the opposite end of the table to Tom, with her sister beside her. Under the general buzz of conversation Emma whispered, 'What the hell is he doing here?'

'I'll talk to you later,' Alix said to her out of the corner of her mouth.

'I hope he's not trying to smarm his way back into your life,' her sister muttered.

Alix frowned and shook her head. Emma threw her a pointed look. As laughter and camaraderie flowed around the table, Alix found herself trying not to stare at Tom too much, but it was impossible not to notice him, the attractive gleam of his eyes, the sound of his laughter and the sight of his hands reaching for bread, some salad and tomatoes, or filling glasses from the carafe of wine.

'Did you guys fit much shopping in?' Fiona asked Yvette and Sophie.

'No, we were so busy we didn't even get near the via Condotti,' Yvette pouted.

'I find that hard to believe,' Dave joked. 'When Fiona goes to

Rome she needs to bring a spare case for the Italian leather bags she loves to amass.'

'The next time you visit Rome,' Sophie said, 'you'll need a spare case for the baby Prada.'

Fiona laughed at her husband's face. 'Don't look so worried, Dave. Not even I could be that extravagant. Though maybe,' she grinned, 'some pretty booties and a cardi or two . . .'

When the meal was over Alix hoped to make her getaway, but Fiona took Emma's arm and announced that as she was the only mother present, she was going to commandeer her to enjoy some baby talk. She slid back the glass doors that led to the huge balcony, which wrapped around two sides of the apartment and offered stupendous views of the Parisian evening landscape. The rest of the friends gravitated outside and, once again, Alix made sure she was sitting as far from Tom as possible, although that was difficult as he got up and moved around the perimeter of the balcony, gazing out into the indigo evening and spotting various landmarks. In another life, at another time, she would have loved to join him there, elbow to elbow, staring at the violet inkiness and the twinkling lights, which sparkled as though some unseen hand had strewn a scatter of diamonds across the evening haze.

Yvette joined her to chat about the Rome shoot, the fabulous clothes and the stressed-out stylist, but Alix was only half listening as a large part of her mind was focused on the guy leaning on the balcony rail and wondering how soon she could leave. Then, as if she was observing it all from a distance, she heard Emma excuse herself and saw her heading for the bathroom. She was still in there when the wine ran out. Dave was sitting back, gently massaging Fiona's tummy, so Tom told him to stay put and offered to fetch another bottle.

With Yvette still regaling her with anecdotes about the latest catwalk stunt, Alix had no opportunity to stop him by offering to replenish the wine herself. He was already going into the brightly lit kitchen and, through the glass doors, she saw him walking across to the small lobby area that housed the bathroom and the utility room.

Just as the bathroom door opened.

This was all so crazy, Emma fretted, throwing a final anxious glance at her reflection in the mirror as she opened the door. She was glammed up, wearing the beautiful silvery top that Alix had insisted she borrow, but behind it all, she was still caught in a black nightmare, scarcely able to believe that a few short nights ago she had demolished Oliver's trust in her and swept his life from under him. And Libby and Charlie were still oblivious to it all. A wave of panic gripped her. She swallowed hard and tried to compose herself, opened the door and came face to face with Tom.

'Emma!' he said. 'How are you? I haven't had a chance to talk to you yet.'

Panic gave way to a blast of fury. 'Talk to me?' she fumed. 'I don't have anything to say to you. We might be out in company having polite conversation, but I took you off my guest list the day you broke Alix's heart.'

He halted, his eyes narrowing. 'I don't think I heard you correctly,' he said.

Emma gave a sarcastic laugh. 'I've never forgotten Alix's face the day she told me you'd dumped her.'

Now he looked perplexed. 'I dumped her? That's news to me,' he said in a silky tone that didn't disguise the hard edge to his voice. 'Just to correct your misconception, Alix was the one who broke up our engagement all those years ago before she hightailed it to London in search of her dreams. And you might find this surprising, but I haven't forgotten it at all. Because I was the one who was made a right fool of.' He nodded curtly at her as he went into the utility room.

Alix was well rid of him, Emma thought. How dare he make himself out to be the innocent one? She walked across the kitchen and stepped out onto the balcony. Although Alix appeared to be talking to Yvette, Emma knew she had been watching for her return, for her sister's eyes gave her away and she threw Emma a panic-stricken glance. She must be concerned that Tom might have upset her in her present low frame of mind, Emma guessed. It was quite a change to have Alix worrying about her. So she smiled and shrugged to reassure her sister that all was well.

The rest of the evening passed in a blur. She chatted to Fiona about her pregnancy. She saw Dave's hand move now and then to brush tenderly across Fiona's tummy – Oliver had done that when she'd been expecting Libby and Charlie. She felt like telling Fiona never to take that love for granted but to cherish every moment of their lives together.

Tom had stopped prowling around and had flung himself into a lounger, from where he observed everyone. Now and again Emma saw his eyes seek out Alix and there was something in the long, hard looks he was throwing in her sister's direction that made her uneasy. Alix, however, didn't seem to notice. She was caught up in conversation with Yvette and Sophie, looking chic and elegant, throwing her head back with a light, graceful laugh from time to time. Emma felt relieved when Tom excused himself rather abruptly, saying he'd an early start in the morning. He kissed Fiona, waggled his hands at the rest of the group and departed.

Later, when they were back in Alix's apartment, Emma was glad to kick off her heels and relax into the sofa. The evening of putting on a good face for Alix's friends had taken its toll and now she felt emotionally drained. Alix was looking at her speculatively and Emma had the instinctive feeling that her sister was keyed up about something.

'What was that all about with Tom?' Alix asked, her light green eyes guarded.

'All what?'

'What was he saying to you?'

'Nothing much. Just some bullshit about you and him. What's he doing with himself anyway? How come he's still in Paris, hanging around with your friends?'

'He knows Marc, and he's here for a few weeks on some photographic project.'

'The sooner he's gone, the better. He's the last person you need prowling around. If we hadn't been in Fiona's apartment I would have given him a piece of my mind.'

'Why? What exactly did he say?'

'What's got into you?' Emma was decidedly uneasy. This wasn't Alix's style. Her beautiful sister seemed painfully fragile. 'God, Alix, you scarcely want to resurrect ancient hurts.'

'I'd like to know what he said to you.'

'I'd rather not talk about it. It was only silly crap that you might find upsetting.'

Alix was silent. Emma watched a range of expressions flit across her sister's face and she was filled with apprehension. Alix eventually said, in a voice husky with emotion, 'Just tell me, sis, please. What did he say?'

'This is really getting to you, isn't it? I'm sorry to be the one to tell you, but if you insist on knowing, Tom is going around with the ridiculous idea that you were the cause of the bust-up between you.'

'How do you know?'

'I told him I'd crossed him off my guest list years ago on account of him breaking your heart – as you do, when someone tramples all over your sister's feelings. He said it was news to him. Alix, he'd the cheek to say that you'd actually dumped him, and that he hadn't forgotten it at all. I don't know how he managed to turn it around so blatantly and make himself out to be the innocent one. How low can you go? He's a right . . .' Emma's voice faltered – Alix looked as if she was about to collapse.

'Oh, God.' Alix closed her eyes, her long dark lashes fluttering and sweeping across her pale cheeks.

Her head dropped into her hands and Emma, by now thoroughly alarmed, swiftly put down her glass and crossed the floor to her sister. She caressed her shoulders, feeling them tremble beneath her hands. 'What is it? You're making me very nervous. It was only Tom, trying to upset you in a backhanded way. He's probably jealous of the great success you've made of your life without him, jealous of your friends and your lifestyle.'

Alix was still shaking and incapable of speech. Her breathing was erratic and it was obvious to Emma that she was deeply upset. 'Calm down,' she said. 'Take a few deep breaths. You shouldn't let Tom upset you so much. If I'd known he was going to have this effect on you I'd have brought you straight home the minute I saw him sitting in Fiona's kitchen.'

Alix still seemed to be in the grip of a painful emotion. She clutched her tummy as though she was in agony. Eventually she raised her face and her eyelids fluttered open. Her light green eyes were translucent with unshed tears and full of anguish.

'Darling, it's okay,' Emma soothed. 'Stop fretting. Just one word to your friends will make sure that you're never thrown together with Tom like that again. I'm sure they'll understand.'

'It's – it's not that.' Alix's voice was choked. She drew a shaky breath. Emma had to lean in closer to hear exactly what she was saying. But she could hardly make sense of it – the words seemed unbelievable.

'Are you telling me that Tom was right?' Emma, shocked, asked. 'That you were the one who called it all off?'

Alix hung her head.

'Is this true? Then why?'

'You assumed,' Alix said, 'that Tom had dumped me, the day I called to your house.'

'Yes, of course I did. You were inconsolable, if I remember rightly.'

Alix shook her head from side to side.

'So it wasn't Tom, it was you,' Emma prompted. 'But why? Was he two-timing you?'

Tears splashed down Alix's cheeks. 'He wasn't unfaithful. Oh, Emma, I can't pretend any more. *I* ended it. It was me. I handed back his ring and I'll never forget the look on his face . . .'

'But why, darling? Although I'm sure you must have had a very good reason . . .'

'Oh, I'm sure I had.' Alix's voice was muffled with tears. She reached for her bag and rummaged in vain for a tissue. Then she gave her sister a tormented look. 'The way I broke us up was unforgivable. So I guess I'm a far worse sinner than you are.'

'Tell me, please. Whatever you did, of course it's forgivable.'

'Want to bet?' Alix lifted her chin and Emma's heart turned over at the expression in her sister's green eyes. Sorrow, regret, pain – it was all there and it plunged Emma back to when a young and vulnerable Alix couldn't understand why her mother wasn't coming home. She caught her sister's hand and held it tightly. 'Don't be afraid. Just tell me what happened.' Even as she said the words, Emma had a flash of understanding. She put a hand to her mouth. 'Oh, God Almighty – had it anything to do with our mother?'

Alix's mouth trembled and she seemed to be trying to control it until it all became too much. Then she threw herself into Emma's arms and collapsed, weeping her heart out.

Chapter 43

'So now you know the whole sorry episode,' Alix's voice wobbled as she drew to a close. She'd sat talking to Emma for what seemed like hours, slow and hesitant at first, then the words tumbling out as she went over the events of fifteen years ago, stopping occasionally to mop fresh tears, refill their glasses and allow Emma to hug her.

'Years ago, I was able to cope much better,' Alix confessed. 'Especially when I came to Paris. London was closing in on me and when I arrived here it was as though I'd left the whole craziness of it behind. I learned to ignore the regrets that woke me up at four in the morning, but lately they've been getting worse and I know they'll torment me for ever.'

'You poor darling, you should have told me the truth years ago,' Emma said, her face full of compassion.

'Sometimes I wonder if it really happened – could I have been so heartless? But I kept some reminders that I just can't bring myself to ditch. Hang on a minute . . .' Alix went into her bedroom and opened her wardrobe door. From underneath cartons of make-up and boxes of shoes, she pulled out a battered green suitcase. She brought it out to Emma, threw back the lid and riffled through the topmost contents of newspaper clippings and letters. Then she found what she was looking for and passed a yellowing piece of paper to her sister with a trembling hand. 'There. That's all I need to refresh my memory.'

'Oh, Alix.'

Alix shook her head. 'I don't deserve your sympathy, no way. Not after what I did to Tom.'

'You should never have kept it to yourself.'

'Actually,' Alix paused, 'I'm kind of glad you know.'

'I'm glad also,' Emma said. 'But I'm really sorry if I landed you in it with Tom. He'll probably come knocking on your door, looking for some kind of explanation as to why I have a different version of events.'

'Right now I don't care about that. I'll fob him off with some kind of excuse, tell him it was a mix-up that I never bothered to put right. That you misunderstood the situation and I left it like that rather than talk about it. Or else . . .' Alix hesitated, 'I could confess and tell him the truth. Maybe he deserves to know. At the back of my mind I sometimes wondered if I should have trusted myself and told him how I felt at the time. If. What if. If only. Sometimes I think it's the most useless and potent word ever.' She sighed. 'It seemed like a signpost when Marc asked me to go to the exhibition. I thought that if I saw Tom again, and got an idea of where he was in his life, I might have some idea of what to do – maybe face my dragon, ask for forgiveness, who knows? But when I did lay eyes on him, up close, the shock of being so near him after all these years, as well as the knowledge of the heartless way I broke us up, punched me in the stomach so hard that I just wanted to run away.' Emma gave her another hug.

Alix drew her knees up to her chin, wrapped her arms around

them and curled herself into a ball. 'But the prospect of telling Tom why I broke off the engagement scares the hell out of me,' she admitted. 'I know he'll be absolutely mad that I didn't trust him at the time.'

'God, Alix.' Emma's face was wreathed with sympathy. 'It's all just too bad. I wish there was something I could do.'

'You've helped by listening to me. You've no idea how much better I feel for getting that off my chest. Anyway, that's enough about me. I'm not going to solve anything tonight. I've kept us up talking and it's already long past your bedtime. As for you, Emma, you should go home to Oliver and start to mend some fences. Believe me, it'll only get more difficult the longer you leave it.'

Emma smiled weakly. 'It's amazing how easy it is to mess it all up. In a way I still can't believe it so I know exactly how you feel. It's like a nightmare that I'm hoping to wake up from.'

'Tell me about it,' Alix said ruefully. 'Just don't let it fester for too long between you. I don't want you looking back full of regrets or if-onlys in ten years' time. When you go home to Oliver, show him how penitent you are. He's still bound to be upset, but staying here isn't going to help matters.'

'I suppose you're right.'

'I *am* right.' Alix summoned a smile.

Emma said, 'I can't tell you how much I admire your determination to put the best side out. When I think of the way I envied you your glittering life, never knowing how churned up you were behind the scenes . . .'

Alix gave her a rueful glance. 'I know. Just goes to show you never can tell. I didn't know what was going on recently in your life, either. But don't forget one thing. You've spent years devoting yourself to Oliver, Libby and Charlie. Surely that has to count for something.'

'I can't bear to think of Libby and Charlie right now.'

'They're great kids,' Alix insisted. 'You should be very proud of them. If they find out what happened they'll be upset, but I'm sure they'll eventually understand and support you both. I can't see Libby and Charlie turning their backs on you after everything you've done for them. You're not infallible, and one fall from grace shouldn't mean the end of your life as you know it.'

Emma smiled a tired smile. 'And can I tell you something, darling sister? I'm so glad you said that because the very same applies to you. One stupid mistake shouldn't darken the rest of your life.'

Alix thought she had cried everything out. Now she felt the sting of tears once more. 'Oh dear, what are we like? Although I still think that what I did was unforgivable.'

'Well, I don't,' Emma said staunchly. 'You were young and vulnerable and, above all, you did what you thought was the right thing at the time. I wish I could make it all better for you.'

'If you want to make anything better for me you'll go home and start talking to Oliver. Anyway, I'll be mad busy for the next few days. I have fashion shoots tomorrow and Friday, and I'm busy most of next week also. Then the following week Hannah will be arriving, and the launch will be on top of me. I'm dying to see Hannah but, God, Emma, I really don't know if I can face this launch.'

'Of course you can.' Emma smiled encouragingly. 'I'm looking forward to your glittery night, and so is Libby. She has the most fabulous dress and she's been looking forward to it so much – it's the highlight of her year. I can't see Oliver coming, in the circumstances, but hopefully nothing will happen to stop Libby. What are you wearing? Do you know who'll be there?'

Alix was glad to change the subject. By now she felt emotionally exhausted. It was half past two by the time she hugged Emma goodnight, took a pint of water into her room, shoved her old case beneath the bed and snuggled under the duvet.

When she awoke the following morning, it took her a while to remember where she was. She'd been dreaming of London and the tiny Islington bedsit she'd rented during her first few months there, the images so vivid and real that she could hear the slight rattle of the window-frame as the traffic trundled by and smell the scent of the fresh herbs and vegetables drifting up from the outdoor displays of the greengrocery shop on the ground floor, all overlaid with the sharp absence of Tom.

Now she lay back in her bed and stretched, the remnants of sleep fading and her mind moving forward to the present, bringing a surge of recollection from the night before. Tom. The heart-stopping sight, through the glass doors of Fiona's apartment, of Emma coming out of the bathroom and halting him in his tracks. Then the calculating glances he had thrown in her direction while she pretended to be absorbed in conversation with Yvette. He had appeared to be relaxed on the patio chair, a glass of wine in his hand, but she had known otherwise. She had sensed the thrumming of his nervous energy and it had chimed a warning bell in her mind: he was like a coiled spring inside, just biding his time and waiting for the right moment to pounce.

She would deal with that when the time came.

Right now she had to shower and dress and face another day, but this morning as she went into her en suite, she was conscious of a sliver of light in the dark corners of her soul. Even though her face was deathly pale, Alix saw a glimmer of peace and acceptance in her eyes.

Emma had listened empathetically while Alix poured out her heartbreak. She'd responded with compassion and understanding. She'd put her arms around her and hugged her tightly. This morning Alix felt a little stronger, as though her sister had restored some of her shattered self-approval.

For, in spite of everything, Emma still felt that Alix Berkeley was worthy of love.

Chapter 44

On Thursday morning when Oliver drove around the corner into Dawson Street, Libby's breath faltered as he almost knocked down a cyclist, veering away at the last second and narrowly avoiding a Jeep driving alongside him.

There was a volley of car horns and the cyclist's raised fist.

If her father's face had been pale before, now it was ashen. The skin was stretched tight across his cheekbones and he seemed to make a supreme effort to pull himself together long enough to get them safely to the car park. By the time they reached it, Libby could see that his hands were trembling as he fumbled with his pass, eventually managing to swipe it correctly and raise the barrier. When he had parked the car and switched off the engine, she made no move to gather her bag and umbrella and get out. Instead she turned to him, summoned her courage and asked what was wrong. 'I know there's something,' she said, braving his wrath. 'It's obvious that you and Mum had some kind of a row.'

'And what makes you think that, Libby?'

'Come on, Dad, you're very unhappy. And Mum jetted off to

Paris in a hurry without giving us any idea of when she'll be home.'

Her father sighed. 'I've no wish to discuss this now with you. I've a full day ahead of me.'

He looked weary and dispirited as they marched up the ramp and out onto the street, going across to the convenience store for their take-out coffee. Suddenly she was gripped with apprehension. 'There's nothing seriously wrong, Dad, is there?' she asked, searching his face for clues, horrified to think it might be more than just a temporary bust-up between them. She might be almost twenty-two, but in the face of her parents' totally uncharacteristic falling-out, she felt like a child, insecure and uncertain, wanting everything to be back to the ordinary, familiar way it had been just the week before.

Her father made her feel all the more uneasy when he said, 'It depends on what you mean by serious.'

Then he stalked off towards his office block, his back rigid. Libby realised then that she wouldn't particularly like to be in her mother's shoes. She walked through the foyer of her own building, trying to picture his face and his possible reaction were she to admit that she hated her job, knew she was on the wrong path in life and thoroughly regretted trying to follow in his footsteps. Her stomach knotted with fresh anxiety and she felt like weeping.

How could she take away his pride in her achievements? Or shatter his illusions?

The week had been difficult in the office, between Tanya breathing down her neck more than usual and a team of auditors who were checking and cross-checking everyone's work. Libby found she was holding her breath when they scrutinised her figures, convinced that some terrible mistake was about to leap out and show her up for the fraud that she was – the Libby Colgan who was pretending to be enthusiastic, committed and dedicated to her job

290

when all the while she felt as though she was in the wrong groove. By some miracle, all her work was passed and she couldn't help challenging Tanya's raised eyebrow of disbelief with a haughty stare.

Today a unit meeting was scheduled for ten o'clock and those meetings were the bane of Libby's life. They would be discussing their quarterly targets and everyone would have to contribute their opinion. On these occasions Libby was always very self-conscious, especially with Tanya sitting directly across from her.

Libby slipped out to the ladies' room to check her make-up, and her hands shook as she added another layer of teal eyeshadow, smudging it so much that she almost rubbed it off. She drew fresh eyeliner in a feathery stroke beneath her lower lashes and applied another coat of mascara. She took a deep breath to calm her nerves. Then she gritted her teeth as Tanya breezed in. Not even her newly acquired Guess purse could raise Libby's spirits.

'All set for the meeting?' Tanya enquired.

'Of course,' Libby said.

'I hope you have your projected targets prepared,' Tanya beamed.

'Yes. I know they're on the agenda.' Libby painted on a false smile.

'The meeting is going to be a little different today,' Tanya said loftily.

'Oh?'

'We're starting with a team-building exercise. Do you know what that involves?'

'Actually, I do.' Libby feigned indifference to cover her ignorance. Whatever it was, it was bound to be dreary and she would hate it.

Later that morning she was pleasantly surprised to find she quite enjoyed it. The conference room furniture had been moved back and everyone got involved, including the managers and the director, Stephen O'Connor, and when they split into two groups, Tanya was in the other. It was silly and fun and they had to be creative and resourceful in solving the puzzle put to them. Libby found herself on her hands and knees on the carpeted floor, alongside Stephen O'Connor, her hands working swiftly as she made silly cardboard cut-outs for her team members. The laughter that resulted was infectious. By the time they came to the solemn business of the day, she was chatty and relaxed, even with the unit managers.

The following morning, however, her dad didn't go to work. Libby had never known him to take an unscheduled day off, but there was no sign of him when she came downstairs at six forty. She presumed his alarm hadn't gone off so she went back up and knocked on his bedroom door, only to hear him say gruffly that he wasn't going into the office until later.

'Now do you believe me?' she challenged Charlie as he sauntered into the kitchen. His hair was sticking up and Libby had a funny protective feeling towards him. For all his burgeoning alpha maleness and his casual nonchalance, Charlie would take any trouble between their parents just as badly as she would. They were in this together. And she was definitely getting soft, she told herself, if she was starting to feel sisterly in her current distress.

'What's up now?' he growled.

'Dad almost knocked down a cyclist yesterday, he's not going into the office until later and Mum's still sending stupid texts. There *is* something wrong. Big time.'

Her words had finally registered. 'Huh? With Mum and Dad? But that's shite.' Charlie's face fell and she felt another wave of affection for him that she tried to squash.

'Yes, it's bollocks,' she snapped, grabbing her bag and shoving it on her shoulder. 'But what's even more shite is that I have to get the bus into work and I'm already late as it is.'

She slammed the hall door behind her. She hadn't really meant that last remark. For all her intentions to reach the office early and have some time to settle down and get her head together before everyone else arrived, thoughts of her parents' marriage being on the rocks were a million times more upsetting than scurrying into the office frazzled and late and incurring Tanya's supercilious smile. She'd seen the lives of some of her friends and acquaintances torn apart by separating parents. She'd seen the layers of unhappiness, guilt and remorse. No matter what age you were, it was always a sort of bereavement.

Then Libby's thoughts shifted gear and rearranged themselves as the bus drove into the city centre. Her parents loved each other. They were great people, honest, trustworthy and reliable. She thought of her mother's sweet smile, and the way her eyes lit up for her father. And there was no denying Oliver's steadfast pride in his wife and family. This was only temporary. Surely there was nothing so terrible either of them could have done that would prevent a reconciliation.

Chapter 45

'What do you think you're doing?'

Emma dropped her bag in alarm. It was Friday evening and she'd arrived back in Laburnum Grove hoping to have the house to herself and some time to prepare before she came face to face with Oliver. But her flight had been delayed and Oliver was already home from work. She'd taken a few steps down the hallway when he emerged from his study, looking, her heart clenched, fraught and dishevelled and as though he hadn't slept all week. He stared at her for several seconds with an expression of loathing. Then his face closed and her insides plummeted.

'Oliver! I'm home.'

'Your home?' He eyed her glacially before continuing in a monotone, 'This isn't your home. You gave up the right to call this your home when you fucked that jerk from the office.'

His words stung, his unusual coarseness telling her more than anything else how deeply distressed he was. His stiff, unyielding stance said that he was still in a sort of shocked denial and hadn't yet plumbed the depths of his anger. At all costs she had to stay calm.

If they were to find any way out of this mess, she had to keep her head and make sure she didn't antagonise him.

'I know you're feeling very angry—'

'How dare you patronise me?' he said coldly. 'How dare you stand there and make assumptions? Get out of my sight.'

'We need to talk,' she said, struggling with her emotions. He was wearing the navy jumper she'd bought him at Christmas. She seized on this as though it had some kind of significance – which, of course, it hadn't, she thought sadly.

'No, we don't,' he said, his eyes hostile. 'The only talking we'll be doing is through our respective lawyers.'

'Oliver,' she said, laying a hand on his arm.

He stepped back abruptly. 'Don't touch me,' he said. He looked so tired and his eyes were so stony that she longed to throw herself into his arms and weep for both of them. She longed to be able to say the right words, do the right things to take that look off his face. It came back to her with the force of a hammer blow that she had put it there with her behaviour. It was all her fault.

'I know what I did was terrible,' she went on, speaking quickly as though to say as much as possible before he cut her off. 'I know I don't deserve your forgiveness—'

'Whatever about forgiveness, what I can't do, ever, is forget. How dare you come back here and show your face?'

'We have to talk about this.'

'There's nothing to say. Our marriage is over and you ended it the night you let some jerk push his dick into you.'

'Oliver!' She felt faint.

His face was bleak. 'But that's exactly what you did. That's exactly what I see every time I close my eyes. My wife getting down and dirty with some arsehole, doing things . . .'

She shook her head wildly. 'It wasn't like that.'

'No?' He stared at her glassily. 'Of course it was like that. You fucked someone else. You destroyed our marriage and broke my trust.'

'I know, yes, but I want to do everything in my power to rebuild it, to rescue whatever I can of our marriage. We can't throw it all away.'

'You already have,' he said implacably. 'I can't look at you without thinking of that night. How do I know it was only the once? How do I know you weren't flirting with him in the office all along, leading him on, enticing him? For all I know you were begging to get into his trousers. You even slept with me after you were with him. How could you have violated our marriage? Actually I don't want to know. I just want you out of my sight.'

His cold, relentless words, delivered with an unforgiving face, were more difficult to deal with than a hot blast of anger. Oliver was impossible to connect with. For safety's sake, he had put himself, his pain and anguish, miles beyond her reach.

Up to now, she'd scarcely cried. A sea of tears had been building up inside her, so vast that it had been impossible for them to find an outlet. Now, as though a dam had burst, they began to pour down her face, trickling into her mouth – she tasted salt – and dropping off her chin.

'Have you . . .' she gulped, 'said anything to Charlie or Libby?'

He was unmoved by her display of emotion. 'No. But that's not because I wanted to keep the show on the road or keep them in painless oblivion,' he said, his voice pitiless. 'I'm leaving that job up to you. I want you to see their faces when you shatter their lives, just the way you've shattered mine.'

'Do we have to involve them?' Her voice was imploring. 'This is our problem, not theirs.'

'Are you joking? They're bound to wonder why their parents have split up.' He made it sound as though it was a foregone conclusion.

His hostile face swam in front of her and she dashed away more tears. 'Oliver, I beg you, not that, please. You've no idea how much I regret what happened.'

'You weren't thinking of me when you opened your legs to that jerk and begged him to fuck you,' he went on remorselessly. 'I bet you had no regrets then. I bet you were panting for it.'

She tried to control her trembling lips. She'd asked for this, she'd expected it, but somehow the reality was far more painful than she could ever have imagined. She took a deep breath and continued, her voice hoarse, 'I told you, it wasn't like that. I didn't really know what I was doing. I was totally pissed.'

He looked at her as though she repulsed him. 'And you think that excuses your behaviour or lessens the infidelity? How pathetic.'

Something flickered at the back of Emma's mind, a smidgen of memory, a fleeting impression of another hallway and whispered, urgent words exchanged; the terrifying feeling that her safe and secure world had been rocked. She shivered, and felt a rush of sadness. The past had reached out to taunt her. Once, this had been her parents. Now it was visited on her.

'Oliver, we can't let our marriage slip through our fingers. We can work through this, go for counselling . . .'

'Are you for real? Do you think for one moment that I want the ashes of this marriage raked over by an inquisitive stranger? Now you've totally lost the plot.'

'I know it's hard for you right now to consider anything like that—' She felt more tears coursing down her face and wondered would they ever end.

'You don't know anything about how I feel,' he said, his eyes Arctic. 'If you did, you wouldn't be standing there now with that pitiable look on your face.'

'I'm here because I value our marriage,' she said, trembling. 'I value what we had, and I'm going to do my utmost to redeem myself and salvage something out of this.'

'You'll be doing it on your own. I'd be happy if I never saw you again,' he said, his voice robotic. 'And I want you out of my sight and out of this house, because I can't stand to look at you.' He turned on his heel, marched into his study and locked the door.

With a heavy heart, Emma carried her bag upstairs and went down the corridor into the spare room, glancing sadly into the bedroom she'd shared with Oliver. It was agonising to see its precious familiarity and to think that one stupid night, just a short few crazy hours, was all it had taken to shatter cherished years of trust and love. Right now, she didn't know if there was any way back. She hadn't for one moment thought it would be easy. But just looking at Oliver, at the expression on his face, never mind the crude words he'd said, had brought home to her just how much she'd hurt him.

She sat on the edge of the bed and tried to control the anguish that rose inside her. Where did they go from here? Maybe Alix had thought it best for her to be at home and on hand to make an attempt at reconciliation, but it was clear that Oliver had a long way to go before he was prepared to start talking. How could she stay under the same roof as him, meeting him in the kitchen, in the living room, in the hallway, when the sight of her made him feel sick and the atmosphere between them was thick on his side with animosity? Never mind the drastic effect raised voices and slamming doors would have on Libby and Charlie.

Libby and Charlie. Her heart sank even further. She would have to tell them something. She picked up her mobile and texted them to say she was home from Paris. Libby replied to say that she'd see her the next day as she was going out that evening straight after work. Emma was still sitting on the edge of the bed when Charlie replied and said he was staying late in college and going on to a party. It was only when she looked at the time of his text that she realised a whole hour had passed without her being aware of it. She got up and walked down to the bathroom, feeling like a fugitive in her own home. She cleaned her smudged eyes and streaky face.

Afterwards, her muddled brain tried to see a way out of the mess. Supposing Oliver had cheated on her, was there any way he could redeem himself? What would she expect of him in terms of atonement? Maybe if she could figure that out, it would be a starting point. For now, surely, the best thing she could do was to give him space and time to come to terms with what had happened. She could go to a hotel for a few days and at least they wouldn't be arguing in front of Libby and Charlie. They didn't need to know anything except that their parents were going through a rough patch. She'd be back in Paris for Alix's launch before she knew it. And after that . . .

Charlie's face mirrored disbelief when she took him aside on Saturday and told him she was getting out of the house for a short while so that she and Oliver could have some time apart from each other.

'I know something's wrong and it's freaking me out,' he said. His voice was unsure and his face crestfallen.

Her heart contracted. 'Yes, I can see that it's upsetting for both you and Libby, and it's upsetting for me and Dad. We're in a situation that we don't like. We will sort it out, Charlie, so don't be worrying,' she said with far more conviction than she felt. Everybody was a loser in this situation. There were no winners here at all.

'I just hope you guys don't split up because that would be crap. I'm a bit old to be going to the zoo and McDonald's on alternate Saturdays.'

She smiled faintly. She knew that the zoo and McDonald's was the least of Charlie's worries. What he didn't want was warring parents, a house divided, remorse, recriminations and everything soured and tainted. 'We're a long way off that,' she assured him, secretly wishing that mere words would make it so.

On Saturday afternoon she spoke to Libby, hating the troubled look on her daughter's face.

'Whatever's going on between you and Dad stinks,' Libby said dejectedly. 'He's going around with a face as grey as the Arctic Ocean and you're sleeping in the guest room. I know you've had some kind of bust-up, but what good will going to a hotel do?'

'I need to get out of his hair for a while,' Emma said.

'Look, Mum,' Libby hesitated, 'I hate to see you both like this. So does Charlie. It's all very upsetting and, well, we're worried about what's going on . . .'

'I'm worried too, Libby – there's no point in pretending I'm not – but it's between your dad and me. I need to give us a little breathing space, then hopefully we'll be able to sort ourselves out.'

'And if you don't?'

'I sincerely hope that day won't come.'

'Are you going to tell me what went wrong?'

'I can't, Libby,' Emma whispered. Her daughter was silent and the look on her face clutched at Emma's heart. 'Don't forget, we have Paris coming up and that's still very much on course.'

Libby's face brightened a fraction. 'Wouldn't it be great if Dad and you made up in Paris?'

'Yes, it would,' Emma said, giving her daughter a hug and inhaling her flowery scent, knowing in her heart of hearts that there was no chance of that happening, not in her wildest dreams.

Chapter 46

Alix knew her moment of reckoning had arrived when she stepped out of a cab to find Tom leaning lazily against the railings outside her apartment on Saturday evening. He was wearing his biker jacket over a pair of jeans and he looked as though he had all the time in the world. The Paris evening was mild, the air was fresh and the blue sky dotted with cotton-wool clouds through which the sun peeped intermittently. For a moment she wanted to ask him to go for a walk with her, perhaps down by the Seine where the surface would reflect a thousand shards of glinting light and the soft breeze toss her hair.

'How did you find out where I live?' she asked, annoyed that she sounded so inane. But he'd caught her off guard and she was tired and dishevelled. She'd been up since six o'clock and had spent the day on outdoor location for a fashion shoot, which had been difficult: it had rained on and off, the model's hair had frizzed and the photographer had grown more and more impatient.

Tom fixed her with an intent yet impersonal gaze. 'I asked Marc for your address.'

Alix bristled. 'And he gave it to you just like that? I'll have to talk to him.'

'Don't blame Marc. I told him you wanted to borrow a couple of my books.'

'I don't see any books. And I didn't think Tom Cassidy did little white lies.'

'I didn't think Alix Berkeley did big black ones.' He held her eyes until she looked away.

She feigned innocence. 'Big black lies?'

'I'm sure you knew to expect me as soon as your sister kindly told me exactly what she thought of me for breaking your heart.' His voice was gritty and rang an alarm bell in her mind. Tom was angry. And, like a dog with a bone, he wouldn't let up until he was satisfied that he'd got to the bottom of whatever was bothering him.

'I didn't think you'd give a damn about ancient history. It's scarcely that important, after all.'

'Maybe not, but I don't like being painted as the villain of the piece when I'm entirely innocent. Now, you've two choices. We can have this conversation out here on the pavement or we can go somewhere more private.'

Alix's thoughts whirled. The only private place nearby happened to be her apartment. The restaurants and cafés that dotted the surrounding streets were bound to be full of Saturday-evening crowds. There was safety in numbers, though, and if things got too hot with Tom she could always make an escape. Although there was going to be no real escape from him until he was completely satisfied with her explanation.

'I suppose you'd better come on up,' she tossed out. The sooner she got this over with, the better.

He was silent as they climbed the steps and got into the lift, kept pace with her as they took the last three flights of stairs. He wasn't the slightest bit out of breath when they reached the sixth floor, she observed. Struggling with her key, she opened the door to her apartment and invited him in, leaving her wheelie-case in the hallway and shrugging off her jacket. Then she felt ridiculously shy as Tom followed her into the living room. What the hell was she doing? This was her private sanctuary. She must have been mad to invite him up here. His very presence was charging the atmosphere, disturbing the peace, his bristling energy some kind of alien force that darted around the elegant interior.

'Tea, coffee, a drink?' she asked.

'Just water, please.'

She went into the kitchen, relieved to escape his brooding presence. She clutched the edge of the worktop and slowly inhaled three long breaths in an effort to calm herself a little and ease the panic that threatened to close around her. Then she returned to the living room with two glasses of water, and handed one to him.

Tom sipped, then put his glass on the low table. 'Are you going to offer me an explanation as to why your sister has a totally different version of events from what really happened between us?'

Alix had rehearsed her lines. 'I don't know what Emma remembers. It was so long ago there's bound to be some confusion.'

'Nice one. Did you really think you could get away with that?' Uninvited, he sat down on the sofa, stretched out his legs and smiled a wintry smile. So far, he hadn't taken off his leather jacket, but he looked at ease in his surroundings and, more dangerous for Alix's peace of mind, as though he intended to sit there for however long it took.

'Hey, come on,' she coaxed, trying to turn the tremor in her voice into a half-laugh, 'it hardly matters any more.'

He fixed her with a beady stare. 'I was expecting that to be your counter-remark. What other platitudes are you going to feed me? How about "too much water under the bridge" or "What difference should it make to us now?" or,' he paused, his eyes glittering, 'the old reliable "We've all moved on"?'

Alix sat down opposite him, her fingers cradling her glass. 'I didn't think this was of any interest to you.'

'Then you thought wrong,' he said in a clipped voice. 'And I'd like the record set straight. Also, I'd love to know why you cast me in the role of villain. So go on, I'm listening.'

'It wasn't intentional. Giving Emma the wrong impression, I mean.'

'No?' His eyes seemed to see right inside her. He sat back and clasped his hands behind his head.

'Emma misunderstood what was going on,' she said. 'I was too upset to put her right.'

'*You* were too upset?'

'Yes. By the time I got talking to her, I was beginning to realise just exactly what I'd done.'

'Really? Go on, this is interesting. I thought you were hell bent on spreading your wings. Feeling smothered? Needing to feel unfettered? Does that sound familiar?'

He hadn't forgotten. Not one word. 'Yes, but I also knew I'd hurt you and I was very upset, distressed in fact. I'd only got as far as telling her that we'd split before I – well, before I started bawling my eyes out. So she assumed, wrongly as it turned out, that you had done the dumping.'

'And why didn't you set her straight?'

'I didn't want to talk about it because it was too painful.'

'Let me get this straight. You were so distressed after you broke off our engagement that Emma assumed it had been the other way around and you were too upset to correct her?'

'Yes, that's more or less it,' Alix said quietly. She shook her head and tried to smile. 'I know it was cowardly and silly. I knew I'd made a ghastly mistake breaking up with you the way I did, and as time went on, I tried to put it behind me and forget all about it. And now,' she hesitated, 'I didn't think it mattered any more.'

'But it does, you see, to me.' He straightened and stared at her with his eyes so full of determination that something jolted inside her. Alix felt the blood drain from her face. It wasn't going to be so easy to fob him off, never mind get him the hell out of her apartment. 'If you realised you'd made a mistake, and you were all that upset and distressed, why didn't you try to contact me before you scarpered?'

Her frantic brain searched for an answer. 'Would you have talked to me?' she lobbed back.

His face was bleak. 'Yes. In fact, I ditched my self-respect long enough to call around to your house on a certain Saturday afternoon.'

'Did you?' she breathed, hardly able to believe this.

'And I really picked my moment. As I reached the top of your road, I was just in time to see you say goodbye to your father and step into a cab.' He fixed her with a look she couldn't fathom. 'It's a sight I've never forgotten.'

A wave of dismay swept through Alix. There was a long silence. 'What's this all about?' She broke it, trying to sound calm and reasonable. 'We're mature adults now, grown up and making our way in the world. You've a successful life. So have I. We've achieved our dreams and got where we wanted. Why should something that happened many years ago impact on us now? I don't understand why you're resurrecting it.'

'Obviously not.' His voice was flat. 'Yes, I'm successful and I love my career. I could quite easily retire now and live in comfort for the rest of my days. But something rankles, some sour taste in my mouth, all because a certain lady saw fit to dump me quite cruelly, when I was younger than I am now and far more stupidly vulnerable. You meant everything to me.' He looked at her steadily, his tone altering. 'I was besotted with you, with everything about you,

305

and from the first time I saw you, I wanted you. I would never have done anything to hurt you. You got under my skin. I felt you were the other half of me, the half I needed to help me *be* me. Making love to you was like nothing on this earth. We were fantastic together. All of a sudden, it was gone. In an instant you took it all away. I'm still at a loss to fully understand why and, saddo that I am,' he grimaced, 'the scars have never really healed.'

Alix's breath caught in her throat. She had always felt he was the other half of her *and* he had meant everything to her. Her scars had never healed either, but they ran far deeper than his because she was the one who had muddled everything up, and was still so muddled that they could never have a future together. 'I'm sorry, Tom,' she said. 'I—' She was unable to go on.

'You said you were distressed at breaking us up, so you did have feelings for me – even then. But I still don't understand why you screwed it all up for us.'

She hung her head and, once more, she spoke from the heart but without giving anything away. 'I told you, I was confused, mixed up, not even sure what was going on in my head, apart from the knowledge that I'd made a mess of everything.'

'So you admit you made a mess of us?'

'Yes, I do. I know I screwed up big time.' She heard the catch in her voice and forced herself to meet his gaze. 'You meant everything to me. When I saw you that time at Fashion Week, it all came crashing back and I just froze.'

'I was so angry when I saw you that I was liable to say anything.' There was a hint of unexpected warmth in his eyes.

This was crazy. Alix strove to compose herself. She couldn't be sitting in her apartment having a conversation like this with Tom. It was almost as inconceivable as the way he was gazing at her. She knew that look, but was afraid to examine its implications too deeply.

'So. Seems like we're two wounded soldiers,' he said, a glimmer of amusement in his face. 'I said something to you the night we went for the meal . . .' He paused, as if gathering his thoughts into some kind of order. She waited silently for him to continue, her heart hammering. 'I talked to you about repairing the damage,' he went on.

Heat flooded her face as she remembered his kiss, and her response.

'It's obvious that you've long moved on and got me out of your system,' he said, 'but, from an entirely selfish point of view, I just wondered if we might do that again to see if it would help and maybe bring me some closure. You see, I've been carrying something about you around in my head for so long that I think I could be just holding onto a fantasy of sorts, a dream that doesn't exist any more. And there's only one way to find out for sure.'

Alix couldn't talk, so she waited for him to continue.

'What do you say?' he asked softly. 'What if you were to humour me and we were to kiss again? Then I might realise there's nothing there after all, and it's about time I got you completely out of my head. I might finally grasp that I've been a fool of the highest order for letting the memory of you linger.'

She felt caught. 'I don't know what to say.'

His eyes flashed with irresistible mischief. 'My dear, the beauty of all this is that you don't actually have to say anything.'

'I don't think it's such a good idea.' She forced the words out, a sliver of cold reality sobering her.

'What are you afraid of?' he murmured, giving her goose pimples as he studied her mouth. 'A few kisses shouldn't mean anything to you. Should it? Not now that you've moved on? Not with all that water under the bridge or— What was the other one? Ah, yes, it doesn't really matter any more . . .'

It was a challenge. In the thick silence something leaped and crackled between them. She must have made a noise, given him an

307

indication of acquiescence, because he was standing up and pulling her into his arms. He cradled her head in his hands, twined his fingers in her hair and looked at her for a long moment. Alix's eyelids fluttered closed against the passion she saw in his gaze. Then she felt his lips dropping soft feathery kisses along her cheekbones, the side of her neck, the tip of her nose, across her forehead and eyebrows. Her mouth felt parched by the time his lips teased hers and all her nerve endings were focused on the sensual feel of him. He deepened the kiss, clasped her tightly to him, and she felt a humming in her veins with a huge ache at the very core of her, an ache that only he could satisfy.

Eventually he drew away. She opened her eyes.

'I don't think this is going to be enough,' he said hoarsely, his eyes dark with desire, 'Problem is, this is not bringing me closure. Far from it.'

She couldn't talk, didn't have to. Instead she snaked her arms around him under his jacket. She felt the hard heat of his body under his shirt, held him close and let him gather her once more into his arms. This time, when he kissed her, she kissed him back with all her heart. She knew immediately that she'd come home. It was as though they'd never been apart. Everything about him was full of sure and sparkling knowledge, a glittering appreciation that life at this very moment was turning out just the way it was supposed to. On a deeper level, everything about him was blazing with a hot, primitive desire that echoed inside her and urged her to slide off his jacket and walk him into her bedroom.

Through a frenzy of snatched kisses, she saw him dragging off his clothes. She barely realised that she was shedding her own – they seemed to shear away from her skin like fragments of another kind of life. When only her black lace panties remained, she felt a suffocating panic. She moved slightly away from him and threw him a startled glance.

'Hey, not so fast,' he murmured, sensing her disquiet and pulling her close again, his hands on her bare skin causing her to shake.

'I'm not as . . . as trim as I was all those years ago.' Her face pinked.

His eyes absorbed the curves of her body. 'No,' he murmured. 'You're even more beautiful than I remember.' He fastened his mouth on one rose-tipped nipple, then the other, and sent quivers shooting around her body. She closed her eyes as a rush of desire flooded through her, so strong it was almost painful. After a while he gently pushed her across the bed against the pillows and continued a line of kisses down her body.

Alix's insides contracted as he slowly drew her panties down her long legs and parted her thighs. She almost buckled when she felt his tongue flicker delicately at the very core of her in a sensual tease. Her whole body tensed. She heard someone moan, heard a long, whimpering sigh, realised what she had said, knew by his gasp that he had caught it too.

'What's that?' he asked hoarsely, as his fingers replaced his tongue, gently massaging the hot, sweet centre of her desire. 'Say it again.'

'Aaaah, Cassidy . . .' It was a sigh from long ago, wrenched from her memory, thanks to the old, familiar way he was playing with her body and even, it seemed, her soul. Although his raw, youthful urgency was now overlaid with skill and tenderness, he was still Cassidy, whipping up her deepest desires.

She reached for him, pulling off his trunks and flinging them to one side. Her heart jumped at the taut, hard sight of him before he laughed, knelt between her legs and hesitated, as though savouring the anticipation. Then he leaned forward and firmly kissed her at the same time as driving himself inside her, fusing her needs, wants and desires so that they were all wrapped up in that glorious moment. He moved deliciously slowly, and then lifted her hips to move harder and exquisitely deeper. She curled her legs tightly around him as her body convulsed, and revelled in the sweet pulsating ripples that seemed to go on for ever.

Afterwards he lay back on the pillow beside her while they caught their breath. Alix was bathed in the sweet moment of afterglow, still shocked and bemused by what had happened. Later, when he was gone, she would try to get her head around it and come to terms with the way her heart had suddenly come alive – although it had never really been dead to him – and her body had responded to his touch.

Then he grinned wickedly in the way that only he could, and said, 'I hate to break the bad news, Alexandra darling.'

Alexandra. His private name for her when they made love, drawing out the syllables in a slow and sensuous murmur. She hadn't heard it in so long, but she'd never forgotten.

He was still talking, 'Although that was incredibly brilliant, I don't think it's going to be enough. You see, it wasn't a fantasy after all.'

Chapter 47

$\mathcal{S}$ he was playing with fire. She was a moth dancing around the dangerous candle flame. She was messing with a self-destruct button. All these hackneyed phrases ran through Alix's head as she pulled on her Cartier sunglasses, drove out of the city and took the A10 for Orléans.

It was bright and sunny on that early Tuesday morning and she was en route to a wedding shoot for a bridal magazine in a château. After that she was meeting Tom. It didn't matter that her sanity was on the line or that she was causing even more heartache for herself. Her peace of mind was immaterial. She couldn't look beyond the next few hours or the prospect of being with Tom again, talking, laughing and making love, watching his eyes as they rested on her, feeling the energy of him sparking her and wrapping itself around her. Who cared if she looked back on her behaviour as foolhardy in the extreme? Right now, being with him was all that mattered.

She'd already seen him since Saturday night.

Somehow she'd found the strength of mind to send him home that night, even though all her instincts had screamed for more and she'd regretted her decision as soon as he'd walked out of the door. She had spent Sunday in a ferment of longing mixed with torment, convinced that there could be no future for them and she would only break their hearts again. Tom had waited until that evening before he'd turned up at her apartment. She'd been half expecting him. That was why she was wearing Calais lace under her white shirt and black jeans, which he'd taken off agonisingly slowly, pausing every so often to watch her reaction to the play of his fingers and mouth. It took him a full hour to completely undress her and Alix was almost weeping with desire by the time he pushed her back across the snowy white pillows. Once more he'd wanted to spend the night, but she'd grasped at every atom of willpower to send him home.

'Why can't I stay, Alexandra? We've a lot of time to make up,' he'd said, trailing a finger around the swell of her breast and giving her a heavy look filled with sensual longing.

'And you want it all now, you greedy thing,' she'd joked, sitting up in the bed and drawing the duvet protectively around her.

'What are you afraid of?' he asked, sending a shiver down her spine.

She half laughed and tried to appear casual. 'Let's not rush anything. This is still so overwhelming and unexpected. It's been a long time and I need to get to know you a little more.' She was talking utter rubbish. It had nothing to do with needing to know him better or the length of time since they'd split. She was grimly trying to rescue herself from falling over the edge and failing quite spectacularly.

'What are you doing this week?' he asked, changing the subject.

'I'm busy all day tomorrow with a couture fashion event, then a wedding shoot outside Orléans on Tuesday.'

'And after that?'

'I'm free on Wednesday and booked up for the rest of the week.'

'Good. What do you say we meet up on Tuesday after your shoot? Perhaps somewhere near the château? I know a couple of pretty villages in that area where there are some nice hotels. We could have a meal and stay over,' he suggested, throwing her a rueful grin. 'If, of course, it's not too overwhelming for you by then. I'll look after the booking. It would be nice to get out of Paris and I'd like to see you on neutral territory. It would also give us plenty of time to talk and get to know each other again. Although I've always known you, Alexandra,' he said, picking up her hand and kissing the soft hollow of her palm. 'You've always been in my blood, in my heart and in my head.'

'Don't say things like that.' She shook her head.

'Sorry. Although I'm not sorry for saying it, just sorry for rushing you.'

Alix bit her lip hard to get a grip on herself as he got dressed, put on his jacket and prepared to leave. He wasn't rushing her. Tom had always been in her heart and head, in equal measures. Yet she found herself agreeing to see him on Tuesday. It would be late afternoon by the time she'd be finished, she told him, deciding to enjoy just one more night with him before she said goodbye. She would forget the past and the future and the shadow between them, just revel in the glory of that one night. It would have to last her for the rest of her life, a night to cherish. Hopefully, too, by Tuesday she would be more mentally prepared to spend the night with him and wouldn't lose sight of her rational self.

She was, of course, kidding herself, Alix mused as her Audi TT surged along the A10. She was looking forward to seeing him, her body already taut with anticipation of his touch, her overnight bag packed with silky underwear. He had only to reach out and touch her lips with his fingers for her to melt into a diaphanous mist where nothing existed but his eyes and the white heat of his body.

The wedding shoot went smoothly. Cécilie, the model, was experienced and the weather was impeccable. There were shots inside the luxurious château and outside in the beautifully landscaped gardens, where Cécilie posed in white and ivory silk, satin and organza dresses.

Later Alix walked out into the warm, blue-skied late afternoon and sped down lanes bordered by lines of elegant poplars and rolling fields of vines, with a swirl of excitement in her heart, until she reached the hotel on the outskirts of the town where she was meeting Tom.

He was waiting for her in the car park. She was trembling with a sudden shyness by the time she cut the engine and stepped out. He was at her side immediately, seemingly relaxed in a white shirt and jeans. His eyes were hidden by his sunglasses, but she sensed from the way he was holding himself in check that he was as nervous as she was.

'You came,' he said softly, taking off his sunglasses and looking intently at her. 'I thought you might change your mind.' He lifted his hand and smoothed back a tendril of her dark hair. He ran his fingers lightly up and down her arms as if to satisfy himself that she was indeed there. Then he cupped her face in the palm of his hand, and kissed her as tenderly as if she was made of fragile china. She remained motionless, reluctant to break the spell.

'Are we staying here?' she asked, feeling a catch in her voice.

He smiled. 'Do you trust me?'

She didn't hesitate. 'Yes.'

'Car keys?'

She was mystified but handed them over.

'I'm bringing you somewhere else, somewhere we can be alone.'

'What's going on?'

'I just feel like going a little further afield,' he said, jiggling her keys in his hand. 'Anyway, you said you trusted me.'

'I did, didn't I?' Alix smiled faintly. What exactly had she let herself in for?

She soon discovered that she'd let herself in for the most magical twenty-four hours of her life.

Tom explained that he'd arrived down in a hired car. Now he fetched a brown leather overnight bag from the boot and slung it onto the back seat of Alix's. He started the engine and took a road that led through the heart of the countryside. Alix was used to travelling in style, enjoying the luxury of private jets and first-class seats as a matter of form, but the trip with Tom across the French countryside, glinting in the sunshine, was exhilarating. She stayed quiet, absorbing it all – the glances Tom threw her from time to time, his hands sure on the controls of her Audi, and the knowledge that they were enclosed in their own private space. After an hour or so he drove into the grounds of a farmhouse, deep in the heart of the Loire Valley. It was a long stone building on a rise, commanding uninterrupted views of the landscape on every side.

'It belongs to a friend of a friend who rents it out occasionally. It's all ours for the night,' Tom said. He fetched their overnight bags and together they crunched up the gravel drive.

It was perfect in its simplicity and seclusion, perfect in the calm stillness that surrounded the property. Outside there were natural wildflower gardens, a square of blue swimming pool bordered by a patio crammed with shrubs, and a tranquil lake shaded by willows. Inside, the kitchen-cum-dining area had exposed beams and a huge stone fireplace, with benches drawn up to a long oak table. Their bedroom had whitewashed walls, simple voile curtains and blue shutters that led to a small wrought-iron balcony. It also had a huge, old-fashioned brass bed. Standing in the balcony, Alix felt she had never been in such a heavenly spot.

Tom came over and wrapped his arms around her. 'Lovely, isn't it?'

She leaned back into him and sighed with pleasure. 'It's gorgeous. And totally unexpected. Thank you for this.'

315

'I just want you to relax away from the hustle and bustle of Paris. I want us to have some time out together. We'll go down for a stroll around the grounds and I have a table booked for later on.'

'A table booked?' She felt a flicker of disappointment, not wanting to leave this lovely place or suffer the intrusion of other diners.

He grinned. 'Downstairs – where else? Don't worry, I'm not expecting you to cook. I have it all organised and the fridge and freezer are full. I just have to switch on the oven.'

She turned and wound her arms around his neck. 'I'm all on for that.'

He lifted her arms away. 'If I kiss you now, you can forget about the walk or food.'

'So?' she teased.

'Much as I'm looking forward to taking you to bed, I'm not that much of a sex maniac –' She interrupted him with a playful punch. '– and I'd like us to have some time to chat and catch up even more. After that, we'll have the whole night to make love. You can't kick me out of bed here.'

'Can't I?'

They went for a long walk, hand in hand through dappled sunshine, Alix overwhelmed with joy at having Tom beside her, the warmth of the evening a caress as soft as thistledown, and the soughing of the trees in the gentle breeze. He led her to a small jetty, helped her into a rowing boat and brought her out across the glittering lake.

Alix felt enfolded in a deep peace. There was just the blue vault of the sky above, sparkling water all around them, and beyond the woods, gleaming in the sunlight. And Tom, laughing and chatting, filling the intervening years, as he guided the boat.

Afterwards they sat outside at the wrought-iron table and Alix lit candles around the patio while Tom turned on the oven and opened a bottle of excellent Bordeaux. Later he served a delicious beef casserole, with salad and crunchy bread, followed by raspberry tart, and they laughed and chatted as the candlelight danced and a violet night dropped down across the countryside. By the time they walked upstairs to the huge brass bed, Alix felt that any separation she'd had from Tom had been wiped away. She felt as close to him as if they'd never spent all those years apart, so close that nothing could separate them again. For a moment as she walked up the stairs with him, she felt a shadow reach out and touch her, but she ignored it.

One night. She had promised herself one night with him and so far everything had turned out perfectly. It was even more perfect when he closed the bedroom door, turned to her purposefully, slowly opened the buttons on her shirt to reveal her wispy bra and murmured in her hair, 'Alexandra . . .'

Much later, they talked into the shadowy, intimate hours of the night, Alix replete in the aftermath of their long, delicious love-making. She watched as Tom rose from the bed and went over to pull back the voile curtains to allow the silvery glimmer of the moon to wash into the room. Then when he lay down beside her something in the moment allowed her reach out her hand, trace the scar along the inside of his arm and ask where it had come from.

He caught her hand, kissed it and held it fast. 'You don't want to know.'

'Maybe I do,' she said softly, raising herself on her elbow.

'I connected with a car door.'

'You were in a *car* accident?'

She sensed his smile. 'Not quite,' he admitted. 'The car door had been propelled into the air and it connected with me as it followed a trajectory to the ground. Only I happened, or rather my arm hap-pened, to cushion its fall.'

'What does that really mean?'

He chuckled. 'I was in the wrong place at the wrong time when a car bomb went off. Gaza. Last year.'

Instantly she felt cold all over as hard reality stalked like a phantom across the warm intimate atmosphere they had created. Tom's job was dangerous. He could have been killed or terribly wounded. And, no doubt, that incident hadn't been his only brush with danger. She had no time to voice her fears, though, for he immediately took her into his arms and held her tightly.

'Don't. Don't think about it, Alexandra darling. Don't imagine the worst or give space to your fears. It's in the past. Over. Gone. All that really matters is now, this moment.'

'How can you say it's in the past?' She rested her head on his chest and listened to the muffled thud of his heartbeat.

'Because it is. I'm more careful now. It was a wake-up call. I don't take silly chances but I'm not afraid to try new things or live, really live, my life the way I want to. And I've no regrets about anything.'

'None?'

'No.' His thumb traced the outline of her lips. 'All those years you and I were apart have just vanished. They don't count any more. What's important is what's happening now. The accident was a wake-up call in more ways than one. I had time to think and reflect when I was in hospital last year. That was when I decided to spend some time in Paris. It wasn't just coincidence.'

'What do you mean?' Her voice was husky.

'What do you think? I still love you, Alix, I always have. And my spies told me you were ostensibly free and single. I wanted to be in the same city as you just in case there was any hope for us . . .'

He shouldn't be talking like this, she fretted, the stardust of the magical evening fading slowly. They had no future. There *was* no us, as in her and Tom, and could never be.

He was still talking, his voice soft in the semi-darkness. 'Then I saw you coming into the exhibition with Marc de Burgh and you looked so elegant and sexy and comfortable with him that I was full of rage.'

'I was with Marc to make Sophie jealous.'

'I was the one who was as hotly jealous as an immature adolescent. And then I heard about your lover boy.'

'You were with Melissa . . .'

She felt him shake with laughter.

'She's married to my cousin. When I saw you with Marc I asked her to stick very close to me. But, Alix,' he went on quietly, 'apart from the fact that I can't believe no one's managed to snap you up, I can't understand why you're still doing the same job. Not that there's anything wrong with your profession – we all need a dash of glamour in our lives – but I know what your motives were behind it, why you decided to spend your life painting pretty faces, and I kinda thought you'd have moved beyond all that by now.'

'I'm happy in my work,' Alix said defensively.

'I'm sure you are. From what I heard you're brilliant at it. I'd just hate to think you're still using it as some kind of smokescreen to avoid showing the real you to the world.'

'That was years ago.'

'Exactly. But you're still held there in a sense and I think it's because you haven't let go of all that childhood hurt and anger.'

He knew her better than she knew herself, Alix thought. The problems of her childhood had never gone away. Yet how could they, when she lived with a daily reminder each morning she looked in the mirror and was discovering even now that she was far more like her mother than she'd ever realised? She'd betrayed Tom all those years ago and she was continuing to betray him with her silence. It seemed there was no escaping her fate. She turned over in bed, lying on her stomach, her body pressed against the length of his, grateful for his presence beside her as she reached into herself to respond to his observation.

'Is that so bad? Does it really matter?' she asked, finding it easy to voice her thoughts in this dark hour of the night, knowing full well that it had defined the course of her life.

'I suppose there are some things in life we never work through,' he said. 'Life is messy and people are complex. Some things defy analysis or understanding, or any clean-cut definition. I'd hate to think you had any regrets. They're such a waste of time and energy. They stop you grabbing the moment and fully enjoying it.'

'Supposing, just supposing, you'd done something you regretted. Maybe something you weren't proud of. How would you go about fixing it, Tom?'

'I mightn't want to fix it. Then again, maybe it couldn't be fixed and I might just want to move on and let it be. I don't mean to sound hard-hearted but, hey, as I said, you get a different perspective when . . .' He fell silent and she tensed, knowing he was thinking about some of the appalling sights he had encountered in the course of his work. He reached for her, and pulled her across the bed so that she lay on top of him, her soft curves melting into his hard frame. Their sweat-slicked skin seemed almost fused together, much in the way her soul felt fused to his.

'Hey,' he said, holding her close, 'it's supposed to be our night together, away from it all. Life is precious and every minute counts. If you do have any regrets, darling, why not just accept them for what they are, put them to one side and get on with living the rest of your life?'

On one level it didn't matter what he said. Her sin was too great to expiate and her regrets went far too deep for any kind of redemption, but his voice was so full of understanding that it warmed her heart. She tucked her head into the curve of his neck and felt his hands gently sliding up and down her back, from the swell of her hips to her shoulder-blades. This moment, now, this wonderful synchronicity with Tom, right through from her body to her heart and mind, would have to last her for ever, she thought, allowing herself to suspend her self-reproach, feel his skin touching hers and revel in the sublime pleasure of it all.

In the morning they were late rising, Alix glorying in the rightness of seeing Tom's face on the pillow next to hers in those first few moments of wakefulness. She lay quietly, drinking in the sight of him, sealing the memory tightly into her mind. Somewhere in the course of the night, the knowledge had slowly spun to the surface that she would have to break her silence and tell him honestly why she had broken off their engagement. It was so wrong to have kept him in the dark that even if it meant he never spoke to her or wanted to see her again, and no matter how difficult it would be, he had to know the truth.

But not just yet.

After a while Tom opened his eyes and smiled at her, his eyes unguarded. 'This certainly beats getting kicked out of bed,' he said, snaking an arm around her and drawing her close.

Later they showered together, slipped on snowy white bathrobes and had breakfast on the patio in the bright morning. Then time seemed to slip through her fingers.

'How are you getting back to Paris?' Alix asked.

'That depends on you,' Tom said, breaking a croissant with his long, lean fingers, 'I could go back in the hired car, or dispense with it and hitch a lift with you.'

So it didn't have to be over just yet. She would allow herself the luxury of his company on the drive back to Paris through the French countryside on this bright, sunny Wednesday. Alix fished her car keys out of her bag and passed them to him. 'I'll do better than that. I'll let you drive.'

She was silent as they headed north, not wanting their time together to be over and greedy for more, feeling a sense of recklessness when she suggested they go out to dinner after Tom turned into her car park. Another few hours wouldn't make much difference to the difficulty of the parting. Afterwards it seemed entirely right and natural to ask him back to her apartment, although Alix berated herself for not having the guts to break her silence.

She had one more night luxuriating in his arms, with his body beside hers, this time in the familiarity of her own bed. Lying sleepless beside him, her heart was breaking as she went over everything again, as she might tell it to him, and agonising that, thanks to her stupidity, he'd surely never talk to her again.

She finally drifted into a troubled sleep, her heart heavy when she awoke the following morning and faced the reality of Tom sleeping in her bed for the first and last time. He woke shortly after her, and he was in a funny, playful mood, tickling Alix until she was gasping for mercy, causing her to roll across the bed. He lunged after her, trying and failing to pin her down and Alix laughed and suddenly twisted away from him, causing him to land heavily on the floor, half caught up in the duvet.

'Wait till I get you.' He was spluttering and laughing. 'I'm going to hold you under that shower until you tell me you're sorry.'

'You have to catch me first,' Alix said, peeping over the edge of the bed and smiling down at him.

Then the next few moments slowly and inexorably unfolded, and slowly and inexorably caused Alix's heart to plummet and the breath to halt in her chest. Still laughing, Tom began to disentangle himself from the mounds of the duvet, thrusting his arms and legs through the soft, downy pile. And Alix watched in horrified disbelief as his attention was caught by something lying under the bed. She felt frozen in time as his laughter changed to a stilled curiosity, and the pieces of her life disintegrated as he withdrew a battered green suitcase.

She'd forgotten to bury it in the depths of her wardrobe after she'd taken it out for Emma.

'Hey, I recognise this. It's the one you brought when you left for London all those years ago.'

'How do you know?' Something pounded into her head.

'I saw you leaving that day. Remember? It was a sight I've never forgotten.'

'Don't open it. Please.' She forced the words out through her trembling lips. She pulled her knees up to her chin and wrapped her arms around them, hugging the duvet tightly to her.

'Why not?'

'Just don't. For God's sake, Tom, you're far too nosy. Just put it back.' She spoke sharply and he threw her a curious glance.

'What's the problem?'

'Nothing. Just don't open it.'

'What's wrong? Talk to me. You're making me feel kinda jittery.'

'I was going to tell you, but not like this.' Her head sank onto her knees as icy fear snaked through her stomach and rose in her chest.

Something in her tone must have alerted him, and told him that whatever was up it was out of the ordinary. Tom reached for his scattered clothes and dressed silently and furiously. Then he came back to where she sat, forcibly pushed down her hands and lifted her chin so that she had no choice but to look into his silvery blue eyes.

'What's there to tell?' he asked. 'What could be so awful that you don't want me to see?'

'Nothing,' she said desperately, her courage failing. 'It's just full of rubbish. Look, Tom, just go. Please. Leave me.'

'I won't go until I find out what this is about. You have me intrigued as to why the contents of an old suitcase should have you so petrified. If, as you say, it's full of rubbish, then it shouldn't be a problem,' he said. With that, he pulled it out, lifted it onto the bed and flipped back the lid.

Alix watched in frozen horror as he looked at the contents. On top of the pile of memorabilia, there were clippings of his magazine and newspaper photographs that she'd collected over the years. Tom laughed. 'So you were checking up on me all along. I find that rather gratifying, darling – there's no need to be embarrassed about that.' She saw his expression change to puzzlement as he lifted out a yellowing InterRail timetable to reveal a small bundle of letters underneath.

'They're just some old letters,' she said, her voice strangled as she reached across to grab them. It was too late. Tom took one glance at the missive from the British Pregnancy Advisory Service and comprehension burst across his face.

'Sweet fucking Jerusalem. I *was* right. There was far more to your departure than a sudden urge to conquer London. I mean, where else do Irish girls in trouble flee to?' His face was twisted with a mixture of disbelief and raw hurt. 'You bitch. You were pregnant, weren't you? Pregnant with our baby.'

Alix let out a cry that came from the depths of her soul.

'You sick bitch,' Tom spat as he hurled the letter into the air. 'You had an abortion, didn't you? You got rid of our child. How could you have done this? Oh, God, it's all making sense now. The worst fucking sense. I can't believe this. *Our child!*'

'No, Tom.' Her voice was so frail that he didn't hear it at first.

'I hope you rot in hell.'

'No, Tom.' She tried to sound a little stronger.

'Oh, yeah,' his voice was choked, 'that's not even good enough for you.'

'I didn't have an abortion.' Alix finally got the words out and he heard her this time. 'I didn't have an abortion, Tom,' she said shakily. 'I made initial enquiries but knew immediately that it was out of the question. I had the baby. Our baby.'

His glittering eyes scorched her face. Then he put his head in his hands and wept. It was the worst sound she had ever heard.

Chapter 48

On Thursday morning in Boyd Samuel, Tanya glided up to Libby just after morning coffee and told her rather snootily that she was wanted in Stephen O'Connor's office. Immediately.

Libby stood up on trembling legs. This was it. She'd been found out. God knew what awful catastrophe she'd caused or how much money she'd lost one of her clients. Stephen's office was at the far end of the corridor and her heart pounded as she mentally rehearsed what to say to him.

Stephen's door was open and he saw her hesitating in the corridor. 'Come in, Libby,' he called, 'and you can close the door.'

She did so, and walked across what seemed like an acre of pale grey carpet. Stephen was about the same age as her father, she thought, sitting on the edge of the chair he indicated and finally realising that he was smiling as though nothing in particular was wrong.

'How long are you with us now, Libby?' he asked, friendly and relaxed as he sat back in his huge leather chair.

Her mind whirled. Was it some kind of trick question? Perhaps this was the way he dealt with problem staff, pretending that nothing was wrong until you eventually dropped your guard. 'About eight months,' she said, her hands shaking.

'Eight months? And you came in straight from college?'

'Yes, Mr O'Connor.'

He shot her a look, 'Good grief, you can call me Stephen. I just asked you in here for an informal chat. I want you to know that I was very impressed with you at the team-building exercise last week. I've also seen some of your work and had a chat with James, your unit manager. I've heard that you're first at your desk each morning, your work is always scrupulously tidy, correct and well presented. You're quick and clever, bright and ambitious, and not afraid to take a calculated risk, within reason, of course.' He fell silent, looking at her thoughtfully. 'You could go far, Libby, and I'd like to think you'd go far with us. You're the kind of innovative, creative thinker we need in these challenging times. I see you have a degree in economics. Have you ever thought of gaining further qualifications?'

Libby was astonished. She hadn't made a gigantic mistake. Quite the opposite, in fact. She was doing okay. She was doing well. She said, 'Yes, I have thought of it.'

'And?'

Libby pulled her thoughts together. 'I've no immediate plans as I wanted to take time out from education when I left college.'

'And rightly so. I can't offer you a promotion, not just yet, but there's a particular Master's course coming up next September that I consider invaluable, and from time to time the company has selected a candidate to sponsor on the programme. This year, despite the cutbacks and the fact that you're not even with us twelve months, your name has come up for consideration. In fact,' he smiled benignly, 'you were a unanimous choice.'

Libby couldn't believe what she was hearing and one of her ears started to burn.

'The company is prepared to fund you and give you the necessary time off for study purposes,' he went on. 'Naturally we'd expect you to remain with us for an agreed number of years afterwards and you'd be strongly placed when promotion arises in the future,' he said, smiling at her, exposing perfect teeth. It was a friendly smile, but Libby realised that it made her feel trapped. 'Have a good think about it, and if you decide to proceed, the college itself has a selection process that, naturally enough, we'd help you with.'

Stephen chatted some more to Libby, as if sensing she was a little overawed. He said he'd need her answer by Monday week, and he asked her to keep his proposal to herself in the meantime. 'We don't want word getting out.' He grinned, looking ordinary all of a sudden. 'You might find yourself slightly unpopular with certain people.'

Libby managed a shaky grin in return and went back to her desk, the beginnings of a headache throbbing in her temples. She smiled sweetly at Tanya, saying she'd had a great chat with Stephen, a very private and confidential chat. In need of distraction, she went out shopping at lunch hour and bought two new tops. Then she ended up leaving the office before half past four as her headache had become progressively worse.

When Libby arrived home, her throbbing head wasn't helped when she pushed open the hall door and heard cartoons blaring from the television in the den.

Ouch. There was no need to have this excruciating decibel level shrieking through the house. Whether he liked it or not, Charlie was going to get a piece of her mind. Still wearing her jacket, parcels rustling, she crossed the hallway and pushed open the door, fully expecting to see her brother reclining on the squashy sofa and staring up at the wall-mounted plasma screen. Instead she found her father slumped on it, his feet on the low table in front of him, a half-empty whiskey bottle resting between his jeans-clad legs, his eyes glued to the screen. As Libby watched, he lifted the bottle and levered it enough to allow a generous measure to flow into his glass. Then he carefully replaced the bottle between his legs and raised the glass to his lips.

'Dad! What the hell is going on?' Libby asked. Any disquiet she might have felt at the state of her father evaporated in the aftermath of the traumatic day she'd had. If anything, she felt impatient with him and his self-indulgence. Skiving off from the office and now wrapping his head around a bottle of whiskey. If anything, she thought darkly, she was the one in need of a bolstering drink.

Oliver turned his head but made no move to lower the volume or take his feet off the table. 'What does it look like?' he asked.

'Like you're very feeling sorry for yourself,' Libby retorted. 'And using that as an excuse to get your head into the whiskey.'

'Don't be so hard on me, Libby.' His words were slightly slurred. 'I took a half-day from the office. Same as you, it seems. Life is tough for me right now. You've no idea how tough.'

'I could say the same about me,' Libby said rashly, her patience finally giving out. 'You've no idea what I've been putting up with.'

'You, Libby?' Her father gave her a glance that was quite shrewd in spite of the amount he'd drunk. 'What have you got to put up with? I thought you led a charmed life. Chauffeured to work most mornings, a good job at a time when so many graduates can't find one, a very busy social life and, until recently, a boyfriend who was most welcome under our roof until you decided to turf him out. No cares or worries, no mortgages or bills to fret your little head about. Just enjoyment and socialising. And shopping, of course, plenty of shopping.' He eyed her carrier bags.

The last thread of Libby's patience snapped. 'That's what you think, Dad. But you have it all wrong, and you're seeing only one side of my life. It's not at all sweetness and light and, right now, I think I'm going to join you.'

'Join me where?'

'On that sofa with the bottle of whiskey.'

'But you don't drink whiskey.'

'Don't I?' Libby went to dump her jacket and shopping in the hall. She returned with a glass and splashed some amber liquid into it, then topped it up with lemonade. She sat down on the sofa, sipped some of her drink and watched the noisy cartoons, conscious of her father's surprise.

'This is the life,' she sighed, plumping up a cushion and fixing it behind her. She slid off her shoes and put her feet on the table, wriggling her toes in appreciation. 'This is far better than staying late at the office.' In a funny way she meant it. It was extremely relaxing to forget about everything for a while, suspend critical judgement and just engage with the funny antics on the screen in front of her.

'Okay, joke over,' Oliver said.

'It's not a joke,' Libby said, the whiskey sending a warming trail right down to her stomach and helping her to relax. 'I'm really enjoying this. I didn't realise how cathartic it was to just dump in front of the telly and stare at cartoons.'

'At least I have an excuse,' Oliver growled. 'I've had to sack Leticia.'

'Sack Leticia?'

'Yes, I caught her in Charlie's bedroom.'

'Snooping around again instead of cleaning? But she doesn't normally come on a Thursday . . .'

Her father rubbed his eyes and gave her a tired glance. 'You don't get it. When I came home early today, I found out that Charlie had bunked off college. And Leticia was in the bedroom. With Charlie. *In flagrante* whatever-it-is. That's why I sacked her. On the spot.'

'Oh.' Libby's head was reeling as she absorbed the full meaning of his words. Despite her father's ponderous voice, and everything that had happened that day, she felt a bubble of laughter inside her. 'Where's Charlie now?'

'He's gone out.'

'No wonder he was boasting he didn't need a free house,' she said, stealing a glance at her father. 'And that's why you're hitting the bottle?' Libby feigned surprise. Then she continued, somewhat riskily, 'Like, it has nothing to do with Mum upping and leaving and having a wild time hanging out in a Sandyford hotel?'

Oliver swirled the contents of his glass. 'Did you have to raise that painful subject?'

'Why not, Dad?' Libby said quietly, feeling fresh resolve. 'Do you think for one moment that Mum's happy? What about me and Charlie? Our parents aren't talking. You're upset, Mum's upset and Charlie and I are at our wit's end because we don't know what's going on. And that's just one side of my crappy life,' she finished softly.

Oliver reached for the remote control and muted the television. Together they stared in silence at the screen. Then, after a while, Oliver said, 'Well, Libby dearest, are you going to tell me about the other side of your crappy life?'

'I can't.' She struggled to contain her restlessness, but felt it simmering on the surface.

'Why not? I might be a little inebriated, but that doesn't stop me being concerned for your welfare – and I saw the look on your face just now. I'd love to wave a magic wand and fix it so that at least someone's happy around here. Come on, help me forget my own woes and give me a chance to be omnipotent for a change.'

'I don't want to disappoint you,' Libby hedged.

He stared at her. '*Disappoint* me? How could you ever disappoint me? You mean everything to me – Charlie too, despite his shenanigans.'

'I'm afraid I might disappoint you with what I want to say.'

'Don't look so worried. The only way you'd ever disappoint me is . . . let's see . . .' He seemed to be groping for words. 'I suppose if you weren't truly happy with your lot.'

'What do you mean?' Libby asked, taking another sip of her drink to ease the niggle of disquiet that slithered around inside her and tried to find a voice.

Oliver put down his glass and folded his arms. 'You might think I'm just indulging myself in cartoons, and you might think I've had a whiskey or two too many, which perhaps I have, and I might not be particularly articulate right now, but for you and Charlie . . . Seriously, Libby, all I want for both of you is that you feel happy and fulfilled in your lives. I'd hate to see you unhappy or doing something because you felt you had to and not because you really wanted to. I hope you'd both have the confidence to be true to yourselves.'

Libby looked into her glass. For all the conversations she'd ever had with her father, she'd never had a late-night bare-her-soul session. She'd never really plumbed the depths of her heart with him, unwilling to be brutally frank with him. This evening was different. It was out of character for Oliver to be slumped in front of the television, never mind indulging in whiskey. Beyond the softening effects of the alcohol, she sensed vulnerability, some kind of defencelessness that he rarely allowed to show. It made it easier to tell him how she really felt, deep down inside.

'Supposing what I really wanted to do was different from what you might expect?' Libby ventured, still not quite sure how much she was prepared to admit to him, even though the alcohol was making her free with her speech and rather light-headed.

'So?'

'So you don't think I should be following in your footsteps?' she hazarded.

'My *footsteps*?' He gave her a long look. 'Libby, is something going on here that I don't know about? Are you trying to tell me something in a roundabout way?'

'I'd like to get back to what you said about doing something only because you really wanted to. Do you think that's important, Dad?'

'Of course it is. The only person you can truly be is yourself. You shouldn't let anyone force you to do something that goes against you. You must follow your own path in life.'

He'd talked to her before about confidence and potential and life paths. She'd listened, but from the perspective of an idealistic teenager had interpreted it as achievement and, given her father's accomplishments, had assumed he meant achievement in an academic endeavour. Now she felt a little bewildered when she heard him equating potential with being true to herself.

'Can I ask you something personal, Dad?' she ventured, emboldened by this new, unguarded Oliver.

'Ask away,' he said affably, pouring a small amount of whiskey into both of their glasses.

'It's about Mum.'

He tensed. 'What about her?'

'Well, going back to when you married Mum, did that seem the right path to you, or did you marry Mum because you had to?'

Her dad gave her a flinty glance. 'I'm not sure what your point is.'

'Or maybe you're afraid to answer me. Because you don't want to admit that you only married Mum because you felt you had to.'

'Good God, what makes you think I *had* to marry your mother?' he asked, his brows drawn together in a frown and his look so direct that Libby felt nervous.

She took a deep breath and wondered why it had taken her so

long to screw up the courage to have this fundamental conversation with her father. 'She was expecting me, wasn't she? I was on the way and Granny said—'

'*Granny?*'

Her throat closed. She'd gone too far. She should have kept her mouth shut – blast the alcohol for lowering her guard.

'Go on – Granny said what? Tell me, Libby.'

Libby bit her lip, took another shaky breath. 'Well, she used to say that you'd married Mum because she was pregnant.'

'Did she now? My mother was sometimes mischievous with her tongue, but don't tell me you believed that?'

Libby remained silent.

Oliver shook his head. 'No. Christ. That's crazy. I can't accept you had such a poor impression of me. Why didn't you tell me? I would have debunked that theory on the spot.'

'I was afraid to. Supposing you'd agreed with Granny? What if it were true?'

Oliver looked sad. 'You have it all wrong, Libby. I married your mother because, above all, I loved her and wanted to spend the rest of my life with her. The fact that you were on the way was an added bonus, a joy. But in no way are you ever to feel that your arrival into the world forced my hand, so to speak. Believe me, you were much wanted and loved. Very much.' He gazed at her for a long, silent moment.

Libby knew what was coming next and braced herself.

'When did Granny speak to you like that?' he asked.

Libby hesitated. 'A few times, Dad.'

'A *few* times?'

'Well, now and then. She told me my parents wouldn't have married only for me. That Mum had, well, kinda trapped you.' Anxious to push the spotlight off herself she rushed on heedlessly: 'I think she said it to Mum also. I kind of overheard—' Too late, she realised from her father's expression that she was making things worse, not better.

'Go on, Libby.'

'Look, Dad, it's all ancient history.'

'Not to me it's not.' Her father sounded much like his usual implacable self, the Oliver Colgan who wouldn't rest until he got to the bottom of things. 'So continue. What exactly did you overhear?'

Libby shrugged as though to cast her words in a more casual light. 'One Christmas – the year that Mum overcooked the turkey, remember? – Granny was a bit sharp with her. She told her how stupid she'd been and how lucky she was to have snapped you up. I thought – maybe I was mistaken, but it sounded like she'd said it to Mum more than once, because Mum just answered her quietly as though she'd heard it all before.'

Her father lapsed into silence. He appeared to be in deep thought and Libby sat beside him, half petrified by her admission yet conscious that something about her life had altered, some little shadow had lifted and that a door, leading somewhere different, had come ajar. But she had no time to think about that now for she'd surely landed her mother in it. Whatever about herself, what had possessed her to bring her mum into it? Yet when her father spoke again it wasn't about her mother. Instead he searched her face and asked her what exactly had she meant about following in his footsteps? What did Libby see when she thought about her true path? Because he was very keen to find out just how different it was from his.

Libby said she'd have to get a glass of water first to clear her head a little, as she didn't want to make things more confused. Her father said he'd have one too, as it seemed that Libby had something important to tell him.

She knew then that there was no getting out of it, that she couldn't fob him off with some half-baked explanation. Funnily enough, she didn't want to. Perhaps it was his reassurance that her arrival into the world hadn't forced him into marrying her mother that gave Libby the strength to take a deep breath and admit that she had made a huge mistake when she decided to go down the road of studying and working in economics.

'What made you decide to study it in the first place? Or can I guess from our earlier conversation that it had something to do with following in my footsteps?'

Libby nodded. 'Yes, Dad, I wanted to make you proud of me.'

'Libby, my pride in you has everything to do with who you *are*, not what you *do*. The fact that you are alive and breathing, and here on this planet, makes me feel immensely happy.'

Libby gulped. 'It was a way of making up for—'

'Please don't say what I think you're going to say. I'm finding this very difficult to get my head around and I wish to God Almighty that I'd spoken to you about this years ago, or that you'd come straight to me when my mother made such hurtful comments. Am I such an ogre that my family are afraid to tell me things that might be important to them?'

'You're not an ogre, Dad. You're so strong and focused, clever and ambitious, that I suppose we don't want to let you down. We look up to you and want to imitate you to some degree. Even if it means doing stuff because we feel we should and not because we want to,' Libby said, trying to explain exactly where she was coming from.

Her father was silent for so long that Libby felt her courage begin to drain away.

Then he said, 'I'm sorry for the angst she must have caused you. And I'd love to know what you really want to do with your life.'

Here goes, Libby thought. 'I'd like to paint,' she said.

'Paint?' Oliver looked surprised. 'Wasn't that your big teenage hobby?'

'Yes, I'd like to draw, to capture things on canvas, feelings, emotions, the whole landscape of life, and not just as a hobby but . . .' Libby hesitated, a little embarrassed by her revelation. 'You probably think that's silly or wasteful.'

'Why should I? Artists, writers, musicians, people who are creatively gifted help to enrich the world we live in, help us make sense of it in some way, and get us through the ups and downs of the day-to-day stuff. Seriously, Libby, if you're unhappy in your career and have a talent for something else, you owe it to yourself to see where you can alter course or make adjustments in your life.'

'I'll think about it, Dad.'

'Do that. Make sure you give yourself enough time and space to think everything through. You deserve the best out of life and to fulfil your talents. I still can't believe the nonsense you were going around with in your head. I'm shocked and appalled.'

For the moment, Libby couldn't admit that she felt more confused than ever. All along she'd privately thought she wasn't much good at her job and was merely treading water. Her chat with Stephen O'Connor that morning had changed that. She was quick and clever at her work, bright and ambitious. They wanted her to further her career and she could go places. Talents that couldn't be ignored. It was all too complicated. Libby sighed. She would think about it later – she had until after Paris to make her decision. She might even talk to Alix. And Mum.

'Did Mum ever say anything to you?' she ventured. 'About what Granny said?'

Oliver gave her a sharp glance. 'Not in so many words, no. Not then, anyhow. But there was something recently . . .' Once again her father fell silent.

Libby's ears pricked up. Something recently? Had it anything to do with their split? If Libby had carried this misconception in her heart, was there any chance her mother had also had some kind of doubt or misgiving? Granny Colgan's sharp words might have found their target in Emma Colgan's heart just as they had in Libby's. She waited for a short while, then went on, speaking almost on instinct, something in her gut urging her to help fix some fences between her parents. 'Whatever about me, it must have been tough on Mum to listen to Granny Colgan. You know how soft she is. It must have been bad enough to find herself pregnant and no mother to turn to. I can't begin to imagine how difficult it must have been.'

Too late, she saw that she was greatly mistaken. Her father stood up abruptly as though he'd been stung. 'She had me to turn to, hadn't she? Problem is, I haven't been enough for her.'

'You know what I mean, Dad. If Mum didn't mention it to you, or wasn't able to laugh it off with you, then she must have been quite hurt. Vulnerable, even.'

'Vulnerable, ha! You haven't a clue what's been going on, so please don't make it worse.'

'Maybe I don't know what's been going on, but I know that Mum loves you with all her heart. *And* me and Charlie,' she said hotly. 'We all come first with her. She bends over backwards to make sure we're happy. I don't know if I'd be able to be as unselfish as her when I eventually have children.'

'You don't know what you're talking about,' Oliver said testily.

'Maybe not, but I wish you two would get together and talk out whatever is causing this rift.'

'I've no intention of talking to your mother,' Oliver snapped. 'Any discussion I'll have with her will be through our respective solicitors.'

'Dad!' Libby was aghast. She'd made a mess of things and her cosy evening had dissolved in the face of her father's hostility. She tried to think of something that would help her to claw her way back to some kind of a truce. 'You can't mean that.'

'I do. Very much so,' Oliver said. 'Furthermore, I'm not going to tell you why any kind of reconciliation between us is impossible. I'll let your mother deal with that and face the consequences. She was ultimately responsible for what went wrong. Ask her the next time you see her,' he said in a wretched voice she'd never heard before. 'Ask her why she betrayed us all.'

Libby jumped as the meaning of his words sank in. 'Betrayed? I don't believe you, Dad. Not Mum. No way.'

Chapter 49

*E*mma sprayed Vera Wang on her pulse spots and practised a shaky smile in the mirror.

Libby was on the way.

Feeling like a fugitive from Laburnum Grove, she'd spent almost a week in this bland, functional hotel that catered mainly for the corporate traveller. She'd spoken to Libby most evenings, had also chatted to Charlie, but Oliver still refused to answer his mobile. She hadn't heard from Alix, apart from a couple of texts to say she was away. Emma had spent her days going for long walks, sometimes driving as far as Greystones, wandering along the great stretch of beach, feeling the breeze tug at her hair, tasting the tangy salt on her lips, other times going up into the foothills of the mountains where early summer was unfolding fuzzy shoots and bringing glimmering evening sunshine across the breadth and depth of the landscape, a landscape she observed from a distance, as though some essential part of her was missing.

It was time in a bubble. Her life was on hold, frozen and suspended. Sometimes she awoke in the middle of the night, jolted out of a restless sleep by the sheer awfulness of it all. Other times she slept on in the mornings, barely able to summon the energy to climb out of bed and face another vacant day.

She didn't know how much longer she could go on like this. Now it was Friday evening; she was flying to Paris early the following week and meeting up with Hannah in advance of Alix's launch. Beyond that, she didn't know what was going to happen.

In the meantime, Libby was coming to see her. Emma had suggested they meet in the hotel bar, but Libby had said she'd rather see her in her room. She was hoping to put up a false, bright front for her daughter, but now, as she sprayed her perfume and looked in the mirror, her face felt tight, the contours pinched and drawn. Not even Alix's magic fingers would have been able to conceal the shadows under her eyes.

She didn't think her morale could sink any lower and she didn't think she could feel any worse until she opened the door to Libby.

'Is it true?' Libby demanded, coming straight to the point, her eyes so hurt and angry that Emma shied away from them.

'You'd better come in.' Emma stepped back from the door.

Libby strode through and stood in the centre of the room. She was wearing a cream swing jacket over navy jeans. Her tumbled hair was sleek and shiny. 'Well, Mum?' The words came out on a sob. 'Is it true?'

'Oh, Libby.' She collapsed onto the bedroom chair and put her head in her hands.

'So it *is* true.' Libby's voice was hushed. 'I can't *believe* this. I thought Dad was making it up.'

'What exactly did he tell you?'

'Does it matter?' Libby's voice was hard. 'We were talking, Dad and I. He said . . . Oh, Mum,' her voice cracked, 'he said you'd betrayed him. *Betrayed* him.'

Emma was silent.

'Mum, how could you? How could you do that to him and mess it all up?' Libby's voice came out like a wail. She subsided onto the other spindly bedroom chair, leaned across the small round table and began to cry her heart out. Emma let her weep for a few moments, too terrified to put a comforting hand on her arm or to attempt to smooth her hair. Eventually Libby raised a tear-stained face that wrenched Emma's heart. 'I don't understand. I mean, *my* mum and dad . . . I can't get my head around all this.'

'Neither can I.' Emma swallowed hard. 'It's a nightmare.'

'*You* feel it's a nightmare?' Libby rounded on her. 'You're the one who caused it,' she said angrily. 'You cheated on Dad. You must have known what you were doing. '

'I didn't. Not really. I was drunk.'

'*Drunk?*' Libby's blue eyes flashed. 'That's no excuse. And all the times you've lectured us . . .'

'I know,' Emma said. 'I made a horrible, catastrophic mistake, Libby. The worst mistake of my life. You've no idea how sorry I am, how hopeless I feel, how much I regret it. I don't think I've slept since it happened. I was so pissed that I didn't know what I was doing.'

'How could you sleep with that on your conscience?' Libby stormed. 'No wonder Dad looks so haggard and miserable.' She glared at Emma furiously then, after a moment, she said, 'What do you mean, "since it happened"? How long ago was this?'

Emma couldn't talk. Her heart hammered against her ribs.

'Hang on a minute . . .' Libby's eyes narrowed and Emma felt weak as she saw her daughter's thoughts come together and flash across her face. 'That weekend,' Libby began, 'when you were wasted . . . after the Friday night you were out with the office gang . . . That was weeks ago! But the *office* gang? God, Mum, I hope I'm wrong, because the most awful thought has just clicked into my head.' Trembling, she rose to her feet and began to back across the room, shaking her head. 'You didn't. It wasn't. *No.*'

Emma knew instinctively that she had to stop Libby leaving. She could hardly see her daughter through her tears, but she followed her across the room. 'Libby, don't go,' she begged, reaching out towards her. 'Please let me explain. It was a terrible mistake.' Her hand brushed Libby's arm.

'Don't touch me,' Libby snapped as she stepped away.

'Please, don't go – I'll never forgive myself for that stupid night, but at least let me try to explain . . .' Emma was sobbing now, huge racking sobs that caused her to bend over and clutch at her stomach.

Libby halted, her hand on the door. 'I don't want to know,' she said coldly.

'I don't blame you if you never want to see me again, I'll fully understand, but please don't go without letting me say how truly sorry I am,' Emma whispered. 'I'd give anything to turn the clock back, believe me, Libby, anything at all. I was stupid and silly. I know my behaviour was despicable. I know I've ruined everything, with Oliver, you and Charlie, the people I love most in the world. I don't care about me any more – I'll have to live with my stupid behaviour for the rest of my life, but I'd give anything to have things back to normal for you.'

Something in her tone, some note of sheer desperation, must have communicated itself to her daughter. Through a haze of tears, Emma watched Libby's face crumple. Then Libby took her hand off the door. 'Oh, Mum, what are we going to do?'

Emma summoned room service when she discovered that Libby hadn't eaten all day. She even ordered a bottle of wine, saying that she'd hardly had a drink since that awful night but they'd both had a shock and needed a remedy. Sitting at the small round table by the hotel bedroom window, she glossed over the events of that Friday night, sparing Libby the details. Libby broke down in tears again. Down below, on the road outside, traffic surged by, and in the near distance, Emma could see the cars coming off the M50, loping and snaking round the slip-roads. It was a sight she was heartily sick of.

'I suppose in a way we all had a part to play,' Libby eventually said in a muffled voice.

Emma shook her head. 'Don't ever think that,' she said. 'I'm the one to blame for this mess. It's up to me and Oliver to sort it out. You and Charlie are in no way to blame.'

'Maybe if we'd been more supportive you wouldn't have been quite so upset over the promotion in the first place and you wouldn't have got plastered. I knew you were disappointed, but I was so caught up in my own goings-on . . .'

Emma shook her head. 'It was my fault and, unfortunately, I don't know what lies ahead. Dad won't talk to me right now and I don't blame him.'

'Dad's in bits, but I'm not going to take sides,' Libby said. 'I just hope you can sort something out. Oh, God, does Dad know who . . .? Or that I . . .?' Libby shook her head. 'I can't bear to think about it.'

'No, your father didn't want any names. And he doesn't know that you . . .' Emma faltered.

There was a short silence.

'By the way, Mum,' Libby said, 'I thought I'd landed you in it yesterday.'

'How?'

'I had a long chat with Dad about stuff and I told him about Granny Colgan.'

'What about her?'

Emma listened as Libby told her about the old lady's frosty remarks.

'Libby, darling! All these years you've been carrying that. If only I'd known . . .' She felt at an acute loss. 'What did your father say?'

Libby looked unhappy.

'It's okay, you can tell me,' Emma encouraged.

'He said that . . . oh, Mum, he married you because he wanted to spend the rest of his life with you and that me coming along was an added joy.'

Emma felt tears prick her eyes.

'So, you see, I guess he still loves you,' Libby went on sadly.

'I know he does,' Emma said softly. 'That's why he's so shocked and hurt. You don't fall out of love overnight. The problem is, Libby, he can't forget what happened and that's the kind of corrosion that breaks up a marriage.'

'What are you going to do?'

'I don't know. But I'm going to try everything to make it up to him. I'm keeping out of his way for now, until the dust settles, then it's over to Paris – you *are* coming, aren't you? I'd hate to think I'd spoil your great night. Your father will scarcely come, but we have to be there for Alix, no matter what's going on in Dublin. You might think she has the big, glitzy life but she's been through a lot, stuff I can't tell you about.'

'Don't worry, I'm all set.' Libby smiled. 'I can't miss that and the chance to put on some glam, thanks to you, never mind staying the night in the best hotel in Paris. And there you go again – even though your own life is upside down, you're thinking of your sister. That's what made me stop at the door, Mum.'

'What do you mean?'

'What's happened to you and Dad, even though it's all so crap, I know you still love us and want the best for us. I know that hasn't changed and I'm feeling so sorry about the whole thing, and kinda sorry for you, Mum. Even though it was your fault, and you were terribly stupid, you didn't deserve for this to happen,' Libby said. She was pink in the face by the time she'd finished and Emma's heart went out to her.

'Thanks, love.' Emma squeezed her hand.

'If it's okay with you, I'm going to tell Charlie. Not everything, of course, but I think he should have an idea of what's going on.'

'Charlie will never talk to me again.'

'He will by the time I'm finished with him,' Libby said stoutly. 'Oh, and guess what? He's not exactly Mr Squeaky Clean himself. I have to tell you about Leticia. And Charlie.'

'Leticia and *Charlie*?'

'Yep!' Libby relayed what had happened.

'You don't mean that was going on under our noses?'

'Apparently so,' Libby said, the glimmer of a smile on her lips. 'But I don't know for how long.'

Despite everything, Emma couldn't help her mouth turning up at the corners. Then she wondered, with a pang, how Oliver was coping. She was actually a little relieved to hear that her responsible, trustworthy husband was hitting the bottle, skiving off work and allowing himself to wallow in the hurt. For it meant, she fervently hoped, that he was moving on from the initial immobilising shock.

Although she still didn't know if he'd ever talk to her again.

Chapter 50

'*A*re you sure I'll get in? They'll take one look at me and know that I'm not even twenty-one,' Charlie grumbled as the taxi sped into the city centre on Sunday evening.

'For the hundredth time, yes. I have that sorted,' Libby hissed. As soon as they climbed out of the taxi on St Stephen's Green, she scrabbled in her bag and removed a small card, handing it to her brother.

'Jeez, you're in the wrong job,' Charlie said, examining the perfectly executed fake ID.

'Tell me about it,' Libby sighed. 'Just don't show it to Dad.'

'Are you for real? Course not.'

'You don't look too bad.' She cast her eye over her brother's indigo jeans and jacket. 'For a brother. I can just about bear to be seen with you.'

'Same here. Can I hang onto this afterwards?' He waved his fake ID. 'It might come in handy.'

'Hang onto what?' Libby eyeballed him. 'I haven't given you anything, right?' It was a balmy evening as they fell into step together around the side of the Green, and Libby felt a quiver of expectation.

On Saturday, she'd taken Charlie to one side on the pretext of checking out his computer and told him what had been going on, feeling a huge rush of sympathy as she saw how shaken he was. She'd allowed him time to absorb the shock, and even cooked him some microwave lasagne afterwards.

'Don't let on to Dad that I've told you,' she urged when he had pulled himself together.

Charlie blew his nose. 'What do you take me for?' he said. 'Of course not. He might guess by my face, though.'

'He'd better not,' Libby said. 'We need to make life as easy as possible for him if we want him to start talking to Mum. I know she was terminally stupid, but don't tell me you never messed things up when you were wasted.' Libby fixed him with a piercing gaze worthy of their father at his most incisive.

'Yeah, right,' Charlie said gruffly.

'Mum's not used to alcohol and she was totally catatonic. She'd never have done something drastic like that otherwise. And she'd never have got that pissed if we'd shown her more support. She still loves us to bits. What do you want for our family? A big, devastating divide? Mum and Dad to get a divorce? We'd have to sell Laburnum Grove. And can you just imagine Christmas and birthdays? Never mind every single weekend?'

'God, no. I want everything to stay the same.'

'So do I,' Libby said, with feeling. 'The Colgan family has to remain intact. We'll have to do our bit to get Mum and Dad back together. They still love each other and Mum loves us the same way she always has. That hasn't changed. We have to get them talking, somehow or other. And, by the way, I'm not taking any sides in this.'

'Neither am I.'

'Good. In the meantime, there's something you can do for me and Mum.'

'Yeah?'

'You'll have to pretend you're on a date with me. Just for a short while.'

They were a bit early, Libby knew, as they brazenly sashayed past the security on the door. One of the beefier guys looked Charlie up and down and asked to see his identification. Libby hung onto his arm while smiling seductively at the guy, and they were waved through.

'Act the part,' Libby hissed. 'Look bored, as though you've been here a hundred times.'

'Are you sure this is the right place?'

Libby looked around at the crowded disco bar. The frenetic atmosphere and thumping music didn't seem so exciting any more. It was all a bit tawdry around the edges. 'This is definitely the right place. Let's just hope he shows up tonight.' She ordered drinks, a Cosmopolitan for herself and a pint for Charlie. And then, after a while, she saw him pressing through the crowds.

She felt a moment of nausea, and forced herself to stay calm and empty her mind of all thoughts. Except the ones of revenge. A lot of what had happened was his fault. He'd not only taken advantage of her mum, he'd had the gall to try to get to her through Libby. Only for that, life in the Colgan household would have continued much as normal, with her dad spared his current heartbreak and her mum learning to move on and accept her mistake. It was a once-off that Libby couldn't help but forgive, having witnessed her mother's whole-hearted regret, even though she still found it difficult to get her head around what had happened.

And it was a once-off mistake that Libby could understand, for it could have so easily been her. Not necessarily with Karl, she cringed, but there had been a few times when she had been the worse for alcohol and anything could have happened. It was all too easy, she knew, to go over the edge and lose your bearings in some mindless place. Sometimes she'd even used her unhappiness in her career as an excuse to get wasted. *Wasted!* How horrible it sounded, never mind the awful consequences it could bring. Luckily enough the worst hadn't happened to Libby – at least, not yet, she silently mocked herself. It was a timely lesson to her, a reminder to be more careful about herself and her drinking. Libby Colgan deserved better than to end up half pissed somewhere she didn't want to be.

'There he is, Charlie, that bloke in the grey shirt.'

Charlie watched him silently. Libby guessed that he, too, was trying to put a lid on his emotions. The he said, 'Jeez, you never told me he was built like a rugby tackler.'

'He plays GAA, just like you. Hang on, wait a minute . . .'

'What's up?'

'See those girls he's with? The two blondes . . .?'

Charlie did a double-take. 'Wow. How did I miss them?'

'They're out of Mum's old office, Nikola and Stacy.'

'Do you still want me to go ahead?'

'Yes, this is even better again,' Libby said, thinking rapidly. 'Forget about the knee in the balls. I've thought of something else that'll make him regret the day he tangled with the Colgans.' And if he did happen to talk about her mum in the office, no one would believe him. She told Charlie what to do and what to say.

At first he was reluctant, in view of his audience of two extremely pretty blondes. 'I can't do that. I'll lose all credibility.'

'Go on, Charlie,' Libby encouraged. 'This is for Mum and Dad. Only you can do it and you'll probably never see them again anyway.'

Charlie downed the rest of his pint and Libby watched as he

made his way through the crowd to Karl. Her brother threw his arm around him and, in a high-pitched voice, told him he was really sorry, *dahling*, for kicking him out of bed the other night but he just wasn't used to such a teeny-weeny willy. Then Charlie turned to Nikola and Stacy and winked. 'Don't worry, girls, you're not missing much,' he said.

Her brother deserved an Olympic medal for sheer boldness, Libby decided. As he made a swift exit, Karl was turned to stone. Stacy and Nikola exchanged flabbergasted glances. They picked up their bags and headed to the ladies' room. And, as Libby had hoped, Karl's eyes swivelled around the disco bar before they came to rest on her.

Libby tossed her long blonde hair, slid off her stool and made a rude gesture with her finger as she marched towards the exit.

Chapter 51

'I didn't think you'd have time to meet me, Alix,' Fiona said. 'This is your big week, the week when you scale glittering new heights. From now on, I'll probably need an appointment to see you.'

'Nonsense.' Alix's eyes were drawn to Fiona's gently swelling abdomen beneath the cobalt blue dress as she sat down on the banquette opposite her.

'All set for Thursday?' Fiona asked brightly.

'Yes – Emma and Hannah are arriving in tomorrow,' Alix said, feeling as though some part of her was detached from it all. 'I'm meeting with Henri on Wednesday for last-minute stuff and to make sure I'm happy with all the arrangements, so the days will fly in.'

'And then we'll have the arrival of all the starlets and celebrities. But don't worry, Dave's all yours. He'll be in the Louis XII early enough on Thursday to look after your hairstyling requirements.'

'Libby will love that,' Alix said. 'She wants to experience everything – the spa, the luxury, the private session with Dave and the launch itself.'

'*And* her famous aunt doing her make-up.'

'That won't cut any ice with Libby. I'm plain old Alix to her, which suits me fine.'

'Still, you're very good to take time out to look after her and Emma on what will be a hectic evening for you.'

'I also promised Hannah I'd do her make-up. And I can work wonders in the space of a few minutes. If I can't look after my own family, what's the point?' Alix frowned. Right then, she didn't see the point in anything.

The waitress arrived and they both ordered *boeuf en daube*, a dish for which the restaurant was renowned. Alix ordered a glass of Beaujolais and Fiona some mineral water. While they were waiting for their food, Alix talked about the launch night, trying to inject some enthusiasm into her voice.

'Alix, darling,' Fiona put a hand on her arm, interrupting her, 'is everything all right?'

Alix looked at her guardedly. 'Yes, why?'

'It's just that— Look, you seem a little down and I don't want to jump the gun or speak out of turn, but according to Marc, Tom Cassidy is going around Paris like his world has come to an end and Marc seems to think that – um – you might have something to do with it . . .'

Alix's head snapped up. She dug her nails painfully into her palm to hold herself in check. 'Forgive me, Fiona, but I'd sure hate to think that this was why you asked to meet me for lunch.'

'No, of course not,' Fiona assured her. 'I wanted to see if you're all set for Thursday or if you need help with anything. But when I heard about Tom and your possible involvement I was concerned, and if there's anything you want to talk about, well, you know I'm on your side.'

Alix laughed to herself. Fiona wouldn't be on her side, no way, if she knew exactly why Tom Cassidy and Alix Berkeley had had a blazing row that ended up with him almost taking the hinges off her hall door as he flung himself through it. Her friend would never speak to her again were she to reveal her terrible deception. 'You can tell Marc to mind his own business for starters,' she said quietly.

Fiona looked crestfallen. 'Sure. If that's what you want.'

Alix was immediately contrite. 'Sorry, don't mind me. I did have a bit of a row with Tom, but I just don't feel like talking about it right now.'

She saw Fiona's eyes widen with a mixture of concern and surprise but she still couldn't bring herself to satisfy her curiosity. The fragile part of her that was silently weeping for Tom and everything else was firmly locked away.

Fiona squeezed her hand. 'I'm here for you, you know that, whenever you want to talk.'

Alix managed to muster a faint smile. 'I do know that, and thanks, Fiona.'

After lunch, Fiona took a cab back to the hairdressing salon, but Alix decided to walk to her apartment. Rain was falling, a light summer rain that misted the city and gently drizzled like pale grey silk. It was her last free day before she was swept up in the pre-launch activities for Alix B and she felt the need to stay out in the fresh air and breathe it in deeply, to allow the soft rain to mist her face and form tiny crystals in her hair as she walked along, trying to arrange her thoughts and mentally close the wound that Fiona had unwittingly opened on a hurt so raw and painful that it throbbed day and night.

It was five long days and five sleepless nights since Tom had slammed out of her apartment, yet if she'd been asked to recall the details of those particular days and nights, she would have found it impossible. His face swam in front of her, so full of outrage and disbelief that it was almost frightening. As she had told him the truth, it was a face that became so full of hurt and confusion that she would have given the world to go back to where it had all begun, when she'd discovered she was pregnant with his child.

The sparkling knowledge that some kind of wondrous miracle was taking place inside her body had been tinged with alarm. Alix had found it hard to believe that such a marvel had occurred as a result of making love to Tom, yet she was terrified by the implications. In those first few nights after her suspicions were confirmed, she'd tossed and turned, her thoughts running from the tiny life forming inside her to the hard reality.

She'd thought it had been heartbreaking saying goodbye to Tom and walking away from him in St Stephen's Green shopping centre. But that had paled into insignificance compared to giving her baby away.

In a north London hospital she'd felt the bulge of the small, wet, slippery life move out of the protection of her body and into the waiting world and nothing had prepared her for just how bereft she'd feel. They'd told her it was a perfect little girl, but she already knew, had known instinctively all along. She listened to the first plaintive wails of her baby as she was placed in an incubator, too numb and shocked to cry, and knowing that a savage, overwhelming grief was waiting to consume her as soon as the shock had worn off. Six weeks later, having seen her baby daughter just once, her gut contracting at the sight of her spiky, jet black hair and screwed-up face, she signed on the dotted line and walked away for ever.

Now, fifteen years later, in her luxury apartment, Alix had sat in her dressing gown and gone through the bald, hard facts with Tom while he recovered from his initial shock and stared at her as though he was unable to take it all in.

Still traumatised by his discovery, she had left her emotions to one side and talked to him in cold, disjointed sentences. From somewhere outside herself, and in a voice devoid of feeling, she had summoned enough resolve to tell Tom how she'd gathered her few savings and gone to London, found somewhere basic to stay and got a job so that she could pay her way and work right up to the birth. Then she had made plans to hand her baby daughter over for adoption as soon as possible afterwards.

'A little girl?'

'Yes, Tom, it was a girl.'

'I don't believe you. You actually had a baby girl, our baby daughter?'

'Yes,' Alix had confirmed, held in the grip of terror at the way things had so suddenly turned on their head that morning. She had got up and searched through the papers in her green case until she came to the document she'd shown Emma. 'Here's the birth certificate in case you need proof.'

Tom shrank away from it as though it was abhorrent. 'I can't bear to look at that right now. It would break my heart. God Almighty, how could you have done this? Where is she now?'

'I don't know. I signed the adoption papers when she was six weeks old,' she told him, sitting down at the table.

He had looked at her as though she was some kind of evil Medusa. 'Did you see her at all?' he pounced.

'Just once. I thought it was best not to form an attachment,' Alix had said, her lips quivering under the strain.

'Form an attachment? Is that how you define it?' Tom was scathing. 'But you forgot about one thing,' he snapped. 'As soon as she's eighteen, she can access her birth certificate and come looking for you. Then I hope she tells you just what she thinks of the monster of a mother who abandoned her at birth.'

'She won't come looking for me. I've put a request for no contact in the file papers.'

'You really had it all worked out, hadn't you?' he had said, his

anger bubbling over. 'You bloody bitch. You'd think you were par-
celling up some kind of nuisance or shitty inconvenience that was
preventing you from getting on with your life and career.'

'I didn't think either of us was ready for it,' she said, grappling for
words as she faced up to him in her apartment. 'I didn't want you
to feel manipulated into a rushed marriage. Tom, you were just
twenty-two. You were barely out of college. Then you were all set
to spread your wings. I didn't want you to feel trapped. It wasn't fair
to tie you down or make you feel responsible when you were so
young and had the world at your feet. I thought it was best for you
to be free to follow your dreams.'

'That's no excuse,' he stormed. 'At the very least you should have
told me and allowed me to have a choice in the matter. Did you
even consider that I might want to know?'

'How could we have coped financially?' She went on to outline
all the questions that had helped her to come to her decision. 'We
were earning buttons. Where would we have lived and how could
we have managed, when it would have been a good while before
either of us was earning any decent money? There was so much
stacked against this tiny baby that it wasn't fair to her. Can't you see?
It was the obvious solution for me, for you, but most of all for her,'
Alix had cried. 'I was doing it for our daughter, Tom, to give her
the best possible start, the best possible life, and I thought it was best
to give her up to a loving home where she was wanted by both parents. Parents who were desperate for a baby and would give her all
the love in the world. Parents with a certain level of financial security who were dying to bring a baby into their comfortable home
and nurture and care for her.'

Tom shook his head. 'That's horseshit. We could have cared for
her and loved her. We would have managed somehow. We loved
each other, we'd have made a go of it. I can't believe you kept it
all from me. It's— Oh, God,' he broke off, visibly overcome. He

struggled to pull himself together. 'I don't know how you could have been so unfeeling. How could you do it?'

Unfeeling? She had been anything but.

'It was our *child*! I can't understand how you could have been so callous, so cruel and so downright hard-hearted. It's beyond my comprehension.' His eyes had been full of pain and contempt as he snatched up his jacket and made for the door.

The room had swayed around Alix, and something had sparked inside her: a nugget of self-respect that dredged itself out of the depths, a refusal to be seen as an out-and-out monster.

'No, Tom, it wasn't like that. You have it all wrong,' she began. 'I did what I did because I thought it was the best for everyone. But I've regretted it every day of my life. Leaving you was the second worst thing I've ever done, and all that crap about a big job in London was just an act, but leaving our daughter was by far the worst. You've no idea how hopeless and wretched I felt, but I thought I was giving her the best life possible. Can't you understand? I panicked, and it seemed the right thing to do at the time. God help me if she ever does manage to track me down, because I don't think I could bear to look at her face. I don't need you to tell me I've been callous and cruel. I know I made a horrendous mistake.'

'Some fucking mistake,' he said savagely.

'There was something else . . .' She hesitated.

'You mean more pathetic excuses?'

'Thing is, beyond everything else, I was scared to death, petrified, terror-stricken, even, at the thought of being a wife, never mind a mother,' she explained, realising that it was imperative to be totally honest with him. 'I'm a carbon copy of my own mum, with her genes inside me. You know I'm the image of her. I was terrified I wouldn't be up to the job, not good enough, or that I might in time hurt and betray you and my daughter. And I couldn't be responsible for that. I couldn't, *wouldn't*, inflict my flawed maternal skills on an innocent child or put her through the kind of betrayal I'd experienced at the hands of my own mother. Now I know that my betrayal was worse.'

Tom had looked at her derisively. 'I can't believe you're using your own mother as some kind of miserable validation for your actions. It sucks to high heaven. You mean you were heedless and too selfish to give a flying fuck about my feelings.'

'No – listen to me, please.'

He stared at her.

'After I moved to Paris, I tried to put it behind me,' Alix went on in a thready voice, feeling as though she was fighting for her life. 'But I've always had a nagging ache for you and there's a day each year, the first of July, when I shut out the world and try to get through it as best I can. Then I heard you were coming to Paris . . . I went to your exhibition because I wanted to see you, to find out how you were getting on, if you were happy, fulfilled, or if there was anything missing in your life. I cared for you, loved you, all those years ago. I thought you wanted to be free. I care for you now. I *love* you, Tom. I'm so sorry for what I did. And you've no idea how much I hate myself, or how much I'll regret it for the rest of my life. I'll never, ever be able to move on from this.'

Something had flickered in his silvery blue eyes, and then it was gone. 'I still think you're an immoral, hard-hearted bitch,' he said. Then he had wrenched open the door and stormed out.

The light misty rain finally stopped as Alix strode past the ter-raced cafés on the Boulevard St-Germain. She hadn't heard from Tom since, but she knew she'd never forget his distraught face.

She couldn't pinpoint the moment when it had dawned on her that she'd rejected and betrayed her child in a more sinful manner than her mother had ever betrayed her. Or the moment that she'd begun to ask herself just how her daughter must feel knowing she'd been abandoned by her mother when she was at her most tiny and vulnerable. They were questions that had begun to tumble though her subconscious and stop her sleeping.

And she'd deceived Tom so shamefully. She'd come face to face with him to see for herself if there were any gaps in his life. Now there was no doubting that she'd opened a chasm of monumental proportions by denying him his daughter. No doubting either that he'd never forgive her.

Chapter 52

'Wow, Alix. This is some fabulous apartment!' Hannah Berkeley exclaimed, standing in the living room and gazing about her in delight. 'I'm so happy for you. Life has been good to my little niece.'

'Yes, hasn't it?' Alix smiled, exchanging a glance with Emma.

'How long is it since I've seen you?' Hannah asked.

'Too long for me and I'm rather embarrassed,' Alix responded, pouring champagne into three crystal flutes. 'At least Emma went out to visit you with her family.'

'That was five years ago, and we had one heck of a busy time, didn't we, Emma?' Hannah said, accepting a glass. 'Here's to the three of us, and to the launch of Alix B. At least it brought us together again.'

'To Alix B.' Emma touched her glass to Hannah's.

'And how is your delightful family, Emma? Will I have the pleasure of seeing them at the launch?'

'Libby's flying in first thing tomorrow morning,' Emma said brightly. 'But you won't see Oliver or Charlie. It's not really their scene and Oliver's up to his tonsils in work.'

Alix silently applauded her sister's brave face.

Emma had flown in from Dublin earlier that day and was back in Alix's spare bedroom. Then Hannah had phoned to say she was alive and well, had landed in Paris that morning from Kuala Lumpur where she'd stopped to break the journey, and had now slept off the rest of her jet lag. She was staying in a boutique hotel nearby and was dying to see her nieces. Alix had promptly invited her over for a meal that evening.

The sisters had agreed before Hannah arrived that everything was great, wonderful and marvellous. There was no point in souring their aunt's visit with details of their messed-up lives. Emma had brought Alix up to date with Libby's visit to her hotel room. Then they had collapsed into each other's arms and shed a few tears.

Alix told Emma that Tom had found out about the baby and was incensed with rage. She was almost incoherent as she described his shock and hurt and the way he had stormed out of the apartment.

'Hold on, Alix, how did all this happen? Did I drop you in it? That time I spoke to him in Fiona's?'

'Not really, I managed to come up with an explanation for that. I've been seeing him,' Alix told her, her long slender fingers lacing and unlacing in agitation, a childhood gesture that Emma was all too familiar with. 'We were getting together. Talking and things . . .'

'Things?' Emma prompted.

Alix's face crumpled. 'You know . . . Then afterwards, one morning, after he'd stayed the night . . .' She couldn't continue.

'God, I'm so, so sorry. You didn't deserve this.'

'Oh, but I did, every last bit of it,' Alix said. 'I've denied him his child, almost fifteen years of fatherhood. How could I have been so cruel?'

'You were doing what you thought was best,' Emma reminded her. 'You gave your baby in trust to a different mother and father out of love for her, so that she'd have the best start in life. At the time it seemed the right thing, the only thing, to do.' They'd talked all this through already, as they'd sat up into hushed, early-morning hours the night that Alix had finally broken her long silence. Emma's immediate reaction had been to reassure Alix that she wasn't quite the demon she was painting herself to be.

'You could also say that I was selfish and careless – too selfish to take on the responsibility of looking after my baby, too careless with Tom's feelings to consider that he might want to know he had fathered a child.'

'Is that what he said?'

'Something along those lines, but in glorious, vibrant Technicolor.'

'I can well imagine,' Emma sighed. 'He was bound to be incredibly angry.'

'I just need to stay in one piece to get through the next couple of days.'

'You'll be fine,' Emma said encouragingly. 'We'll both be great. I feel I've spent enough time beating myself up over the last few weeks. I need some light relief. Let's put everything to one side for the next forty-eight hours or so and enjoy your moment of glory. It'll be fun and glamorous – and to hell with it! Oliver can wait.'

'Right.' Alix summoned a grin. 'The same goes for Tom.'

Hannah was looking great, Alix thought as they sat around the table until late in the evening, catching up on everyone's news. At sixty-nine, she was still the same feisty person who'd temporarily given up on her travelling dreams to help look after her two little nieces. Although her hair was now a silvery grey, to Alix's eyes she hadn't aged a bit. She wore it in a short funky style, for ease of management, which gave her a youthful aura and brought out her heart-shaped face and soft, delicate skin. She'd retired from nursing four years previously and was now enjoying a busy, action-packed life.

'I've been meaning to come to Europe for a couple of years,' she admitted. 'This launch was just the excuse I needed. I'm staying in Paris for a week, then going to visit some old nursing friends in London and, depending on how things go, I might squeeze in a quick trip to Dublin.' She smiled at Emma.

'Sounds good, Hannah,' Emma said.

Looking at her sister's face, Alix swiftly changed the subject. She poured more champagne. 'This toast is for you, Hannah. I don't think we fully appreciated what you did for us in putting your life on hold. I sometimes wondered if you ever felt aggrieved about giving up your best years when you should have been looking for romance and relationships and perhaps a family of your own.'

Hannah smiled. 'Not at all. To me, you were an instant, ready-made family. Remember, I was almost forty. I think if love and marriage had been on the agenda for me I would have found them by then. Thing is, girls, life was different thirty-odd years ago. Back then, women of my age were most definitely on the shelf. Thank God all that's changed. Look at you, Alix, you're thirty-six, -seven? Yet you'd never be labelled a spinster or on the shelf – your gener-ation has pushed back the boundaries and is making the most of everything, living life to the full. Careers, family, social lives, the works! Even my generation has benefited in the long run, and I like to think that seventy is the new fifty. And I do have a friend back in Melbourne. His name is Richard. Marriage isn't on the cards, not now, but that's not to say there isn't a touch of romance in my life!'

'You were very generous, all the same, to look after us the way you did,' Alix said.

'To be honest, I wasn't quite the martyr you might think,' Hannah went on. 'The arrangement suited me, you know. I never admitted it, but I'd had a few disappointing relationships and I was pretty fed up with men and my life in general, so in a way you were just the tonic I needed.' Hannah's face softened. 'And it was the least I could do for you and for Andrew. I don't have to tell you that he was really gutted by what happened. And for you pair, losing your mum at such a young age was a terrible blow. So it was good to feel useful.'

They'd never really talked to Hannah about the tragic events of that weekend, Alix mused. It was a subject that was strictly off limits, and although as they grew up Hannah had told them many times how much their mother had loved them and how proud she would have been of them, the sad details had never been discussed. Hannah, much like Andrew, seemed to have put up an invisible boundary that warned them not to cross into forbidden territory. They knew that she had always been close to her brother, so it was obviously painful for her to discuss the way he had been betrayed by his beautiful wife and the tragic consequences. It was painful for Alix now to grasp the devastating consequences it had had for her. 'Well, thanks to you, Hannah, that blow was considerably cushioned for me and Emma. We were blessed that we had you to turn to,' she said.

'Andrew and I tried to put on a face and keep life as normal as possible for you,' Hannah smiled.

She wasn't the only one who'd been busy making faces, Alix thought ruefully. How many people went through life putting on an act? And who, exactly, did it benefit in the end? She rose to her feet. 'Right. Time for food. Who's for some moussaka? Served with dressed green salad and crusty, buttered bread?'

'I trust you prepared it yourself and from scratch,' Emma joked.

'Absolutely,' Alix laughed. 'You can give me a hand and start pouring that bottle of Cabernet, and we'll make plans for tomorrow. I'll be meeting with Henri to go over last-minute arrangements for the launch, so I want to make sure you two are kept out of mischief.'

'I'm hoping we'll go shopping, Emma,' Hannah said. 'You know your way around Paris far better than I do.'

'You're on,' Emma smiled.

The following morning, Emma met Hannah for coffee and croissants in her hotel, and after a couple of hours drooling over the designer shops in rue St-Honoré they went for lunch in a brasserie off the Champs-Élysées. When her grilled salmon arrived and the waitress had left their table, Hannah took a deep breath and asked Emma if anything was troubling her.

Emma's heart lurched. 'What do you mean?' she asked.

Hannah's eyes were full of concern. 'Maybe I'm wrong, I hope I am, but I can't forget the look on your face when I asked about Oliver yesterday evening and talked about visiting Dublin. And I've a feeling you're not really with me today. Is everything okay between you?'

Emma put down her fork and took a sip of water. 'I didn't want to talk about it. I've been putting it on hold until Alix's launch is over. But Oliver and I—' Her pretence of nonchalance collapsed. 'Oh, Hannah, we're in trouble and our marriage is on the rocks.'

Hannah was visibly distressed. 'Oh dear, that's too bad. What happened?'

Piece by piece, thanks to Hannah's soothing voice and her sympathetic face, Emma unburdened herself. 'I still feel physically sick when I think of it,' she said. 'Just a crazy few hours have ruined everyone's lives. God, Hannah, how could I have let it happen?'

'You didn't set out on purpose to do it. People do silly things in the heat of the moment. You poor thing, you must have suffered so much these past few weeks. But remember this, Emma, no matter how things work out with Oliver, you'll always be Libby and Charlie's mum.'

'I didn't realise how perfect my life with Oliver was until I wrecked it.'

Hannah gave her a rueful smile. 'Life isn't perfect, honey, ever. If it was, it'd be very dull. I wish I could turn back time for you and make it all right again, but the only people who can do that are you and Oliver.'

'Oliver doesn't want to know me any more. He wants a divorce.'

'You mean he imagines he does. Naturally enough, he's not thinking clearly right now. He hasn't a clue what life would really be like if you pair split up, or if you were to pull apart the hundreds of familiar little ties that bind you. There might be difficult times ahead for you and Oliver, but I've no doubt that if you love him you'll make it work. You'll find a way through this, believe me.'

'The thing is, Hannah, he said he could forgive me, but he'd never forget. He said some terrible things.'

'Of course he did,' Hannah smiled. 'What you have to do is make him understand that all those years of marriage are worth far more than a few silly hours with some klutz.'

'You see, that's another part of the problem,' Emma said, feeling a swelling in her throat, 'I'm not all that sure if I am the love of his life. Sometimes I think Oliver just married me because he felt he had to.'

'Oh, Emma, don't be carrying that idea around in your heart. I always thought Oliver was mad about you.'

'Not any more. He can't stand the sight of me. Nothing will ever be the same again.'

After a while Hannah said candidly, 'Well, no, it won't be the same. Right now Oliver is hurt and angry, so naturally he's lashing out at you. But time is a healer, and eventually his anger and hurt will abate a little – you can't keep up that full-on level of emotion indefinitely. But irrespective of what happens, you can't go back to the way you were. What you have to do is find some middle ground with Oliver, make some adjustments and find a new way of relating.'

'I can't see that ever happening,' Emma said.

'Hey, come on.' Hannah patted her shoulder. 'Where's my little warrior? You can't just give up. You have to fight for what you want. You have to impress upon Oliver that you want to spend the rest of your life with him, that you still desire him, that you're still his exciting, sexy wife and you love him to bits. The last thing you need to do is to turn your back on him, whether through guilt or shame. Okay, you made a mistake, but you're still a very valuable, loving person. Don't ever lose sight of that.'

'I don't feel very valuable right now.'

'No, of course you don't,' Hannah said. 'The first thing in all this is you have to accept that was happened was an unfortunate mistake but it doesn't make you a criminal. If anything, I bet you appreciate Oliver all the more.'

'I do,' said Emma, tears pouring freely now. 'I never knew what I had until it began to slip away from me.'

'I'm not trying to pry, Emma, but something else must have driven you to this. You're not the kind of person who goes off the deep end on account of a disappointment over a job.'

Emma sighed. 'You're right. Things haven't been great between myself and Oliver. He's been too wrapped up in his job and taking me for granted. I only found out afterwards that he's had work problems of his own.'

'So it's a wake-up call for you both. You have a better appreciation of Oliver, you know how very deeply you love him, and he'll have a chance to prove that he can rise above his pride because he loves you in return, which I've no doubt he does. Make him listen to you so that he can see the extent of your remorse, and come to understand that you feel so remorseful because you love him with all your heart. Thing is, Emma, it's not as if you're looking for your freedom or hoping for more one-night stands.'

Emma shuddered. 'God forbid.'

'That's something else you have to impress upon Oliver, that you still find him sexy. He's probably imagining all sorts of exciting things, all manner of sensational tricks you got up to with this – whoever he was.'

'Karl,' Emma supplied as nausea rose in her stomach. 'And it wasn't like that. I can't even remember it properly. It's just a haze. Ridiculous, isn't it, to think I threw away my marriage on account of a couple of fuzzy hours of sex?'

'You haven't thrown away your marriage. It's been damaged, certainly, but it's still very much worthwhile. If you're strong enough, stop punishing yourself and go out there with confidence, self-belief and all the love you're capable of. You can come through this with Oliver.'

'Talk about history repeating itself,' Emma said sadly.

'Don't think like that either.'

'That's something else that crossed my mind in the middle of all this mess. I'm every bit as bad as my mother.'

Hannah frowned. 'Your mother worshipped the ground you walked on, Emma. Both you and Alix were infinitely precious to her, as well as Andrew.'

Emma felt a sudden pang for her mother, a pang that found a thirty-year-old echo in her heart and brought her back to the eleven-year-old girl. 'Well, she had a funny way of showing it,' she said, the pang subsiding under a flicker of anger.

'Your mother,' Hannah enunciated slowly, 'loved you all so much that she was readily prepared to forgive and forget. She was prepared to put that – that trouble behind her and move on with Andrew and her girls.'

Emma was quiet for a few moments. 'Funny, you and I have never really talked about that awful weekend when Mum died, but maybe you don't know everything that led up to it. Maybe Dad didn't tell you. Maybe he spared you the worst details because he didn't want to speak badly of Mum.'

Hannah had a strange, puzzled look in her eyes, Emma noticed. 'I'm sorry, you've lost me,' Hannah said. 'I've never spoken to you in detail about that terrible weekend because I found it extremely difficult to raise the awful subject with you and Alix. But please be assured that at no time, ever, did Andrew speak badly of Camille. How could he when she was prepared to forgive his infidelity, even going so far as to set out herself on that fateful journey to insist that he came home?'

I have to go out, darling. Helga will keep an eye on you. Look after Alix for me, won't you?

Emma felt something icy slither down her back and reach around to clutch her stomach in a tight grip. She was almost afraid to ask, to voice the words, and her tongue grappled awkwardly with them, but they had to be said. 'What are you talking about, Hannah? What do you mean by my father's infidelity?'

Chapter 53

*I*t was going to be okay, Alix told herself as she treated herself for once and took the lift all the way to the sixth floor. The inexorable machine of launch night was steamrolling along, scooping her up and sweeping her along regardless. She'd met Henri that afternoon and was impressed with the efforts he and the team from Aurélie were putting in to ensure that the following night would be a mega-success.

'You just have to turn up and be yourself, Alix,' Henri said. 'We want you to relax and enjoy your big moment. All the right people have RSVPed in the affirmative, which is very reassuring.'

Right now, as she opened the door, the launch was just over twenty-four hours away and she was relieved to be getting it out of the way. For the sake of everyone else she would have to look as though she was having a marvellous time. Privately she was touched that Hannah had come all the way from Australia for her great night and that, according to Emma, Libby was barely able to contain her excitement and couldn't wait to show off her fabulous dress. Even Emma was doing her best to be happy, although her heart was mangled beyond belief. Alix owed it to them to be her happy, cheerful self. But the big bright smile was wiped off her face when she walked into her kitchen to find both Emma and Hannah looking at her as though something dreadful had happened.

'Hey, what's with the long faces?' she asked with forced cheer. 'I thought you'd both be on top of the world after your shopping spree. Unless your credit cards were maxed out before you started!'

'We need to talk,' Emma said, rising to her feet. 'And Alix,' she went on softly, her face full of an unnerving compassion, 'I'm afraid that this is going to come as a shock.'

The blood drained from Alix's face. 'I don't think I can take any more shocks. I've just about had a bellyful.' Then she realised that her mask had partially slipped and Hannah was listening. 'Sorry, Hannah, it's just . . .'

'It's okay, Hannah knows, I've told her. Everything. I had to,' Emma explained, looking so concerned that, by now, Alix was thoroughly alarmed.

'What's up?'

'It's about Mum.'

'Mum?' Alix sat down. 'What about Mum?'

'I'll let Hannah tell you,' Emma said.

Alix turned to her aunt.

'There's no easy way to tell you this,' Hannah began, her eyes full of anxiety. 'I gather that you also believed it was your mother who was unfaithful.'

'Well, yes, of course,' Alix said acerbically. 'I saw the newspaper headlines in the kitchen when I went to get some milk. It was Mum plastered all over the papers, running off with her toy-boy lover when the accident happened.' She watched Emma and Hannah exchange solemn glances. 'Why? What's going on?' Her voice rose and she stared from one to the other. Her sister looked as though she was trying to stop herself from crying, which further distressed Alix.

'That silly Helga had no right to buy those tabloids. They weren't supposed to get past the front door,' Hannah fumed.

'They were poking out of the bin.'

'The right place for them. The thing is, darling Alix, both you and Emma were terribly mistaken.' Hannah's voice quivered.

'Mistaken? But surely a sex scandal can only mean one thing.'

'You see, pet, it was never your mother. She was entirely innocent. There was a bit of a scandal, unfortunately, but the student in question was John's girlfriend, Clara, and the teacher involved was, in fact, your father.'

'*What?* You're joking! No. *No.*' Alix rose to her feet, her hands fluttering wildly. 'Tell me this isn't true!'

'I'm afraid it is, darling,' Emma said, coming over. Alix was conscious of her sister catching her hands, hugging her, making her sit down and passing her a mug of hot, sugary tea. Alix hadn't even noticed her getting it ready. 'Sip this slowly. You've had a shock. Hannah told me this afternoon, so I've had a while to absorb it.' Emma had to hold Alix's hands around the mug as they were shaking so much.

Alix took a gulp of hot, sweet tea. She shuddered uncontrollably. 'I can't believe this. It's not possible.' Emma's arms went around her again, holding her, steadying her, her firm, supportive grip confirming more than anything else the terrible truth behind Hannah's words. Alix felt the whole landscape of her life crashing together inside her, then shattering into tiny pieces. Eventually, when the shaking had subsided a little, she looked at Hannah. 'Dammit, Hannah, how did we get it so terribly wrong?'

'All I know, Alix, is what I pieced together from your father and Clara afterwards. She was introduced to your father, whom she already knew from the university, when she and John both called to your parents' home to discuss some project work with your mother – you know the way your parents' door was always open to students . . .'

Alix gave a horrified cry and Hannah stopped. 'Go on, Hannah,' she said, somehow dragging up the words even though she didn't want to know this fresh new heartbreak.

'Clara obviously took some kind of fancy to Andrew, because when her boyfriend broke it off with her, she threw herself at your dad.' Hannah sighed. 'Andrew, unfortunately, succumbed to temptation and, in a fit of remorse, confessed all to your mother before leaving home that Friday evening.'

'I remember there was a dreadful row,' Emma murmured, her eyes shining with unshed tears.

'Then Clara, the little upstart, told her ex-boyfriend what she'd done. I think she was trying to make him jealous. He was a decent young lad and, naturally, he was appalled. He tried to phone your father, heard he wasn't at home, and eventually persuaded your mother to give him the number of the hotel he was staying in, just outside the village. John then talked to your father, whom he held in very high regard, and he was so upset at what had happened that he offered to call over to your mother to apologise in person on Clara's behalf . . .' Hannah paused.

'So Mum *was* going to get Dad when – when the accident occurred,' Emma said gently as she held Alix in a tight embrace.

'Yes, your father didn't want to appear back home in case there was another row in front of his young daughters, so he suggested that if Camille wanted to see him and talk things through in private, John should bring her over to the hotel . . .'

'This is appalling.' Too stunned to cry, Alix's voice broke. 'I still don't understand how we got it so wrong.'

'It was an easy mistake to make,' Hannah said. 'After the accident, most of the locals were reluctant to talk to the tabloid reporters. They were horrified by what had happened, of course, and even more disgusted by what they viewed as a gross invasion of privacy. The bare facts of the accident were obvious, but there was confusion over everything else, except for a few careless murmurs that gathered legs and arms and found their way into the tabloids, which, naturally enough, I kept well away from Andrew. Most likely Clara talked a little, as she was totally histrionic about it all. Unfortunately both you and Emma saw those awful headlines and jumped to the wrong conclusion.'

Alix shook her head. 'I just can't take this in. It's weird. All these years . . . and when I think of the mess I've made of everything, it's just crazy. It beggars belief.' She stood up abruptly, moving out of Emma's embrace. Hugging herself, she went across to the long, elegant windows where the evening was drawing in. Up in the indigo sky, beyond the silhouette of the rooftops of St Germain, a thin crescent moon was etched quite perfectly.

Somewhere out there, Tom was going around Paris in a ferment of anger. Somewhere out there, on the other side of the Channel, their daughter was growing up without knowledge of her birth parents. And she, Alix, had made a monumental mistake that had changed all their lives. She closed her eyes. It was far too much hurt and pain. Far too much to take in.

'Alix, please don't beat yourself up,' Hannah said.

She whirled around from the window. 'How can I ever forgive myself?'

'Darling, please don't punish yourself. You did what you thought was the right thing, the best for everyone, and nobody can fault you for that, least of all yourself.'

'Oh, yeah?' Alix said harshly. 'This really compounds my absolute stupidity. As for Mum, all these years I've been thinking badly of her. And what about Dad?'

'Obviously he hadn't a clue what his daughters were thinking, any more than I did. But I don't have to tell you that he never recovered,'

Hannah said. 'He'd never wanted to hurt his precious daughters or Camille. He spent the rest of his life in a welter of regret.'

'I guess he did,' Alix said, remembering his haunted face. 'Funny, isn't it? He was the one who betrayed us and I should hate him, yet right now I don't feel anything for him.'

'I'm partly to blame as well,' Hannah sighed. 'Andrew was devastated by Camille's death and I tried to spare his feelings by helping him to brush it under the carpet. Maybe if we'd talked some more, the truth would have come out long before now. Come here, my darling, let me give you a hug.'

Alix stared at her aunt for long moments, then allowed her to envelop her in a hug, burying her face in her aunt's warm body and sobbing like the seven-year-old child who'd lost her mum.

Later, when Alix had somewhat recovered from the shock, they moved into the living room and sat talking, reminiscing about their childhood and their mother, seeing everything from a fresh perspective. Alix felt so weary that she relaxed into the cushiony sofa with her shoes kicked off and her legs curled up under her, letting Emma and Hannah's gentle concern wash over her like a soft balm.

'It's off to bed for you after this,' Emma said when she drained the last of the wine into Alix's glass. 'You need a good night's rest before tomorrow. And we're definitely shoving everything to one side, putting our best foot forward and going out there all guns blazing. Alix Berkeley will look sensational and so will her sister. You should see her dress, Hannah – it's the most divine Cavalli silk creation. Forget the A-list guests and the mega-stars, Alix is going to steal the show.'

In spite of her sore heart, Alix couldn't help smiling at her sister's enthusiasm. With Emma and Hannah by her side, maybe she would get through the next twenty-four hours. After all, she'd have the rest of her days to come to terms with everything, including the spectacular way she'd messed up her life.

'But first,' Emma said, putting down her glass and rising to her feet, 'if you'll excuse me, I have to make a phone call.'

Libby answered the phone in Laburnum Grove.

'Hi, Libby, all set for tomorrow?'

Her mother sounded cheerful, Libby thought thankfully, as though she was determined that nothing would spoil the following night. 'Hi, Mum, yes, I'm trying to hold back on the excitement. Wait till I get to Paris and ask the cab driver to bring me straight to the Louis XII. I've been practising the phrase in my best schoolgirl French. Practising all my French, actually, to make sure I don't miss anything. This could go to my head, you know. How are you and Alix?'

'We're fine. I just need to talk to your father, Libby, if you can get the phone to him. Is he there?'

'Dad? Yes, he's here, but why can't you try his mobile? Or send him a text? I'm not sure if he'll talk to you . . .' She didn't want to be caught in the middle between warring parents.

'Sorry for dragging you into it, Libby, but his mobile is switched off.'

'Switched *off*? I don't believe you.'

'That's the message I'm getting. Look, I really need to talk to him. It's important.'

'Okay. I'll see what I can do,' Libby said resignedly.

'Thanks. You're great, and roll on tomorrow. I can't wait to see you in your fantastic dress. It's going to be brilliant.'

Her father was in the den with Charlie, watching Sky Sports. Libby's heart thumped as she held out the cordless handset. 'It's Mum. She's calling from Paris and she really needs to talk to you.'

Oliver stared straight ahead.

'Dad! Stop acting like a four-year-old,' Libby said, exasperated.

'You have to see what Mum wants. She'd hardly have phoned looking for you if it wasn't important.'

Her father stared at her and she could see a muscle moving in his
cheek. Then he reached out and silently took the phone. He stood
up and walked out of the den. Libby collapsed onto the sofa beside
Charlie and inwardly sighed with relief.

'What's going on?' her brother asked.

Libby shrugged. 'Haven't a clue. All I know is that I'm all set for
Paris tomorrow, quaffing champagne and rubbing shoulders with
celebrities and supermodels.'

Charlie gave her a quizzical look. 'How come I'm not going?'

'Charlie, for God's sake, Mum asked you ages ago but you said
you weren't interested. Surely you've heard us talking about it on
and off?'

'Yes, but I thought it was something to do with make-up. I
didn't realise there was going to be supermodels *and* champagne. I
guess I wasn't listening properly.'

Libby rolled her eyes at his downcast expression. Then her father
walked back into the room. They both fell silent and stared at him.
If it was possible to show confusion, bewilderment and surprise all
at once, then that was the look Libby saw in his eyes.

'What are you staring at me like that for?' Oliver asked belligerently.

'How's Mum?' Libby said.

'She's fine, up to a point,' he growled.

'What's up?' Libby persisted. 'Dad, I know by the look on your
face that she's not okay, so there's no point in pretending. And
Charlie and I know everything.'

'Everything?' Oliver faltered.

'Well, most of it. We know why you and Mum aren't talking.
And we're not taking any sides. We're hoping you'll be able to sort
it out like two mature adults.'

'Not so fast, Libby.' Oliver's voice had a dangerous edge. 'These are people's feelings you're talking about, not some multinational takeover.'

'Sorry,' she said, a little discomfited.

Oliver ran a hand through his hair. There was slightly more silver at the temples, Libby noticed, and fresh grooves in his face. 'We're just trying to help, Dad,' she said. 'Charlie and I would do anything to get this family back on the road again. Wouldn't we, Charlie? We're just glad you spoke to Mum this evening.'

Oliver sighed audibly. 'It's not as simple as that. And your mother's phone call . . .'

'Yes?' Libby waited.

'It had nothing to do with what's wrong between us, although in a roundabout way . . .' He trailed off. 'God, I just don't know what to think.'

And Libby and Charlie sat frozen as their father slumped onto the sofa.

'What is it, Dad?' Libby asked quietly. Charlie lowered the volume of the football match after the warning look Libby shot him.

Oliver folded his arms. 'Something weird's happened. Something your mother has lived with for thirty-odd years didn't actually take place. It was the greatest misreading . . . Turns out it was her father all along, not her mother.'

'You're not making sense,' Libby said. 'And I'm going to Paris in the morning for the glittering launch night, so if there's anything I need to know . . .?'

'I quite forgot,' Oliver said. 'You don't know the circumstances of her mother's death, do you?'

'Other than she was in an accident and . . . I suspect there might have been some sort of scandal,' Libby said.

'But not the scandal we thought it was.'

Libby plumped up a cushion and stuck it behind her back. 'So I was right – it was a scandal. I only guessed that because Mum never talked about it. In that case, Dad, I think you'd better tell us everything.'

Libby had to ask her father to repeat the whole thing twice, she was so shocked.

'Oh my God, poor Mum! Imagine that happening to you at eleven years of age. *I* thought it was bad enough when my parents . . . well, you know . . . had a bust-up.' She glanced sidelong at her father. 'But at least I'm an adult. Mum was only a young child. And to find out now that she'd been wrong! And she's still trying to sound cheerful on the phone so that tomorrow night will go well. I'm so glad I'm seeing her. I just want to give her a big, huge hug.'

'So do I – want to see her, I mean,' said Charlie.

'Yeah, right. You just want to get your hands on the supermodels and champagne.'

'It's not that. The house is empty without Mum. I know she was mega-stupid,' his face reddened, 'but I just want it to be back to the way it was before . . . I miss her to bits.'

'Charlie, you can't just wave a magic wand and turn back time,' Oliver said, seeming at a loss in a way Libby had never seen him before. It was impossible to equate the dejected man now flopped on the sofa with the driven and suited-up Oliver who left the house to precision timing each morning. In a moment of intuitive empathy, she suddenly saw him in a different light: as a man instead of her dependable father. She wondered if her dad was really happy and fulfilled in his career, or if he was caught up on some kind of a treadmill that had evolved over the years of fatherhood, mortgages and bills. A treadmill he put up with and made the best of simply because he loved them and wanted the best for them. Something she and Charlie would probably try to emulate if and when they had families of their own. Did anybody ever follow their real dreams, she wondered, or did it mostly come down to doing what was expected of you and putting other people first?

She still hadn't told her father about her chat with Stephen O'Connor. She had to come to a decision by the time she returned from Paris. And in this, she knew, she was on her own.

'Tell you what, Charlie,' Libby said, turning to her brother, 'Mum could do with a bit of support right now after a shock like that, so why don't you come to Paris with me? You could get Dad's ticket transferred to you. Would that be okay, Dad?'

Oliver seemed to rouse himself. 'No, Libby, actually it's not okay.'

Chapter 54

*E*mma accepted a chilled flute of champagne from Alix and reminded herself to pace her drinks. There would be plenty more where this had come from. It was late afternoon and, from what Libby had told her, she would need all her wits about her as the evening progressed.

Oliver was here.

'This will help settle your nerves.' Her sister grinned, clinking her glass to Emma's.

'How about me?' Libby asked, her voice muffled in the huge warm towel swathed round her head.

'Later,' Emma said. 'You can't sip champagne at the same time as Dave styles your hair.'

'Says who?' Alix said, handing Libby a fizzing glass.

'Guess I can work around it,' Dave said as he positioned a chair in front of the large ornate mirror and invited a tent-shaped Libby to make herself comfortable.

Hannah sat back in the period armchair, looking elegant in navy blue Lanvin. 'I'm beautified so I can have all the glug I want.'

They were in Alix's suite in the Louis XII, where Alix had just opened the first of the magnums of champagne that had been sent up, complete with ice bucket and crystal flutes. 'From Henri,' she'd said in answer to Emma's unspoken question as she peeled the foil and expertly prised out the cork.

Emma slowly sipped the sparkling wine. She hadn't seen Oliver in almost two weeks, the longest time they'd spent apart since they were married. And now, according to Libby, he was in Paris and would be at the launch that evening.

'We all came over on the same flight, Mum,' Libby had told her when she arrived at the hotel, alive with excitement and anticipation. 'Dad and Charlie have gone to check out Paris and they're going to have a look at the Stade de France.'

'They're *both* here?'

'Yeah – Charlie wanted to come because he misses you, and Dad told us about your phone call last night and everything that happened with your parents, so we know you've had a bit of a shock and need some support,' Libby said, giving her a hug.

'We'll talk about it again. In the meantime, Alix needs your support far more than I do today,' Emma said, holding her daughter close and breathing in her light, floral perfume.

'Then Dad said he was coming as well because, after Leticia, he couldn't very well leave Charlie unsupervised with all those models and free-flowing champagne. But that's only an excuse, Mum,' Libby went on conspiratorially. 'I think he really wants to see if you're all right after yesterday's news, but he won't admit it. Not even to himself. And I know that you and I are sharing one of the sumptuous bedrooms in this fantabulous hotel, but if anything happens that you and Dad . . . I can always bunk in with Charlie,' Libby finished, her face a little pink.

'That's very generous of you,' Emma said, 'but I can't see it happening, darling.' Champagne flute in hand, she went over to the cheval mirror in the corner and looked at her reflection. Dave had styled her dark hair, flicking it out from around her face and jazzing it up at the back so that it was sexily elegant. Alix had given her a smoky, seductive look using Alix B so that her skin seemed natural and translucent and her eyes were darkly evocative. She'd decided to wear the Helen McAlinden lilac cocktail dress, which gracefully skimmed her contours.

She wondered if Oliver would think she was beautiful.

Alix was working on autopilot, glad to be busy. She'd made up both Hannah and Emma, her fingers and brushes buffing and blending and swirling. As soon as Dave had finished styling Libby's hair into a blonde, tousled cascade, she would transform her niece with pale, dusty mauve and shimmering gold on her eyelids and lashings of black mascara, keeping her lips and cheeks soft and dewy fresh to balance the look. She'd seen Libby's dress and agreed that the black velvet mini was sensational and just perfect for her.

Estelle, her agent, was on the way, and Fiona was lying down, as she needed to conserve her energy for the night ahead. Alix felt like lying down as well, closing her eyes and waking up when it was all over. She'd scarcely slept the night before, despite her sister's advice. Emma and Hannah deserved Oscar nominations for the way they were being falsely bright and cheerful to keep her buoyed up for the star-studded evening. Yet she knew her sadness surrounded her like a cloak, for despite her best efforts at putting on a good face, Fiona had spotted it when she'd arrived at the hotel earlier that afternoon. 'Alix? You look as though someone's just died.'

Alix felt as though her defences were in ribbons around her. 'So I should, because that's precisely how I feel.'

Fiona looked alarmed. '*Mon Dieu*. What's happened? Is it Tom?'

'Good grief, no. It's what didn't happen that's the problem.' Alix gritted her teeth and enlightened her on how she'd discovered the true circumstances of her mother's death, leaving out any reference whatsoever to Tom or London. Fiona was suitably shocked – and she didn't know the half of it, Alix thought grimly.

'This is unbelievable,' she sounded subdued, 'and all those years you carried the wrong idea . . . You have my sympathy, Alix. That was truly a shock.'

Alix felt as though she was made of filigree glass, ready to snap at any moment. 'I just want to get through today and this evening. After that I'll have all the time in the world to think about it.'

Fiona gave her a hug. 'Good for you. Tonight is *your* night, Alix. Don't let anything take that away from you.'

Dave still had to do her hair, but her floor-length Cavalli gown with the asymmetric hem was ready and waiting to encase her in rippling silk, much as she had dragged herself out of bed that morning and encased herself in the falsely bright persona that would get her through the next few hours. Downstairs the team from Aurélie, backed by an army of PR, design and media people, were transforming one of the elegant hotel salons into a fitting showcase for Alix B. Soon an avalanche of paparazzi, celebrities and VIPs would be thronging the salon, plucking drinks and canapés from circulating waiters with silver trays, while flash bulbs popped in their faces and they strove to be seen with the right person.

Alix had finally arrived.

She swallowed some champagne and beamed at Libby. 'Well, pet, are you ready for your fun, chic look?'

Chapter 55

'Alix, this is amazing,' Emma breathed, taking in the sumptuous salon with the glittering Venetian chandeliers, the tables artistically arranged with cleverly illuminated make-up products, the upbeat background music and attentive waiters with trays of martinis and Cosmopolitans, gourmet canapés, caviar blinis and sushi, who threaded through the milling crowd. Along one side of the room, tables and mirrors had been set up and were being manned by the Aurélie beauty team, who were giving make-up demonstrations and handing out small gift bags. Emma didn't have to recognise faces to know that she was surrounded by an impressive array of models and celebrities. It was in their confident air, the way they projected themselves and paraded their beautiful gowns, mini-dresses, basques and chiffon. 'I didn't think it would be quite so ravishing.'

'Didn't you?' Alix's eyes gleamed. 'This is Paris, honey, where everything is *de trop*. Libby looks fantastic.' She nodded to where her niece was chatting to Estelle and Hannah.

'So do you.' Emma admired the fluid lines of the watered-silk gown and matching platform sandals. Dave had textured Alix's hair, studding it with tiny diamanté clips that sparkled and twinkled like stars every time she moved her head.

'Here come Sophie and Yvette,' Alix said as her friends wafted gracefully through the crowd and waved excitedly at her.

'Is that Marc with them?'

'Yes, it is,' Alix said.

'Did you think Tom might come?' Emma murmured, sensing Alix's disquiet.

Alix shook her head, shooting glittering prisms into the air. 'No way. This isn't his scene and, anyway, he can't stand the sight of me right now. *Bonsoir*, Sophie, Yvette.' She moved forward to embrace them.

Libby appeared beside her. 'Isn't this fabulous, Mum? But there's no sign of Dad or Charlie.'

'It *is* fabulous and you look lovely,' Emma said, smiling at her.

'I feel lovely,' Libby said. 'Hey!' She pointed to a tall, statuesque girl with cropped hair and finely chiselled cheekbones. 'Is she who I think she is?'

'I guess so. Why don't you ask Alix to introduce you?'

'Charlie will go mad – he's missing all the fun,' Libby laughed as she moved closer to her aunt. 'Speak of the devil!' She shot a glance at her mother. 'Here they come.'

Emma gripped her glass as she saw Oliver and Charlie moving through the crowd. Oliver was trim and handsome in silver grey Hugo Boss and Charlie looked the part in a black shirt and trousers.

'Hi, Mum,' Charlie said.

Emma sensed his awkwardness at coming face to face with her, now that he knew exactly what she'd been up to. 'Hi, Charlie,' she said quietly, silently begging his forgiveness. 'Thanks for coming. You look really smashing. Paris had better watch out.' There was a moment of hesitation and when her son leaned forward to give her a quick hug she felt her heart splinter into tiny pieces. Libby smiled with relief, pressed a flute of champagne into her brother's hand and bore him off in the direction of the Amazonian models. Leaving Emma with Oliver.

She prickled with anxiety. In spite of the crowds around them, the noise and the background music, she felt as though she and Oliver were the only people in the salon. 'Hi, Oliver, you're looking well,' she said. Close up, it was obvious that he'd had as little sleep as she'd had over the last few weeks.

Her husband's face was impassive. 'I came over with Libby and Charlie to keep an eye on them.'

'Good idea.'

Silence fell between them as the chatter and music swelled around them.

'I had a bit of a jolt yesterday,' she said. 'Hannah's news was astonishing. I phoned you because I felt you should know about it.'

'I'd say it was surprising, all right.'

In her brief phone call to him the previous night, she'd just outlined the bare facts. For Alix's sake, as well as Libby's enjoyment and excitement, she'd held herself together all day. Now she felt a powerful longing to drop the false front and weep on his solid, familiar shoulder for all the years she'd carried mistaken beliefs in her heart and blamed her darling mother for an act of betrayal she'd never committed.

'Can we talk?' she asked. 'Somewhere quieter?'

'I'm not sure about that, Emma.'

At least, she realised with relief, he was making eye contact with her, as well as being civil. 'I don't mean about the situation between us. I just want to talk to you about Hannah's news.'

He gave her a long, measured look, then swept his eyes over the room for Libby and Charlie. Emma followed his gaze. They were laughing together at something Yvette was saying, Charlie's eyes full of flirtatious adoration. Emma said, 'I think we can leave them for a few moments, don't you?'

'A few moments, then.'

They moved through the crowd to the foyer and, feeling the need for fresh air, Emma led him out to the courtyard. It was pretty, with tubs of scented flowers and greenery and dotted with tables where clusters of people were over food and drinks. Emma walked across to a quiet corner table. She could have done with fetching her wrap to throw over her dress, but now that she had Oliver to herself she was unwilling to interrupt their moment together.

'I was telling Hannah about us,' she began when they were both seated, 'telling her that despite my best intentions I'd turned out like my mother.'

Oliver's expression was wintry. He brusquely waved away the attentive waiter.

'One thing led to another,' Emma continued, picking up a stray coaster and twirling it between her fingers, 'and right out of the blue, Hannah passed a comment about my father's infidelity. Gosh.' She shook her head. 'I didn't know what to think . . . all those years Alix and I were mistaken.'

It was strange talking to her husband, acutely aware that everything about him was so dearly familiar to her yet now removed and coldly remote. Her eyes scanned his neat dark hair, his keen eyes, the breadth of his shoulders in his suit, and her mind was awash with memories of those recent nights in Paris when their bodies had passionately meshed together. She blinked back tears, swallowed hard and went on to fill in the details of that long-ago weekend, as Hannah had related them. 'The thing is, Oliver . . .' She was glad that he waited silently while she grappled with her thoughts. 'It's affected Alix rather badly, but that's another story. However, I don't feel any differently about myself. I'm still Emma Colgan and the fundamentals are the same. I'm not emotionally tied to the tragedy that happened to my parents and I haven't been for a long time.'

'And is that good?' he asked a little stiltedly.

'Well, yes, and no.' Emma considered what she was about to say. Oliver was still sitting opposite her and she ached with need for him, freshly aware of her utter insanity in allowing their lives to be shattered. Then she said, 'I haven't been standing in the shadow of my parents – but actually, Oliver, I've been standing in yours.'

'Mine?' Oliver flashed her a look of disbelief, which was no less than she'd expected. 'What did I do?'

Emma almost changed her mind, but she made herself continue. 'After Hannah lifted the veil on our misconceptions, it showed me how important the truth is in certain situations, so I think you should know the truth about us. Or, rather, me in particular.'

'What truth?' His eyes narrowed.

'After my mother's death, in those early years, I was vulnerable and insecure. You came to my rescue and changed all that. Then you offered me a whole new life by agreeing to marry me when I was pregnant.'

'I'm not going down this road,' he said curtly. 'I told you, I'm not here to discuss our shambles of a marriage.'

'I'm not asking you to discuss it, but I do want to straighten out a few things and make you aware of them.' Emma took a deep breath, knowing there was right in what she had to say. 'You see, I haven't been totally honest with you. I never admitted that all those years ago I deliberately became pregnant. And I did so because I knew you'd offer me marriage and all the security that being married to the dependable and ambitious Oliver Colgan would entail.'

Oliver was startled. 'What are you saying?'

Emma met his astonishment unflinchingly. 'Your mother was right about me. I did trap you into marriage. Very deliberately.'

He was clearly stunned. 'I don't believe you.'

'It's true. You see, I never thought that someone like the attractive Oliver with his good background and brilliant future would look twice at the troubled Emma Berkeley and her dysfunctional family. When we met all those years ago and started a relationship, I pushed my personality to one side. I was overcome, overawed, by you. I was terrified the day might come when you'd grow tired of me and want to move on. I was afraid you wouldn't think I was proper marriage material, afraid that I didn't really deserve someone like you. Then I stopped taking the Pill.' She paused to collect herself. 'That's why I made every effort all these years to be the best wife and mother, sometimes ignoring my own needs, which was also wrong of me. That's what I've spent my life making up for – the way I deceived you and forced you into marriage. It had nothing to do with my own mother's behaviour, which I now know I totally misunderstood. But that's it. My confession. Twenty-two years later.' Her voice finally cracked.

There was a long silence.

Oliver looked perplexed. 'Good grief. I don't know what to say. This is . . . I never guessed . . .'

'I know how you feel. I was like that yesterday when Hannah dropped her bombshell.'

Then Oliver asked, rather cuttingly, 'Did you love me at all or just see me as a meal ticket for life?'

'The truth?' Emma asked.

He gave a short, mirthless laugh. 'I'd imagine that anything else is futile.'

'I was crazy about you,' she said. 'I loved you then, albeit in my own selfish way, I love you even more now and, whether you believe it or not, I will never stop loving you.'

Oliver stared down the courtyard. 'This is unreal. What's happened to us? To our family?'

'I guess we're going through some kind of baptism of fire right now,' she said. 'I've had time to think in the last couple of weeks and I came to realise that I haven't been open or honest enough with you. Neither have I voiced my needs properly. As well as all that, I was wrong to cast you in the role of rescuer and me as the damsel in distress. It meant I never really felt as though I was your equal. Then I let you get away with thinking you had to be the all-powerful family provider, strong and in control, instead of it being a joint effort between us. I'm not just talking about the breadwin-ning side of things. I mean sharing everything with me, including worries, work problems, your defeats as well as your triumphs, and not keeping me in blissful innocence about stuff that might affect our relationship . . .'

'I hope you're not attempting to shift some of the blame for what happened onto me?' he said coldly.

'No way,' Emma said. 'I accept total responsibility for my stu-pidity. I'm just saying that I'm sorry if you felt you couldn't be open and honest with me because, thanks to my expectations and your well-meaning but misplaced determination to save me any worries, you didn't want me to see a more vulnerable, human side to you.'

'Who says I have a vulnerable side?'

'I do.'

He looked away, but not before she saw defencelessness flash across his features. *Oh, Oliver . . .* She felt a rush of tenderness for him and longed to hold him close, breathe his scent and show him just how much she loved him.

'I don't know why I'm even sitting here discussing this with you,' he said, gazing into space.

At least, Emma told herself, he was discussing it, and talking to her as though she was a normal enough human being and not some kind of hated, evil adulteress. He hadn't stormed off in a huff. She became aware of the luminous quality to the evening. The sky was changing colour, the air becoming still, the aromatic scents rising more intensely from the flowering bushes. She watched the play of golden light sparking off windows fronting the courtyard that told her the sun was slowly setting.

'Do you know what I'd love to do?' she said on impulse. 'If I had a magic wand, I'd love to turn back time to that Friday morning. Or else I'd love to watch the sun that's sinking into the west right now and let all our baggage and complications sink with it. Wipe the past clean and start from scratch with just the good stuff. Because I believe our marriage deserves a chance and there's lots of good stuff buried beneath this muddle, only it's hard to see right now.'

Oliver shook his head. 'No way. That's asking too much of me, far too much. I don't know if I'll ever get to that stage.'

She would have to tread infinitely carefully, Emma knew. 'Then could we at least begin to talk?' she asked, gazing at him from under her eyelashes. 'I don't mean tonight. Tonight is for Alix, Libby and Charlie. I mean when we get back to Dublin. Talk about how we might begin to sort out our complications? One way or another? We will have to sort out stuff, Oliver. Even if it means breaking up our home and our lives together, selling Laburnum Grove and going our separate ways. We can't leave everything hanging in limbo indefinitely.'

Oliver was holding himself very tensely. 'I'm still very angry with you,' he said, 'and I don't know what the future holds for us.'

'Neither do I, and I expect you to be angry,' she said. 'I'm incredibly angry with myself, and I know how utterly devastated I'd be if the situation was reversed.'

There was a loaded silence. Their eyes collided and held for a long, unguarded moment of silent communication. She saw it all reflected in his, the hurt of her betrayal, his injured pride and the exhaustion she longed to wipe away. By the time Oliver broke his gaze, Emma felt dizzy.

'I suppose we'll have to talk eventually – but be warned,' he said. 'I'll probably shout and rage, and I'm not making any promises whatsoever.'

'I'm not asking for promises,' Emma said. 'Just talking, even shouting, is a start.'

Anything would be better than a cold, remote silence. She wanted Oliver's raw emotions out there, she wanted to hear his legitimate anger and listen to his fury, and break down the barrier of his wounded pride.

'Okay,' he said in acquiescence. 'Tonight is for Alix and the kids. We'll start dealing with stuff when we get back to Dublin, right?'

Relief flooded through her. As they rose to their feet and left the courtyard, Oliver still holding himself rather stiffly yet walking by her side within touching distance, Emma felt as though a welcome chink of light had opened in the wall between them, sending a ray of hope to her heart.

When Libby saw her parents slip out of the salon, she sent up a prayer that somehow they might sort themselves out. Anyone could see that they loved each other. Surely that meant everything.

'Hey,' Charlie nudged her and nodded in the direction of a tall, statuesque girl. 'She's some stunner. Is she . . .?'

Libby winked at him, passing him her camera. 'Stick close to Alix and she'll introduce you. Take loads of photos. I'm just going out for a breath of fresh air. I won't be long.'

It might be the most glamorous, glitzy party she'd ever been invited to, she looked fabulous and she was enjoying herself immensely, but for a moment she felt an overwhelming need to escape the pretensions, the exaggerated air-kissing and overdone bling. Alix and her friends were lovely and natural – it was just the hangers-on and Z-list socialites that were giving her a pain. The party would go on for hours. No one would miss her for a short while.

That was how she found herself slipping upstairs to her bedroom to take off her spiky five-inch heels, shove her pedicured feet into a pair of comfy Converse runners, and grab the only jacket she'd brought, which happened to be the distressed indigo denim she'd worn on the flight from Dublin. She passed through the ornate lobby out into the cool air of the evening, almost bumping into a man who was jumping out of a cab at the entrance to the hotel. He must be somebody who was somebody, Libby decided, as a member of the waiting paparazzi leaped forward to talk to him. The man gave Libby a keen, inquisitive glance, as though he thought he knew her, but Libby was quite sure she'd never met him before. She'd have remembered the unusual shade of his silvery blue eyes.

In her chic, fun party dress, with her jacket draped over her shoulders, Libby headed out into the Paris evening, the air deliciously cool after the heat of the salon. The hotel's white frontage shone against the background of a darkening sapphire sky. Libby headed down the boulevard in the direction of the Seine. The evening was drawing in, the western sky aflame with shades graduating from the deepest bronze to rich tangerine to a pale, shimmering gold. The last prisms of sunlight were gracefully dancing through the leaves on the trees. She reached the river and paused, feeling suddenly alive in the beauty of the evening. Then she crossed over the river and strolled along the Left Bank.

She'd seen them before, had walked by them on other visits to Alix in Paris, but now she was filled with a fresh curiosity as she strolled past stalls of assorted books and paintings. Her eyes were drawn to a riot of colour and shadings, to canvases full of blurry passion and others with precisely executed pencil work. She looked back at the western sky and wished she could somehow capture it, here, now, this very minute.

'You Eenglish?' an elderly artist asked as she drew near. Libby knew he'd been observing her meandering progress. He probably wanted to sketch her, this posh young madam in her Converse shoes, with frilly tulle peeping from under the hem of her D&G party dress, topped with a denim Hilfiger jacket. She'd had her hair styled by Dave and her make-up was Alix B at Aurélie. She was staying in the Louis XII. How much more A-list could you get? And what did it matter anyway? Who gave a toss? Not her, for one.

'No, Irish,' she corrected him.

'Dubleen?'

'That's right,' she said, halting to look at his work. 'Hey, that's fantastic,' she said, overawed by his lively and unusual depiction of a bridge over the Seine, the waters dancing in the pristine morning light, the colours muted yet coming together in a life of their own.

'You like?'

'Yes, it's really lovely, but I can't buy it.' She started to move on. She'd no money with her, was afraid he might think her interested enough to buy it, and hated the thought of letting him down. In any case, she could hardly transport the canvas home on her scheduled flight.

'You don't need to buy to take pleasure from looking at it,' he said in his accented English, standing back to allow her more room to view his work.

She stood for a few moments in the calm of the evening, peering at his vibrant painting. 'It must be great to capture your feelings like that.'

'Ah. I'm happy you see it comes from the heart.'

'Sometimes I'd love to paint,' she admitted, tendrils of her long blonde hair lifting in the light breeze.

'What ees stopping you?' he asked.

Libby hesitated for a minute. Then her thoughts crystallised in the mellow evening. She gave a half-laugh. 'Nobody but me, come to think of it.'

'Well, then, you need only to select your subject and pick up a brush.'

'Back home, I have a very good job,' Libby admitted, wondering why she was talking like this to a perfect stranger, but it was all part of the capricious moment, something to do with the liberation of her mish-mash of clothes and that she'd slipped out of an over-whelmingly glamorous party for a breath of air. 'My job takes up a lot of time and energy, and I'm talented at it. My boss wants me to go further, but I don't know if that's where my future path in life is supposed to be. Or if I should give it up, change direction and start to paint.'

'That's an easy one to decide.' He smiled.

'I don't know how you can say that when I'm finding it all very difficult and complicated.'

His wizened face broke into a hundred creases and his periwin-kle eyes sparkled as he smiled a wise smile. 'That's because you, my little one, are at the start of your life and I'm nearing the end of mine, when things become very clear.'

'I see. So what do I do?' Libby asked. 'Draw up enormous lists with positives and negatives? Go on some kind of Zen retreat to reflect on my great purpose? Have late-night talks with my friends and family?'

'No, it's far easier than that, and it should take just a few min-utes.'

She felt he was humouring her and she was starting to feel annoyed. 'I'm talking about the rest of my life. How could it be so easy?'

'All you have to do,' he said, 'is something very simple. Find out what makes you cry. Then you'll know.'

Libby stood in the dusky tangerine magic of the early-summer evening and thought for a few minutes. She felt something gleam inside her. Then she grinned. 'Hey, cheers,' she said. 'I guess I can live with that.' She knew what answer she'd be giving Stephen O'Connor on Monday morning. She only had to look at the wash of colours around her to know what moved her to tears and she felt a new and exciting energy surge through her.

It was going better than she'd expected, Alix thought, even though her face ached with the effort of constant smiling. She graciously accepted the third or fourth glass of champagne that someone pressed into her hand. Henri had told her that Aurélie were thrilled with the launch and deeming it a terrific success. The salon was crowded with the right people, and Anika looked sensational. A couple of the fashion houses were climbing all over her and vying for her attention.

Libby had temporarily disappeared. So had Emma and Oliver, for that matter, but now they were back and chatting to Marc. Knowing them both so well, she could see the slight distance and awkwardness between them, but at least they were together.

Charlie was having a ball. Her nephew didn't half cut a good figure and he was deep in conversation with the latest Italian cat-walk sensation. Flirtatious conversation by the looks of it, Alix decided. So, all in all, a successful night with just a couple more hours to get through before she could legitimately slink off to bed.

She was moving across the room to chat to Fiona when she spotted Tom and her heart kicked against her ribs.

Chapter 56

*A*lix didn't know how long he had been there, for even as he made his way towards her, his progress was impeded by well-wishers and acquaintances who stopped him for a few words. She looked around wildly to see if there was any escape, but there was nowhere to hide. Eventually he broke free and made straight for her.

'Tom!' she faltered. 'I didn't expect to see you here.'

'No, I guess you didn't.' He was casually dressed in his leather jacket and jeans, and his hair was messy as though he'd been running his fingers through it and had forgotten to smooth it down. He obviously hadn't intended putting in an appearance at Alix's posh evening when he'd left his apartment.

'Have some champagne,' Alix babbled, at a loss.

'I'm not here for champagne.' His face was set.

He was here for revenge, she immediately thought. He was going to denounce her to the whole gathering as the monster she was, a far cry from the honest, incorruptible make-up artist whom Aurélie had signed up to launch their glittering new product. 'What is it, then?' She tried to breathe slowly – there was little or no air in the room.

'I can't talk here,' Tom said, his eyes absorbing everything from the celebrities to the tables where the make-up was prominently displayed, the huge posters and merchandising material emblazoned with the legend 'Alix B at Aurélie'.

Alix's heart fluttered in her chest and her hand went to her throat. 'The foyer,' she said. 'We can talk there.' She picked up her silk evening bag and they moved from the busy, noisy salon out to a corner of the cool, marble foyer.

'I'm on my way to the airport,' he began. 'I asked the cab driver to take a detour by this hotel.'

'Why, Tom?'

He seemed agitated all of a sudden. 'No, forget it, it's probably the height of foolishness. I'm just being stupid and delusional.'

'You're here now so you might as well tell me.'

He looked at her directly. 'I heard about your mum,' he said, a little subdued. 'Fiona phoned me because she thought for some reason that I might want to know.' There was a question in his eyes.

Alix groped for words. 'I didn't tell Fiona about us, but I gather you were talking to Marc and word got around.' She laughed mirthlessly. 'As regards my mother, I only found out the truth from Hannah yesterday.' She lifted her chin a fraction. 'So now you know how absurdly, incredibly, ridiculously stupid I've been.'

He held her gaze. 'I was going to ignore Fiona's phone call,' he went on, as though she hadn't spoken, 'but . . .' He was still looking at her thoughtfully and Alix felt a shiver in some hidden part of her.

'But?' she prompted, striving for composure.

Tom half turned. 'Forget it,' he said dismissively. 'Just write me up as a sad case.'

'Okay.' Alix began to move off, feeling that she was stepping away from the only person who mattered to her right now.

'Wait.' He touched her bare arm, causing shivery sparks to dance along the surface of her skin. His expression was unreadable.

'Tom, if you're looking for more apologies, or you've come here to turn the screws on me, I can't say any more to you than I already have,' Alix said wretchedly, 'and I'm not prepared to plead my case with you any further. You've heard my full confession and you know how remorseful I feel. You can multiply that by ten when I start to come to terms with the gut-wrenching implications of Hannah's revelation.'

'That's why I'm here,' he said candidly. 'I'm shocked at and furious with you, Alix, but I'm putting that to one side for now because, foolish as I am, incredibly absurd as I am, and ridiculously stupid, you're still under my skin, in my head and heart . . .'

Alix put a hand to her mouth to stifle a cry. He hadn't changed. At some intrinsic level he was the same endearingly honest Tom she'd fallen in love with at the age of sixteen.

'I keep seeing your face and hearing your voice as you told me what you did,' Tom went on. 'I'm still full of a burning rage, but I was just beginning to understand how cut up you were about everything, and how difficult it must have been, when Fiona phoned and told me about your mum. I know more than anyone just what heartache that will mean to you, so I guess I just want to tell you I'm sorry it all turned out like this. That's it. I'm finished being foolish and absurd. Now go back inside. At least you've made a success of your career. It's your big night and people are waiting for you.' He nodded across to the open doorway of the salon from where party noises wafted through to the foyer.

'Where are you going?' she asked, sensing the slight thaw in his demeanour towards her.

'The airport. I'm sure you'll be relieved to hear I'm quitting Paris and getting out of your hair.'

'How could I be relieved after everything that's happened between us? Where are you going?'

'London, of course. What you did is one of those things that defy analysis, but all that matters to me now is that somewhere out there I have a living, breathing daughter. That to me is utterly stupendous, brilliant and marvellous. I'm not wasting any time in finding her. Neither am I wasting any energy in regrets. I know her date of birth and her mother's name, so it should be a starting point.'

'A starting point? Tom, have you any idea of what you're talking about? It would be like looking for a needle in a haystack. Besides, there are rules and regulations . . . You can't just barge your way through these.'

'I don't care how long it takes. Or what hurdles I have to jump. At least I'll be in the city where she was born, and hopefully still lives. And for God's sake,' his voice shook, 'don't look at me like that.'

Her breath caught. 'Like what?'

'I don't know but it's making me feel all jittery.'

'Take me with you. Please.'

He laughed. 'You don't get it. I'm going now. This minute. I've a cab waiting outside. You have a party to go to. There are more than a hundred guests waiting for you. This is what you've been working towards all your life. This is your dream.'

'I don't care. It doesn't matter. I have other dreams that are far more important.' The words tumbled out. She meant every one of them.

He gazed at her in silence. Aurélie's PR would come looking for her in a moment, as she'd be needed for more photographs. Out of the corner of her eye she saw someone heading into the salon carrying a huge bouquet of flowers. More guests hurried across the foyer, sending out a waft of perfume, their heels click-clacking on the polished surface. She saw Libby coming in through the entrance, looking beautiful.

'Please, Tom,' she cried, filled with the rich certainty that, above and beyond the sparkling success of her career, her life was precious and still held a measure of promise. But it wasn't something intangible, beyond her grasp. It was here, now, in the foyer of the Louis XII, in Tom's silvery blue eyes as they regarded her quizzically, in his body as he inclined towards her with all his taut attention and mercurial energy focused on her.

And, beyond that, it was somewhere in London.

'Why can't we call a temporary truce and suspend hostilities for a while?' she implored. 'I want to help you find our daughter. It's the least I can do. I can show you where she was born, bring you to the agency that arranged the adoption and get some advice from the social workers about making contact with her and her adoptive parents. We'd have to find out if it's appropriate and in her best interest. I know she might hate my guts, but that's a chance I'm willing to take. After that you can do whatever you like with me.'

Something passed across Tom's face. Something playful. 'Are you serious? You want to come to London with me? You'd walk out of here right *now*?'

'Yes, right now.'

'As in this minute?' His eyes flickered over her body encased in its beautiful gown.

'Would we have time to swing by my apartment so I can jump into a pair of jeans? And grab my passport?' Alix asked, feeling heady with jubilation, already opening her silk evening bag and checking for her key and her mobile. 'I could book a seat on your flight en route to the airport.'

He looked bemused. 'I don't know why I'm even thinking of going along with this. As I said, I'm furious as hell with you, but what the heck? I always knew life was bloody crazy. *I'm* bloody crazy. We're tight for time, but maybe we could spare five minutes. If I ask the cab driver to step on the gas.'

'Yes, oh, yes, please, Tom.'

*

Libby didn't know what to think when Alix grabbed her arm and told her she was leaving.

'You're leaving?' she spluttered. 'How come? What's up?'

'I've no time to explain. Just tell Emma I'm going to look for Alexandra. She'll know.'

The man standing beside Alix jerked his head around as though it was news to him. Libby recognised him as the man she'd passed outside the hotel earlier on.

'You called her Alexandra?' he said.

'Yes, Tom,' Alix breathed.

'Why?'

'It reminded me of you. Of us.'

'Something else . . .'

'What?'

'All this,' he gestured towards the salon, 'your profile up in lights . . . all the fame and publicity. And this is only the start. Surely you realised she might become curious if she noticed the similarities of your names when she eventually has access to her birth certificate? Even if you requested no contact?'

'I didn't think of it at the beginning,' Alix said, 'but lately I half hoped that she might, and it made me feel very scared . . . Does that make sense?'

The man called Tom took Alix's hand and Libby realised they had completely forgotten her presence. She liked the look in his eyes as they rested on Alix. Whatever they were talking about, she sensed it was very important.

'Totally. I'm scared also,' he said. 'So we might as well agree that we're in this together. But just for now. Later I'll decide what I'm going to do with you.'

Libby gave a discreet cough. From the back of the foyer, someone emerged from the salon and called Alix.

Alix planted a swift kiss on Libby's cheek. She looked, Libby thought, as though she was lit up from within. 'I have to run,' Alix said. 'Go straight to Emma. You know what to tell her, don't you? I'm going to start looking for Alexandra. With Tom. Oh, and, Libby?'

'Yes?'

'Wish me luck!'

Then, in a swirl of sapphire blue silk, with diamanté twinkling in her hair and prisms glittering off her platform sandals, Alix lifted the skirt of her beautiful gown and hurried across the foyer hand in hand with Tom. Libby followed them outside and watched them dive into a waiting cab. Alix waved out of the window and blew her a kiss as the cab screeched away from the kerb.

A couple of paparazzi were idling outside. They jumped to attention when they grasped the identity of the departing couple and, thanks to her recent French revision, Libby followed every word.

'Hey! What's happening? Wasn't that Alix going off?'

'It must be a stunt – part of the launch extravaganza. She'll be back. Probably by helicopter.'

'Who's that blonde babe? Is she Peaches Geldof?'

'I'm not sure, but I think she's sporting the latest boho-chic look. Isn't that skirt amazing with the jacket?'

They were talking about her. Libby turned to face them, drew herself up to her full height, and savoured the moment. 'I'm actually Libby Colgan,' she said, rather majestically.

'Libby *who*?'

'Who's she? Did you ever hear of her?'

'Don't worry if you haven't heard of me. Yet.' Libby smiled sweetly as a flash bulb exploded in her face. 'Just watch this space.'

Then she strolled back into the hotel.

Epilogue

Eighteen months later

*T*he tiny village didn't know what had hit it. Nestled deep in the heart of the Irish countryside, it normally enjoyed a quiet, peaceful existence. All that changed when the wedding of Alix Berkeley and Tom Cassidy took place at 1.00 p.m. in the quaint, stone-clad country church on a day when cerulean blue skies seemed to stretch for ever and sunshine gilded the last traces of autumn.

They could have sold the rights to *Hello!* or *OK!* and preserved their privacy on the day, some people said. But the groom, who was mistaken by a few villagers for a rock star, was heard to say in the local pub that the media had to earn a living somehow, so long as they kept a respectful distance, and that was how the locals got to mingle with the glitterati and witness the excitement at first hand.

Everyone agreed that the bride looked stunning in a Synan O'Mahony lace and organza creation. The bridesmaids, one blonde, the other dark-haired, were both beautiful in raspberry silk mini-dresses. And everyone was overawed by the tall, glamorous models and celebrities who flew in from abroad and flocked to the occasion. Most people recognised the French-born Sophie even if they didn't know her by name. Others took their eyes off her amazing face long enough to spot the diamonds sparkling on her left hand. They later found out in press coverage of the event that she was newly engaged to Marc de Burgh, a famous Belgian fashion photographer, who had also attended the wedding, and that the blonde bridesmaid was a promising, emerging artist called Libby.

Then there was the couple with the little boy, also big celebrities, to judge by the way the cameras sought them out. She had fabulous red hair and her husband pushed the buggy while the child slept throughout the ceremony, blissfully unaware of the fuss and flash bulbs. However famous they were, and despite their air of foreign glamour, the locals caught traces of their Cork accent and agreed that they were most definitely Irish.

After the church service, the reception was held in the ballroom of the nearby refurbished Ashwood Manor. There wasn't much in the way of a photo opportunity here, or a chance for the locals to brush shoulders with the glitzy guests, so most of them returned home. Three or four of the more intrepid photographers hung around outside the manor, just in case a late arrival turned up or anyone famous decided to stretch their legs between the vintage champagne reception and the sumptuous meal.

But all was quiet. They spotted the bride's sister and her husband slipping out of the hotel as the afternoon was drawing in, when the sun was a golden ball in the sky. He took her hand in his as they strolled along a path that led through to the gardens facing the westering sun.

Someone saw the bride's nephew at a bedroom window, but he firmly closed the curtains before they caught any glimpse of his companion.

And then, just before the photographers packed up and went home, the bride and groom emerged from the side of the hotel along with the tall bridesmaid with the dark, spiky hair. The groom brought his camera and, for a few private moments stolen from the afternoon, the bride and her bridesmaid posed for him, laughing and hugging each other against a backdrop of cypress trees etched against the apricot sky.

In deference to the groom, they decided to refrain from capturing his private moment. But although nobody was quite sure of the identity of the bridesmaid, and they bickered as to whether she was a fashion model, a film star or a close family friend, they all agreed on one thing: she had the most amazing silvery blue eyes.